wonderlight

A LOVE STORY

TINA SPENCER

To those fighting their way out of darkness

And to all the closeted hopeless romantics:
Lachlan is for you

"I wish I could show you,
when you are lonely or in darkness,
The Astonishing Light
of your own being."
- Hafez

author's note

Before you embark on an adventure to Scotland, I want to let you know that this book contains themes and subject matter some may find triggering. There is mention of SA (in memory), depression, and anxiety. For a full list of content warnings, please visit www.tinaspencerbooks.com.

As well, Canadian/ British English is used throughout the novel to stay authentic to the characters and the locations in the book.

Take It Away - The Used
Crawling - Linkin Park
Underwater - Rufus du Sol
Gordon's - Gnoss
The Merry Sisters of Fate - Lúnasa
Somewhere I Belong - Linkin Park
Perfect Storm - Duncan Chisholm
Ocean Eyes - Billie Eilish
Drifting Away - Audien, Joe Jury
Into You - Ariana Grande
Open End Resource - Andrew Bayer, Alison May
No Place - Rufus du Sol
Halo - Beyonce
Freeze - Kygo
Falls - ODESZA, Sasha Alex Sloan
After You (feat. Calle Lehmann) - Gryffin, Jason Ross

prologue

AVERY

Five years earlier

Dr. Samson's office is the stereotypical therapist's office. Warm light, fuzzy burnt orange couch, and yellow cushions. He's got too many plants crammed in this space, and his bookshelves are the vibrant colours of the rainbow. It's like he's trying to jam happiness down your throat just by sitting here.

I thought he was a child psychologist when I first met him.

The room smells like pages from old books. It's kind of perfect, actually. The guy is educated and well-spoken. And he understands things without making me feel like shit about it. That's why I've stuck with him for this long. Even if he goes all philosophical on me once in a while.

It's been just over a year since I started working with Dr. Samson. The days blend together, an endless blur of monotony, and I continue to leave this office empty-handed. I haven't gotten better and I'm starting to think I never will. Maybe I'll forever roam this world as a mere shadow of the person I used to be.

"Are you going to say anything, or are you going to pick at your nails until there is nothing left but bone?" Dr. Samson sits across from me in his usual attire of jeans and grey sweater. His go-to look is comfortable-chic and he never holds anything back. He also never asks me how something—trivial or monumental—makes me feel.

Thank God for that.

I grind my teeth, biting into the flesh inside my cheek until the metallic taste of blood fills my mouth. It's a great distraction but a dangerous one. Replacing one type of discomfort with another. I shift in my seat, the fresh scars on my inner thighs rub against the rough fabric of my jeans, providing a new sensation to fixate on.

"I don't know what you want me to say. Feels like I haven't made any progress. If anything, I'm getting worse. And to top it off, I've been having this one recurring dream lately, and when I wake up I can't get enough air. My body is literally trying to suffocate me."

Dr. Samson doesn't take notes. He watches me. Listening intently.

"How long have you been having this new dream?"

My eyes fall to the ground. If I look up at him, I won't be able to go on. Talking about this shit never gets easier. It's like staring up at a monstrous mountain, knowing you'll never take a single step. Coming to therapy is torture, when you'd rather be anywhere but inside your head.

I exhale heavily. "Showed up about two weeks ago and inserted itself into the regularly scheduled roster of nightmares I get to choose from. I have a good selection now. Variety."

Dr. Samson patiently waits for me to tell him about my dream. He never asks. It's up to me to talk. I have the choice to share or stay silent the full hour I'm here every week. Having the choice is apparently an important part of my healing journey.

The sooner I do this, the sooner I can leave.

"It always starts at the same place. I'm drowning, stuck deep underwater. My lungs are burning but I keep swimming up. Reaching, pushing, kicking but I can never reach the surface. I'm so close, but there is something preventing me. Something I can't see or feel. An invisible forcefield. I thrash, swim harder, scream, yet somehow don't choke on the water. Nothing works. Finally, I realize I'm not going to make it. And as soon as that hits me, something grabs my ankle. I always look down, watching the darkness drag me to the bottom." I take a deep breath, remembering the aggressive panic attack this dream caused me two nights ago. Cold sweat collects at the base of my neck.

"Interesting and wonderful. Promising progress, Avery." Dr. Samson offers me a bright smile, while pushing his glasses up the bridge of his nose.

"Excuse me?" Has he totally lost his mind and needs a therapist too? I just told him that I was dragged down to the bottom of the ocean to join Davy Jones in his locker, and he says that's wonderful?

Clearly I'm missing the obvious humour in my dream about drowning.

"You're looking for your Wonderlight." He leans forward, resting his arms on his legs and smiling, acting like he just told me the sunny forecast for next week.

"What the fuck is that?"

"I was hoping you had at least skimmed my book *Healing After Trauma*, but I guess not." He sighs, straightening up and leaning back in his chair. "Wonderlight is a term I created to describe a state of consciousness in one's healing journey. A moment of complete awe for the light. The light you seek to find but cannot see when you allow the darkness to become you. Wonderlight comes before hope. And once you reach out and touch it, you allow the light to spread through, the glow slowly transforms you, paving the path through the darkness. It's the hue of light right at the edge. But you need to open your eyes in order to see it, touch it, feel it. To let it heal you."

What a load of philosophical bullshit. I didn't even understand half the crap that just came out of his mouth.

"Wow, Samson...you should become a poet or philosopher. That was some deep shit you just shoved in my face." I snort.

The darkness hides me. It protects and shields me from everything I hate about myself. Everything I've become. Anger feels good. It helps me forget how broken I am. I hate the light. It represents everything I'll never have.

Dr. Samson ignores my hurtful words.

"Your mind will continue to replay what your heart hasn't learned to heal. You can't see Wonderlight until you're ready, Avery. There is no shortcut or easy way out of the dark. We see what we choose to see. And right now, you're choosing to keep your eyes shut and let your demons become you. In your dream, you tried to reach the surface, but you couldn't. That tells me that the invisible barrier holding you back is you. So you gave up when it got too hard to process and allowed the darkness to drag you back down." His words cut through me like glass as I try to hold back tears.

"It's not a choice. The fear, the pain, the memories from that night, the panic attacks from the dreams. I don't choose any of them. Why would I want to torture myself?"

Dr. Samson remains calm. Unwavering in his emotions. He is in complete control of himself. How does he do that? Had to be a class he took or something.

"You are letting the physical control you. The darkness

inside your head is there because you're allowing it to stay. To control your thoughts and remind you of the pain. You're allowing it to continue to hurt you by not choosing to heal. The longer you disconnect, the further you will fall from yourself. You have to open your eyes in the dark, otherwise how will you see Wonderlight?"

My skin feels hot as tears slide down my cheeks. I wipe them away quickly with the back of my hand, eyes blurry as I pick at a fresh scab beside my thumb.

What if I can never let go?

"You have to surrender to the pain, the suffering, the past that still haunts you two years later. Learn to love the broken parts of yourself. When you do that, when you let go of the emotional turmoil and the fear...only then will you find the light."

Pressing my face deeper into the donut hole, I close my eyes and force my body to relax.

Except, it is impossible to relax. My nerves are on edge, and I can't shake the feeling that I am in the wrong place at the wrong time.

How was I going to last through this for an entire sixty minutes?

"How are you doing? Are you comfortable, Avery?" the nice massage therapist asks as she flattens a warm blanket on my back, tucking the edges down the sides of my body.

"Great, thank you," I say, my words muffled as I speak into the tiny hole on the massage table. I shift my weight, trying to get comfortable, but it's no use.

Soft spa music fills the space as sage and eucalyptus incense burn in the corner of the room.

How do people relax on demand? It's impossible for me to shut my brain off.

Amy gets to work, kneading and pushing at the sore muscles in my back. I was ill-prepared for this last-minute spa day John, my boyfriend, surprised me with. He planned the entire thing, claiming I needed a relaxing day at the New Nordic spa that just opened up outside of downtown Toronto.

Who was I to say no, even though I'm not a big spa person?

Apparently John had booked it months ago, hoping for the two of us to finally spend some time together, but of course, he couldn't make it. His re-election campaign is not going too well, so he had to spend the entire weekend at the office.

"Are you here alone? With friends? A partner, perhaps?" Amy asks quietly while she works the kinks out of my back muscles.

God, that actually feels so good.

It's weird to engage in conversation while I'm barely clothed under a sheet, but silence can make people uncomfortable. Unless you're an introvert. We love quiet time a little too much.

"Uh...here on my own. My boyfriend organized a weekend getaway for us but he couldn't make it so he changed it to a solo spa for me."

"Aw, that's sweet. Sorry he couldn't make it. Have you guys been together for long?"

"Three years."

Amy coos, "He sounds like a true romantic."

John doesn't have a single romantic bone in his body. He is thoughtful and caring, but not romantic. If I was to label him as anything, it would be a workaholic.

I'm to blame for the no-romance stuff, not him.

I hate romance. It's not real and it only belongs in story-books. And he has always known that so we keep our relation-ship very real.

But lately we've become a bit more distant.

John and I haven't seen one another in a long time. He's so busy with work, we never spend time together anymore. We brush by one another in the mornings when he's rushing off to work. Sometimes I feel the bed dip when he gets in late at night. Today was supposed to be our opportunity to reconnect but his job took priority. Something about a new fire that needed to be put out.

I can't pinpoint exactly when we became roommates, but every relationship goes through this. We respect and care for one another, and sacrifices need to be made right now in order for him to pursue his dreams.

Sometimes I'm still not sure how I ended up in Toronto living with John in our (technically his) apartment. I was a shell of a person for so long, but somehow a friendship bloomed between us in college. Is it the story book love story my mother always said a person should strive towards?

No, but I never wanted that to begin with.

I don't think I could ever be with someone who expected a grand type of love. I'm not even sure I'm capable of experiencing emotions in that way. Love is unrealistic. It's a miracle I was able to hold down a relationship after what happened to me. I was broken beyond repair. And after years of therapy and medication...and time, things finally started to feel a bit more normal. I started to move on with my life.

John was a good friend when I needed one. He waited patiently as I worked through my past trauma. It took me a long time to even fathom the thought of someone touching my hand. John never rushed me. He never asked why I was so withdrawn, and I never said the words out loud but I think he figured it out. There were so many opportunities to leave but he never did.

I've only ever told my story out loud to one person. Well, technically two people know.

Dr. Samson got me to say the words as an exercise, to help me gain power over what happened to me. A way to move on. It was one of the hardest things I've ever done. Becca (my closest friend from childhood) knows what happened, but I never uttered the words out loud to her.

Dr. Samson was my father's twentieth and final attempt at finding me a therapist. I was depressed and he insisted I speak to a professional. I wasn't eating and Dad just chalked that up to depression too. Thankfully, Samson turned out to be exactly who I needed. I never felt judged or broken when I was sitting in Dr. Samson's office. He always made space for me.

"Any plans for the rest of the weekend?" Amy asks, trying desperately to fill the silence with small talk.

"Probably just going to go to bed early with a good book. You?"

Amy chuckles, her firm fingers press into my lower back, and I hold back a groan. I have been working too many hours recently, and sitting idle at my desk for long hours is doing a number on my body. Amy is actually my favourite person right now. Even if she talks too much.

"No dinner plans with the boyfriend?"

A lot of focus on John today. Maybe I should set them up.

Yes, because girlfriends think about setting up their boyfriends with other women.

What is wrong with me?

Let's not go there today.

"He's probably going to be working late. He's a city councillor and running for re-election."

"Oh wow, you must be so proud!"

Amy steps away, squeezing a bottle as she pours more oil on her hands. A second later warm fingers press into my back, gliding down my spine.

"He's very good at his job." I huff out as Amy pushes on my lungs.

Working as a city councillor is more than a full-time job.

The energy and passion John puts into his work are unmatched.

I fully support him.

Always have, always will.

FEELING zen and actually relaxed for the first time in what feels like a decade, I pull out my apartment key. But before I can even insert the key, the door flies open with a suddenness that startles me. Standing in the cramped foyer, dressed in his customary work attire, is John. His impeccable sense of style is evident, the fresh black suit and crisp white button-down shirt perfectly complemented by a solid navy tie. His hair is combed back, with just the right amount of hair gel.

The perfect Toronto councilman.

"Oh, hi. Wasn't sure you'd be home." I tuck my key back into my pocket and step into the apartment.

John offers me a tight smile before glancing down at his watch. He is likely heading to work.

On Sunday afternoon.

But he seems...off. Maybe a bit nervous.

"I thought you were going to stay at the spa for the day."

"Only so much I can do there by myself. The massage was great, thank you."

He offers me a curt nod, avoiding my gaze.

"I was just about to head out but I'm glad you're here, actually. Can we talk?" He steps into the hallway.

"Sure. Everything okay?" I drop my bag on the floor, and the door gently clicks shut behind me. Bending down to take my shoes off, I notice two silver hardcover suitcases and a matching carry-on tucked neatly at the end of the hallway.

Those are my suitcases.

What is going on? Are we going on a trip?

That's not like him. And he wouldn't book a trip during re-election when he didn't even have time to join me at the spa today.

A sour feeling in the pit of my stomach grows.

"What's going on, John? Why are my suitcases out?"

He finally looks up at me, but it's like I'm staring at a blank wall. No, it's worse. He's got a calculated poker face on. I call it his councillor greeting.

"Avery, let's sit."

Something is definitely off because I'm suddenly speaking to Councillor Cooper. His voice and demeanour speaks a type of professionalism that sends a chill down my spine. My initial instinct is to turn around and bolt out the door, but I remain rooted in place. Watching him stride towards the living room, as I follow him like a lost puppy trailing behind its master.

John sits on the grey couch, straightening his tie as I drop on the black lounger across from him. My heart is beating a thousand miles a minute.

There is a telling look on his face and suddenly, I know everything is about to change.

The feeling is similar to the one from that terrible night seven years ago. The night that irrevocably altered my entire world, leaving me shattered and forever changed. All it took was one person, one moment, to extinguish my light. There are certain times in life when you can almost hear the crack that eventually implodes your world. And I know this moment will be one of those times—the kind of moment that will shift the course of my life forever.

CHAPTER TWO

avery

"A re you going to say something?" John asks.

I can't even look at him.

I'm concentrating on not throwing up at the moment.

Words are sort of not a priority, unless you want me to vomit all over your over-the-top Urban Barn floor rug, John.

Now that I think about it, almost everything in this apartment belongs to him.

John comes from money, old money. His parents live in the rich area of Rosedale in Toronto and John's dad bought him this condo in downtown Toronto when he moved back. When John offered to pay for most of the furniture, insisting his parents wanted to give us a good start, I didn't fight him all that much. Even then, when I thought we would be something, I knew that his parents were doing this for their son.

John was born and raised in Toronto. He moved to Vancouver when he received a scholarship to the University of British Columbia. We met in second year and quickly became friends. Unlike most people in their early twenties, John always knew what he wanted to do with his life. While everyone else was partying, he was spending hours studying at the library. I would know because I was there too, burying myself in books so I wouldn't have to think about how badly I wanted to disappear. Back then, I was too lost in my grief and books helped me escape reality.

It was always his plan to move back to Toronto after college. He would get a fully paid-for condo and could follow in his father's footsteps. The Cooper family name means something here.

I was surprised when he asked me to go with him to Toronto. To come here, to a new town, and start over. His life was all planned out. Everything was lined up for him, and my life was the total opposite. I was in complete shambles inside and out. It took me an entire week to think about it. Becca even sat me down and forced me to make a pros and cons list.

Her list was filled with cons.

Looking back now, I should have listened to her.

"I didn't mean for this to happen. It just kind of did. Are you really surprised? We have been headed towards this for a long time." Okay, that catches my attention. And apparently sparks my growing rage.

Focus. Please Lord, don't let me throw up right now. It would be funny later, especially if it was on him, but not right now. I'm embarrassed enough as it is.

"Right," I say.

A big chunk of my life is blurry. Including helping John furnish this place. He handed me his credit card and I shopped for him like a good little girlfriend. Happy couples shop for furniture together when they first move in. They don't send their girlfriend alone to buy literally everything for their home.

The red flags were always there. I just decided not to see them.

"Can you say something? I'm not saying what happened is okay, but we barely see one another anymore. I mean, we haven't even been intimate for a year." His scratchy voice pulls me out of my thoughts. Was his voice always this annoying? He sounds like a man-child who didn't quite make it all the way through puberty.

"Maybe if you were here more often or weren't fucking someone else we would have," my voice doesn't sound like it belongs to me.

Is this really happening?

It took me a long time not to recoil at his soft touch. I hated the way it reminded me...even though it was nothing like that night. The only way I could stand to have sex with John was if I took control and didn't look at him directly. It always had to be dark in the room. I hated the idea of him watching me, or anyone else looking at me when I was at my most vulnerable. What if they could see the ugly parts of me from that night too? What if they hated all those parts as much as I did?

I highly doubt he calls it the forever kind of love when he has Jessica bent over his office desk.

John waves his hand in front of my face.

Yes, I keep zoning out.

What did he expect me to do when he told me he's been cheating on me for a year?

What did he say again? Oh right, long time coming.

I nod my head vigorously. Sure, blame me for your decision to begin cheating.

That makes sense.

"Do you love her?" I'm glaring at the two wooden stools tucked under the thin kitchen island when the words just fall out of my mouth. I didn't mean to ask him that question because it changes nothing. Love has nothing to do with this.

Not for me.

Well, you could have said anything but that.

He starts talking but I just keep doing inventory of what's sitting in the apartment. The only things belonging to me are my desk and bookshelves in the spare bedroom which we converted into my office. I work from home, so I needed a dedicated place to work, and John graciously offered me the second bedroom when I moved in.

The spare bedroom is now filled with books. I turned the room into my personal little haven. During the day I sit at my desk and work. On evenings and weekends, I lounge on my giant poofy floor chair and gorge on novels. I even added some twinkling lights to combat the winter blues during the colder months.

"Do you really want to know the answer to that question, Avery? Won't it just hurt more?" he asks casually, like he's asking me about pulling a splinter out or something.

I don't know, John, but let's find out.

I nod, still not looking at him.

"Very well." He pushes a box of tissues across the coffee table towards me.

Bold move, and very presumptuous of him. As if he's worth my tears.

Asshole.

Should I be crying?

A normal person would likely turn into a puddle of tears after finding out their boyfriend has been cheating on them for the past year. And he's kicking me out of our home so he could be with her. I should be inconsolable but I find myself oddly unmoved, save for the rage directed towards myself. How could I have been so blind to miss all the fucking signs?

Here I was thinking he was my long-term plan while he was getting his dick wet elsewhere.

Glancing up at him, I take in his cool composure. He's been planning this for months. He had the nerve to push a box of Kleenex to me. I lean over, pushing the box right back. I want to tell him to take the box and shove it up his ass but I keep my mouth shut.

He glares down at the box, coughing.

"Yes, I love her. At first it was just a fling since it was easy. She's always been there for me, working tirelessly on my campaigns. She's so passionate about what we do, the difference we make every day. I don't know, somewhere along the way it just sort of happened. We became friends and then it turned into more. I thought it would fizzle out over time, but it didn't." Even though I want to punch him in the face, his words still cut into me like a surgical knife.

"How romantic for you both," I murmur while nodding, like we're agreeing on a kitchen remodel and trying to decide on a colour scheme. I look around as his words eventually grow heavy, settling on the furniture like a layer of fine dust.

He says more things, and they don't resonate in my mind because I'm distracted again. Something about a genuine connection and not intending for them to fall for one another. Utterly useless trivialities that mean nothing to me.

I'm honestly just trying to figure out how I missed something this big for so goddamn long. He was barely home, even on weekends. He kept buying me stupid shit and randomly coming home with flowers. It was all there and I chose to turn the other way. I'm always the paranoid, untrusting, emotionless one, and somehow, I missed this.

I guess I let the feeling of safety drown out the rest.

Bile threatens to climb up my throat, but I force it down.

"Did you hear me?" His voice now repulses me, just like his face.

I take in his features for the first time in a long time. His face is round and soft, a veil of innocence still cast over him even though he just turned twenty-seven. He's a pretty boy by definition. Short, perfectly styled blond hair. Never a strand out of line. He strives for outer perfection since he's always in the public eye. Dark brown eyes that are a little too close together. He shaves every day and never misses a workout, even though his schedule is always jam-packed. Well, maybe not as packed as I thought it was since has time to fuck Jessica at work, or maybe it's just that he's adopted a new type of cardio. Although, if memory serves me right, being with John never lasted longer than a few minutes.

He's not much of a giver.

Great catch, Jessica.

And he's an inch taller than me, putting him at a whooping five-foot-ten. I was never allowed to wear heels around him since he said it made him feel small. Time to go shopping, I guess.

It's funny how none of these red flags appeared as flaws until this very moment. I liked his kind heart and his quiet nature. How he always seemed to do something thoughtful for me. How much he cared about serving his community, and how important it is for him to be viewed in a certain light. But now that I sit here, with all the lies unwrapped neatly in front of me, I realize that every event he booked for me, every trip, every gift, every 'staycation' and shopping spree was just a cover up.

It was a way to assuage the guilt.

"I don't know what you want me to say. I'm mostly mad at myself for being so blind that I didn't even see the signs. I thought you were caring and thoughtful, but it turns out you just sent me away so you could pack my bags for me. At least you had the decency not to sleep with both of us at the same time."

His eyes fall to the floor, his fingers turning and twisting in his lap.

"You're a coward." I loosen the anger, allowing it to flow freely out of me.

His eyes flash up at that declaration. "Don't talk to me like that. I've been nothing but kind to you," he spits.

The impulse to laugh is too strong and I don't suppress it as the sound pierces the air around us. John looks at me like I'm deranged. The audacity.

"Kind?! Is it kind to cheat on your girlfriend for a year and pack her shit and kick her to the curb? You blindsided me! I still have my coat on, and my hair is damp from the spa you forced me to go to." I stand, needing to put some space between us.

"It's not like that."

A laugh erupts from my throat. This one dripping with sarcasm. He glares at me through narrowed eyes.

"Fuck you, John." I turn and head to my office.

Storming inside the room, I expect to find it bare and boxed up, but everything appears to be just as I left it. Walking over to my desk, I yank on cords and pack up my workstation. After all, I need my work laptop and a few things before I can get the hell out of here.

John hovers by the door. The air is suddenly thick as it presses on my lungs. Moving quicker, I start shoving things into my backpack.

"I didn't touch your office."

Well, isn't that a relief. Thank you, jackass.

Is he expecting a grand gesture or something? He had an emotional and physical affair with someone else, and this is what he chooses to say to me right now. He doesn't bring up the fact that he lied or wasted my time. He just stands there, watching me. As if I'm going to attack him if he gets too close.

Oh God...did he bring her here while I was away? Did he sleep with her in my bed?

I'm definitely going to be sick.

I obviously met her on more than one occasion. He works with her. She had dinner at our house a couple of times. I bet his close colleagues all know about it too. A conversation from a few months ago pops up in my head. I remember sitting at the dinner table across from him, nursing my cup of peppermint tea while John reheated his dinner. He came home well after ten p.m. most nights, but I would always have his dinner there so he could eat something healthy. I remember joining him that night, and he barely said two words to me. Somehow the topic of sex came up, and he told me his work was so stressful that it was affecting his libido.

That couldn't have been more than four months ago.

Months and months of lies.

Once the election is over, let's sit down together and plan a much-needed vacation. Do you want to go to the Caribbean? Mexico? Bahamas? Maybe Greece?

He fed me endless lies while he was sleeping with Jessica.

The bastard was likely making the same plans with her.

I fucking hate liars.

I move towards my bookshelves and stare at my collection of novels, promising to return to them while I grab my e-reader and sketchbook. Swallowing the huge lump in my throat, I turn to the door, hoping to shoulder-check John on my way out but he gives me plenty of space.

I don't look at him as I make my way towards my bedroom. I bet he's counting down the seconds until I leave.

Jessica is probably waiting in the stairwell with her own bags, ready to move in.

"Don't you or that woman touch my books. I'll come box them up and take them along with my shelves and desk. I'm not sure when but I'll be back."

"Of course. I'll keep the door closed until you get your things," he mumbles from somewhere behind me.

It would be so easy to let my rage run wild. I want to throw everything around and wreck his entire apartment before I leave. It would feel really good to trash the contents of his fridge all over the kitchen floors. It would be liberating. But I can't set the anger free, not when it threatens to consume me. I'll just shove this part of my life down, to the pits of my soul until it becomes a distant memory.

I'm good at avoiding things. Actually, I'm great at it. I think I could probably give TED talks about avoidance. I mean, no one should listen to me because I have enough baggage to load a plane, but that's how qualified I am.

The king bed is perfectly made. Throw cushions sit neatly on the slate grey comforter I washed two days ago. The house is in tip-top shape, and I'm sure it's because Jessica is coming over.

Why does that thought make me feel so sick? Half the closet sits empty. A clean split down the middle, waiting to be filled. All traces of me are gone, just like that. In a matter of hours. It was that easy for him to get rid of three years. Longer if you count our relationship back in Vancouver.

I open all the drawers, making sure nothing was left behind.

It's all empty...like I was never here.

"Everything is packed for you in the suitcases. I'll text you sometime next week and let you know when you can come by for the rest of your stuff. You can hold on to the key for now. But please, don't show up randomly."

Translation: don't come by unannounced since Jessica will be here.

Rage vibrates through me like an old Honda Civic trying to start up in the middle of winter. He's so calm. Not a trace of guilt or remorse on his face. His eyes are ice cold and void of any emotion.

I am such an idiot.

"Where the hell am I supposed to go, John? Everyone I know is in Vancouver. You've had this planned for a while. Do you expect me to sleep on a park bench? I need some time to figure out my next steps. Why don't you go stay with your girl-friend while I find a place?" The words come out louder than I expect them to.

I can't wait to get the hell out of here but I refuse to go unprepared. I've been stashing away money for months now, and it will help me secure a new place to live. But finding a new home takes time, and time is the one thing I don't have. He offered no warning, no consideration for my future. Instead, he blindsided me and threw a bucket of ice-cold water right in my face as soon as I walked through the doors.

Briefly, I consider calling my dad, but I'd rather sleep on a park bench than do that right now.

John runs his hand down his face, exasperated from dealing with me.

"You're right." He sighs, pulling out his wallet. He digs out a card, holding it out to me. "Stay wherever you want. I'll cancel the card by the end of the week."

"You're giving me your credit card?"

He shrugs, like I just asked him if he likes Tacos. "Consider it a parting gift."

"Fuck. You." I hiss.

He doesn't say anything, his eyes simply find the floor

again. Snobby rich asshole, thinking he can do whatever he wants and then use his daddy's money to fix it.

I snatch the card out of his hand, turning away, but he places his disgusting palm on my shoulder, stopping me. I draw back, nudging him off.

"I hope one day you'll understand and be happy for me."

I don't look at him. Don't utter any words as I walk across the apartment, grab my things and head out the door.

And the worst part, I can't feel anything as I leave the place I called home merely hours ago.

I expected to be in pain by now, to feel the weight of my heart breaking into pieces. But instead, all I feel is numbness, a cold void that permeates every inch of my body. It's as if I'm watching this entire day play out from a distance, detached and aloof. All I'm missing is some popcorn.

I should be crying, but the tears refuse to come. The only thing that remains is a sense of familiar emptiness that echoes through my soul.

Broken doesn't even begin to describe me anymore.

Everything feels dull when you've been walking around in complete darkness for most of your life. Perhaps that's my problem. What happened to me in that parking lot years ago ruined me so badly that I can't even feel broken hearted over something like this.

I thought I had made progress. Regained some emotional connection and stability. But it turns out, I don't even know who I am. The old me would have caught on to his deception well before now. Old me would have cared, cried a little, maybe even pulled over and bought a tub of Rocky Road ice cream.

The old me would not have been with someone for so long just because it felt safe. The old Avery was romantic and full of hope, like my father. She dreamt about getting married one day and having a bunch of kids. She was full of light.

When it was all over with John, I got in my car and drove off. Didn't dare glance back to take one last look at the apartment complex on Queens Park.

This place. This city, it never really felt like home to me. It always felt temporary, like a clock was ticking in the background, counting down the moments, until my timer was up. I was trying to force myself to be someone I'll never be. It's time I stop trying to fit into an uncomfortable mold. No one is ever going to love someone as ugly and fractured as me.

I'll be alone forever.

It's better that way.

No expectations, no disappointments, no waiting around. No lying or cheating.

No one to suddenly make me homeless.

Lesson learned. Thank you, universe. A warning sign would have been nice. I would say for next time but there won't be a next time.

John's credit card digs into my hip, burning a hole in my pocket. I shouldn't have taken it. I'm not sure I'll even use it. But why shouldn't I? One last gesture from good ol' Johnny boy. Because he's just so 'kind' to me and always has been.

Fuck that guy. On second thought, I will use his card.

I drive around aimlessly, not knowing where to go or what to do with myself. I should look for a hotel, but the thought of sitting on a cold bed in an empty room stewing in my own thoughts makes me want to... No, I can't even go there.

I need a distraction. Go somewhere far away from here.

I don't feel heartbroken. Not in the way I thought I would. Maybe betrayed and embarrassed for being so oblivious. After all, I'm the idiot that left her family and friends in Vancouver and uprooted her entire life for a guy. At the time, I thought a fresh start would do me some good.

Boy, was I wrong.

And on top of that, I have no family or friends here. Not really, all my friends are John's friends. I should have invested more time building my own circle in Toronto, but I was fine with simply existing.

I should go back to Vancouver and forget about the last three years of my life. But the thought of going back to Vancouver like this breaks my heart more than finding out John was cheating on me.

How twisted is that?

I should have stayed in therapy. Dr. Samson gave me the option to continue seeing him virtually after I moved. We tried for a few months but it just wasn't the same. And I was doing better. Time had healed a lot of my wounds so I stopped making appointments. He emailed me a few times but eventually, that ended too.

Home brings back terrible memories for me. Memories I worked so hard to shed. It reminds me of a time when I was beyond repair. A time when I didn't know if I would make it out alive. Darkness ravaged me for years. Vancouver reminds me of the old, weak me and all the emptiness that came along with that. I'll face it one day but not today.

Maybe I can convince my dad to move somewhere else. A fresh start for both of us. He's been talking about retiring. It would be perfect timing. I'll just have to suck it up and call him.

And tell him about John and the fact that I am suddenly homeless.

Shit.

Maybe I don't have to call. I could just book a ticket and

show up. *Surprise, Dad, my ex-boyfriend is a piece of hot garbage, just like you always predicted. Congratulations, you were right. Now deal with your pathetic twenty-six-year-old daughter while she tries to figure out where to go from here.*

I groan, pressing my forehead against the cold steering wheel as I wait at a never-ending red light.

When did everything become so unbearable?

It wasn't always like this. I used to be bubbly and outgoing, but life slowly chipped away at me. First my parents' divorce, then my mom abandoning me for love and lust. Then what I refer to as D-Day—my dark day.

And here I am again, completely alone in a city where I have no one to turn to and nowhere to go. At least I tried, right? If I ever see Dr. Samson again, I can proudly tell him that I tried. For three years, I tried to fit myself into a square peg when I'm clearly a triangle.

I thought it would finally set me free.

But what if I can't fit in anywhere?

You don't belong. You never belonged.

The shadow whispers in my head, filling me with hateful words. I wish I could quiet my mind for just a second. A second of silence. I shove the voice aside, focusing on the moment.

What do you want?

The impossible question that keeps nagging at me, one I don't have an answer to.

I want to fill the gaping void inside my soul. I'm tired of feeling stuck, living in fear and doubt. I want to be brave, do scary things, and take risks. I want to rediscover the woman I was always meant to be, the one who loves herself and knows she's enough. I want to heal, to break free from the chains of the past, and embrace the light.

I want to stop running.

My chin trembles with all the emotions rippling through

me. God, I don't think I've ever truly loved and accepted myself. Not in the way I've needed to.

How can anyone else love me if I can't even love myself?

Dr. Samson's voice whispers in my head.

Spend the next three minutes letting the emotions run free. Don't block them out. Imagine them as a small wave moving up towards the sandy beach. Watch as the water runs past your ankles. And then, just as quickly as it came, feel it pull away and back into the ocean. Let the emotions and anger wash back out to sea. Let go of what you cannot control or change.

I repeat my old therapist's words in my head again and imagine myself at the beach, my toes sinking into the cold sand. Until finally, my breathing slows down.

My body begins to relax.

Breathe in. Breathe out. This, too, will pass.

Once upon a time, I became who I needed to be in order to survive, to see another day. I put up walls and lived within the small confines of my mind. The thought of starting over feels impossible right now but living this way is no longer an option. I need to break free from the past, from everything that's been holding me back.

What better time to start than now? When my entire life is sitting in suitcases in the back of my car.

I can go anywhere, start over.

Pressing my foot on the gas pedal, I drive away from the darkness that's been haunting me for years.

CHAPTER FOUR

avery

I pull up to the ticket machine and press the giant green button. Ignoring the aggressive thumping in my chest, I snatch the parking slip and place it on the dashboard. The yellow and black partition raises.

No going back now.

Technically, I can peel out of here the same way I came, but I'm not going to.

This feels right.

I feel a little buzzed, even though I haven't had a lick of alcohol. I have no idea where I'm going yet, but it's not back to Vancouver. I need some time before I can face my dad.

Before I can face reality.

I make a mental note to text him and Becca as soon as I can. Before I board...or maybe after I land because I don't want anyone trying to talk me out of this.

I park my car close to the doors and stare at the grey concrete wall in front of me with the giant yellow F3 written on it. Pulling out my phone, I take a photo of the yellow letters because I'm not sure I'll remember it later with the adrenaline running through me right now.

Taking a shaky breath, I pull the visor down and pop open the small car mirror. Sometimes, I don't know who is staring back at me. I don't recognize myself, like I shouldn't be in this body. I stare back at a set of sad brown eyes. My eyes are darker than normal and my hair is still damp, pulled into a messy bun on the top of my head. Curls desperate to break free. My skin is dull, lacking color and emotion, which seems to be the theme of the day. My lips are puffy and chapped. The side of my lip is close to opening, I was probably chewing on it while driving.

Terrible nervous habit.

I look like shit but I don't care enough to do anything about it. I've never really thought much about my appearance. Brown hair, olive skin, brown eyes. It's all dull and mundane. I have my dad's large eyes and his thick hair, but my colour palette and the rest of me looks just like my mom. And I hate that a little bit.

She's beautiful. Too bad it's only surface deep.

I remember the guilt I felt after my mom left. Dad took it incredibly hard. She was the love of his life, and one day she decided she didn't want us anymore.

A few weeks after she left, I think I was around nine at the time, he called me down one morning for breakfast. We hadn't sat down together to eat since Mom left. It felt weird to sit at the table without her. Dad had made pancakes and just as I dug in, he burst into tears. I had never seen him like that before. He reeked of alcohol as he sat there, staring at me. He said I reminded him of her. I hid in my room for a few days after that because I didn't want to make him cry again.

I've been saving up for a long time. One of the many perks of being an introvert in a new city is you get to stay home and save money. I can go anywhere and support myself comfortably for half a year, but I'll have to figure out my work situation. Thankfully, I can work from virtually anywhere in the world being a web developer. They just prefer to have advance notice if you move, but I'm hopeful my boss will make an exception. I'll have to sort out my hours with her and figure it all out when I get to wherever I'm going. Maybe I'll take a vacation. I haven't taken time off in three years, after all.

I take one last look at the pathetic woman staring back at me before I step out of the car. My legs feel heavy as I haul my bags, lock the car and make my way to departures at the Toronto Pearson Airport.

Doubt fills my head as the wheels on my suitcases gurgle in the background. Maybe I should just go to a hotel and sleep on it.

I have no plans.

Zero.

I'm free to go somewhere and spend quality time with myself. I may never get this opportunity again. I would really like to look in the mirror and not hate the woman staring back at me. If I head to a hotel, I'll just be thinking about my old apartment and my ex-boyfriend having Sunday dinner with his new girlfriend.

That's not going to happen, not today.

I'VE BEEN STANDING in front of three giant screens for what feels like an eternity. I glance at my watch, and it's almost seven p.m. Didn't I get to the apartment in the early afternoon? It feels like this day will never end.

Where do I want to go? Correction, where do I NEED to go?

No sunny locations with happy couples plastered to one another. I love the ocean, but I can't be around that. It'll just remind me of my piteous little life. I'd like to go somewhere green and quiet. It's the middle of September, which means it's generally the slow season in most places. No place with attractive men in my face. Somewhere colder, but not too cold. Lots of scenery and beautiful landscape.

I'd love to sit somewhere for hours with my sketchbook.

Los Angeles - no

Mexico - no

Paris - the city of love...hell no

Amsterdam - maybe

Geneva - I would love to go to Switzerland

The screens flash to black simultaneously for a second, before new destinations pop up.

That's weird. I've never seen it do that before.

Glasgow.

A silent buzz tickles down my arms. Something tugs inside me, and without a doubt I know where I want to go.

I've never been to Scotland, but I have always been infatuated by it.

Scotland has everything. Historically rich cities that hold such contrast to the wild landscape. A land of rugged beauty and deep history. Rolling hills, haunting castles, misty mountains capped with snow, countless glens, valleys, and sparkling streams. The country has always stirred something deep within my soul.

It's an artist's dream.

And maybe the perfect place to finally heal.

The closest to Scotland I ever got was Ireland. It was our last family trip, unbeknownst to me at the time. My dad had a business trip, so my parents decided to extend our stay and we explored Ireland for a week. It was where I had some of my best childhood memories. And two days after we got home, my parents sat me down and told me they were separating.

Scotland feels like the perfect place to start fresh. To make new memories just for me. The land of mystery and magic, where they say the past and the present intertwine.

Maybe I can find some of that magic too.

I make my way over to the airline desk, where an older lady, with a sleek blonde bun and perfectly painted pink lips is typing away on her computer. Her strong perfume slaps me right in the face. It smells very similar to Chanel No5, my mother's signature scent.

"Hello," I utter softly, already feeling bad about interrupting her.

"Hi," she says without looking up at me. I notice she doesn't have a name tag. When she finally glances up, she narrows her eyes and offers me a tight smile.

"Are there any seats left on the Glasgow flight taking off at eight-thirty?"

"You don't have a ticket?" She looks behind me and takes note of my suitcases.

"No."

She takes a deep breath. Definitely annoyed with me. Would it help my situation if I told her I was freshly dumped? "I think that flight may be full, but let me take a look."

Her nails clack loudly on the keyboard.

"There are only two business class seats left." She looks up at me and smiles, her head tilting to the side.

"Sorry," she says, pouting.

Rude.

"That's fine. I'll take one." I hand over my passport along

with John's credit card. I make sure to plaster on the biggest smile I could muster up. She doesn't reach for my things.

"It's $3,500." She says coldly.

"That's fine."

"Very well," she mutters, reaching over to grab my passport and credit card.

I take a deep breath, looking down at my shaky hands. This is absolutely fine. John told me to spend his money. He didn't specify where I could stay.

My pulse refuses to slow down.

I should just cancel the whole thing and turn around.

"When do you intend on returning?"

Shit...

"I'm not sure. Can we say six weeks and leave the option open for changing the flight if I need to?" I ask hesitantly.

"That will cost extra." All traces of the previous fake smile is completely gone.

"Okay."

What am I doing?

Not thinking clearly, it seems.

Thankfully we don't exchange any more words and she gets to work. A minute later she reaches for my bags, and I help load them on to the conveyor belt. She types some more on her keys and then hands me my boarding pass, passport, and John's approved credit card.

"Thank you." I smile at her, but she doesn't even look at me as she motions for the next person in line to approach her desk.

Good riddance.

I exhale the breath I was holding this entire time as I head for security.

The next couple of hours are a blur. I fly through security, which is a tiny miracle all on its own. I grab some food and pick up a new book before heading to my terminal. I pay for everything with my own money and seriously consider cutting up John's card. It didn't feel right using it for the flight like that.

I barely have time for a bathroom break before they announce boarding.

I smile at the kind flight attendants as I make my way to my seat. I've never flown first class before, so this is so exciting. I quickly pull out my phone and fire off a text to my dad and Becca. And as soon as the texts are delivered, I turn my phone on to airplane mode.

I'll happily deal with the I-told-you-so messages when I land in Glasgow.

I'm dreading the conversation with my father, but I know Becca will have my back. We've been friends since we were five and we only grow stronger every day. Even though she is still in Vancouver and I live in Toronto, we still text and call almost daily. She's like the sister I never had. The type of person who would drop everything for the people she loves. If I had called her from the airport and told her to meet me in Scotland, she would do it no questions asked.

I would have kept a few more friendships if it hadn't been for John demanding I uninstall all my social media. He didn't want any stories popping up and surprising him when he was on the campaign trail. His family already didn't use social media, unless it was run by their office. I agreed, so I lost contact with my other friends. Over-time, people got busy with their own lives and forgot to stay in touch.

No social media. Never really cared much for TV. I barely socialize and might as well live in a cave with my books for the rest of my life.

You'd think after years of therapy I would be a bit better at all of this. Maybe if I had put in more effort I wouldn't be so lonely.

A kind flight attendant pauses by my seat, smiling down at

me. "Would you like a drink, miss?" She is holding out a warm, rolled-up towel and I reach for it eagerly. She has a hint of a Scottish accent, and hearing it is already making me feel better.

"I'd love a whisky. Thank you." I unravel the hot towel and place it on my face. The warmth radiates deep into my pores, forcing me to relax into my seat. I take a deep breath, filling my lungs with the calming minty notes.

But no amount of warm towels could contain the excitement and wonder for all that awaits me in Scotland.

A fresh start. It's about damn time.

CHAPTER FIVE

avery

I arrived in Glasgow three days ago and I'm already sick of myself.

The loneliness is itchy and uncomfortable. Almost convinced my dad to fly here while I was talking to him on the phone last night. We could use a nice vacation, lord knows it's been forever, but I couldn't ask him.

We've been talking more since I got here, more than we did when I lived in Toronto. Dad was a lot happier than I thought he would be at my change of scenery. I don't know why I thought he would be upset, but he was proud of me for doing something for myself for once.

Becca was absolutely ecstatic. Apparently, she has always hated John and only put up with him for me. She offered to join me in Scotland and has been scouring the internet looking for cheap flights. It's tempting, but I need to be alone for a little while.

Really alone.

Uncomfortable-in-my-skin alone. And she understands that.

The first day was a write-off. I spent it nursing a bottle of whisky from a grocery store while staring at the four beige walls in my hotel room. I did the one thing that I emphatically didn't want to do in Toronto. Guess it didn't matter where I ended up, I was going to mope for a whole day regardless.

I got drunk, looked at flights, contemplated reinstalling all my socials but decided against it. I scrolled Expedia looking for flights back to Vancouver before I passed out. Waking up the next day with a raging headache was not part of the plan and I swore to never drink again.

On day two, after my headache subsided, I ventured outside for a bit. Grabbed a couple of new raincoats and a pair of hiking boots. It was nice to get out and explore close-by neighbourhoods. Glasgow is the perfect blend of old and new. Some buildings have been preserved and are oozing with rich history, and some are new with a modern aesthetic.

Everyone here walks with purpose. It's a busy city and easy to blend in, even though I'm sure I look like a lost tourist, relying way too much on my iPhone to get me places. I was outside all day today and even sat at a coffee shop alone. My day was spent mostly reading, exploring, and filling a few pages of my sketchbook. Walked around a few small museums and actually managed to keep myself busy.

The days are fine, but the nights since I left have been slow and treacherous.

I spend a lot of my nights in the hotel room alone, drinking and eating. It's just not a good combination and I'm starting to think I need to get out of the city. Away from everyone and everything.

I glance at the clock and it's just after four-thirty. I got back twenty minutes ago but I can't stay in this room all night. I order an Uber and decide to make tonight my last night in Glasgow.

Bothwell Castle is only a fifteen-minute car ride from central Glasgow.

Tomorrow I'll head to Edinburgh.

Twenty minutes later I step out of the Uber, and a large medieval castle in ruins greets me. The place is deserted, the air feels cleaner, and there is a heavy silence around me instead of the bustling city noises.

"You know Ubers don't come back here, and there are no taxis. You'll have to take the train back," the driver kindly informs me.

"Thank you. That's good to know."

My feet sink into the wet grass as I make my way towards the castle entrance. The walls are weathered, and the stones are uneven. It feels as though a large gust of wind could push the entire thing down. I wander around the empty courtyard, taking in the sight of the old stonework.

According to an information board, construction of the castle began in the thirteenth century. Bothwell played a key role in Scotland's Wars of Independence, changing hands several times. Lots of people lived and died right here. And on and on the historical information reads.

Climbing up a nearby stairwell, I enter a second floor that's open to the sky. Running my hands on the rustic red bricks I feel scribbles tickle the pads of my fingers. Names scratched into the walls in all different shapes and sizes. I can't help but wonder how many ghosts roam this land at night.

It doesn't take me long to walk the grounds and explore the rest of the castle. I've seen everything, including a room full of ancient artifacts. A few vases, utensils, and old plates from when the castle was bursting with life centuries ago.

I make my way out of the castle, walking down a lonely gravel road. Trees stand tall above the road, swaying in the wind as colourful leaves cover the ground. Something about this spot resonates with me.

I sit on the grass and pull open my sketchbook.

The sound of charcoal scratching the blank paper fills the air, erasing my thoughts with each stroke. My mind always tiptoes away quietly with a charcoal pencil in my hand. I took up sketching after my parents' divorce. At first, it was a way for me to ground myself and focus on something else, but over time it became something I loved to do.

The lone path and burly trees come to life on paper. I run my finger along the image to blend the shadows. Once I'm satisfied with the picture, I mark the bottom edge with the location and date.

As I leave the castle grounds, the streets turn into Scottish suburbia. Houses tucked away neatly from the road, each appearing to have a different size and age. I'm jealous of the owners of these homes. Their backyard overlooks a castle. A perfect marriage of old and new, tucked away in this small corner of Scotland.

A part of me wishes I was born into a different time. A time when life was simple. Maybe love was more prevalent too. A type of love that burned a fire in your soul. I've read about it. Who hasn't? Books are filled with tales of all-consuming love. A love so great that one can simply not exist without it. Too bad it's all fiction.

Why do we want things we can never have? Why do people write about something that don't exist?Maybe so we could all feel something for a little while. Slip into a different world full of hope, love, lust, and passion.

That's why I like reading romance novels. They help me forget who I am. And I discover what deep emotions like love and intimacy might feel like. I've never been in love and I've never desired sex in the way others do. Likely because of the man who raped me and turned sex into something hideous.

It took years of therapy to rid myself of the nightly terrors and panic attacks. It took even longer to go back to doing normal things, like going somewhere alone or dating or even being intimate with someone. It still doesn't feel right. It never has, and I've never been able to turn my brain off during sex. Which means I've never been able to climax with a guy. I'm not sure what that says about me but at least I became a master at faking it. I don't think John ever caught on, or maybe he did and that's why he went looking for Jessica.

It's all just about release, and if I can't escape my thoughts, then it's not really an enjoyable experience. I mean, I went an entire year without having sex with my boyfriend and didn't even notice.

No, that's a lie. I did notice. I just didn't care.

It doesn't matter anymore.

That chapter of my life is permanently over.

As it's my final night in Glasgow, I didn't want to spend it cooped up in my hotel room, drinking alone. So, I decided to visit the Piper Whisky Bar, which is a short walk from where I'm staying in George Street. Although I'm alone, I'm excited to immerse myself in the vibrant bar culture that Scotland is renowned for.

A week ago, I wouldn't be found dead at a bar or restaurant by myself. Hooray for small wins.

I pause in front of the bar, staring at the ancient wooden door, wondering if I should turn my ass around and walk back to my hotel.

Get over yourself.

I pull on the handle, leaving my fears and insecurities at the curb. The smell of stale ale and cigarette smoke burn my nostrils as soon as I step inside. The room is dimly lit, casting a glow over the patrons huddled around large wooden barrels scattered on cobblestone floors.

Suddenly, I am transported back in time to old Scotland. Well, what I imagine old Scotland would be like based on the history books I digested in university. Laughter and loud conversation drown out the Scottish music playing in the background.

I spot the large bar in the back of the room and feel a wave of anxiety as I make my way over to an empty stool. The smell of fries and vinegar surrounds me like a warm hug, as a waitress walks by with two plates of fish and chips. My stomach grumbles, and I'm reminded that I barely ate today.

I stick out like a sore thumb, but I try to avoid making eye contact with anyone. There is an impressive collection of alcohol lining the wall behind the bar. And a huge selection of whisky.

The bartender looks up from cleaning a glass and nods in my direction.

"Hiya! What are you having?" He's short and sporting a buzz cut. It looks like he spends most of his free time at the gym. Large tattoos line his hands, crawling up his wide arms and past his skintight black shirt.

I lean on the table, scanning the vast collection of golden liquid bottles.

"Whisky for sure, but you have so many, I don't know which one to choose." I offer the bartender a meek smile, hoping he'll decide for me.

He grins, instantly reaching for a bottle and pouring a small amount in a glass. "Try this one, it's new. Remarkably smooth with a hint of cinnamon and smoke."

Nervously, I lift the glass to my lips, noting the inviting aroma as the rich amber liquid meets my tongue. Complex flavours of smoke, citrus and cinnamon linger on my palate, smooth and pleasant. I feel the warmth of the whisky spread through my body, and I can't help but take another sip.

"It's amazing. I'll take a glass."

The bartender nods, pouring me two fingers' worth in a

simple whisky glass. I take notice of the logo on the bottle. *Anam Cara*...sounds Gaelic. A gold ring sits behind the name with a beautiful symbol. I haven't seen a logo this intricate before.

"I'm Archie. Let me know if you need anything else," he says, sliding me the bill.

"Thank you, Archie." I smile at him, settling further into my seat and feeling content.

See, being alone at a bar isn't so bad.

With every sip of whisky, I feel more at ease. As I take in the lively bar, I can't help but feel a sense of familiarity and comfort, even though I've never been here before. I'm not sure if it's the new whisky or my bravery, but I feel good.

Archie walks back to take my card, and his eyebrows raise in surprise when he notices my already empty glass. "You like it then?" He laughs.

"Oh yes, may I get another? Thank you."

When Archie comes back with more whisky, I order the mouthwatering fish and chips that whizzed by me earlier. The bar is alive with energy, music, and joyful chatter as more people crowd inside. I take a deep breath and glance around, realizing I'm the only one here alone. The weight of that thought presses down on me, like a boulder sitting in the center of my chest.

I steel myself, deciding to make the most of my solo experience. But a bit of virtual company won't be a bad thing either.

I pull out my phone and fire a text off to Becca. Looking at the time, I realize she must be asleep. It's still very early in the morning in Vancouver right now.

Alone with my thoughts once more.

Just as I'm about to put my phone away, it vibrates in my hand. I scan the screen and my heart sinks at the name. A slow panic rushes through my blood.

JOHN

Why the fuck am I getting international charges in Scotland? Did you leak my card info online as payback?

It's fine. *Channel your anger.*

ME

You told me to find somewhere to stay, so I did.

JOHN

Wow, Avery. I told you to find a hotel, not fly to Scotland.

My fingers tap across the screen with violent speed. I want to tell him how much of a piece of shit he is and how my whereabouts are no longer his concern. All the words I want to say to him appear on the screen, boiling my blood. I pause, my thumb hovering over the send button but then, I delete it all.

Bubbles appear on screen.

JOHN

Do what you need to do…I'm cancelling the card. When will you be by for your things?

He's waving a very deflated truce flag. He can shove it up his ass.

ME

I'm not sure.

Why do I feel guilty? I have no reason to feel guilty. I'm not a user, was never with him for his money. Our relationship was never about that and yet, I still feel dirty for using his card. I shouldn't. He cheated on me. Other people might have left with damages, but I just grabbed my stuff and walked out.

I shouldn't let him make me feel bad about this.

Maybe I should thank him for the accommodations?

I grunt, slamming my phone down on the bar.

"Rough night?" A deep, raspy British voice draws my attention.

I glance over my right shoulder to find a tall, well-built man dressed in tight jeans and a black T-shirt standing behind me. Every inch of his arms are covered in tattoos, and some ink pokes out above his neck line, crawling up to his strong jaw. My eyes rove up, finding bright green orbs staring down at me. Mr. Handsome has stubble on his face and blond hair that's pulled back into a bun. He's sporting a vicious smile and a silver lip ring in the corner of his bottom lip.

I bite my cheek, trying to hold back a laugh imagining John's face if he were to see me talking to this guy right now.

His preppy personality could never.

"Rough week," I utter before taking another swig from my glass.

"You first." Mr. Handsome takes a seat on the stool beside me, looking sideways trying to get Archie's attention.

"You might need a few drinks first." I say.

He laughs, just as Archie approaches us, glancing at me with a concerned look. My new friend orders a beer, and I offer Archie a tight smile, letting him know I'm okay. He nods, walking to the beer taps.

I get a prickling sensation and turn to see Mr. Handsome staring at me. Not in a subtle way, as if he's trying to picture me naked. His eyes travel down to my chest, and he licks his lips.

Well, that's not what you want.

I shift in my seat, turning my body away from his obnoxious gaze.

"Whatever it is can't be that bad." I don't look at him. Instead, I focus on Archie as he approaches holding a tall pint of beer. Placing it in front of the man sitting next to me.

The man I suddenly want to run away from.

"Bad enough that I'm sitting here alone talking to a complete stranger," I murmur into my drink.

A beat of silence passes, and for a second I'm hopeful he may just get up and leave.

"That's a good thing. Otherwise, you wouldn't have met me."

Good grief. This is just getting better and better. I should have ordered in and stayed at the hotel.

Maybe I'm way past help. I don't need a therapist, I need a mechanic for humans. Shouldn't I want to rebound with a random hot, tattooed guy at a bar? But the mere thought makes me nauseous.

"My ex won't let me see my kid. Today she messaged me saying she is filing for sole custody. In a fucking text message. That lad is my everything, and she wants to take him away from me. What kind of bitch does that?"

Keeping my eyes on the glass shelves in front of me, I can't help but wonder what he did for her to want to take his kid away.

I pause. "I'm sorry, that must be tough."

It's quiet again. The silence is uncomfortable and heavy.

The bartender makes his rounds, and I thank the heavens for the welcome interruption. Archie asks if we want more drinks, and I open my mouth to answer, but Mr. Not-so-handsome beats me to it.

"You bet, mate. And another one for her too." Archie nods and walks away quickly.

I'm not sure a third whisky is such a great idea right now.

"Your turn." His knee nudges mine before I register his words. I shift my body away from him.

It was just a friendly nudge, no need to panic.

"I still want to know why a beautiful woman is drinking at the pub alone." He observes me while sipping his beer.

I sneer, shaking my head and exhaling slowly. "Fair is fair, I suppose."

I play with my glass, watching the liquid swirl round and round.

"I decided to take a spontaneous vacation after my long-term boyfriend confessed to having a year-long affair with another woman, whom he is evidently in love with." The words hang heavy in the air. I watch him carefully, waiting for his unwanted pity or judgement.

But he doesn't give me either. Instead, he laughs. His voice booms across the loud bar, turning a few heads around us.

"That's fucking brutal, mate."

I can't help but laugh because he's right. My life is a joke.

One big fat joke after another.

My food arrives and I eagerly pop a fat fry in my mouth, groaning. This is the best fry I've ever had. Why do chunky fries taste so much better in the UK?

Mr. Not-so-handsome coughs, choking on his sip of beer.

"What?" I pop another fry in my mouth.

He shakes his head, smirking. "His loss, especially with sounds like that coming out of you."

My eyes bulge and I almost spit out my food. Brown curls fall around my face, covering my heated cheeks.

What sound?

"Want to get out of here?" He plays with his lip ring, tipping his chin towards the door.

"What?"

His green eyes fall down at my full plate of food. "You can eat after."

Excuse me? After what?!

"I don't even know your name." I laugh but it sounds more like a nervous sputter than anything else.

He shrugs. "You don't need to, sweetheart."

Desperation is oozing out of him, making his lack of game entirely too evident.

"As tempting as that may be—" I cut into a piece of fish "—I think I'll eat my food and get some sleep, alone. I've had a long day."

He reaches behind his head, pulling the hair tie out and running his hand through his thick wavy locks. I bite my lip to keep from laughing. Does this typically work on other women? Was the hair ploy his Plan B?

He winks, sticking his tongue out at me, and I suddenly lose my appetite.

"I'll make it worth your while. Don't you want to forget all about that ex?"

I push my plate away and snicker to myself.

I think I'll get this to go and head back to my room. I still have some whisky back in my very beige hotel room, but at least it's quiet there and less hair waving in the breeze. I look down the bar, trying to spot Archie.

"Sounds great, but I've sworn off men for the foreseeable future. Thanks for the offer, though." I raise my glass to my lips, chugging the rest of the whisky.

"Fine. Your loss." He shoots up from his stool, throws some cash down on the bar, and walks away without looking at me once.

We didn't even exchange names, and he wanted to take me back to his place.

Jesus, I'm definitely in the wrong time period. What happened to subtle smiles and gentle compliments? Stolen glances and heart flutters? If this is the reality of dating, I want nothing to do with it.

Archie walks over a minute later, scowling at my full plate of fish and chips.

"Everything all right with the meal?"

"Oh yes, it's delicious. Can I actually get it to go?"

"Aye, not a problem." He takes a step before pausing and turning to face me.

"I shouldn't be saying this, but stay away from that fella. He's no good company." Archie looks behind me and I don't have to turn around to know who he's referring to. But eventually my curiosity gives in and I turn to see Mr. Not-so-handsome, leaning on a table facing five young women. He says something, and they all burst out laughing. There is a beautiful redhead, playing with her hair as she stares intensely at him. I bet she'll be the lucky one he takes home.

I turn back towards Archie. "You don't have to worry about me. I already told him no, that's why he's over there."

Archie flashes me a brilliant smile. "Good. You seem like one of the smart ones."

A few minutes pass, and I finally make my way to the pub doors, clutching my cold takeout in my hand. My eye catches on Mr. Douchebag as he works his hands through his locks, buttering up his next prey, which happens to be the redhead who was entranced by him earlier. He doesn't even notice me walk past him.

I push through the doors and smile to myself as a cold gust of wind yanks my hair in my face. If tonight solidified anything to me, it's that I'm definitely not interested in being with anyone for a very long time. And when the need strikes, there are tools that don't require a warm body and they never miss the spot.

CHAPTER SEVEN

avery

Every single piece of my heart will forever belong to the beautiful city of Edinburgh.

I wasn't expecting to fall as hard as I did. But as I walked down the Royal Mile—the city's most famous street that leads to the Edinburgh Castle—and gazed upon the castle perched proudly atop the hill, I knew I was done for. I spent hours exploring the castle and its network of courtyards, dungeons, and halls dripping with endless tales. I watched the sun as it bathed the castle in orange and golden lights, casting a magical flare over the city. I'll forever remember how the sight took my breath away.

The entire city of Edinburgh feels so much more than just winding streets and medieval architecture. Every corner, every street, every building feels like a living, breathing part of Scotland's rich history and identity.

I spent all of yesterday exploring. Edinburgh is a theatrical grace set in between intricate ridges and vast hills. Tall buildings and spires of dark stone welcomed me at each corner. I walked around, discovering haunting cemeteries perched in the middle of the narrow streets. From every angle, this place appears like a work of art. I tried to capture every moment on paper. My wrist hurts today from all the sketching.

I feel like this place has kickstarted my pulse. I haven't travelled the entire world, but I'm certain Scotland is one of the most beautiful places on Earth. And I can't wait to see the rest of it.

I ended a full day of exploration standing atop Arthur's Seat and watching the sunset. It was poorly planned on my part since my legs were burning by the time I climbed down from the highest point in Edinburgh. But the breathtaking views of the city and surrounding countryside were well worth the burn.

Thanks to many years of running, I had no issues climbing up the trail. The hike was strenuous at parts, but it was well marked, and a great way to take in the natural beauty of the hill. Though, it was the sunset kissing the hill that stole the show. I had never seen colours so vibrant swirling in the sky up close, it felt as if I could reach out and smear my fingers through the bright colours.

I was entranced as I gazed upon the setting sun. It happened so fast. Within twenty minutes, the colours disappeared, as darkness edged its way in, taking hold of everything. Swallowing the light. Everything slipped away as I took it all in and just sat in the moment, trying to capture the stillness and the sound of the wind in my heart.

I fell asleep that night with anticipation buzzing in my mind. It has been so long since I have felt truly excited about anything.

AS I MAKE my way to the car rental place this morning, a renewed sense of energy propels me. The anticipation to get to the highlands has me skipping my morning coffee, which is unheard of for me.

"You're all set, Ms. Harris. You can extend or shorten the rental through the link in the email we sent you. If you need anything else, call the number on here." The clerk hands me the car keys and motions to the number on the keychain.

Thankfully it's slow season and I have no issues securing a car.

"Thank you."

I walk out and find the green Citroen waiting by the curb for me. It was the only automatic they had at Budget, which is helpful, but it doesn't stop the sudden fear creeping in as I realize I have no experience with driving on the other side of the road. Hopefully I don't end up in a ditch within five minutes of driving.

I take a deep breath and open the door, stepping into the clean vehicle. It's nothing fancy, but it's perfect for me. My little adventure companion. I have to head back to the hotel, check out, and grab my bags before I can make my way out of Edinburgh.

IT'S JUST after ten in the morning when I pull away from the hotel and head towards the highlands. According to my phone, Isle of Skye is roughly five hours away. I can do that easily in one day, but there is so much to see in between. I make a last-minute decision to leave Isle of Skye for the very end. So I change the route to Glencoe quickly before the light turns green.

As I continue to drive, the scenery in front of me changes from the bustling city to the peaceful countryside. Rolling hills and lush greenery stretch out as far as the eye could see. The clouds loom overhead, casting a gloomy shadow over the land-scape. I didn't bother checking the weather app earlier. It doesn't matter, I dressed prepared for a typical rainy day in Scotland.

I relax into my seat, immediately taking comfort driving down quiet country roads. And honestly, the opposite side of the road driving is not that bad once you get used to it. Especially on secluded roads.

My first solo adventure, and it only took me twenty-six years to get here. Most women my age are getting married or having kids...but not me. I ran away to Scotland to find a piece of myself and honestly, it might just be the first right decision I've ever made. I don't feel like I'm missing out. I would rather be here than trapped in a hopeless relationship with a ticking time bomb attached to it.

Getting lost in these open fields feels so freeing.

I just wish I had done it sooner.

But I don't think I was ready until now. The extra nudge from John is what I needed to end up here.

I stopped in Callander on my way up for lunch and heard some tourists raving about the various hikes in Glencoe, depending on time and difficulty. According to the eager group, the views are beyond impressive and warrant a full hike.

One Google search later, and I have plenty of trails to explore today.

I'm deciding over which route to take on my drive when the vast hills of Glencoe appear in the distance. They're breathtaking, even from afar. Pulling the car over in one of the lookout spots, I quickly step out of the vehicle, not wanting to miss this for another second.

I gape at the Three Sisters standing tall before me. The tips of the hills kiss the clear blue sky, like a trio of angels guarding the vast expanse of Glencoe. The sheer magnitude of the landscape takes my breath away. The sun shines down, casting a golden hue over the land and highlighting every variety of green that could ever exist. Lush wildflowers carpet the landscape. It's beautiful.

The place demands undivided attention, emanating a powerful feeling of awe and stillness. Glencoe exudes a quiet, yet undeniable force that makes me feel both humbled and uplifted.

My fingers itch to sketch, but I push the urge aside. Not here; I need more time and somewhere quiet. I linger for a little bit longer before excitement buzzes under my skin, urging me to go immerse myself. I snap a couple of pictures and jump back in my car.

As soon as the door closes, my phone begins to ring. I connected my Bluetooth to the car before I took off for the highlands. Becca's name flashes across the small dashboard as her unique ringtone fills the small cabin.

Even with the international phone plan I signed up for, this is going to cost me a small fortune if I let her talk for an hour. And Becca can easily talk for an hour. She has a talent for turning a ten-minute conversation into two hours, without you even noticing.

"Hey, Becs!"

"Oh my God, are you actually in Scotland? You did it? I'm so fucking proud of you."

"You're still in shock, huh?"

"Yes! You finally took control and, fuck, John was a sack of potatoes. I'm so glad you dropped that heavy load."

I cringe, sitting further back in the driver's seat and staring out at the landscape. "More like he dropped me."

"Best thing he ever did, I swear."

I laugh. "Thanks."

"We both know you weren't going to do it. You were too comfortable, hiding away."

"You're right." I sigh.

"I'm always right; we've established that. Listen, when am I coming? Because you know I'm going to. I'm bringing a hot Scottish man back with me."

"Good luck. Actually, you'd probably find the perfect guy and I'll keep attracting assholes. I have a magnet or something."

"No...you just need to let go a little. That's all."

There is a long pause on the other line and I stare at my phone, wondering if I lost her. But then I hear her exhale. "Listen, I'm mad that you didn't invite me but I get it, girl. You need this. You have for a long time. I know you're not a big talker but that doesn't mean I don't know you and I think you've been putting this off for too long. We both know you have. I guess, I'm just happy that you're finally spending some time with number one."

I hold my breath. "Becca..."

"No, don't. Just...focus on you, Avery. Okay? Promise me? And when you're ready, shoot me a text and I'll book my flight."

"I promise." I smile.

"Good. Please take care and maybe find some Scottish eye candy and take some photos for me. Mama needs her fix."

And she's back. "I won't be going near the opposite sex. Actually, I just left Edinburgh and I'll be spending a lot of time with trees and hills."

"Boring. Not my thing."

"I know. Okay, I have to go but I love you."

"FaceTime later?"

"Absolutely."

"I love you, Aves."

CHAPTER EIGHT

avery

I find the trail carpark easily. Cutting the engine, I grab the keys and turn to snatch my backpack from the back seat. Making sure to bring my sketchbooks, extra charcoal pencils, and my water bottle.

Glencoe's vastness immediately pulls me in. Its natural beauty is unlike anything I've ever experienced. There is also dark history amongst these hills. The Jacobite rebellions of the eighteenth century left a haunting mark, and you can feel it in the whistle of the wind. I don't know how else to explain it— some parts are eerie. The odd hiker passes me by, sometimes going the opposite direction but for the most part, the trail is secluded. It's a quiet comfort knowing other people are roaming around and I'm not completely alone.

I spot a few red deer in the distance, grazing, and they pay me no attention. I thought the silence and distance from other people would bring unwelcome memories, but I feel oddly at ease being here.

As I make my way through a wooded area, the sound of my boots crunching loudly is the only thing I could hear. Suddenly,

I emerge from the trees into a clearing, revealing a vast lake. The water is so still it appears like a mirror, and in the distance, I can see the majestic Sisters of Glencoe.

This is the perfect place to stop and sketch.

Setting up camp close to the water, I pull open my sketchbook and turn to a new page. The wind blows through the field, creating a soft rustling in the grass as gentle waves lap against the shore. My fingers take over, flashing across the white page as dark lines come to life. My mind quiets and I'm transported to another place, melting into the strokes with each passing minute.

Another gust of wind blows through, pulling my hair in front of my face. Dark, brown strands rustle in and out of view, blocking the landscape. Minutes turn into hours as the world slowly slips away. I don't exist outside this field. This moment. This sketchbook.

In the distance, a small rainbow bridges one hill to the next. The colours melt into one another, like a brilliant watercolour painting. The rainbow grows darker by the minute, vivid and full of life. I've always admired rainbows. They represent a sudden ray of hope after a storm.

A new beginning.

The sky turns grey and my fingers are covered in black charcoal before I'm finally satisfied with my drawing. I grab a pencil and glance up to finish any detailing I may have missed. My eyes catch on a tall figure dressed in black, staring out at the water.

Weird, I didn't hear anyone coming, but then again, I was too absorbed in my work.

I don't know how long he's been standing there, but I can't seem to take my eyes off him. He stands tall and wide, like a statue. His hands are tucked somewhere in front of him, and he's pulled his hood up. In my experience, people who stare out at the water for long periods of time are often lost, searching for answers they cannot find.

I consider leaving as old fears begin muttering in my ear, urging me to run. But the mysterious person hasn't even noticed me, I have no reason to run.

I avert my gaze, focusing on my sketch. But my eyes keep wandering towards the dark silhouette standing against the incredible scenery. I try to ignore him, focusing on the jagged peaks and the way the light falls on the water. I work on the lines and the shadows, trying to capture the essence of the landscape. When I finally finish, I put down the pencil and let out a deep sigh. The stranger is still there, but for some reason I don't feel as uneasy.

I reach inside my bag without looking and pull out my water bottle. While making a mental note of all the flaws in my drawing, I unscrew the lid and take a large swig.

Except it's not water, and I start choking as whisky burns down my throat. A coughing fit ensues as I stare down at the half-full bottle of Anam Cara in my hand. I don't remember putting this in here.

Shit, this is probably illegal.

I quickly shove the bottle back in my backpack and reach for my water bottle this time. I drink half of it in one go and finally look up, hoping no one caught that.

The dark figure is gone, and the landscape sits beautifully open to me once more.

A wave of relief washes over me as I pick up my sketchbook again. The whisky was actually nice, after it stopped trying to choke me to death. Especially with the constant wind and the chilly air seeping into my bones. I'm pretty sure no one cares if you drink out here. I reach for the whisky, sipping on it slowly as I detail the lake.

If they do, I'll just apologize profusely like a good Canadian.

I can't drink too much, though, or I'll never find my way back to the car. One more small sip. Letting the bottle linger on my lips, I tip it up as a gust of wind presses against my already cold cheeks.

"That's beautiful." A deep, velvety voice startles me.

I jump up, finding the same mysterious man by the lake now standing in front of me.

"Jesus Christ!" My hands are shaking. My fight or flight is definitely activated and my heart is beating so fast, I'm certain I'm going to empty the contents of my stomach.

Actually, he's towering and that says a lot. I'm tall, five-foot-nine to be exact, which is considered Amazonian in some places. But this guy is a new level of tall, he has to be six-foot-three, at the very least.

He takes a step back, alarmed by my reaction. "Sorry, lass, I did not mean to frighten you. I heard you coughing and I came close but then I got a wee bit distracted by your art." He's sporting a black cap, sunglasses, and his hood is firmly in place on top of his head.

He looks like he might have just robbed a bank.

"You shouldn't creep up on someone like that. Especially in an open field. I'm pretty sure I was close to needing CPR." I turn around, needing an extra second to catch my breath.

I should pack up and leave if he's planning on sticking around. My heart is still beating a thousand miles a minute.

"You're right. I'm sorry. Figured you saw me standing by the loch earlier." His voice is as rich as my whisky, laced with honey and an unforgettable subtle Scottish accent.

"That doesn't make it any better."

I can feel him standing behind me still. Feel his eyes watching me as I try to collect my things on shaky legs.

"Can we start over? My name is Lachlan and I mean you no harm. I give you my word."

I give you my word. I love that he just said that. The literature loving bookworm in me is geeking out hard right now.

I consider his words but there is no part of me that trusts a complete stranger.

I watch as Lachlan walks to the edge of the blanket, sitting on the damp grass. He rests his arms on his knees, practically making himself small, as he stares up at me. He's got a great facial structure, but that's about all I can see. Most of his face is hidden by the shadow from his ball cap and the sunglasses he doesn't need to wear.

"It's okay—honest mistake. The place is yours. I was just heading out anyways."

"You don't have to leave. I can leave." He says.

I would like to bottle up his voice and take it home with me as a souvenir. I could honestly listen to this man read out every line in the phone book. An unfamiliar surge flows through me and my breathing halts, having nothing to do with being scared. Actually, the fear that should be growing stronger is dissipating.

"No problem at all!" My voice comes out a little scratchy.

I stand in place, staring down at my things on the small navy blanket I shoved in my backpack this morning. I should leave, now.

Lachlan turns, his body facing me as he pulls down his hood and removes his cap. He pauses for a second, staring out at the water, like he's second-guessing himself. Then, he slowly removes his sunglasses and looks up at me.

Wow. Just...wow.

He's unequivocally gorgeous.

His hair is a deep chestnut brown with small splashes of red. Shorter on the sides but longer on top. Just enough length to curl in all the right places, or run your fingers through it.

Square jaw, strong high cheekbones, beautiful full lips, and he's got the bluest eyes I've ever seen.

Eyes as blue as the ocean capture me instantly, making me feel bare and exposed.

Where did this man come from? Did Scottish Gods spit him out of the lake?

Words, I need words. I'm staring at him, no...I'm gaping.

My breath catches sharply in my chest, as if a rope has wrapped tightly around my lungs, twisting further the longer I gaze into his eyes. It's like he can see into my soul. They're a deep blue, like the middle of the ocean, with lighter hues mixed in. The sort of crystal blue you'd find on the sandy shoreline on a gorgeous sunny day. Looking into his eyes is like staring into the vastness of the sea.

A single drop of rain lands on my cheek, snapping me back to reality.

"It's ok, I'll go," I stutter, widening the opening of my half-empty bag.

Just don't look at him again and you'll be fine.

He laughs, and the sound makes my stomach flutter. Lachlan grabs my sketchbook, and starts to flip through it.

"Are you an artist?" God, that voice mixed with that face. It's just not fair. Might as well hand me a towel because I'm seriously going to start drooling.

Get it together.

"No." I say.

"You should be, this is amazing." He glances up at me.

"Okay. I really should go. I have to go. I need to leave, like right now. You stay though. You're good."

For the love of God, stop talking.

I think I'm having a stroke, why can't I hold a conversation with this man?

He carefully folds my book and holds it up to me. I yank it

a little too hard, throwing it inside my bag. Dropping to my knees, I begin to grab pieces of charcoal and pencil scattered around the blanket. Lachlan helps me without words. He's so close, the smell of pinewood and soap envelops me.

"I'm sorry if I ruined your day. I sincerely didn't mean to scare you. If I had known it was going to force you to pack up and leave, I would have stayed away. I don't usually have this effect on people."

My head whips up. "And what kind of effect is that?"

I shouldn't challenge him but the way I reacted to his sneak attack is completely justified. Was he expecting for me to congratulate him?

He seems to think about this for a few seconds, smiling at me like I'm missing something obvious. "Just hasn't been my experience personally, usually I'm the one that runs."

"I'm not running. And also, kind of arrogant of you to say that." Typical response from an attractive guy.

His laugh bellows across the lake, taking me by surprise. The rain starts to pick up and I shove more of my things into my bag. At this point, I don't even care. I can organize everything at my next stop.

"It's not every day I run into a grumpy tourist who's not afraid to speak her mind." He smirks.

I narrow my eyes at him. "It looks like you could use a bit more bluntness in your life." This time, I hold his gaze.

Lachlan grins slyly, nothing but trouble and challenge in his eyes, as he lifts a brow, waiting for me to look away.

"I can't argue with that, lass."

Ugh fine, he can have the win. What does it matter? I'm leaving in a matter of minutes.

I reach for the whisky bottle at the same time as him. His large palm presses into my hand, sending a sudden jolt of electricity through my body. The sensation grows in strength, like an angry wave, causing my heart to race and every inch of my skin to tingle. It's as if a live wire has been set loose inside me, awakening something deep within. The current grows stronger, swirling under my skin and turning my blood ablaze.

The sensation is unlike anything I've ever felt.

Our hands break apart, his smug expression vanishes as he stares deep into my eyes, searching for something. I feel his gaze pierce into my soul. It's intoxicating. My hand trembles as I press it against my chest, trying to calm my racing heart.

CHAPTER NINE

lachlan

What the bloody hell was that?

I have never felt something like that before.

It felt like my entire body came alive, all at once. Everything faded away as soon as I touched her. It was the strangest feeling, blinding yet exhilarating. I am struck by the way it moved through me.

It wasn't like the type of shock you feel when you grab a blanket fresh out of the dryer—a small static shock from the heat. No, it was nothing like that. This felt like a sudden flash of light, forcing my body up through cold, dark water as I came up for air.

The aftershock from her touch still lingers on my skin. A reminder that I didn't imagine what just passed between us.

And she felt it too.

I'm still out of it as I watch her pack the rest of her things, in a weird daze I can't seem to snap out of. I should say something.

Think.

And her eyes, God, her eyes.

It's not that they're beautiful, or breathtaking. They are but that's not what captivates me about them. It's the way she looks at me, so deep and still, as if she is the first person to see me, or understand the words I'm speaking. Like, I've been communicating in a different language my entire life, and no one has understood me until now. I saw something else in her amber eyes, something familiar, an uncanny sea of darkness. So raw, that I found myself wanting to reach out for it.

What the fuck does that even mean?

I don't know. Maybe I hit my head on a rock. Maybe this is a dream.

"You can keep the whisky." Her voice comes out more breathless than before.

Don't mind if I do. I need a fucking drink after that. I bring the bottle of whisky to my lips and take a long swig. Avery's surprised gaze slips to my neck, as she watches the bitter liquid slide down my throat. Her lips part slightly and I notice her shuddering breath.

I have the sudden need to taste her lips, bite into the plump flesh as I leave kisses down her neck.

What the hell is the matter with you?

The smart thing to do right now would be to get up and leave. Store this away as an interesting interaction with an unlikely stranger in the hills. But my curiosity gets the better of me as I keep my arse planted on the wet grass. Besides, she's just about packed up and ready to get the hell out of here. Far away from me.

The big scary man dressed in black. Of course she's skittish; I would be too. Who creeps up on a woman like that?

She doesn't even know who you are.

That's why I stuck around in the first place. She doesn't recognize me, which is a welcome surprise. For a brief moment, I forgot who I was and why I'm roaming these lands. Forgot about my life, the never ending loneliness, the fact that I don't really know who I am anymore.

There is something in her eyes that made me take pause, forced me to look at her, to search for...I'm not even sure. I sound deranged, even to myself.

I planned this hike last week. I packed and prepared for it. Mid-week is always quiet, less chance for me to run into groups of people or tourists. I have a long list of places I want to hike through in the highlands. Hoping to get too lost to come back one day. Maybe I'll build a cabin in the woods. I'm used to hiding, actually. So much so that I've become really good at being invisible.

But then, I saw her sitting there. I had to see what she was working on up close.

She was an enigma, and I couldn't take my eyes off her. A small crack fused back together when she looked at me, as if she could see me. It felt like before...

This is strange. I don't do this.

"Where did you get this?" I hold up the small bottle of Anam Cara whisky.

She doesn't look up at me this time. "Edinburgh."

"It's good." I say, knowing exactly what the whisky is or where you can buy it. Even though I barely had anything to do with it. Except for taste-testing the products and signing off on a few things. It was so long ago, I hardly remember any of it.

The rain pounds down, smacking the surface of the loch with a harsh intensity that reverberates through the air. I don't know what compels me to keep talking to someone who has no interest in conversing with me.

"You know, Anam Cara means soul-friend in Gaelic." Her amber eyes cut to mine but she doesn't say anything. "It origi-nated in the early Celtic church, referring to an ancient and

eternal bond of souls. Someone you confessed your most trea-
sured secrets to, who made you feel like you belonged."

A type of bond that transcends. A rare connection.

"That's beautiful." She whispers, never taking her eyes off
me. I watch her throat as she swallows. "Truly, truly beautiful.
But I have to go."

"So you said, many times." I trace over the logo on the
bottle with my thumb.

She finally stands. "I would say it was nice to meet you but
I would be lying. Enjoy the whisky."

Ouch. Can't say that doesn't hurt.

I mimic her movement, standing up and smiling to myself
at her sharp tongue. No one ever talks to me like that.

The corner of her mouth lifts but she turns her face, hiding
her smile from me.

"Can I get your name? So I can properly thank you for the
half-empty bottle of whisky?"

She lingers for a moment longer, gazing at the loch and
drinking in the scenery before finally slipping her arms through
the straps of her bag. As she does, my eyes roam over her,
absorbing every detail to memory. Her lips, full and slightly
swollen, as if she has been biting on them nervously. Her dark
hair, damp and curly, framing her face in a way that makes her
look even more stunning. I notice the way her eyes soften, and
the warm golden hue of her skin that complements them so
perfectly. It's clear that she respects the natural beauty around
her, and for a moment, I feel grateful to be standing here
with her.

"It doesn't matter. We'll never see one another again," she
says, her eyes locking on mine for one last time.

CHAPTER TEN

avery

Fury of nervous emotions coil in the pit of my stomach.

It's just the whisky.

A ghost of a smile dances on his lips as he takes a step towards me. My heart picks up the pace, starting a solo drum session inside my ears. It's so loud, I can barely hear myself think.

"Goodbye, then," he says, threatening to drown me with his eyes.

"Bye." I get out and force myself to turn around.

Breathe in, breathe out. This, too, will pass.

Focus on one step after the next.

My sodden boots sink deeper into the ground with every step. The drenched fabric of my pants clings to my skin, weighing me down as I trudge across the field to the tree line and the path that leads to the carpark. The rain intensifies, assaulting me from every angle. Its unrelenting fury stirs something within me, and before I know it, I'm running, pushing against the resistance of my waterlogged clothes.

I don't know why I started to run. It's not like he was stopping me or I felt threatened by him. Quite the opposite; I felt safe. Something about him was familiar and maybe that's what urged me to pick up my speed.

Reaching the trees, I look behind me one last time. The image of this Godlike man, glued to the same spot with his eyes curiously on me, will forever be ingrained in my mind. His black clothes appear darker and shadows fall all around him, his face sullen and curious.

What the actual fuck was that?

It doesn't matter. The only thing that matters is I did the right thing and got the hell out of there.

A part of me screams for me to turn around and go back, but that voice only forces me to run faster.

By the time I reach the carpark, the electric pull from his touch feels like the remnants of a dream.

CHAPTER ELEVEN

avery

When I got in my car, I planned on driving until I couldn't anymore.

I pulled up the Maps app on my iPhone, and followed the winding roads until I found the ocean. And then I kept driving; allowing the countryside and the landscapes to distract me from myself. It seemed like a good idea at the time.

But now it's dark and I'm beyond exhausted.

Highway hypnosis is a real thing and it's actively trying to kill me. Even rolling down the windows and allowing the cold night air to smack me around proved unhelpful. I'll need to stop soon to avoid ending up in a ditch somewhere.

Squinting at my phone, there seems to be a small village coming up. I'm not certain I'll find a place this late at night but it's worth a try. If not, I'll sleep in my car.

I press 'accommodations' on my phone and select the first option that pops up, as I fight back an aggressive yawn. *Corran Inn and Pub*, please be my saviour.

The road becomes narrow as stone houses with thatched roofs line up one after another. To my right sits a vast and strikingly dark stretch of twinkling water. Shadows of black mountains frame the large body of water. According to my phone, this is Loch Hourn. If it's this scenic at night, I can't imagine what it looks like during the day. Will it give me the same sense of awe and wonder as it does in the quiet night?

"You have arrived at your destination," Siri announces cheerfully.

I slow down, craning my neck as I stare up at the grand and imposing building. The inn appears historic, even at this time of night. It's screaming cute country Scottish with its white stone, slate roof, and tall black chimneys. There are symmetrical windows framing the top and bottom floors. The front of the inn is gripped by a large, arched doorway, framed by two white columns. This extension perfectly separates the inn and the adjoining pub. A wooden sign above the door reads "Corran Inn and Pub."

This is definitely it.

There is a well maintained garden in front of the inn, with a black and grey cobblestone path leading up to the entrance. Flowers and green shrubs are planted in beds along the walkway.

I quickly kill the engine, smooth down my frizzy hair, and step outside. I don't want to be too hopeful in case they send me packing, because the possibility of sleeping in my car is very real.

Inside the inn is bright and welcoming, with a large grey marble fireplace tucked in the corner, surrounded by two chairs and a faded red couch. The smell of firewood wafts through the air, filling my nostrils with its warm, woody aroma. The comforting warmth in the room feels so good against my cold skin. It's exactly what I need after hours of driving in wet clothes.

I'll happily volunteer to sleep on that red couch if they don't have any accommodations available.

Approaching the front desk, I press a dainty gold bell and notice a musty sea scent. There is a short, dark hallway tucked in the corner behind the front desk, which I assume leads to an adjoining pub.

An older woman appears from the same dark hallway a minute later. She's already smiling, no trace of fatigue on her face despite the ungodly hour. She has dark grey hair and thin glasses that sit on the tip of her nose, and sweet, rosy cheeks. Her eyes are bright blue, and full of light.

"Good evening, fit like?" She asks, with a thick Scottish accent.

What did she just say?

"Sorry, silly tourist over here...do you mind repeating that?" I cringe, feeling like an idiot already.

The sweet lady laughs, waving me closer to the table. "Sorry, lassie, how can I help you?"

Her smile genuinely warms my heart. It's rare to find someone who has an innate talent for making others feel comfortable, but this lady is one of those people who effortlessly exudes warmth and kindness.

"I'm wondering if you have any rooms available for tonight? I've been on the road for some time, and could really use a place to stay. I don't have a booking."

"Aye, dinna fash, love."

Huh? The only words I picked up are *aye* and *love*. Which does not help me in this situation.

She laughs, likely due to the panicked expression on my face, while I try to decipher the meaning behind her words.

"I have one room left." She says.

Thankfully, I understood that and if it was appropriate to hug this sweet lady, I would.

"Perfect, I'll take it," I say cheerfully as I slide my credit card towards her.

"How long will ye be staying with us?"

"Not sure, a few nights? Can I extend my stay, or do you have another booking? I'm happy to leave whenever you need me to."

She glances up at me from her computer, her eyes pinned on me cautiously, as if she's trying to decide what to do with me.

"You know what? I have another room I can give ye. We don't typically offer it to guests, but it's not attached to a reservation, so ye can stay longer, if ye fancy."

"Sure, that sounds great. Thank you, again. You've just saved me from having to sleep in my car." I say, pressing my hands together in front of me like a prayer.

"No problem at all, love!" she exclaims. "The room faces out towards the loch. It's grand, ye'll love it."

"Perfect." I sigh in relief, allowing the stress to finally ease off my shoulders. All I want to do right now is take a hot shower and climb in bed. I can figure out my next move tomorrow while I explore the village of Corran. I need to find out exactly where I am in relation to everywhere else.

I'll look through the map tomorrow, see which key points I missed while I was rushing to get away from Glencoe...away from him.

"Do ye have any bags?" The kind clerk looks behind me at the empty floor.

"Yes, I do. They're in the car. Just wanted to make sure you had room first."

"Brilliant. I'll need a bit of time to check ye in. Do ye want to grab yer things? Ye can park yer car behind the inn." She passes me my credit card. "I'm Ailith, by the way."

"Nice to meet you, Ailith. I'm Avery, as you already know."

I wave awkwardly, glancing down at my card with my name printed on it. "Thank you for your hospitality." I turn, rushing out the door to my car. The cold September night air pricks my skin, clinging to my damp clothes and forcing me to move faster. I pull my bags out and place them near the front of the inn as I re-park the car.

When I walk back through the door, I look up to find Ailith standing behind the desk, holding an ornate black key. One of those round giant ones, the size of your palm with circular swirls.

"You're all set, Avery. Are ye hungry, lass?"

Food: another thing I completely neglected today. I don't want to put her through any more trouble, but just then my stomach decides to growl boorishly, the sound echos throughout the room. I cough, a feeble attempt to cover it up which only makes Ailith burst into laughter. I'm pretty sure my face is the same colour as the red tartan drapes, hanging by the windows.

"The pub next door is open, but the kitchen just closed for the night. Thankfully, it's my kitchen, so I'll fix ye up a sandwich, if ye fancy that."

She must be an angel. "I'd love that."

"Braw."

Ailith beams and I smile back, pretending like I understood what she just said. Do they have dictionaries for Scottish slang? If so, I'll need one.

"Ye go on and get settled and I'll be right up with yer food. You're in room number five, on this floor. Just through that hallway on the other side, at the very end."

I glance down at the metal key in my hand. "Is it just one room key to get in and out?"

"Aye. Don't lose it or it'll cost ye extra." Ailith winks as she heads towards the hallway behind her desk.

Grabbing my things, I look behind me in the direction Ailith pointed. Despite the single flickering light further down, the other hallway is not any brighter than the one Ailith disappeared through. An eerie sensation creeps down my spine, causing goosebumps to pimple along my arms, as if the shadows are watching my every move.

I walk slowly, my eyes drawn to the intricately carved patterns on the ornate wooden doors leading to the rooms. Four wall sconces provide dim lighting, casting tall shadows lurking in the corners. Oh my God, what if this place is actually haunted?

Stop being such a baby.

I'm sure the owners meant to preserve the authenticity of the original structure when they renovated the place. Because it's definitely been updated, the front desk and the outside of the building appear brand new. I glance behind me, half expecting a ghost to pop out at me.

Picking up the pace, the small wheels on my suitcases rumble against the cobblestone floor. A large metal number five hangs beside a door at the end of the hallway, right next to a flat stone wall. I'm one of the last rooms which means I have to make the trek down this dark hole multiple times a day. There is another door across from mine, room number six.

I work quickly to unlock the door, feeling cold air brush against my back. Grabbing the brass handle, I throw my shoulder against the heavy door and stumble inside.

The room is small but cozy, with a countryside charm that is reminiscent of the highlands of Scotland. The ceiling is low and the walls are covered in thick stone. Dark polished wood lines the floors, and a thick red rug sits in the centre of the room. A four-poster queen bed, with a woolen comforter and plump pillows is tucked against the back. A red tartan blanket lays neatly on top of the white comforter. And a small fireplace sits in the opposite corner of the room, welcoming me with open arms. This might be the cutest room I've ever seen.

There is a large painting of Glencoe above the bed.

Thank you for the reminder, universe. You're a jackass.

And there is no TV, which might be the best thing ever. First room I've stayed in that didn't have a television in the bedroom.

I pull my bags inside and close the heavy door. There is a small bathroom right by the door. With clean white tiles, a small rectangular sink, mirror, a toilet...and in the far corner, taking up the majority of the space in the bathroom is a white claw-foot tub and shower combination.

My sore muscles groan at the sight of it. I can't remember the last time I took a bath.

I have to stay here long enough to enjoy that tub.

A soft knock on the door makes me jump out of my skin.

No peepholes in the door. Of course not, why would there be? The door is a piece of art. No one in their right mind would drill a small hole into it.

"Avery?" Ailith's soft Scottish voice calms my nerves as I twist the lock and open the door.

She holds out a plate of food. "Here ye go, lass. Ham sandwich and crisps. I hope this can hold ye over 'til the mornin. Kitchen opens at six for breakfast."

"Thank you, Ailith, for everything."

"Oh, it's my pleasure, love. Eat and get some sleep. Let me know if ye need anything in the mornin."

Ailith turns but stops abruptly, looking back at me.

"Before I forget, this is a small family-run inn, so the doors to the inn are locked from two to six in the morning. Except for Fridays and Saturdays, when we're open all night. Ye can get to yer room from the pub, though, which stays open later."

I nod, making a mental note of everything.

"My husband, Duncan, and I run the pub and inn so we're always around. Don't be shy to get me if ye need anything. Duncan looks like Father Christmas, and he's a big fella. Ye can't miss him."

I smile at her warmly. "Thank you, Ailith."

Ailith pauses for a split second like she's trying to think of anything else she might have forgotten to tell me.

"Goodnight, lassie." And with that she was off, disappearing down the dark dungeon.

I triple-check the door is locked before I inhale my food and decide to test out the bath tonight. The water fills up quickly as I undress from my damp clothes. My body immediately relaxes when I step in, the hot water washing away the day. I close my eyes, take a deep breath, and ground myself.

Everything is okay. Tomorrow is a new day, with new opportunities, adventures, and new beginnings.

My muscles relax as I sink farther into the tub. Taking a deep breath and trapping it inside my lungs, I submerge my body underwater. The pressure is invigorating, making my skin prickle with joy. Everything quiets as I focus on the underwater bubbling sounds.

Lachlan's blue eyes flash in front of me. I feel the radiating heat from his body as his eyes trace up my neck, to my jaw, and my lips. An electric force, similar to the one I felt at Glencoe settles under my skin. I sit up, gasping for air.

CHAPTER TWELVE

avery

The morning glow from the sun bleeds around the edge of the curtains. I stretch my sore body as the events from yesterday slowly trickle in. I don't think I've ever crashed so hard in my life. Even if there were ghosts roaming the halls outside my room, I doubt they would have been able to wake me.

Usually when I fall into a deep sleep, I'm jolted awake in the middle of the night by a terrible nightmare. Coming down from a panic attack while half asleep is equally mortifying and exhausting. Half the time I'm disoriented while trying to get enough air, so that I don't pass out. It's one of the reasons why I don't go anywhere without sleep medication.

Dr. Samson always said nightmares were my body's way of coping with the trauma, since I refused to acknowledge it head-on. After being trapped inside your own head for too long, you start to crave the dark.

Samson used to say that my mind didn't care, if I wasn't going to address my problems, then it would take control at night. That never made sense to me. Shouldn't my body want to protect me? We're conditioned that way for other types of pain, so why not trauma or abandonment?

Samson called it trauma overload, and the panic attacks while unconscious was a way for my body to lighten the load. It got a lot better when I moved to Toronto, but I still get the occasional nightmare.

This morning, I'm thankful for a dreamless night of sleep.

I roll over, looking at the time on my phone. It's just after nine in the morning.

I desperately need coffee.

But first, a quick Google search to find out a bit more about Corran.

"Corran, Loch Hourn. A hamlet on the northern shore of Lochalsh in Inverness-shire in the Highlands of Scotland. Corran is at the end of a minor road, about one kilometer past the village of Arnisdale. Population: 8,574 (2011 Census). Despite its small size, it is the largest town between Helensburgh and Fort William and during the tourist season the town can be crowded by up to 25,000 people."

A Tripadvisor page suggests there are various walking paths, trails, lochs, and deep forest hikes to explore. Just the type of seclusion I'm searching for. Only me and the highlands so we can get to know one another intimately. Corran is also close to Fort William, Inverness, Glenfinnan, and Isle of Skye!

Looks like I'm in the right place.

THE PUB next door looks like the stereotypical village Scottish pub.

I step inside, breathing in the delicious aroma of coffee and fried potatoes. The walls are adorned with the familiar tartan tapestries and photographs of the highlands. Two wooden beams run across the high ceiling, accentuating the rustic small-town atmosphere. The bar is long and wide, running down the length of the pub. Behind it on the back wall, sits rows of gleaming glasses and various liquor bottles in all shapes and sizes. There are booths and tables spread throughout. There is even a pool table tucked in the back and a place to play darts.

This must be THE pub in town.

I spot Ailith buzzing around, serving food and morning coffee, as I make my way towards one lonely booth tucked away in the back corner. It's the only booth without a window or light above it. The seat is large and covered in brown faux leather. I slide into the far corner and pull out my laptop.

Ailith is at my table a few moments later. Holding a full pot of coffee. She hands me a mug and gives me the Wi-Fi password before I get the chance to ask for it.

"It's always the first question around here. Folks love to be connected."

If I didn't love her before, I sure as hell do now. I thank her and sip on my steaming coffee, with hints of hazelnut that feel like a giant hug.

"Did ye sleep well, lass?" Ailith smiles, seeming perfectly relaxed and in no rush, even though she's probably up to her eyeballs in work.

There is something about the countryside that forces people to stop and enjoy the fleeting moments. City people don't do that. Everyone is rushing from the minute they wake up until the second their head hits the pillow at night.

"Yes, it was wonderful. Thank you so much for taking me in, and for the sandwich. Please let me know what I owe you."

Her grin widens as she places a laminated menu in front of me.

"Don't be silly, it's no bother. I wouldn't have wanted ye to go to bed hungry. Ye looked a bit rough when ye got in, and I noticed yer clothes were sodding wet." Amongst many things, Ailith is also very perceptive.

Rough is the correct term, Ailith. I was running away like a madwoman through Glencoe trying to get away from a very handsome Scottish man.

I don't say that though. "Thank you, that's really kind of you."

"Do ye need a minute to look over the menu?" she asks.

I nod.

"Take yer time. I'll be back."

Logging into my email, I scan the breakfast menu, while my incoming messages load in my inbox. I'm not that hungry, so I order pancakes when Ailith strides back to my table.

I take out my headphones, open up my Spotify playlist, and focus on my ticking work inbox. There are a couple of emails from my boss updating me on my work situation. I texted her when I got to my hotel that first night in Glasgow. I wasn't sure I could work while in Scotland, but she assured me it will be fine. She has to submit some paperwork, and once that's approved, I can put in as many hours as I'd like. Since the company I work for is an international company, it's easier for me to continue working abroad.

Being a contractor is a bit risky, but I have a lot of leeway and freedom with my schedule. I have been pulling a lot of hours the last few months since John was so busy with his re-election campaign...or rather, his new girlfriend. My boss was very supportive when I mentioned I would be taking a much-needed break.

I look at some of the available projects and favourite a few for later. Maybe I can stay here longer and get some work done in the meantime. Corran seems like a good anchor spot in the highlands. And that way, I won't have to dip too much into my savings.

I'll need to think about finding a place when I get back to Vancouver too. Although, Dad will probably force me to stay with him. He's still in our old four-bedroom home in the suburbs of Burnaby. I tried convincing him to sell the place and move to an apartment downtown, but he won't hear of it. I think it's because of the good memories he had in that house. It was the first house he and Mom bought together, where they got married, brought home their daughter and it was also the place he got his heart broken. I personally wouldn't want the reminders, but we're not the same. Not when it comes to the affections of the heart.

Closing down my work email, I start making a list of all the places to visit while staying in Corran. My pancakes arrive not long after. I eat slowly, completely lost in all the trails and hikes available around me. It's an endless adventure for a nature lover. There are too many places and not enough time.

A drop of syrup lands on my laptop while I am busy skimming a blog post. I reach into my bag, blindly searching for some wet wipes when my hand grazes the metal spine of my sketchbook.

I flip it open. The smell of dried charcoal hits my nose, as I look at the black-and-white image of Glencoe. But I don't see the landscape, I just see his face.

I flip the page, but Lachlan is plastered all over my sketchbook.

Even the streets of Edinburgh remind me of him. It doesn't make any sense.

Frustrated, I flip open to a blank page in the middle of my book and grab a pencil. My eyes landing on the stone walls, and I begin sketching the pub in my line of view.

This hobby is my escape, and I'm not allowing the memory of some guy to take that away from me.

I turn up the music and get lost in the details as the image begins to come to life. That's my favourite part. When all the lines and shadows finally take shape, going from nothing to something.

To a memory etched in time.

I don't notice Ailith until I see coffee being poured into my mug in my peripheral vision. Glancing up, I find Ailith squinting down at my drawing. She's so focused, that she almost overfills the mug. Rüfüs Du Sol's *Underwater* continues to blare from around my neck. Ailith sets the pot of coffee down on the table and reaches for her glasses resting atop her head.

She leans in closer, her eyes widening with curiosity.

"Oh, my heavens...Avery! That is a bonnie picture. May I?"

I can feel the heat radiating off my face, like a small furnace as Ailith pulls my sketchbook towards her, studying my messy drawing.

"Oh lass, I'd love to have this. I can hang it in the pub."

She wants my distraction sketch that belongs at the bottom of a trash bin.

"Ailith, it's honestly so rough and it's not even done. I was just doodling." I try to reach for my book, but she's got her finger firmly pressed on the bottom edge.

"Nonsense. I love it."

Sure, she's just trying to be nice. I don't see what she sees in this random waste of paper, that I started drawing in hopes to distract my thoughts away from a certain person. Drawing has always been a personal hobby, and having others see my work leaves me feeling exposed. As if they will judge me negatively for my personal art.

It wasn't always like that though. When I was in high school, my dad convinced me to get into a couple of junior showcases and galleries. It was a fun experience and the feedback was positive. But back then I used to paint with colour. There was light and wind in my work. I don't paint anymore, and I only use black charcoal when I sketch. So much of my past started to seep into my work, and I didn't want anyone to see that part of me. That's the thing with trauma, it steals all the light and colour, replacing it with black ink.

"Avery?" Ailith's hand touches my shoulder and I realize I must have zoned out.

"Um...sure, if you like. It's not finished though. Can I leave it with you once it's done? I need to fix it."

She waves her hand in front of her, like she's trying to get rid of my negative thoughts. I can't help but smile at her.

"Stop doing that. I love it." She pinches my cheek and I jerk at the contact. "Such a sweet lass, especially when you're as red as a tomato."

I laugh. A full blown, genuine airy laugh with sound. I haven't heard myself laugh in so long, it sounds strange coming out of my mouth.

"So you're not a full-time artist?" Ailith takes a seat across from me.

"No. I'm a web developer. This is just for fun." I say, pointing to the half-completed sketch.

"Well, ye could have fooled me." Ailith scans the pages of my sketchbook as I watch her face. She seems in awe, taking in the familiar sights of her magnificent country. Ailith smiles, the corners of her eyes crinkling softly. She's got so many laugh lines and I love that about her. It makes me feel like she spent a lot of her life happy.

"These are really good." Ailith glances up at me periodically, a smile glued on her face the entire time. "I am impressed."

She finally slides the book to me and I quickly slip it back in my bag.

"Thank you."

"Your job is on the computer then?" She nods to my laptop sitting on the table.

"Yep. Mostly a lot of web design and maintenance for worldwide clients." I bring my coffee mug to my lips.

"That's handy. Sometimes I wish I was younger so I could learn to navigate that complicated machine. I've been fighting with mine for ages, trying to fix the inn's website." Ailith leans her palms on the table and stands up. "Do ye want anything else, lass?"

"No, thank you."

"Stay as long as ye like." She winks and heads towards the bar.

Glancing around, I notice the place has filled up quite a bit since I arrived. There seems to be a good mix of tourists and locals, busy with their morning routines. My eye catches on a tall figure standing by the edge of the bar sporting a thick white beard. I assume that's Duncan, given Ailith's description of him. Just then, Ailith walks around the bar and he leans down, giving her a soft kiss on the cheek.

Definitely Duncan.

"Lachlan, lad! Welcome back." Duncan booms from behind the bar, and my heart sinks at the sound of that name.

I reluctantly follow Duncan's eyes.

It can't be.

The blood drains from my face.

It's him. The guy I met yesterday at Glencoe.

Why is he here?

My chest tightens with each pounding heartbeat as I watch Lachlan approach the bar. I squeeze my shaky hands in my lap, trying to control my emotions.

What are the chances?

I can't flee right now. I'll have to walk right by him, and there is no way he won't see me. I assume he's from around here if Duncan called him by name. Does he live in Corran?

Good grief, I ran away from him just to end up in his town.

Lachlan's laughter spills out, sounding lighthearted and warm, as I talk down my thundering heart. I turn to my laptop and pretend to look at something, but nothing is registering.

I need an escape plan.

Get it together.

The waiting becomes unbearable, and I glance up quickly to see his back facing me as he talks to Duncan and Ailith. Broad shoulders, black ball cap. He's wearing a thin sweatshirt and blue jeans. I can see his defined back from all the way over here. Does this guy live at the gym? Maybe he's a fisherman.

Please don't let him see me.

Better strap on your runners, girl.

Maybe I should head for the airport and go to Spain or France or somewhere that's not here. Alaska. That seems safe. No hot weird Scottish men in Alaska, right?

He tilts his body, slapping Duncan on the side of the arm as they both laugh at something. I can see all of him now. The butterflies in my stomach flutter aggressively, making me feel sick.

His head turns, as if he could sense me somehow. And his eyes instantly lock on mine from across the room.

CHAPTER THIRTEEN

avery

My body is frozen. I want to run, to hide, to look away, but I can't move. I'm rooted to the booth, powerless to do anything else.

His expression falls as I finally avert my gaze, a sudden sense of shame causing me to recoil.

With shaky hands, I decide to send an email to my dad.

Hey, Dad - I'm in the highlands...about to shit my pants.

Delete, delete, delete.

Not even a minute later, I hear his boots approaching the table.

"Did you follow me here? Who sent you? Was this Edgar's idea?" Lachlan snarls.

His deep voice commands attention, but it's the anger coursing through my veins that has me looking up at him.

"Excuse me?! Follow you?"

"Get. Out. Now." He growls.

His eyes are dark, cold, and distant as he places his hands on the edge of the table and leans in close to my face.

"You do not want to play this game with me, lass. Did

Edgar send you? If he thinks— " Lachlan hisses through clenched teeth. His voice is low, but the rage in his eyes could light this entire place on fire.

Too bad for him, I have a wicked temper. "Listen, asshole, I don't know who you think you are, or who you think you're talking to but you need to get out of my fucking face right now."

Unlike him, I don't try to keep my voice down. Lachlan pushes off the table, as the corner of his mouth lifts up into a vicious smile.

"Such a filthy tongue for a bonnie lass. Is that why you left so quickly yesterday? Because I wasn't meant to see you? Did I blow your cover? Feel free to run now."

"Okay, that's it..." I move to push Lachlan's obnoxious body out of the way when Ailith shoves herself in front of him. I halt, almost knocking into her.

"What's this?" Ailith looks in between us.

"This—" but he doesn't get to finish his sentence.

"Ah, so you met Avery, then. Good, I was coming over to introduce you. She checked in to the inn last night. Poor lassie was soaked head-to-toe when she walked in. She must have been caught in the rain and had mud all along the back of her trousers." Ailith smiles tightly, placing her hand on Lachlan's cheek.

Lachlan moves his head back, his eyes ping-pong between me and Ailith like he's trying to understand the words that just came out of her mouth. I'm not sure why Ailith even provided him with that much detail.

"She showed up last night?"

"Aye. She did. Now leave the young lass alone. She was not bothering ye."

Lachlan flinches and Ailith turns to face me, reaching for my clenched fist. "Lachlan here is my nephew. He works at the inn and pub when needed. If ye see him in the halls and need anything, feel free to flag him down."

Lachlan turns and storms away.

"Your nephew...he's your nephew? Do you want me to leave? He told me to get out. I'm not even sure why he got so angry at me. I didn't even say anything."

Ailith steps closer and reaches up, grabbing my shoulders. I realize she can't be any more than five-foot-three as I stare down into her eyes.

"Absolutely not. Pay him no mind. He must have thought ye were someone else."

No, he recognized me and remembered me. You don't approach someone you don't know with that much hate and anger.

I didn't steal from him or hurt him, it doesn't make sense for him to charge at me like that. How could I have followed him, if I got here first? Contractor, Edgar? Maybe he did mistake me for someone else...or maybe he has short-term memory loss. What are the chances that we would run into one another again at some random inn in a small fishing village in the highlands?

Apparently I forgot to leave my shit luck back home.

None of the pieces add up, and it's going to eat away at me slowly.

I turn back, quickly grabbing for my things and leaving more than enough money to cover breakfast. Ailith steps to the side, but I feel her eyes on me. I crush the stray tear into my palm before dragging my bag over the seat.

"I'm so sorry about that. I honestly don't know what just happened." I get out quickly, unable to bring myself to even look at her.

Before Ailith has a chance to say anything else, I run out.

I'VE BEEN PACING my room, trying to compartmentalize my emotions and figure out my next step. My eyes fall to the open suitcase laying on the floor. I should just leave, forget about all of this and go to the next town. Continue my adventure and never think about that asshole ever again.

Once a runner, always a runner. Do you run every time things get hard because you couldn't run that night?

Stop. I order myself but it's no use, the anxious thoughts are always there, living rent free in my mind.

I spot my running shoes in the corner of the room. A run will help. Nothing like a bit of lung burn to silence the hateful thoughts. I quickly change into my workout clothes and head out the door.

I recall seeing a lighthouse not too far from here. I round the corner, walking in that general direction as I zip up my sweater. I pull out my headphones from my pocket.

As I reach for my phone, an axe cuts through the air, drawing my attention. There is a lush shrub fence running on the side of the inn, blocking the back of the building from the rest of the street.

My feet slow down as I peer through a ten-inch gap in the fence. There is a tall man on the other side, holding an axe with a small mountain of chopped-up firewood in front of him. He's in jeans and a white T-shirt that hugs his chiseled back beautifully. The veins in his strong arms pop as he holds the axe slack in his hand.

What is it with this place? Of course, there is a random

highlander chopping wood in the middle of the day. If only Becca was here. She would have a field day with this.

I decide to send her a text.

ME

> I found the gold mine you are looking for.

You were about to start your run. Plug your headphones in and get going.

In a minute.

I'm standing here like a creep, watching this man as he bends down to reposition a new piece of wood. He straightens his stance, raising the axe up in the air. His muscles bend and flex as the axe comes down with great force. A deep grunt escapes his mouth upon impact. Two pieces of wood thud silently to the ground.

Why was that so hot?

This place is making it incredibly difficult to not think about sex.

Completely distracted by the view and my own thoughts, I shift slightly to get a glimpse of his face. My ankle rolls and I curse, trying to catch myself from falling on my ass.

That was close.

I straighten up and rotate my ankle, making sure I didn't injure it. Glancing over my shoulder, I pray no one caught that.

Lachlan's piercing blue eyes knock the breath right out of my lungs.

I should look away, need to look away but then he raises the bottom of his shirt and wipes the sweat from his forehead, keeping his eyes glued on me the entire time. I trace his sculpted chest and the visible six-pack that tapers down to his defined waist. There's some kind of ink winding its way around his back, but it's gone before I can see what it is. My traitorous eyes continue to travel down, zeroing in on his defined V. A black strip of Calvin Klein boxers sits right above his jeans, and the sight has me taking in an uneven breath. Every piece of him appears to be carefully hand-crafted by God.

My breathing is ragged as my eyes crawl back up to find him still watching me—his eyes filled with ice-cold fury. The side of his mouth ghosts up for a split second before he walks towards me.

"Haven't had enough? Do you want a photo?" he spits.

Say something. Anything. Pick a word and just say it. Or don't, walk away. Just start running.

No. No more running.

"If I find out you're stalking me, I'll fucking have you fired before nightfall." He narrows his eyes, making sure to drag out the last bit like I don't understand English.

Stalking him? That's enough to snap me back into place.

"Stalking you? Who the hell do you think you are? You seem to have some deep-rooted mental issues. So how about we stay away from each other, okay?"

Surprise flashes in his eyes, but is quickly replaced by an emotionless gaze. "Aye! Sounds good to me. And if you decide you want to run off to the next town, that'll be grand."

"Fuck. You." I spit, turning on shaky legs as I walk to the end of the street.

No one has ever infuriated me so much. I've never lashed out at someone like that. Not wanting to give him the satisfaction of seeing me run again, I wait until I'm out of sight before breaking off into a sprint.

I hate him.

THE LIGHTHOUSE in Corran is evocatively beautiful. Something about it tugs on my heart strings, like it's calling out to me, with its white cylindrical tower, black roof, and yellow wraparound balcony. The windows in the black lantern room are a mix of green and red.

With every step, my feet sink deeper into the yellow sand as I approach the water. The gentle lapping murmurs of the loch help slow down my thoughts, allowing me to take a mindful breath. Reminding me to let go. The thoughts, the questions, the uncertainty—let it all go.

Breathe in. Breathe out. This, too, will pass.

I have always been fascinated with lakes and oceans. The fact that they can hold nothing and everything all at once. Instilling a sense of calm on the surface but underneath there are things we cannot see. Life, movement, darkness, and uncertainty. I stare out at the water for a long time before turning around to face the lighthouse. There is a stark white lodge tucked in the back, surrounded by lush trees and mossy mountains. It's three times the size of Duncan and Ailith's inn, with four chimneys sticking out from the roof. Tall windows surround every side of the white building.

I should come stay here, forget about Lachlan.

I didn't come here to start a fight with a delirious stranger, or to cause trouble for anyone else. I just wanted to escape, a chance to heal myself. And no one gets to take that away from me, not even me.

If Lachlan is bothered by my existence, then he can go somewhere else. But for now, I'm staying put.

I'm done running from my problems.

I'm ten minutes late as I approach the oversized boardroom in the Glasgow office. I did it on purpose, knowing it'll irritate the fuck out of Edgar. Pulling open the heavy oak doors, I slip into character, rolling my shoulders back and tipping my chin up.

Black suits stand simultaneously as I make my way towards the head of the table. Henry is already seated and my chair is pushed out for me. I spot a few people glancing down at their wrists, checking their precious time. Not sure if it's a tactic to make me feel guilty. Too bad I don't care.

None of these wankers would have a job if it weren't for me. I've lined their pockets for years, but they don't acknowledge that, and it sure as hell doesn't stop them from treating me like I'm a mindless man without thoughts and opinions. They like to pretend they own me.

"You're late," Edgar declares from the other end of the table.

"The drive from Corran is not short. You're lucky I even

came, considering I'm on a break." I glance at the file folder sitting on the table.

"Perhaps you should consider moving back to your residence here in Glasgow, and take day trips out to the countryside," one of the suits says.

"Perhaps you should start the meeting and not concern yourself with my geographic location." My voice carries harshly across the table. Henry twitches nervously in his seat, cutting me a warning glare.

He hates these meetings, especially when I become confrontational and he is left to deal with the aftermath.

The office chair squeaks loudly against my black leather jacket as I sink into it. I flip open the folder as a monotone voice fills the room. This meeting could have easily been done over the phone or by email. But Edgar demands that I attend in person. Another clause in the contract I overlooked.

Henry leans in close, the sharp smell of his cologne burns my nostrils. I need to remind the lad that less is more.

"You should have taken the car with my driver, like I advised. You would have made it on time," he whispers, disapproval laced in every word.

I narrow my eyes at him, and he looks away immediately, pretending to pay attention to the speaker, while smoothing down his tie. Most people can't hold eye contact with me for very long, and Henry never lasts longer than a few seconds.

Henry and I have been working together from the beginning. He saw a rare potential in me while I was living in London. He changed my life, and I've had a lot of opportunities because of him. Access to money which opened a lot of doors for me. But I've also never hated myself more than I do now. Is it all related? Who knows. But if I had a chance to re-do it, I would choose a different path.

"Mr. Moore, any further thoughts to our suggestion from

the last meeting?" An old bald man draws my attention from across the table. I recognize him from previous meetings, but his name evades me.

Last meeting. Nothing of importance comes to mind. I rake my hand through my hair.

"Please refresh my memory."

"We discussed expanding the business. Introducing new products, perhaps a new liquor line. We're thinking tequila. It would be a smart financial next step, especially since your whisky is growing a fan base in America right now. We also discussed purchasing land here in Scotland. Perhaps a golf resort in the countryside, tied in with the whisky inspired by your roots. Your name alone would draw in plenty of tourism and business." He clears his throat, throwing that last bit out quickly.

Aye, I remember now. I also recall telling them that I wanted to scale back and using my name was not up for discussion. This idea reeks Edgar. He's trying to make up for the recent opportunities I've turned down.

"I will be investing in a golf resort, but my name will not be on it. I was clear about that last time. As for the other matter, you can continue to focus your efforts on the existing whisky business. I'm not interested in expanding to other liquors at this time." I lean into the table, resting my elbows on the cold wood, while keeping my eyes trained on the man.

He flinches under my hard gaze, glancing at Edgar before turning back to me.

"Sir, it's already been discussed and Edgar has approved the plans. For your benefit, we think..."

I stand up. "I am on a break. You are all aware of this, and yet you still try to pull me into work on a daily basis. Calls, emails, meeting requests, proposals, new contracts...I already signed off on business plans for the next several months.

Nothing is changing until I come back, and unfortunately for you all, you need my signature to move forward since it's my name you want."

Edgar clears his throat, preparing to tear me down. But I'm ready for it. He may scare a lot of people, but he holds no power over me. Not anymore.

"We have to pivot with the change in market. It's our responsibility to ensure we are taking advantage of every opportunity. The world won't wait around for your return, Lachlan, and we can't afford to either."

"Great. Do it without me, take my name out and do whatever you want."

"That's not how this works." Edgar snarls.

"Then put a pause on it, or follow the plan." I stare right into Edgar's eyes, not backing down.

He smiles, running a hand down his perfectly pressed suit. "And how long are you planning on extending your holiday? It is a holiday, since I took the liberty to ensure there are no threats to your well-being. But here you are, pulling a disappearing act. Your behaviour is tiresome, Lachlan."

Vacation. Bloody bastard has the balls to use that word when he was the one dealing with lawyers and the police. My knuckles turn white from the way I'm pressing my fists into the table.

"I don't need to give you a—"

Henry coughs loudly.

"We're still discussing Lachlan's return date. We're hoping for another two months at most," Henry speaks up, his voice shaky. Management doesn't like to wait around for anything. I'm sure Henry is getting shit from Edgar on the daily about my return. But my terms were crystal clear from the beginning. Edgar can try to control me all he wants but I looked over my contracts; and although I can't step away without losing everything, I'm entitled to a temporary leave of absence.

Edgar stands, buttoning his jacket as he takes slow steps towards the boardroom doors. "I suggest you figure it out quickly, Lachlan. You have obligations you need to fulfill. Contracts you signed. I'm not a patient man."

He doesn't look back as he walks out the door.

Another power move played in front of everyone to make me look insignificant, and without options. He doesn't care if I drop dead tomorrow as long as he gets his money. Edgar is Hades dressed in an Armani suit.

I don't acknowledge his departure, as I face the others. "I know you're all aware of the recent troubling events that took place. I'm dealing with that. All you need to concern yourself with right now is Anam Cara. Keep things status quo until I return and in the meantime, I'll discuss the golf establishment with Henry. Remember, you work for me."

I grab my bike helmet off the ground.

"From now on, if you have any questions or concerns, please direct them to Henry. If he cannot answer them, he will loop me in. Oh, and I won't be attending these in-person meetings anymore."

I hear mumbled agreements as I stride out of the room. The door opens behind me but I make my way down the marble floor, heading for the elevators.

Hurried clicking shoes follow me.

"Lachlan...I thought we were going to meet after the team meeting. We need to discuss other things you've been neglecting." I ignore Henry's voice, focusing on the elevators at the end of the hall.

Henry stops beside me, waiting for an answer while he catches his breath. He puffs out his chest, trying to gain a few extra inches. He's not a short guy, maybe a handful of inches shorter than me. But I'm six four and I tend to naturally look down at people when they're standing this close. Henry's the only one that seems offended by it, as if I had a say in my height.

"I'm done. You heard what I had to say in that room. It applies to you too."

"That's not how this works and you know it."

I lean down, looking directly into his eyes. "It is right now. So fucking deal with it and stop texting me. I'm on a temporary leave of absence."

The elevator dings and the doors slide open. I step inside, pressing the key for the garage.

"You're making a big mistake. This is going to stall you or ruin your career and you won't be able to recover from it." Henry clutches the file folders desperately against his chest.

I wait until the doors are almost closed before looking him dead in the eyes, "And what if I don't want it anymore?"

The metal doors shut and the elevator begins its descent. I can't wait to get back on the road and away from here. Every time I'm back in the city, I find myself counting down the seconds until I can leave. It's a terrible feeling and I know staying in the highlands is not a sustainable long-term plan but I need some time to figure everything out.

All the decisions that I have yet to make. Decisions that will change my life forever. But things have already changed. Everything is different and nothing matters anymore. I don't care about any of this. I don't care about the money. I just want to drive to the other side of the country and lock myself in a cabin in the woods. Away from everyone and everything.

I just need to forget all of this for a little while. Figure out how to stop drowning.

The elevator doors open to the underground parking garage. I pull my helmet on and head straight for my motorbike.

I was supposed to stop by the house and take care of a few things, but the only place I'm going right now is back to Corran. It'll be late by the time I arrive but it's fine. Not like I have anyone waiting for me. When you've been alone for so long, time tends to lose its significance. The thing about being truly alone is that it's not just about physical isolation. That part I crave, especially with my career. It's the state of mind that drains your soul, a feeling of emptiness so deep that it slowly starts to suffocate you. And you don't realize you're choking until it's too late.

My bike roars to life as I pull out of the parking garage, needing to get away from the city before the anger completely crushes me.

CHAPTER FIFTEEN

avery

I haven't seen Lachlan for three days. Three days of quiet and comfort. He probably left, which works perfectly well for me.

I've been spending my days puttering around Corran. Making small day trips to nearby waterfalls and trails. Exploring small villages, and really immersing myself in nature with my sketchbook in hand. My mind quiets down when I'm trucking through the fields, nothing else exists and I feel so incredibly small. Finally finding a bit of peace in my own skin.

I've been dying to go to one of the famous beaches in Scotland. And today I woke up early, packed my bag, and headed out to Sanna Bay Beach.

The drive to Sanna Bay Beach, which is situated at the most westerly point in mainland Britain, mostly consists of waterfront views. It's the most picturesque drive I could ask for. And for some reason, looking at all that water reminded me of a conversation I had with Dad not too long ago.

He came to visit me in Toronto for a week and one morning when we went out for breakfast, he brought up philosophy and the purpose of life. Which somehow led to me telling him I wanted to be cremated when I die. At first, he wouldn't even entertain the conversation, he never likes to talk about sad things.

But death is inevitable. A certainty for us all, just like the rising and setting of the sun. Everything must end, sooner or later.

I told him I wanted my ashes to be spread in the ocean. Not that it would be his decision but I wanted him to know. He didn't say anything for a long time and then he nodded. He knew it's the only place that I feel the most at peace with myself.

I never told him what happened to me when I was nineteen and I don't think he ever figured it out. I chose to keep it hidden. No one was allowed to inform him or my mother, I was an adult and I got to make that decision. It was the only part of that night I had control over.

And my mother, well she wouldn't have figured it out either way. She wasn't around. By that time she was living abroad with husband number three. She never called, never texted, never emailed.

But my dad was there, and he witnessed the way depression ravaged me from inside out. He tried everything to help me, but I could never bring myself to tell him. I knew if I did, it would destroy him beyond repair. And he was already so broken from Mom.

I would meet with Dr. Samson weekly, and afterwards Dad would take me to the beach. We would sit by the ocean for hours, staring out at the water. He waited patiently for me to open up, but I never did. I just couldn't. The guilt from that will always weigh on me. I caused him a lot of sleepless nights, but it was better for him to think I was having a mental crisis than to learn the whole truth.

That part of my life feels like so long ago now.

Approaching Sanna Bay, I am speechless by the raw beauty of the cliffs surrounding the ocean, towering in the sky covered in prolific moss and wildflowers. I can't get out of my car fast enough as I park and shoulder my bag. The path to the beach is narrow, but as the sandy expanse of the bay comes into view, I feel like I've left Scotland entirely.

This place looks like the Caribbean.

The white sand is soft and powdery as it crunches beneath my feet. The shallow turquoise water hugs smooth rock beds as they lay open on the beach. Perfect for climbing and gazing out at the clear blue seas. There are sand dunes covered in tall wispy grass everywhere. A little piece of heaven on Earth.

There is a bite in the wind as it blows in from the sea. I breathe in the smell of salty ocean air as it whips through my hair. Slipping off my boots, I sink my feet in the cool sand, feeling the vibrations from the waves in my toes.

The beach is long as it stretches around the sea. I start walking, looking out at the distant islands and their peaks covered in mist out on the horizon. The place is completely secluded. Aside from the sounds of seabirds and waves ebbing, there is nothing else.

Effortlessly peaceful.

How can one country have absolutely everything? It's magical.

I could spend forever here. I could start new. There is nothing holding me back, no one waiting for me. Aside from my dad and my best friend, I have nothing back home. But let's be real, it hasn't felt like home in a long time. My throat tightens as the weight of my loneliness hits me out of the blue. But I've been alone this entire time, haven't I? I just chose to ignore it because it was easier.

I could be alone here.

No, I have to go back. My family is in Vancouver, my life is there. I can't run from my past forever, and being here will hopefully allow me to heal enough to go back and not be reminded of that night.

Before I know it, I've spent the entire day at the beach. Walking, reading, sketching, I even watched the clouds go by for a couple of hours. My thoughts lulled to nothingness. It's amazing what being near water can do for someone like me.

I thought about leaving but when the sun began to set, I climbed a dune that led to a low-lying cliff at the edge of the sea.

The sky begins to change colour, dark splashes of orange and yellow paint the sky, with purple hues bleeding in the background.

I glance down, watching the water crash wildly against the jagged rocks. Dr. Samson's words from years ago echo in my head.

The number one thing that makes your anxiety worse is avoidance of your fear. Your anxiety forces you to back off. It makes you believe the worst thing is waiting for you on the other side. But in reality, you'll only set yourself free if you let go. Truly let go. Don't allow those thoughts to control you. The only way you can do that, to let go for good, is to face your demons, Avery. Only you can take back your life.

So much easier said than done, Samson. When do you ever really have control?

The colours in the sky intensify as they fall into the water. The soft glow of the sun casts down on me.

I remember the sunset from that night too. I remember looking at it with *him*...from one of the campus buildings. The deep hues of purple and how they projected on the fluffy clouds as the sun began to set over the university campus. I focused on the sky that night when I lost a part of myself. I tried to picture the colours of the sunset as he held me down, pressing me into the sharp concrete floor. As he took everything from me. My life completely changed within hours. All my hopes and dreams bled out, seeping into the bumpy concrete right in front of my eyes.

I allow my thoughts to drift back to that dark parking lot. To the hours before, and the smell of stale smoke lingering on his clothes. The cigarettes didn't bother me. I had seen him sitting in the back of the lecture hall, with an unlit cigarette tucked behind his ear. He was outgoing, charming, and the life of the party. And for some reason, he was interested in me. He was well-spoken, confident, and a complete monster in hiding.

I remember the bruises he left on my body. No matter how long I spent wiping away at my skin, they didn't fade for weeks. Reminding me over and over again until I stopped looking at myself in the mirror.

I couldn't stand the sight of me. It was my fault, after all, wasn't it? I had trusted someone I barely knew and stayed late on campus. I had allowed him to follow me, to walk me to my car. Where he decided he wanted to rape me. Turns out, he wasn't even a student at my university. I was the perfect prey.

Pulling my knees up, I hug myself tight as nausea roils through me. I can still smell the smoke on his body. Hear the belt clanking to the ground. The sound of his zipper. Panic slithers in my blood as my pulse quickens.

I can feel everything as if it were yesterday. Trapped in an awful nightmare I can't escape.

But it's my mind that's doing this. Keeping me trapped in an endless loop of horror.

I can't change the past or what happened to me. I can't go back, so why can't that be enough? It doesn't define me. Why do I continue to allow it to steal more of me? Knowing these thoughts have left me helpless for far too long.

Let it go.

Long breaths in through the nose, slow breaths out through my mouth. Slow and calculated as I force myself to focus on the waves. I picture releasing the dark box filled with memories from that night. Watching as it shatters against the sharp rocks below my feet. The pieces sinking, pulling farther away from me with each wave. Darkness fades deeper into the bottomless sea.

I'm not that scared, helpless girl who couldn't leave her house anymore. That girl would have never come to Scotland alone. She couldn't sit alone at an empty beach, exposed and raw. She would have been too scared. Constantly looking over her shoulder.

My sobs take hold, shaking me to my core. I drop my legs and brace my hands on the edge of the cliff as I starve for air. The rough edge of the rock digs into my palms and I relish in the new pain, a temporary escape I can focus on.

A loud wave crashes on the rocks below and a gust of wind pulls me back in. Slowing my breaths and helping me focus on the ocean instead of the panic attack threatening to consume me.

I won't let the past control me anymore.

I want to be free, to choose myself. To let go of the pain from that wicked night and release it into the sea. To spread the ashes of the broken girl I used to be, watching the pieces disappear into the water. Wave after wave, farther and farther away from me.

I want to bury that piece of me.

The tears slow. My breathing grows shallow as a cold calm finally takes hold of me.

CHAPTER SIXTEEN

avery

Mentally drained, I climb out of the rental car and head for the inn's front entrance.

The drive back from Sanna Bay beach took longer than expected. I need a shower and twelve hours of sleep. My stomach grumbles loudly, reminding me to eat something if I want to continue to keep up with these long excursions.

I walk inside the inn and the smell of fried fish has me salivating. The interior side door to the pub is open, and Scottish music spreads through the small foyer. There might be a band playing live music at the pub tonight. Maybe I can order food to go and listen to the band while I wait.

Rounding the corner, I step inside the pub, spotting Lachlan immediately.

He's leaning against the bar, his back pressed into the mahogany wood as he tips his head back, laughing. There are three outrageously beautiful women standing in front of him, completely absorbed by Lachlan.

As if he can sense me, he turns his head, and his ocean eyes lock onto mine. For just a brief second, everything slips into the shadows and it's just me and him. In a crowded room full of people, he's staring at me as if we're the only two people left standing.

His mouth quirks, and the girl in the middle leans into his chest, running her perfectly manicured fingers down his body. But he doesn't take his eyes off me and I can't bring myself to look away. We're held together by an intense staring contest.

He turns his head in the direction of the ladies he's with, but not before throwing me a cold, ruthless grin. He reaches out and pushes the blonde's hair away from her face.

It's when he starts to lean into her that I turn around, heading straight for my room. I could swear I hear his laughter follow me.

I don't know what his deal is or what kind of game he's playing but I want no part of it.

I JUMP at the sound of loud banging. My heart beats erratically in my chest as I take in my surroundings. I'm lying in the middle of my bed, with the fire still lit and my bedside table lamp on. I must have snoozed off.

And I'm still in my towel.

Fantastic.

Thud. Thud. Thud.

Rolling over, I check the time on my phone. Twelve in the morning.

I sit up, rewrapping the towel around myself as I make my way to the door, realizing it barely comes to my ass. The knocking grows louder. Who the hell...

"Hold on! Wait...who is it?" I whisper yell against the door.

"Lachlan. Open up." His deep Scottish voice, thick with honey, calls from the other side of the door.

"What do you want?" I hiss.

"Open the door."

"Do you have any idea what time it is?"

"Open the fucking door, Avery. I don't have all night."

I'm worried he's going to wake the entire place.

"Then, leave." I grind out.

Silence, and for a second I hope he's leaving.

Thud. Thud. Thud.

I nearly fall back.

"Fine. I'll go wake up Ailith." He says.

This jackass, I swear to God.

I open the door a few inches, hiding my body behind the frame. Lachlan is standing there, all of his six-foot-something solid frame leaning against my doorframe. His arms are crossed at his chest and he looks utterly annoyed. He's so close to the door that I have to back up. The smell of whisky and bad decisions rolls off his body.

Of course, he has to lean against the doorframe like that. How else would God laugh at me?

He's ditched his hat. His thick, brown hair is slightly curled, like he's been running his hands through it all night...or maybe someone else has.

Not like that's any of my concern.

I notice the takeout container in his other hand.

Even in the dark hallway, the shadows dance stunningly on his body.

I push away my inappropriate thoughts and readjust the scowl back on my face.

"Ailith gave me this, told me to bring it to you. Just open the door all the way so I can hand it to you and leave." He lifts the container of food.

Wouldn't Ailith have been long gone by now? He just threatened to go wake her.

"At this time of night?"

"Aye, she didn't want you to go to bed hungry."

"How does she know I went to bed hungry?"

"Avery," he warns. The way his voice drops when he says my name does something to me.

Traitor. I say to myself.

"Thanks. Just leave it on the ground."

I move to close the door, but he pushes off the frame and places his hand on the door.

"Will you just take it?" His mouth tightens.

"Fine." I swing the door open. "Give it here."

He freezes, all the irritation from a second ago vanishes from his face. His eyes travel down my body, moving slowly as they pause at my exposed legs, reminding me that I'm practically naked. Standing in front of this man who despises me.

I watch his throat move as he swallows, before his eyes zero in on my mouth, and I realize I'm biting my bottom lip, practically chewing on it. Lachlan's eyes dilate as he takes a deep breath.

"Did you poison it?" I ask.

He takes a step back, holding the container out to me, like he's trying to put as much distance between us as humanly possible. "Take the food or I'll drop it."

I almost want to call his bluff.

"Thanks...asshole," I mutter under my breath.

My fingers brush his as I reach out to grab the food. A jolt of electricity slides through my body, shocking every nerve ending as it steals my breath. *There it is again.*

Lachlan stares at his hand, a bewildered expression in his eyes. "Fuck," he breathes.

His eyes cut to mine for a second too long, before he turns and walks three steps away. Opening the door directly across from mine and steps inside.

Room number six.

The door thuds loudly as he slams it in my face.

I remain there, stunned as I stand in my damp towel, clutching the food container to my chest.

He's staying at the inn? And across from me?!

Great. Fantastic.

He's going to murder me in my sleep one of these nights.

I don't understand how we went from Glencoe to this. Is it because I bruised his precious ego when I quickly packed up my shit and left? Or maybe he thinks I'm a psychopath who ran off but then followed him here. Why would I do that? He's not the first hot guy, big freakin deal. Also, I showed up here first. He didn't tell me where he was staying, how could I have followed him?

It doesn't matter. He's clearly made up his mind and what he thinks of me is none of my concern.

I scowl, closing the door and locking it. Chucking the container on the table, I whip the towel off and get dressed for bed.

He didn't have to bring me the food if he couldn't stand the thought of seeing me. I mean, he made that perfectly clear earlier when he locked eyes with me from across the pub, with his hand on some woman.

Perhaps he can't say no to his aunt, or maybe he was...

Stop it.

The guy knows exactly how to put me in the worst mood.

I'm going to find Ailith in the morning, thank her for the food and see if she can move me to a different room.

I sit at the table and open the container to find a turkey sandwich, cut-up cucumbers, and a handful of fries. Ailith might be the only one here that actually cares about me. She is so thoughtful. Maybe she asked Lachlan to bring me the food hoping it will smooth things over between us.

Valiant effort, Ailith. But that's a lost cause.

I finish eating, do my nightly routine, and lay awake in bed for hours, staring at the ceiling. I'm too frustrated to fall asleep. Eventually I give up and pop a sleeping pill. I used to take them regularly, but I haven't needed them in quite some time.

Why couldn't Lachlan be bald, or fat, or anywhere but here?

I wish I never met him.

If I know anything for certain, it's that I want nothing to do with my grumpy Scottish neighbour across the hall. And he's not going to force me to leave, not when this means more to me than a spontaneous holiday.

I picture Sanna Bay Beach at sunset and the sound of soft ocean waves as my eyes begin to grow heavy with sleep.

CHAPTER SEVENTEEN

avery

I walk into the pub after sleeping the morning away, thanks to knockout sleep medication. But now it's the afternoon and I'm groggy as hell. If I don't have coffee soon, a raging headache will shadow me for the rest of the day.

The place is near empty except for a few tourists and young waiters prepping for the evening.

There is a young woman behind the bar, putting away glasses and rearranging liquor bottles. She has long, straight strawberry-blonde hair that drapes down her back. She looks to be in her early twenties, maybe even younger. With bright green eyes and a white smile.

"Hiya!" she exclaims.

"Hi, is Ailith here? I didn't see her at the desk," I say, pointing behind me towards the inn's front lobby.

"Aye. She's in the kitchen. I'll go fetch her. Are you Avery?" Her Scottish accent is similar to Ailith's but much lighter, and her smile reminds me of Ailith too...warm and comforting.

"That's me."

She extends her hand. "I'm Elizabeth, but my friends call

me Elle. Nice to meet you, Avery. Ailith has told me all about you."

I feel my face grow hot, as I reach over and shake her slightly damp hands. "Nice to meet you."

As Elle turns and disappears into the back, I quickly scan the room, my heart racing with hope that Lachlan is not around. The last thing I want is to have this conversation with Ailith with him close by.

Elle reappears a minute later.

"Ailith is making bread, she said you can go see her in the kitchen."

Oh, that's different. I would have thought guests weren't allowed to wander through the kitchens.

"Okay, are you sure?" I say reluctantly.

"Aye, go! All good." Elle puts away a glass, and moves up the partition, waiting for me to step behind the bar.

"I work here three times a week and some weekends. My family and the Hills go back, so any friend of Ailith's is a friend of mine too." Hill...that must be Ailith and Duncan's last name.

"Thanks. Ailith has been so kind and welcoming. I'm glad I stumbled upon this inn when I did."

She nods with understanding in her eyes. "Ailith is wonderful. Let me know if you want me to show you around or grab tea some time. If you end up staying for a while, that is."

"I would love that."

People here are so incredibly nice. I wonder if Ailith had something to do with this too. Maybe she has a soft spot for lonely travellers? First the sandwich, now a new friend. I think I'll take Ailith home with me when I leave Scotland.

"Grand! The kitchen is that way." Elle points at the narrow opening behind me.

I walk down the short hallway towards the kitchen, spotting Ailith as soon as I step through the arched doorway. She is standing at a large island, kneading dough on the smooth metal countertop. She glances up at me, a wide smile spreading across her rosy face.

"Avery! Lass, how are ye? Ye been hiding in yer room or just exploring our wonderful wee village?"

"Good morning...or afternoon, I should say," I backtrack, grabbing a curl and twirling it around my finger nervously. "A bit of both, but mostly exploring."

"Brilliant." Ailith nods, both of her hands plunged into a large dough as her fingers push and pull. "Do you need something, sweetheart?"

"I just wanted to find you and thank you for the food last night. You really didn't have to do that. But thank you for thinking of me. I really appreciate it."

Ailith looks up, her brows pull in confusion as she wipes her hands on her apron.

"Sorry, lassie, I don't follow."

"Food delivery to my door at midnight. Brought over by a very annoyed Scotsman who can't stand the sight of me...ring any bells?" I laugh, glancing around anxiously and trying to bring light to the already awkward conversation.

Ailith approaches me, pursing her lips as she shakes her head slowly.

"I didn't send food to yer room, Avery. I didn't see ye yesterday, but Duncan said he saw ye leaving in the morning. Figured ye were just touring around and ate while out. Who brought ye food?" she asks, suddenly perturbed.

"Lachlan did. I was just trying to be funny about the upset Scotsman bit...it doesn't matter." This is embarrassing, why did I think it was a good idea to come here? I could have thanked her later in passing.

Ailith blinks at me.

"He said you sent him over. Turkey sandwich, cucumbers,

and fries. It was all so delicious. I'm sorry, I feel a little silly now."

I watch Ailith's expression completely change. Concern and confusion melting away as a smile pulls up in the corners of her mouth. She turns, walking over to the sink and filling up a glass with water.

"Sounds like this was Lachy's doing. I never send him to deliver food to guests. Especially not late at night." She winks.

I blink quickly, as if there is a lash poking my eyeballs. There must be some sort of link here I'm missing. He wouldn't willingly bring me food.

"Do you want some coffee?" Ailith asks.

"I'd love some." I exhale.

She walks to the coffee maker sitting on the counter, grabbing two mugs from the open shelf above her head.

"It may not seem like it right now but Lachlan doesn't hate you. He's working through something just now." Ailith says, grabbing cream and milk from the fridge. "I'll have a word with him."

A slow dread fills me. "No, honestly. It's okay. I can handle him."

"Are ye sure? He's staying across the hall from ye." Ailith glances up, peering over her shoulder at me.

Yes, I know. I don't think either one of us is happy about that. Maybe that's why he was pissed off...

"Yes. No..." I blurt out. "I don't know."

Now would be a good time to ask her for a different room.

But this feels like an olive branch. Even though he doesn't want me to know that.

Have you forgotten that you don't like the guy?

"Why don't you take a seat?" Ailith motions to the two stools tucked at the edge of the island.

The kitchen is large and has an industrial-size fridge and stove. There are lots of open shelves hanging from the walls, instead of traditional cupboards, which makes the entire place feel larger. The shelves hold plates, bowls, cups, and mugs. Even pots and pans. The few cabinets are weathered white with black knobs. Plain white granite covers the rest of the U-shaped kitchen.

Ailith slides a mug towards me, and I cradle it into my hands as we both take a seat.

"What's really troubling ye, Avery?"

I glance down at my black coffee. "It's nothing, I just don't know what to make of it. He seemed irritated last night, upset that he had to come to my room. And if that wasn't the case, then why was he so grumpy? Our entire exchange has been weird since the beginning. I'm not sure if he told you, but we met at Glencoe and it was very brief. And then I left and drove until I decided to stop here for the night."

I look up to find Ailith watching me carefully, nodding along, like she's familiar with everything I'm saying. Lachlan must have filled her in, but there is something else she's not telling me. A certain wariness in her eyes that's keeping her from speaking.

"Sorry for bothering you with this. You barely know me and he's your nephew, so I should just shut up," I mutter, feeling worse about the whole thing.

Ailith reaches over and lays her hand on my arm. "Don't ever apologize for the way ye feel, lass. Does he make ye uncomfortable?"

"No." And that's the honest truth.

"Do ye want to leave Corran?" she asks.

I blink at her, trying to read in between the lines. I bite my lip, a slow shake to my head.

"Then stay and don't pay no mind to anyone else. Lachlan

has been through it and he has issues trusting people, but it's nothing personal. I promise."

We sit there for a bit, drinking our coffee as I think about everything Ailith just said...and purposely left out. She goes to stand and groans, her hand flying to her back.

I reach towards her, but she waves me away.

"If my mother were alive and sitting here, she would tell me to quit moaning, but my body is getting too old for all of this." Ailith motions to the space around her. "My legs grow tired quickly. Duncan says I should sit at the desk, focus on the site, but I'd rather have back pain from standing than spend a minute working on that darn website. I don't know how ye do it every day."

"The website?" I say, cocking my head to one side.

"Aye. Duncan has been complaining about our booking system and wants me to fix it. But I can't stand the damn thing. Gives me a bloody headache." I tip back the last bit of coffee in my mug.

"Do you want me to take a look at it?" I like Ailith, and if I can help her out in any way, it'll make me happy. She's one of those rare people that actually cares. She just sat here and listened to me, while I complained about her nephew. Most people would have told me to go fly a kite.

"Oh no. Dinna fash."

"Dinna fash?" I ask, feeling blood rush to my cheeks.

"Ah...means don't worry." Ailith shakes her head, smiling.

Look at that, I just learned something new.

"I'm serious, I'd love to help. It would be no trouble for me to take a look, or even build it for you."

"We can't afford the cost of that, lass." She frowns.

"Let me worry about that. You've been nothing but kind and I'd love to help you out."

Ailith contemplates it for just a second, before her face

lights up. She places her mug down on the counter and leans in, pulling me into a tight hug. I sit frozen in my seat for a second before deciding to hug her back. I can't remember the last time someone gave me a genuine hug.

Can't remember the last time my own mother hugged me like that. I choke down the pinch in my throat.

"Oh, Avery, ye have no idea what this means to me," she exclaims, pulling back to look at me.

"It's nothing, honestly."

"It's everything, Avery."

Her words tug at my heart. Ailith showed me kindness from the moment we met, and made me feel welcome in a new country. The website is nothing compared to that.

"Duncan is going to be so happy to hear about this. You've saved my marriage, lass." She winks and I can't help but laugh. I doubt something as feeble as a website would ever bring down a marriage that's lasted this long.

Ailith picks up our empty mugs, pausing. "Listen, Lachy's a good lad. I practically raised him when my sister passed. I'm sorry if his first impression with ye wasn't good, but give him time."

Whatever he's going through doesn't give him the right to take it out on me. I sigh, twisting my hands in my lap. My initial reaction is to shut her down but I don't want to ruin this moment.

"You mentioned earlier he's going through something. What is it?"

Ailith walks the mugs to the sink. "I'm sorry, that's not my story to tell."

I stand up, pushing the stools back in.

"Thank you for the coffee, Ailith. I should go."

"Anytime," she says over her shoulder.

"Avery..." Ailith calls, pulling my attention back to her.

"Duncan and I live in the white house right next to the inn. Do ye want to come by later and grab some of my work books, for the website?"

"Of course." I smile.

She smiles back and faces the sink. And that's the end of that.

I leave the kitchen, passing the bar and wave goodbye to Elle. She beams brightly at me, waving her arm, before turning her attention to a new customer.

Maybe I was too quick to judge him, or maybe he needs space to work through his shit and I'm just an unpleasant distraction.

CHAPTER EIGHTEEN

avery

The rain has been relentless for a week—not just a light mist or a soft drizzle, but a constant downpour that shows no sign of letting up. Ordinarily, this would upset me since I can't really go anywhere, but my work visa was approved four days ago. And I've been holed up in my room working to pass the time.

Elle and I have been spending a lot of time together too. She's been helping me with the inn's website, providing information whenever I hit a roadblock. She's worked here for years and has lived close to Ailith and Duncan her entire life. Her mom and Ailith have been best friends since they were kids, and Ailith treats Elle like her own. It makes me wonder if Ailith and Duncan have children of their own. But they've never mentioned it and I've never asked.

Elle is a ball of bright light, filled with the kindest energy. She radiates the type of optimism that draws you in. It's funny how close you can get to someone in a matter of days, clicking with ease as if you are two puzzle pieces finally reconnecting. Elle is eighteen, young and innocent. Full of ambition. She's taking a year off to work before she moves to Glasgow to attend university.

I rub my shoulder, trying to take out the kink in my neck as I slouch farther down into my chair. This little wooden table is not ideal for hours of work. I would go for a run, but it's still pouring out. I love running in the rain but all my workout clothes are currently drying from this week's deluge.

My phone vibrates on the table.

ELLE

Are you planning on leaving your room today? I thought you were on holiday, you're the worst tourist. Come down to the pub for a dram, I'm working tonight.

I smile, standing up and walking over to my bed.

ME

Listen, if you miss me, just say that.

ELLE

Would you come if I said I did?

ME

I'm tired and need a shower desperately. Tomorrow?

ELLE

You have thirty minutes before I march over and knock down your door.

I laugh, rolling my eyes at her theatrics.

ME

It's only 7:30, and I've been working all day.

ELLE

It's Friday night, people like to celebrate the weekend around here. It's going to get crowded soon and I won't be able to spend much time with you. Get down here. Not up for discussion, mate.

ME

Okay, sheesh…so bossy.

ELLE

What is a 'sheesh'?

ME

You're cute <3

Dropping onto the bed, I rest my face against the cold comforter. A nap actually sounds great right about now. But so does a drink, and some food. After a quick shower, I glare at my open suitcase that is still laying on the floor. Opting for skinny jeans and a tight, long-sleeve black top with a V-neck that's cut a little too close to my breasts. I second guess myself four times before giving up, and deciding to wear the damn shirt.

All my T-shirts and sweaters are dirty. Laundry is at the top of my to-do list. I stare at my reflection, realizing I'm over-dressed for the pub, but it's fine. After inhaling some food, and maybe a couple of drinks, I'll head back to my room.

Putting on some mascara, lip gloss, and mousse in my damp hair, I rush out the door with two minutes to spare. That should win me some brownie points with Elle.

Chatter and laughter ooze from the pub as I approach the inn's front foyer. Scottish music is blaring in the background and the place is packed. Right as I enter, the pub doors facing the street fly open and a giggling group walks in. I spot Elle behind the bar and head for the empty stool directly in front of her.

She squeals, pulling me in for a mandatory hug. "I'm glad

you came on your own. I really didn't want to have to break your door down," she says, planting a kiss on my cheek.

"I'd like to see you try. That door weighs a ton. I'm sure it's from the fifteenth century." I lean back, sitting on the metal stool.

"I'm stronger than I look." Elle winks, opening her arms wide and turning toward the full stocked shelves behind her. "What'll it be tonight?"

"Let's start with beer, please." She grabs a tall glass and walks over to the beer taps. She narrows her eyes, studying me up and down.

Her gaze lingers on my clothes. "You look fit. Hoping to meet a young lad?"

"No. I just haven't done any laundry yet, and I'm running out of clothes." I groan, heat floods my face as I pull on the top of my shirt.

She hands me my beer and leans in close to my face. "I'm sure I can find you someone fetching. It might be nice to have a man warm up your bed tonight. Unless you prefer lassies, or both. Whatever you fancy."

"Elle!" I yelp, my face growing hotter by the second.

"Wait, unless there is someone waiting for you back home?" she gasps.

"Absolutely not." I laugh a little too loudly.

"What?"

"Nothing." I avert my gaze.

"That bad?" She says quietly.

"Mhmm."

"You HAVE to tell me now. You can't be all mysterious about it."

I snort, pointing at the bottles of whisky. "You're going to have to get me something much stronger than beer for that story."

Elle perks up at that. Filling up a whisky glass with two fingers' worth of Anam Cara and sliding it over to me without hesitation.

Wow, I was only joking.

"On me." She says.

I sigh, knowing there is no way she's going to let this go. I shoot back the whisky. My throat catches fire and the entire thing almost comes back up but I quickly reach for my beer, chasing it down.

My stomach protests, the liquor burning everything in its path.

Elle starts laughing but then, her head tilts up and her eyes land somewhere behind me. She's got the biggest smile on her face, and I'm just about to turn to look at the object of her admiration, when the hairs on my body rise. The scent of pinewood and men's soap brushes by me tenderly.

I focus my eyes on Elle, watching her cheeks turn red and her eyes sparkle. I just hope he doesn't sit next to me.

The urge to run back to my room grows strong and I actually contemplate it but I'm here to see Elle. If Lachlan has a problem with me, he can leave.

Strong arms come into view as Lachlan takes a seat two stools down. Slowly sipping my beer, I keep my eyes glued onto the collection of liquor bottles lining the glass shelves. Maybe I should try a different whisky tonight. I've been obsessed with Anam Cara and haven't tired much else. When in Scotland!

Elle busies herself with Lachlan, exchanging words while she pours him a beer. I try to listen to their conversation but it's too loud in the pub.

Probably for the best, I shouldn't be eavesdropping on their conversation.

I steal a quick glance at him, watching as he flashes a big smile at Elle. The sight of it gnaws at me, leaving me feeling confused and a little angry. It's not that I care about his opinion of me—in fact, I don't particularly care whether people like me or not. But there's something about the way he shows kindness to others while actively hating me that leaves me unsettled. It's the insatiable desire to understand what I did wrong, even if it doesn't really matter.

He turns, striking blue eyes cut to mine. Elle leans on the bar, still looking at Lachlan as she continues to talk, oblivious to our heated hate stare. And I just stare back at him, holding my ground like I have something to prove.

"Oh, Lachlan! I forgot to introduce you to my new friend. Avery, move closer so I can talk to you both." Lachlan drops his eyes.

"I'm good, thanks," I shout back.

Elle's brows furrow, realizing neither of us are moving. She walks over and grabs my drinks, placing my empty glass of whisky and full pint of beer right beside Lachlan.

For fuck's sake.

I blink at her and she puts her hands on her hips, arching a brow at me. Eventually I stand up and sit on the stool next to him, careful to leave enough space between us.

Elle is younger than me, but somehow thinks she can boss me around, and I let her get away with it.

"Avery, this is Lachlan...Ailith's nephew, and Lachlan, this is Avery...she's travelling from Canada. Avery is helping Ailith with the website." Elle grins, thinking she's introducing us for the first time. Bless her happy little heart.

I take a deep breath, preparing to deliver the bad news when Lachlan stretches his hand in front of me. "It's nice to meet you, Avery. Welcome to Scotland."

I stare at him, then blink several times, trying to find the humour in his voice but he's completely serious. Pretending like he doesn't know me.

That's fine. I'll go along with it. I just need more alcohol.

I press my hand into his, shaking it firmly as the feeling of live wire licks against my palm, crawling under my skin. I breathe through the shock this time, fully expecting it before our hands meet.

Lachlan clenches his jaw, yanking back his hand. It's just as intense for him as it is for me, but he fights it every single time.

"Nice to meet you," I breathe out.

I turn towards the bar, taking a large sip of my beer. "Elle, can I get another whisky?"

She nods, exchanging a curious look between me and Lachlan. Elle hands me my whisky and I empty the glass, again. This time the burn isn't as intense.

Elle claps her hands excitedly. "I have a feeling I'm going to like drunk Avery."

I wink at her.

"How did you two become friends?" Lachlan angles his body, half facing Elle behind the bar. His question is for me, but I stay quiet.

"We met last week here and I started helping Avery with the website. Ailith has been so much happier since Avery agreed to do it for her." Elle runs down the bar, disappearing in the kitchen.

"Is that so?" His deep voice coats my skin. I nurse my beer, avoiding his eyes.

"Yep," I say right as Elle walks back.

"Avery, I ordered you a burger and salad since you haven't eaten all day," Elle announces to me before she turns to Lachlan. "She's been cooped up in her room, working away on her laptop. I convinced her to come out tonight. And now I'm worried she's going to get pissed drunk and throw up everywhere."

"Hey! That's rude. I can hold my own." Elle just laughs, patting my hand, like I'm a small child.

"I'm surprised Avery is interested in making friends. Aren't you leaving soon?" Lachlan's eyes burn a hole into the side of my face.

"You wish." I murmur.

"What?" Elle says at the same time.

The urge to punch him in the face right now is so strong.

Lachlan turns, shaking his head. Slipping out of character already? If you're going to pretend you don't know me, you should stick to the script.

Elle squints at him angrily as she leans on the bar, turning her gaze on me.

"So tell me about the lad back home." She says eagerly.

"There is no *lad*." I say, making air quotes with my fingers. I reach for my beer but Elle wraps her fingers around the glass, pulling it away from me.

"Sounds like there might be, or at least a story. No more alcohol until you tell me what happened. Is that why you're here?"

"No! And that wasn't the deal!" I sigh, resting my chin on my hand.

"Let me take a wild guess, there is a man back home waiting for you to love him. Maybe even a proposal, but you won't give him the time of day because you're scared of commitment. So, you decided to run off to figure out what you really want."

Elle heaves out a sharp breath and I turn to Lachlan, who is glaring at me with a knowing smirk.

My heart begins to race and my face contorts with hot fury. It feels like his words slapped me right across the face.

"Did I get it right?" he continues, adding salt to my open wound.

"Lachlan! What the fuck?" Elle shouts.

"You don't know what you're talking about." I snap.

Anger bubbles under my skin, begging me to release it. I've never been great with controlling my temper, even though I've tried quieting that part of my mind for years now. Anger is quick, relentless and unforgiving.

It doesn't help that every interaction I have had with this insufferable man since Glencoe has been painful. He doesn't deserve to know the truth, but the whisky is coursing heavily through my veins, making it hard for me to keep my mouth shut. And for some reason, I don't want Elle to make an inaccurate assumption about me.

Lachlan leans in closer, his elbow resting comfortably on the bar.

"Are you sure? Or was it so spot on that it hit too close to home. Admit it, you love to run, lass."

"Why do you even care?"

He laughs, shrugging as he turns away and faces the bar. Done with this conversation, bored with my existence once again.

Elle gives me a sad look, as she busies herself by refilling my whisky glass. She mouths 'I'm sorry'. But I can't let this go. I'm raging and the words spew out of me.

"You want to know about my amazing lover back in Canada, Elle? The one who sadly couldn't be here with me," I say with fake enthusiasm, keeping my eyes on Elle.

She blinks at me, looking like a deer caught in the headlights.

"I uprooted my life and moved across the country three years ago, far away from my family and friends, for a guy. I supported his career, was there for him, moved into his house, furnished it, cooked for him. I respected him and cared for him. And then three weeks ago I walked into our apartment to find my bags packed and sitting by the door. He told me he had been having an affair for the last year, and that he was in love with her." I sip my whisky, watching the pity grace Elle's eyes.

I can't stand it when people look at me with such sad eyes, feeling sorry for me and my pathetic life. That look is isolating, only makes me feel helpless, weak and alone. I'm full of regret, for opening my mouth in the first place and for allowing Lachlan's words to get under my skin.

"Oh...Avery. I'm so sorry...you didn't have to." She reaches for my hand, but I pull it back, tucking my hands in between my crossed legs.

I don't want to push her away. Not over something like this.

"It's okay. It was honestly the best thing that happened to me." Elle nods, looking over at Lachlan shamefully. I know he heard me. I said it loud enough for him to hear all of it. I hope he feels awful about it and for being so quick to judge me.

The silence hangs heavy between us, even though the pub is filled with laughter, music, and chatter.

I turn my stool to the right and scan the crowd.

Maybe I should hook up with someone. It's been a long time, and honestly, the whisky and beer are making me feel really good right now, despite my disastrous oversharing.

My eyes land on a guy sitting across the bar at a two-person table. He is leaning back in his chair, watching me. Dark blond hair, almond eyes—they look light, but I can't tell the colour from this far. He's built, but on the leaner side. Maybe a runner or swimmer. His features are softer—baby face as Becca likes to call it. I don't know how long he's been staring at me, but I decide to wave at him.

He smiles, raising his pint at me. He's cute and doesn't look like he's from around here. Too bad I don't have random hookups with strangers I meet at pubs.

"Avery, bonnie lass! So nice to see ye at the pub during the night. I was worried there for a second." I turn my stool around and find Ailith standing beside Elle, holding a plate of food. She sets my burger and salad in front of me.

"Thank you, Ailith. Always nice to see your smiling face." I laugh, feeling a little dizzy as I grab a piece of lettuce and pop it in my mouth.

She rests her elbows on the bar, stretching her back.

"How's the website coming along?" she asks, and I give her two-thumbs up before digging into my burger.

"Is she sloshed?" Ailith turns to ask Elle.

"Is sloshed drunk? If so, then noooo. But the food is really good. Thank youuuuu!" I exclaim, reaching for my whisky, but Ailith is too quick.

Maybe I am a little tipsy. How many glasses of whisky have I had?

"Give her some water," she barks at Elle before turning her attention to Lachlan.

He's sitting quietly, facing the bar and looking deep in thought.

"How's things?" Ailith asks him.

He nods, not looking at her.

"What's the matter?"

"Nothing."

"Yer meeting go all right?" I watch the conversation between him and Ailith while taking another giant bite out of my burger. Lachlan tilts his face to the side, lowering his voice.

Rich, buttery notes of garlic and cheese explode in my mouth, and I have a small moment with my food.

Lachlan slides his empty beer glass over to Ailith as they continue their quiet conversation.

"I should get back. Ye need anything else, Avery?"

"Nope. Thank you, again," I mumble in between bites.

Ailith nods, tapping her knuckles on the bar. She begins to

walk away but pauses, turning to face the three of us. "Before I forget, you're all coming to supper on Tuesday. I'm roasting a chicken."

I start to shake my head, chewing faster so I could protest with words, but Ailith puts her hand up to stop me. "I don't want to hear it, lass. So don't bother. It's not up for discussion. You're comin'."

She points her finger at Lachlan. "And you, be nice."

I watch as Ailith disappears down the bar. Placing my half-eaten burger on the plate, I grab a napkin, aggressively wiping my hands and thinking about ways to get out of this upcoming dinner.

I don't belong there. These people are family and I'm an outsider, a tourist simply passing by. But Ailith has the biggest heart on the planet and has decided to welcome me into her home. Likely because I offered to build her website. How can I kindly turn down the dinner invitation without offending her?

Surely I can sit through one dinner with an unbearable human. I'll just ignore him, and I'm sure he'll do the same. Like he is right now.

This won't be the first time I've had to sit through an uncomfortable dinner. I used to tag along whenever Mom would invite me to lunch or dinner to meet one of her boyfriends. I would keep my mouth shut, stuff my face, and smile whenever she spoke to me.

This is different though. This is for Ailith.

I pick up my fork and start stabbing my salad.

I could try to be nice to him, even though he doesn't deserve it. Not after what he said to me.

"How long have you known Elle?"

Lachlan turns, looking twelve shades of dejected, and my heart twists uncomfortable at the sight of his sullen face.

"Since she was born," he utters, turning back to his beer.

"She lights up when you're around. Before you decided to be a dick, that is."

He's looking at the bar, but a soft smile curls at the corner of his lip.

"She's like a sister I never had. Annoying, persistent, and adorably innocent. Ailith and her mom have been friends since they were little." Lachlan turns his head, the warm affectionate glow still on his face as he watches Elle serving drinks to a group of friends.

Elle laughs with the group, sliding their drinks to them with complete ease. She's a carefree type of happy. I wish I knew what that feels like.

"I know. She told me."

I stuff my overloaded fork in my mouth again and chew. The bar is flooding with people, and I doubt I'll be seeing much more of Elle for the rest of the night. Everyone is busy keeping the crowd happy. I push my plate away and consider leaving, even though the night is just starting for everyone else.

"Where in Canada are you from?" Lachlan asks.

"Vancouver. Toronto. No...Vancouver."

Lachlan nods, considering my answer. "Are you going anywhere else after Scotland?"

"No."

"So, you're just a solo tourist?"

I raise my brow at him. "Yes, as opposed to what?"

His eyes flicker to mine with curious, reflective energy. But he simply shakes his head, not answering me.

Lachlan slips off his stool. His arm brushing my back as he walks by. He jumps over the bar, standing in front of me and he bends down, reaching for something below the counter. When his head pops up, his eyes instantly find mine, causing my heart to pound in my chest.

There is something about the blue in his eyes, something I'm incredibly drawn to. Something I don't yet understand.

A minute later, he's back on his stool beside me. Opening a brand-new bottle of whisky and filling two glasses. He pushes one towards me with the back of his hand, careful not to touch my skin.

"Sláinte," he says, raising his glass to his lips.

"Sláinte," I repeat back, taking a sip of the golden-brown liquid. Sláinte is the equivalent of "cheers" in Scotland, and it might be my new favourite word.

How is it that with just a single look he has the power to light my entire body on fire?

I wonder how easy some things must be for someone like Lachlan. He could captivate anyone with eyes like that. I'm sure he doesn't have issues with women cheating on him, or leaving him for someone else. Well, unless he's a total asshole to other people too, but I don't think he is that way normally. I've seen the way he talks to Elle, Duncan, and Ailith. Even strangers in the pub. The girls from the other night. Maybe he doesn't like relationships. Maybe he prefers to be alone, having a different woman occupying his bed every night.

Discontent brushes down my spine—whispering words I don't care to hear. I tamper down the thoughts, refusing to acknowledge them. I don't know him well enough to make those kinds of conclusions. And I don't really care to find out, either way.

Another sip of whisky and more of those sticky, confining thoughts start to fade away.

"I'm sorry about before," Lachlan's deep voice pulls me out of my thoughts.

Has hell frozen over? Is he apologizing to me?

"You're talking to me?" I glance at him.

He shifts on his stool, taking in an exhausted breath. "Aye, about what I said before. I...I shouldn't have...it was unkind for me to assume."

Guilt is a powerful thing.

He waits for me to acknowledge his apology, maybe tell him it's okay and that I forgive him. His eyes carry a deep familial sadness, one that calls to me, begging for me to unravel it.

Don't they say broken souls have a way of recognizing one another? Maybe that's what this is. Maybe that's why every time he touches me I feel an intense surge of electricity coursing through my veins, squeezing the air out of my lungs.

Everything blurs around me as I allow myself a small moment to get lost in those eyes. My fingers tingle, wanting to reach out and touch him. I don't know how long we remain still, lost in one another's current.

I could swear a spark of darkness ripples in his ocean blues, calling my name.

CHAPTER NINETEEN

avery

"Hi there," a strong voice pierces through my thoughts, dragging me back in.

Lachlan blinks, his gaze breaks away from mine and his cold mask falls back into place. I avert my own eyes, taking in a deep, slow breath to steady myself. The weight of the whisky in my body seems to intensify as I turn towards the voice.

It's the guy I waved at from the other side of the pub.

"Hi." I say, forcing a smile. I completely forgot about him.

The man takes a step closer to me.

"I noticed you're drinking whisky. Got you a Jack Daniel's." North American accent, maybe American.

I let out a bitter laugh, amused by the irony of that. "Thank you."

"What?" He stares at my mouth, smiling.

"I'm just surprised they sell Jack Daniel's here. Scotland is known for their whisky. Isn't the imported stuff more expensive?" Shit, I sound like a snob.

"Woah...usually when I buy a woman a drink, she doesn't

scold me or ask me how much it costs. But you're hot, so I'll let it pass," he retorts, winking at me.

"Gee. Thanks." I roll my eyes.

He lets out a shrill laugh. The scent of sour vodka rolling off his breath turns my stomach.

"Looks like you need a good taming."

Did he just fucking say that to me? Or did I hallucinate it? The nerve.

"I bet the wildest thing you'll ever tame is a house cat," I spit back.

A deep, full laugh bursts from Lachlan.

Shit, did I say that out loud?

I turn, watching Lachlan's body shake with laughter, as a smile creeps up my face. That was a good comeback, even for me.

"You're a funny girl, aren't you? I'm Mike." He says, ignoring Lachlan completely as he takes another step, his eyes dropping to my chest.

There is something about his glare that triggers me. Dark memories from a distant past flash before my eyes, and all the humour and backhanded compliments from before are replaced by a deep sense of fear.

I've seen that look before.

"You have a good night," I stutter on a shaky breath.

Mike sneers, sliding the Jack Daniel's to me. "Why don't you take a drink, baby? It'll loosen you up. You clearly need it."

Panic churned in my stomach, as a thousand anxious voices whispered in my ears. For a moment I sat frozen. I couldn't think, couldn't speak, couldn't breathe. The fear was choking the air out of my lungs.

Deep breaths, it's going to be okay.

I have to stay here. If I try to leave, he might follow me to my room. That's not something I'm willing to risk, especially after how much I've had to drink. I don't even want him to know I'm staying here.

The inn.

What if he's staying here? What if he's already seen me around? What if he won't leave?

I'm drowning.

"I've been watching you from across the room since you walked in. Tell me your name."

My skin crawls. "I'm good."

Glancing down the bar, I pray to make eye contact with Elle or Ailith. I don't spot either one of them. I pull out my phone, angling it away from Mike, and send a quick text to Elle.

"Are you here alone? Are you staying at the inn?" Mike leans into me, whispering close to my ear, as his clammy fingers wrap around my elbow. I jump back, hitting Lachlan's shoulder without intention. I breathe out an apology in his direction.

I need to get away.

"Please don't touch me."

Mike steps back, raising his hands in the air, and laughing like this is all a joke. "Woah, okay. Not here, I get it, babe."

He reaches out, brushing my cheek.

I slam my eyes shut, taking short laboured breaths. "Don't... touch...me."

My right leg falls off the stool, as I stumble out of my seat. Standing on shaky legs, my back hits a solid body. I glance up to find Lachlan's furious glare pinned on Mike.

"You better take your fucking hands off her, mate, before I cut off all your fingers and shove them up your arse," Lachlan snarls, accentuating every single word.

"Why don't you mind your own business, pal? I've got it."

My knees grow weak and everything starts to appear hazy.

Lachlan pulls my back into his chest, wrapping his arm around my collarbone. His close proximity should alarm me but I only feel a small amount of comfort knowing I'm not alone.

He leans down, his lips hovering above my ear. "I've got you. Just breathe for me, okay?" His voice is soft and gentle.

I nod against his chest.

Lachlan presses his thumb into the delicate skin on the inside of my wrist. His touch jolts me, the simple act is so subtle, yet commanding. I focus on it, chasing away the chaos inside my head.

"She's with me. Why don't you go back to your drink?" Mike says with a dismissive grin.

"Back the fuck off and get out of my pub."

The people in the pub are blissfully unaware of the shit show taking place around us. Meanwhile, I feel everything crashing into me. Every vibration, every word, every fear, every frantic beat of my heart telling me to run and hide.

"Your pub? I don't see your name on it." Mike steps closer, nudging my shoulder as he stares up into Lachlan's eyes.

"Go ask the burly lad behind the bar if you don't believe me." Lachlan's head jerks to the side. "Besides, the lass looks real comfortable in my arms. Wouldn't you say? Back off and leave her alone."

"Fuck this shit. Bitch isn't even worth the effort," Mike seethes, reaching for the whisky glass he originally brought for me. He tips it back all at once.

Lachlan steps in front of me, using his body to shield me.

The empty Jack Daniel's glass slams on the table. Mike shakes with pure outrage as he reaches around, trying to grab at me. But before his fingers get anywhere close to me, Lachlan's fist plummets into his nose.

In a matter of seconds, chaos breaks loose right in front of me. Lachlan has Mike in a chokehold and Mike is scratching, trying to get free. They bump into a table while I stand there, completely useless, and in shock.

"Both of ye. Out. NOW," Duncan roars, appearing from thin air. He cuts an imposing figure, towering beside them like a goddamn Viking warrior.

Lachlan releases Mike and takes a step back, his arms hanging limply at his sides. Duncan gestures towards the pub doors, beyond which lies the dimly lit street. Mike shuffles towards the exit as Lachlan trails behind him, his eyes trained on Mike's retreating form.

My mind screams at him to stop, to abandon his reckless pursuit. I don't want him to get hurt. Yet, the words refuse to come out of my mouth, remaining lodged in my throat like an invisible boulder.

Duncan casts a fleeting glance in my direction before following the duo.

"Don't let him get in a fight over this. Please," I call out to Duncan.

He gives me a single nod.

Soft hands grasp my arm and I flinch, looking down at Ailith.

"Come on, love. Let's go." She gives me a weary smile. I clutch her hand hard, letting her guide me back to my room.

CHAPTER TWENTY

avery

Ailith offered to stay with me, but I insisted she go back to the pub. The place was packed and the night had already gone to shit. I didn't want to add to her stress. She sat with me on the bed for a few minutes, a hesitant expression on her face, before she reluctantly stood up and walked out.

It's been hours and I'm still pacing my room. Every few minutes I stick my ear up against the wooden door, listening for any movement on the other side.

Where are they?

Quiet, muffled voices draw closer. I stop breathing, pressing my face against the door.

"Yer a numpty! What were ye thinking? What if Mike had recognized ye?" I detect Duncan's thick Scottish accent.

A long beat of painful silence passes. I listen for Lachlan to say something but he doesn't utter a word—no anger, no smart remarks, just...nothing.

"Start using yer head! You're acting like a fuckin' wean." Duncan booms, his anger ripples through the door.

A wrecking sensation tears through my chest. I have no idea what a wean is, but it can't be good if Lachlan is this quiet.

This is all your fault.

Before I have a chance to change my mind, I pull open the door, taking in Lachlan's bloody cheek and hand, as he leans against the stone wall.

"Shit, are you okay?" I walk towards him, but he turns his body, trying to give me his back.

I gently grab his swollen, red hand and he winces.

"I'm fine. It's just a cut." His voice is hoarse.

His cheek is swollen and bleeding. There is a deep cut on his lip and his hand is all messed up.

What the fuck happened out there?

"This is not okay. Let me fix it. I have a first-aid kit in my room."

Lachlan pulls his hand away, turning for his door. "It's all right. Go to sleep."

I step into his line of sight, blocking his door. "Please. Let me do this. I feel terrible," I whisper, urging him to look me in the eye.

"I'll get ye some ice. Let the lassie fix ye up," Duncan mutters and he begins to walk away.

Lachlan looks doleful as he reaches behind me for his door handle. I can't let him leave like this. Without another thought, I grab his uninjured hand, feeling his body flinch at the sudden contact. But he doesn't pull away.

"Please," I choke out, my voice barely a whisper.

He takes a slow breath and his jagged eyes land on mine. I don't wait for him to change his mind. Working quickly I guide him to my room and motion for him to sit on the edge of my bed. To my surprise, he doesn't fight me on it.

I walk over to my backpack and pull out the first-aid kit I always carry around with me. Grabbing a clean hand towel from the bathroom, I run it under hot water and get straight to work.

Lachlan's shoulders are drawn in and his eyes are fixated on the cold fireplace, distant and far away. If I wasn't there, he wouldn't have fought with that worthless piece of shit. Or maybe if I had kept my mouth shut and didn't acknowledge Mike, he would have left us alone.

Laying everything out on the bed, I try my best to ignore the hurried beats of my heart. Stepping close to Lachlan, I gently grab his chin and lift his face up. I feel his eyes on my face, but I focus on his bruised cheek as I press down the warm towel, dabbing off the blood. I grip the back of his neck, and his hair brushes against my fingers, charging the kinetic pull between us.

Lachlan's body responds instantly, going rigid as his breathing becomes shallow and quick. The air around us seems to vibrate with tension, as if crackling with electricity.

"Am I hurting you?" I whisper.

"No."

We've never been this close, and it all feels too much. This intense need rushes through me, muddling my thoughts. It almost hurts, being this close to him and wanting to touch him everywhere. Or maybe that's the alcohol talking as it works its way out of my system.

I work quickly, pressing the cloth lightly into his cheek and ignoring the way my body lights up beside him. As if a single touch will set me aflame.

His soul crushing eyes stare into mine, so intense that I struggle to remember what I'm doing or why I'm standing here. His face is mere inches away, and my eyes fall to his lips. Something strange is happening and I don't know what to make of it, as a range of conflicting emotions swim through me.

You need to focus.

I jerk his face to the side, needing a break from his eyes as I finish cleaning his cheek. Stepping back, I fold the towel and glance down at his lips again. Lachlan leans back on his hands, remaining patient and composed.

It's me that seems to be falling apart.

I fill my lungs with air. "I'm going to clean your lip, you have a pretty big gash."

"Okay." He nods.

I need to get closer to him to access that cut properly. This was such a bad idea. Someone else should have volunteered to do this since I seem to be having a brain malfunction.

Just take care of him for saving your ass and send him on his way.

I step towards him and he widens his legs, allowing me better access. Making sure my body doesn't touch his, I lay my hand on his good cheek, pressing my thumb under his chin. God, he smells good.

This is torture, absolute fucking torture.

The guy is likely sitting here, counting down the seconds until he can leave. Meanwhile, I'm dreaming about wrapping my body around his until the smell of pinewood infuses into my skin. I shake my head, trying to rid myself of these thoughts as I lean down, taking a closer look at his busted lip. It's deep but thankfully the bleeding has stopped. My thumb brushes the bottom edge, as I press the rag down. Lachlan lets out a deep sigh, and the sound shoots straight to my core.

What is wrong with you? The man is literally bleeding.

"Are you okay?" His question catches me off guard.

"Am I okay? I'm not the one with the cut up face."

"At the pub, you were...frightened. Did you run into him before tonight?" His eyes search mine but I drop my gaze, trying not to think about the crippling fear and the power it holds over me. Even after all these years.

"No, he just reminded me of something I'd rather forget."

Lachlan's arm stretches out, but just as quickly, he retracts it. As if a sudden recollection corrects his movements. My shoulders sag at that. Partly out of relief and partly out of disappointment. I hate myself for that.

Straightening my spine, I keep my eyes on his lip. "I'm sorry about all of this."

"You have nothing to be sorry for." His warm breath skates across the palm of my hand, sending shivers tiptoeing down my spine.

"You shouldn't have said anything, or gotten involved."

"He is an atrocious pig. I wanted to gut him for touching you. He's lucky Duncan was there to stop me."

I blink at him. "Don't say that. It's not worth it. I'm not worth..." I shake my head, unable to finish my sentence.

Lachlan studies me for a long time, causing every hair on my body to rise. He doesn't say anything and I'm convinced that's the end of our very short conversation. I finish cleaning his lip and step away, walking to the bathroom to rinse out the bloody towel.

I stare at my reflection in the mirror. My cheeks are flushed and my nipples have hardened, pressing through the material of my bra and top.

Jesus Christ, Avery.

I blame the alcohol. I'll clean his hand, patch up his cheek and lip, and then we can go back to not speaking to one another.

I walk back into the room and sit on the bed, pausing before I reach for his messed up hand. It's in really bad shape. His knuckles are swollen and dried blood is caked on his skin. I smooth out his fingers and rest his hand on my leg, nudging the towel into his skin and repeating the same motions as before.

It's eerily quiet and my thoughts are too loud.

I glance up after a few minutes, surprised to find him watching me.

"I would do it all again. And so much more, because you're worth it. He should have never touched you," he breathes out.

Goosebumps break out across my arms. My hand stills as I look into his eyes, reminding myself to breathe.

The door swings open, causing me to jump and nearly fall off the bed. Duncan looks between us as he walks towards Lachlan, holding out a bag of ice.

"Ye did good, lassie." Duncan says, inspecting Lachlan's injuries.

I take the opportunity to patch up his face, placing two small butterfly closures on his cheek and wrapping his hand in gauze.

"There isn't much I can do about the lip, but I'll put a thin tape at the bottom to help the wound close." I lean in, holding my breath while I tape his lip.

"Make sure ye ice that cheek, Lachy. Ye dinnae want to ruin that braw face o'yers, or ye'll have a lot of folk ragin'." Duncan leers before turning around and walking out my door.

I grab all the extra material and put away my first-aid kit.

"What did Duncan mean by all that?"

Lachlan stands, refusing to answer me.

"Thank you," he murmurs before stepping out and shutting the door behind him.

The weight from the night finally settles over top of me. Feeling everything and nothing at the same time, I turn on the fireplace and strip out of my clothes before climbing into bed. My tears flow freely, soaking the pillow underneath my head.

I dreamt of him and the ocean that night.

CHAPTER TWENTY-ONE

lachlan

Tightening my grip on the rubber handle, I take a deep breath, raising the axe above my head and throwing it down in one swift motion. The blade cuts deep into the wood with a satisfying thud. I repeat the movement over and over again, listening to the rhythm of the swings as chips of wood fly all around me.

When I first got to Corran a couple of months ago, Ailith asked if I could start chopping firewood. They go through a ton of wood every week and Duncan explained it's more cost-effective to buy the logs in bulk and split them yourself. My first instinct was to throw money at the problem. I offered to pay for pre-chopped wood but they said no, so I reluctantly agreed to do it.

I thought I would hate the repetitiveness of it. That it would be exhausting. The hours of swinging, bending, and lifting just to break wood in smaller pieces. But after a few sessions, I was hooked. Craving the focus and the outlet it provided for my anger. I drive all my pent-up temper into each swing, using the full force of my body to split the wood. To push out the nothingness.

I'm so tired of the constant rage, and the loneliness that comes with it. Tired of the need to resist, push back, avoid everything around me. I'm so tired of pushing away anyone that comes near me. Who I am, what I am— like I have no control. I've been out here a lot in the last week. Trying to sort through my punishing life and now, there is something new occupying my thoughts.

Someone I refuse to let myself think about.

But last night, something broke inside me when I saw the crippling fear in Avery's eyes.

The fucking bastard was harassing her, over and over. Touching her, teasing her. I couldn't just sit there and do nothing. Especially when her entire body started shivering with undiluted fear. It was as if she wanted to absorb into herself, and run at the same time. People don't act that way for no reason, it was a trauma response.

I've been mad since Glencoe. I don't need a reason to dislike someone; it's a feeling and it doesn't require any explanation. I could pretend it's because she showed up at the pub the next day and raised all my red flags, but that's only half of it. Watching her run from me like that fucking pissed me off. Not because she owed me anything, but because I felt something on that field and I couldn't understand how she didn't. Maybe I am really losing my mind. The pull was gravitational, and when she looked at me, it felt as though she could see me. Really see me...the version of me I want to be.

Bloody hell, get over it already.

It doesn't matter. Thinking about Avery is a complete waste of time.

"Knew I'd find ye out here again. I reckon we have enough wood to last the month, laddie," Duncan says, leaning against a nearby tree holding a pint of ale. I've never seen the bloke drink water. Pretty sure his main diet consists of beer and whisky.

"I'm trying to get ahead. I want to camp in the highlands soon and might be gone for a few days." I lay the axe on the grass, wiping my brow with the back of my sleeve. The gauze Avery placed on my hand is falling apart, covered in sweat and dirt. But that's a good thing. Maybe I'll finally stop thinking about her every time I look down at my hand.

"What's troubling ye today, Lach?"

Duncan is a man of few words, but he misses nothing. And he only speaks when necessary.

"The usual crap."

"Still haven't decided what yer gonna do?"

I shake my head. "No, and coming here hasn't cleared anything up. It's given me space to breathe but nothing else."

Duncan jerks his head towards the bench by the back door, indicating he wants to talk. He's the only one that hasn't talked to me about work yet. I'm sure Ailith has filled him in—those two don't hide anything from one another. But Duncan respects the power of time like no one else. Growing up, he would give me space to process things, only stepping in when he thought I needed it.

I feel the conversation coming and this is the first time his timing is wrong. I don't need help. I need a time machine.

Duncan sips on his ale, his eyes focused on the axe hidden in the grass. "I think ye already have yer answer, Lachlan, but you're no wantin to confront it."

A dark laugh comes out of me before I can stop it. "You're wrong."

"Am I? Or are ye resorting to yer anger to cope with yer problems again?"

My brows furrow. "It's not that simple and you know that. He's made it impossible for me to get out."

"Laddie, ye ken I love ye. Aye, treated ye like ma own bairn, which is why I cannot lie to ye," Duncan hesitates for a second. "You've been livid for so long, over things completely out of yer control. Ye couldn't done anything to help your ma when she took ill, ye chose a career ye thought ye wanted but grew to resent. And now ye cannot find a way out, so yer ignoring it and letting yourself sink into yer rage. Yer angry at a lassie ye ken nothin' about and pickin' fights with randie strangers. Yer letting the anger devour ye."

I turn away, not wanting to look at him anymore as my chest tightens. Because deep down, I know Duncan is right. I have been angry for so long, but it's better than feeling everything else. It's better than rotting away or turning to other hurtful hobbies.

"Don't ye reckon it's time ye stop punishing yourself?"

I grit my teeth. "It wasn't a random stranger. He was fucking harassing her. Touching her after she told him to stop. You would have done the same."

"Aye, I would. But I think it means more to ye than that."

"Bullshit."

I'm fuming but I don't dare show it, not when he just gave me shit about my anger issues. I've been alone for so long, everything has turned inward. Rage feels good, it's productive, it drives me forward. I got everything I thought I wanted, needed even. But the dream in the spotlight quickly faded to a nightmare, and now I have nothing left but worthless rage.

"Is Avery who ye thought she was?" Duncan asks, throwing a curveball at me by changing the subject.

"No. I had my team look into her. She was telling the truth."

"Ye gonna say sorry and quit acting like such a bawbag?"

I shoot him a withering look. Since when does he care about a random guest at the inn? So what, she's developed a bit of a bond with Ailith and Elle but that's not something Duncan ever concerns himself with.

"No, why would I? She's just a tourist. She'll be gone soon."

Duncan drinks the last of his ale and stands up, smirking down at me.

"Just a tourist?"

I hate when he starts talking in riddles. Just come out with it.

"Aye. What are you getting at?"

"Stop swimming against the current, Lachlan. Let go for once, it may do ye some good." He turns, disappearing through the back door.

I walk over to the pile of logs, picking up my axe, and line up the next piece of wood.

Stop swimming against the current.

There is nothing here to explore. She's leaving and I fucked everything up the minute I yelled at her, ordering her to leave. I had valid reasons, even if they were rooted in paranoia. Still, there is no going back from that and no point in trying, she is only here for a short time. Exploring Scotland for however long before she goes back to her life in Canada.

Not to mention the fact that I can't be with anyone right now. I won't. No one deserves to be pulled into my mess.

A stitch twists in my stomach.

I couldn't fall asleep last night thinking about Avery. The way her fingers grazed my face, as she carefully cleaned my wounds. Her touch was so soft. I noticed the way she held her breath, trying so hard to make sure not an inch of her body brushed mine. My fingers itched as I held back the urge to wrap my arm around her waist and pull her close. She smelled like summer, a heady coconut and vanilla scent I still can't seem to get out of my head. And those sad whisky eyes looked at me, as I felt something blooming in my chest. In that moment, I wanted nothing more than to take her fear and pain away. I wanted to know what broke her so I could fix it with my bare hands.

I know how this sounds, but I can't deny the connection or whatever it is that's making me feel this way. It's just there, and it doesn't need to be acknowledged or actioned. I felt it the moment I looked into her eyes at Glencoe, but she is a passenger and nothing more.

Just a tourist.

CHAPTER TWENTY-TWO

avery

After the incident with Mike at the pub, things seemed to settle back into their natural rhythm, as if the whole ordeal had never occurred.

I'm not sure what I hoped would happen; after all, I barely know anyone here. I'm just a mere guest, passing the time until I leave for Canada. And someone else will take my place, as if I was never here. Despite all that, a small part of me yearns for Elle to acknowledge what happened, or for Duncan to say hi as pass in the hallway, or even just a moment's respite from Lachlan's obvious avoidance.

I thought maybe after I tended to his wounds we would become acquaintances or some shit like that.

But it seems like I'm the only one who likes to hold on to things for days. Mulling over details, conversations, stolen glances, and every gentle touch. Always the oversensitive thinker. It's one of the things I hate most about myself, highlighted in yellow on my long itemized self-loathing list.

I find myself constantly glancing down the hallway every

time I leave my room, unable to resist my growing curiosity. However, each time I pass his door, it remains shrouded in darkness, and not a single sound emerges from within. Where does he disappear to when he's not here?

It's none of your business.

Tonight is the dreaded dinner at Ailith and Duncan's house. I tried to come up with an excuse or pretend I'm going to be out of town, but Ailith wouldn't hear of it. Apparently the dinner is for me since I helped with the inn's website. I'm praying to all the Gods that Lachlan will continue his MIA streak.

Elle plops down across from me at the booth.

"How's things?"

Her blonde hair is up in a low ponytail today, the soft golden colour bringing out notes of green in her hazel eyes.

"I'm fine." I say, flipping over my sketchbook.

"You seem sad." Her brows pull together, lips pressing into a thin line as she rests her arms on the table.

"No, I'm great. I'm just nervous for tonight's dinner. I feel like I'm imposing."

Actually, I feel like I'm in limbo and I should maybe move on from Corran.

"Oh, Aves, don't say that." Elle reaches across the table, grasping my hand tightly. "You could never impose. We've become friends, have we not? And Ailith adores you. We all want you there."

I snort. "Not everyone."

"Aye...everyone."

I really don't want to get into this with her. "I'm sure you've noticed, but Lachlan is not my biggest fan."

Elle shifts in her seat, averting her eyes. Apparently she doesn't want to get into this with me either.

"What?" I poke.

"He likes you just fine. Why else would he defend you?" Her eyes shift up, suddenly rounding in surprise. As if she's discovered a hidden treasure.

She leans in, whispering. "Do you fancy him?"

I blink at her, wondering if she heard me a few seconds ago when I said the guy does not like me.

"Are you serious? Of course not! We have a very comfortable hating relationship."

She bellows, her lips forming an O. "You so do, you're blushing!"

What? I reach out and touch my cheeks, which sends Elle off into a fit of uncontrollable laughter.

"You're insane. This conversation is over, and I never want to hear about it again."

I down my coffee, grabbing my sketchbook and pencils off the table.

"It's not nice to lie, Avery. Where you going?" She's still laughing.

"I'm heading to Morvich for the day." Elle opens her mouth, about to cut me off but I know exactly what she's going to say. "Don't worry, I'll be back by dinner."

I tidy up my breakfast plate and mug, planning to drop them off at the kitchen on my way out.

"Do you want me to come with?" Elle asks unenthusiastically.

"No, you have to work, and I need some alone time."

She smiles at that, even though she offered to come with me. "Can you do me one, small favour?"

"Depends what it is."

"Can you share your location with me? In case of an emergency, or if you get lost in the woods. The highlands are big and you're not from around here."

Elle's small act of concern warms my heart, as a light

flickers inside my chest. Excluding my dad and Becca—who are always just a call or text away—no one has cared enough to check in on me like that. It's as though she's finding new ways to burrow herself deeper into my life and my affections.

"How can I stay mad at you when you go and say things like that?" I hand her my phone and she smiles brightly at me.

I'll admit, knowing there is someone here looking out for me is comforting. If I go missing or faint in the woods, Elle will be able to see where I dropped off. I take a deep breath, feeling better about venturing out on my own. I've been hesitant to explore further out the last couple of days, thinking Mike may still be around here.

Elle finally stands, handing me back my phone. "Make sure the phone is on at all times. And I expect regular status updates."

"Why do you need status updates if you can see where I am?"

"Don't be cheeky, and do as I say."

"Yes, Mom." I squeeze her cheek, giggling and she swats my hand away.

I forgot how nice it feels to be surrounded by good-hearted people. I never felt that way around John's friends, family, or colleagues. Always needing to look a certain way or pretend to be proper and put together. Always discussing highs, and denying any lows. His family only respects accomplishments. I feel like I can be myself around Elle and that's all she expects from me. She pulls me in for a hug, her scent of lavender and sunshine casing me.

"Please stay safe, Avery." She pulls back, grasping my shoulders, and giving me her best serious glare.

"I promise."

She nods, a brilliant smile back in place as she grabs the

plate and mug out of my hands. "I'm heading to the kitchen. I'll take these."

"I don't mind. I can do it."

"Go and stop arguing with me." A playful bite in her tone.

"You know I'm older than you, right? What happened to respecting your elders?"

Elle just laughs and walks away.

"Have fun!" she yells over her shoulder.

THE DRIVE to Morvich is picturesque like the rest of the highlands. Winding roads turn into small villages by the water, surrounded by abundant green mountains in the distance. It feels like I'm trapped in a painting. Today would be a great day to actually get lost in the woods, a perfect reason to miss the upcoming dinner. My stomach twists uncomfortably just thinking about seeing Lachlan again.

After that electrically charged night of wound care, I have no idea what to expect.

Morvich is everything I hoped it would be. A hiker's dream. Spectacular wilderness in the West highlands, including the famous Falls of Glomach and the Five Sisters of Kintail. I wanted to make the trek to the falls first, but a quick Google search last night proved it to be an impossible task for today since I have to be back in Corran by six. Maybe I'll come back later this week, stay overnight in a hotel.

I drove right to Mam Ratagan, a pass from the famous Shiel Bridge over the village of Glenelg, which provides the most breathtaking view of the Five Sisters of Kintail. Rolling hills, veiled in a peaceful mist, stretched out as far as the eye could see. The mountain peaks by Loch Duich nearly drove me off the road. I didn't think it would get more picturesque, but I was wrong...once again. The scent of wildflowers whipped around me, mixed with the cold, salty tang of the sea. The view seemed to stretch on forever, a validation to the rugged, untamed beauty of Scotland's highlands.

I parked the car and walked to a bench, overlooking the loch and the five mountains. Somehow, this landscape makes it feel like anything is possible. As if in another world, under a different sun, I could be anyone else. I could start over.

I'm not religious, but this feels spiritual.

It's as if I'm standing on the highest rooftop, staring out at the rest of the world. It feels like everything is within reach, as contentment and peace wrap itself tightly around my heart. Binding me to the views I imagine only something heavenly could create. Something that's not part of this world. The mountains sit side by side as they stretch beyond the lands, surrounded by blue waters and the clear skies, not a single cloud lingering in sight. The glens below are embroidered with shades of emerald and gold.

If I could describe the feeling of lightness, it would be this. Standing at the edge of this hill and looking out at the land-scape below, there is no room for darkness. Nature won't allow it. Your heart can't feel it, not here.

I sketch it over and over again. Trying to etch this feeling deep into my body, shoving it into every piece of me, every corner of my mind. But no matter how many sketches I complete, I can't even begin to scratch the surface of what this place feels like. What it means to be here right now. Like I was always meant to be here. Despite the hurt, suffering, abandon-ment, and loneliness I've endured throughout my life, I can't shake the sense that everything will be okay. There's something about the way the sun glows over the horizon, casting warmth and light across the landscape, that fills me with a sense of belonging. It's as though I've finally found my place, and all the struggles I've faced were simply leading me to this exact moment.

And I know that whatever my future holds, I'll finally be able to face it.

CHAPTER TWENTY-THREE

avery

Clutching the bottle of wine tightly in my arm, I take a nervous breath and knock on Ailith and Duncan's bright teal door. My breathing is erratic and far from calm, and it feels like acid is eating away at my stomach lining.

It's just one dinner. It will be over before you know it.

The door swings open and Elle's already grinning like she hasn't seen me in years. She grabs my hand and yanks me into the cozy foyer. I nearly face plant into her chest.

"You're right on time!" She pulls me in for a hug. I have never met someone who likes to hug as much as this girl.

"How was Morvich?" she says into my hair before releasing me, and I step back, handing her the wine bottle as I unzip my coat.

"I wasn't ready for that kind of greeting." I smile.

"Sorry, I'm just chuffed you're here."

I blink at her. "Chuffed?"

"Happy, excited, delighted. Take your pick."

I chuckle, hanging my coat. "Morvich was amazing. Like everything else here."

There is a tall mirror hanging on the wall by the hooks, causing me to catch a glimpse of myself. It's getting easier to look back at the girl staring at me. I feel good today, and I'm happy I made it back in time to take a shower and get ready without rushing. Back at the inn, I decided jeans and a simple button-down white top would be appropriate for a casual dinner. I even had time to put on a little bit of makeup and curl my hair properly. I may look like my mom, but I definitely inherited my dad's round curls. He used to have the most beautiful loose ringlets when he was younger.

I nervously glance down a long hallway that ends with a closed stained-glass door. There is a set of wooden stairs to my right, which I assume leads to a loft upstairs.

"You give this to Ailith," Elle says, pushing the bottle of wine back into my arm. She raises a brow, inspecting something on my shirt.

Her hand whips out, unhooking the first couple of buttons on my shirt.

"What are you doing?" I grab her hand, but she resists, accidentally pressing her palm into my breast.

"We're not at church. You're bonnie, stop covering up."

"You're eighteen, stop that!" I swat at her hand, but she dodges me.

"Aye, and you're twenty-six, stop acting like an eighty-year-old."

My mouth drops wide open as I gape at her.

"Who am I trying to impress here? Ailith?!" I mutter.

Elle smirks at me, taking a step back with an approval in her eyes. I look down and three buttons are popped open. The white lace of my bra is on full display, along with my cleavage.

Absolutely not.

"You look fit," Elle says, sounding pleased.

"You're awful. Duncan doesn't need to see my boobs while eating his dinner," I say, buttoning up my shirt.

I manage to close one before Elle's hand wraps in mine and she pulls me down the hallway.

"Don't you dare touch that shirt," she scorns through a fit of laughter. She has one of those contagious laughs, like Phoebe's from *Friends*. It makes me smile no matter the circumstances, and right now is an unfortunate time to smile because it only encourages Elle.

The sound of dishes clattering and running water grows louder as we approach the stained-glass door, which I assume leads to the kitchen. Elle halts, turning to face me, looking way too hyped up as if she's had twelve energy drinks.

"How much coffee have you had?" I say.

"Only four. So you had fun today? All on your own?" She says, grabbing her hair and pulling it up into a messy bun on top of her head.

"Yes. Have you been? What am I saying...I'm sure you have. You live next door."

Her lips quirk and she shakes her head. "I've never been to Morvich or Kintail. Well, we've driven through it many times, but I've never stopped to see it up close. Usually I'm napping in the car."

"You're shitting me!" I glare at her, stupefied and not sure I believe the words coming out of her mouth.

Her shoulders lift and she giggles.

"Okay, we're going. Me and you, we're going to hike the Five Sisters and see the Falls of Glomach...up close," I state, mentally planning out our entire mini-trip but Elle bursts out laughing, as if I just told a joke.

Is she drunk already?

Before I can ask her, the door swings open from the other side and Lachlan steps out, nearly bumping into Elle's back.

My heart leaps up my throat, causing a sudden surge of tingles rushing through my veins.

"Bloody hell," he retorts as he takes a step back and leans against the doorway. He's almost too tall, filling the entire space while keeping the door propped open.

Realizing I'm staring at his body, I force my eyes up, only to find his gaze fixed on me, a quizzical expression on his face. My cheeks heat up with a sudden flush.

Get it together.

I didn't think he'd actually show up, but here he is and looking as good as ever.

With a clean-shaven face, his high cheekbones and defined jawline are accentuated, giving him a striking, chiseled look. Soft waves of tousled hair fall across his forehead, adding a touch of casual charm to his appearance. But it's his eyes that catch my attention, bright and captivating as ever, drawing me in with their intense gaze. His lips are full and supple, perfectly complementing his rugged beauty. The swelling on his cheek has subsided, and the cut on his lip is scabbed over, leaving only faded marks that somehow make him even more desirable.

"I'd like to see the day Elle goes hiking," he says, smiling at me.

He is smiling at *me*. I need a moment.

Elle slaps his arm. "It's rude to listen to other people's conversations."

"You're standing outside the kitchen door blethering loudly. It's hard to ignore your obnoxious voice, Ellie bear," Lachlan crosses his arms.

"Sheep-shagging bastard," Elle gasps, shoving past him and disappearing into the kitchen.

Leaving me alone in the hall with him...

A deep chuckle rumbles through Lachlan's chest as he

steps back, taking up his position against the doorway. Blocking me from following Elle.

"Avery," he states.

The sound of my name rolling off his tongue feels like an aphrodisiac.

Stop it.

"Hi," I whisper, tucking my hair anxiously behind my ear, as I stand there awkwardly.

The corner of his lip twinges up for a split second before it disappears.

He's acting strange.

I take a steady step towards the kitchen...closer to Lachlan, hoping he'll move. But he doesn't. And I pray to God he can't hear the sound of my heart thundering in my chest.

"Your face looks good," I say, glancing at his cheek.

His lips split into a wide smile. "You think I look good?"

I blink at him. Is he...flirting with me? No...I must be hallucinating this conversation.

"No... I meant the cut on your face looks good. Looking better, than how it looked the last time I saw you. I mean, considering the beating you took and all. Sorry about that again...anyways, it's a lot better...I wasn't saying you look better...your face, you know. Not that you look bad...oh never mind." I stammered off.

If I were to put my hands up to my cheeks right now, the pure heat would burn my fingers. Someone hand me a shovel so I can dig my grave already.

Lachlan's grin widens, completely happy to witness the disaster that is me right now. The air grows thicker between us as I take another step forward. I extend the wine bottle, pressing the end of it into his chest.

I need to get to the other side of that door.

The wine bottle should be the perfect buffer as I step into him, but he still doesn't move.

Lachlan is an immovable rock, and I'm standing dangerously close to him, with his eyes casting down on me, causing my knees to grow weak. I feel him everywhere, my skin tingling with anticipation.

Elle's eyes pop up from the corner as she grabs Lachlan's shoulder, pulling him away from the doorway.

"Give her some space."

Lachlan's eyes burn into me as he steps aside, making room for me to walk by him into the bright kitchen.

My thoughts are hazy after that interaction. He's acting weird, completely unlike the Lachlan I know. And that look in his eyes is quite the contrast to his typical hatred-filled gaze.

CHAPTER TWENTY-FOUR

avery

Ailith doesn't hear me come in, busy stirring something, as she stands above an ornate forest green stove. I place my hand on her small shoulder, and she glances up, a radiant smile breaks loose on her face. The wooden spoon she's holding thuds against the pot, and Ailith turns, pulling me in for a tight embrace.

"I'm so glad yer here, sweetheart. Thank ye for coming."

My chest warms and I swallow the lump in my throat. And to think I was considering skipping out on tonight when Ailith is so incredibly happy to see me. Me, out of all the people. The random tourist staying at her inn.

"Thank you for having me." I croak.

I hand her the wine I brought and she takes it eagerly. I don't know why her kind gestures always make me so emotional. Probably because of the bus-load of mommy issues I carry around.

Ailith uncorks the wine and grabs five tall-stemmed glasses from the counter. She walks to another swinging door on the opposite side of the kitchen, pressing her back into it.

"Everyone out of the kitchen, unless you plan on finishing dinner for me."

Lachlan and Elle pause their conversation, heading towards Ailith. She holds out the wine bottle and glasses as Lachlan approaches, pressing them into his hands before he walks out of the kitchen. Elle grabs my hand, leading us out and into the open-concept dining room. The house is clean and fresh, with modern finishes.

There is a large rectangular space that incorporates the open-concept dining room and living room. Grey hardwood floors with white and brown accented furniture are placed throughout the space. This is not at all what I expected from Ailith and Duncan. I pictured them living in an old historic home with touches of rustic furniture, similar to the inn's aesthetics. White and brown shelves line three walls in the living room, overflowing with all kinds of books. I'd love to poke through their collection at some point tonight.

Duncan is lounging lazily on a brown leather sofa with a beer in his hand, watching soccer on the TV mounted above the fireplace. I say hi, waving awkwardly at him and he gives me a nod, lifting his beer up at me in acknowledgment. I have come to learn that Duncan is a man of very few words.

On the opposite side of the room, sits a large dining room table with a brown buffet pressed up against the back wall. The buffet is an antique piece, chipped wood and frosted glass cover its exterior, like it's been in the family for generations. Ornate pottery pieces and trinkets sit neatly on the dustless shelves.

Lachlan and Elle take their seats at the table, side by side, joking around like siblings. The room echos with their laughter, bringing a smile to my face as I take in their easy interaction. Just as a random pang of jealousy hits my side. I miss the effort-lessness of being completely yourself with someone, knowing they will accept and love you no matter what. The only person

I am this close to is Becca, and I haven't seen her in so long. I miss my best friend as I stand here, watching them.

I start to make my way over to the table when Ailith storms into the room. Carrying a large serving dish with a golden roasted chicken and vegetables surrounding it. I step out of the way, making space for her as she places the heavy dish on the table. Ailith then rearranges the table, placing me right across from Lachlan.

Fan-fucking-tastic.

I offer to help, needing to be anywhere but at the table. But Ailith refuses, running back to the kitchen. I contemplate following her anyway.

"Avery, sit down. You're making me uncomfortable." Elle motions to my new seat, while sipping on her glass of white wine.

I take an exasperated breath, pulling out my chair and taking a seat. Making sure to avert my eyes from the man sitting directly in front of me. Keeping my hands under the table, I start picking at my cuticles.

Ailith walks back in with two more dishes of food, one containing mashed potatoes and the other a tower of fluffy Yorkshire puddings.

"Duncan. Telly. Off." Ailith hollers and Duncan grunts as he stands, turning off the TV. He follows Ailith back into the kitchen.

How much did Ailith cook?

They walk in a minute later, carrying more mounds of food. There is enough here to feed a small village. Everything looks fantastic as Ailith and Duncan take their seats on the opposite ends of the table. Duncan opens a new bottle of Anam Cara whisky, pouring a small amount in five crystal glasses, as Ailith hands around the bottle of wine. I guess everyone is double fisting drinks tonight.

The whisky glasses are circulated around the table before Duncan raises his glass in the air. Everyone follows suit, including me.

"Sláinte!" Our voices blend together, loud and boisterous as we raise the whisky to our lips.

Notes of smoke and cinnamon crackle on my tongue, the burn hitting my nostrils as the liquid slides down my throat. A different flavour palette than the one I've been drinking at the bars. It's delicious, smoky with subtle hints of citrus. Something about it reminds me of the highlands. I savour the sip and take another before setting my glass down.

Ailith starts circulating the food around the table.

"Avery, Elle mentioned ye visited Morvich today. It's where Duncan proposed, ye know? We have fond memories from there," Ailith tells me, while serving chopped-up carrots on her plate.

"I'm not surprised Duncan would choose that spot. It's gorgeous. I didn't have enough time to explore the whole area, but I'm planning on going back to hit up a few hiking trails. Elle is coming with me," I say, winking at Elle who gives me a coy smile and drops her eyes to her plate.

Ailith glances at Duncan before they erupt into a wild laughter.

"If ye can get Elle to go hikin' with ye, I'll let ye drink at the pub free o' charge for the rest o' yer stay." That's the most words I've ever heard Duncan say at once. His accent is thick and hard to understand in some parts.

"Seriously? You hate the outdoors that much?" I grab the carrots from Ailith, shovelling a spoonful onto my own plate.

"She cannot stand anything to do with the outdoors. But Lachy is off his head about hillwalking. Ye might wanna take him with ye," Duncan says, nudging his head toward Lachlan.

Lachlan's eyes already on mine, sparking with pure mischief as he studies me, a smirk pulling at his lips.

Oh sweet Jesus. That is a lethal look.

"Aye, I love to hike," he states, raising his fork to his mouth.

Nope.

No.

Absolutely not.

"That's okay. I'll go alone," I murmur, looking away and smiling at Ailith who is too busy cutting into her chicken to pay attention to me.

"Why don't ye want to go with Lachlan?" Duncan eyes me curiously, his white bushy brows furrowing together. "I'd far rather take him on a day-long hillwalk than Elle. She'll just drag ye back, moaning the hale time. That is, if ye can talk her into comin'."

"It's true. I'm great company. I also bring snacks," Lachlan's voice is laced with humour. "And whisky, I know how much you like a wee bit of whisky while touring," he whispers that last part, winking at me.

A fray of tingles follows his wink, landing right in between my thighs. Where is the old Lachlan and who the hell is this guy? I remind my raging body that this is a performance and this man does not like me.

"Weren't ye planning on going up there for a couple of days to hike, Lachy? Ye mentioned wanting to stay in that cabin in the woods ye love so much," Ailith pipes up.

Oh, for God's sake. My cheeks heat and I probably match the grilled tomatoes on everyone's plate right now.

"Aye," Lachlan nods. "There are some great trails, but they're long. It's best to stay overnight. Can pack more into the day staying close by."

Why is he doing this? He knows I would never go anywhere with him.

"Why don't ye take Avery with ye?" Ailith says, moving her fork in between the two of us.

Ailith, please, for the love of God, stop talking. I beseech you.

"Only if she wants to come with. What do you think, lass, care for an adventure?" Lachlan utters with a devilish smile on his face.

Think. Think. Think.

Just say no.

"Sounds great." I fake a smile and cut into my chicken, a bit too aggressively.

I kick Lachlan's leg under the table, causing him to choke into his glass of wine.

"It's settled then," Duncan states.

"Am I off the hook?" Elle laughs and I throw daggers at her with my eyes. She shrugs, pretending like I didn't need her to step up. She could have saved me by agreeing to come.

I continue scowling at Elle, and she beams back at me, clearly oblivious to the gravity of the what just happened. I sigh, popping a roasted potato in my mouth. Notes of garlic and rosemary cradle my tastebuds, and I can't help the groan that slips from my lips.

"This is all so delicious, Ailith, thank you."

Duncan and Elle both nod in agreement. I turn my head and catch Lachlan staring intently at my mouth. Self-consciously, I run my finger along my lip, wondering if there's food on my face. I notice Lachlan's gaze lingering until he finally snaps out of whatever thought was holding him hostage. He averts his eyes and starts shovelling food into his mouth, avoiding any further eye contact with me.

"I reckon you ditch the outdoors and come dancing with me. We can visit one of the new clubs a few towns down," Elle speaks up and it takes me a second to realize she's talking to me.

"I don't dance. And I certainly don't go clubbing."

"Why? Are you celibate, Avery?"

This time, it's Duncan who chokes on his whisky. He punches his chest a few times, trying to catch his breath.

I'm going to kill her.

I place my fork down and dab my mouth with the cloth napkin. "I'm too old to go clubbing with an eighteen-year-old."

I wish a black hole would appear in the floor and swallow me up. If I thought I was blushing before, I can't imagine what my face looks like now.

"Don't be daft. You're a wee lassie, I'd love to be twenty-six again," Ailith says.

I'd rather spend my energy getting lost in the woods than drinking my face off into oblivion. I tried that once upon a time and it didn't go so well. Alcohol is a downer and if you're already depressed, it's a bad combination.

"It's just not my scene," I admit.

Everyone is silent for a couple of minutes. I pick up my whisky and take a large swig, thanking the universe for putting an end to that awkward conversation.

"What is your scene?" Lachlan asks.

Spoke too soon.

It's clear to me that Lachlan's attitude has changed. He vanished for awhile after the night of the fight, returning with less hatred towards me? Something's not quite right, and I can't put my finger on what he's after or what kind of game he's playing. I've dealt with angry Lachlan before, but I don't know how to handle the charming version of him. It's disorienting, and I find myself constantly on edge, wondering what he's going to say next.

I stare back at him, unable to think of a response under his weighted gaze.

<h1 style="text-align:center">CHAPTER TWENTY-FIVE</h1>

<h1 style="text-align:center">avery</h1>

Thankfully Duncan puts me out of my misery.

"The whisky is real great, laddie. I'm thinkin' this might be the best flavour yet." Duncan inspects the whisky through the glass, like he dropped a ring inside and he's trying to find it. "How are the sales coming along?"

Lachlan shifts in his seat, a nervous twinge in his face. "Good, going well."

"Brilliant." Duncan nods, sipping on more whisky.

"You work for the company?" I blurt out.

Lachlan glances at Ailith quickly, before his eyes cut to mine.

"I own it."

Wait, he owns the whisky company?

"Anam Cara? You own Anam Cara?"

"Aye, it's wonderful ain't it?" Ailith says proudly.

The same whisky I've been obsessed with and practically threw at him at Glencoe. I remember him telling me about the meaning of Anam Cara in the field that day, as I was hurriedly packing up. I figured he was just trying to fill the awkward silence but now…

"Oh, wow. Small world," I breathe out, staring off.

"What?" Elle asks, twisted curiosity in her eyes as she glances between Lachlan and I.

"Avery had a bottle of it at Glencoe when we first met." I kick him under the table again, his eyes fly to mine.

I don't think he realizes that he just outed himself. But Elle certainly doesn't miss the comment.

"I thought you met the other night at the pub. I introduced you two and you said it was nice to meet her," Elle turns her body towards Lachlan, swinging her arm behind her chair.

I shove a piece of chicken quickly into my mouth, hoping to avoid this conversation altogether.

"No, we met before. If you can even call it that."

"Avery, why didn't you say anything?" Elle forces me to look up.

I open my mouth to answer her, but Lachlan interject.

"Because there was nothing to tell. We didn't know one another. I didn't even know her name until I got to the pub. She ran off like a scared cat and somehow ended up in Corran. I thought maybe she was—" Lachlan's voice drops off, his words falling flat against the table.

I ran away from him because I felt something.

And that terrified me.

"Maybe I was what?"

He blinks several times. "It doesn't matter."

A fork clatters on a plate.

Ailith and Duncan exchange a look, shifting in their seats. Elle suddenly loses interest in the conversation. A heavy silence drapes overtop of the table, and it suddenly feels like I walked in on a very private family conversation.

Elle coughs, breaking the silence. "I have some news. I've

decided to start school early. I'll be going to Glasgow in January."

"Oh, that's wonderful, Elle!" Ailith stands from her chair and walks over to give Elle a hug.

"Is it still all right if I stay at your place in Glasgow, Lachlan? Surely, you'll be back home by then?" Elle smiles, nudging a very silent Lachlan.

So he lives in Glasgow. It's remarkable how little I know about this man.

"I'm not sure that's a good idea. We can talk about it later," he says to his plate.

Elle glances at Ailith and gives her a sad, knowing smile.

Could this have something to do with what Ailith said the other day in the kitchen? About Lachlan dealing with something right now? It must be, otherwise, why would he be living here if his main residence is in Glasgow.

I turn to Elle. "Are you going to focus on electives since you're starting in the middle of the school year?"

The tension slips from Elle's eyes as she smiles, picking up a bread roll from the basket in front of her. "Aye, that's the plan. And in September I'll start with the freshmen. My councillor said I'll be done sooner than my graduating class, which will be brilliant. I can even take summer classes to speed things up, if I wanted to."

Feeling someone's gaze on me, I quickly glimpse in Lachlan's direction. My pulse picks up as I look away, trying to distract myself by focusing on Elle, who's receiving compliments from Ailith. I avoid Lachlan's hypnotic eyes—the same ones that pulled me under in a dream a few nights ago. I woke up drenched in sweat and longing for something I haven't thought about in a very long time.

One hour turns into two as we continue talking and drinking well after dinner. The conversation shifts to the inn and upcoming shipments, schedules, new hires...so I finally muster up the courage to excuse myself and walk over to the living room. I've been wanting to look through their book collection all night.

The bookshelves are bursting with all types of literature. Classics, contemporary, history, mystery, self-help, but it's the entire shelf dedicated to romance that catches my eye—my guilty pleasure. I start sorting through, picking up a book here and there, reading the back, flipping through the pages. I find a book tucked in the back, opening to the middle, I read a few sentences and quickly realize it's pure erotica.

Ailith likes smut?!

"What are you reading?" Lachlan's hoarse voice startles me. The book in my hand drops, landing by my feet. Lachlan bends down, glancing up at me as he picks it up off the floor.

"You like romance?"

Nothing to be ashamed of, this book belongs to his aunt. Why should I be embarrassed about finding it, or reading it?

"I do."

He flips through the book, seeming to find an exciting excerpt because he slowly looks over his shoulder, making sure his family isn't near by.

"So does your aunt, apparently." I say, smiling to myself.

His eyes remain on the page, and a hint of pink kisses his cheeks. The man is blushing.

I bite my lip, trying not to think about how hot he looks standing next to me, reading. What is it about hot men and books?

"Do you believe in all this stuff? The happily ever afters?"

"No, I don't." I say bluntly, picking a new book off the shelf.

"But you read romance?" he asks, raising a brow at me.

I shrug. "It's a form of escapism. Just because I don't believe in love, doesn't mean I can't enjoy reading about it."

His brows shoot up. That seems to pique his interest.

"You don't believe in love?" His voice tips oddly.

"Nope." I pop the P, opening another book.

"Some people do end up finding their person and growing old with them." His arm brushes my shoulder as he shifts, putting the book back and grabbing a new one.

"Are you speaking based on experience?" I ask, holding my breath.

He peers down at me. "Not personally, no. But I've seen it."

He tries to grab the book I'm reading out of my hands. But I don't let go, causing my body to lean into his. He's searching my eyes, as if they hold all the answers to his questions. It's not the first time he's looked at me like this.

"How can you be certain love isn't real?" His breath falls on my cheek, sending my heart into overdrive.

I let go of the book and take a step away from him. "Believing in love is like believing unicorns exist. It's fictional. A complete trap and I have no interest in wasting my time finding it."

I reach out for a new book at the same time as he does. Our fingers collide, as a familiar pulse rushes through my body. I lose myself in the feeling of it, craving the buzz of it more and more each day.

"I'm going to go help Ailith and Elle in the kitchen."

I steady my shaky knees as soon as I walk through the kitchen door.

Duncan and Ailith are at the sink, one is washing, the other is drying. And Elle is busy putting away the leftovers into glass containers. They all glance up at me as I make my way inside the kitchen.

"Lass, we were just talking about ye," Ailith declares.

"Oh?" I walk over to Elle and start helping.

"I took a look at the website today and it's brilliant. Thank ye so much. I meant to say that at dinner, but it slipped my mind. The booking page is a thing of dreams." Ailith says.

"Aye, thanks lassie," Duncan echos her sentiments, without glancing back at me.

"I'm happy I could help."

"When ye get a chance, love, can ye show me how it all works? Ye may have to show me a few times because me memory is not as good as it used to be when I was a wee lass," Ailith confesses.

"Of course, no problem."

"It's lucky you decided to stop in Corran, at our inn. Not just for Ailith and Duncan here, but for me too." Elle leans into me, wrapping her arm around my shoulders. A bright smile on her pink lips.

"Oh you guys, you're going to make me cry. It's me who's lucky to have met you all," I choke out and Elle tightens her hold on me.

This little family has made me feel so welcome in the short time I've been here. I didn't feel a fraction of that living with John for the last three years in Toronto. Three years I spent locking myself up in an apartment waiting for a man who never wanted to be home. Never fitting in with his family or friends. I thought I was the problem, that maybe I didn't need the human interaction. That I was better off without it. But after coming here, I realize I was just incredibly lonely.

Looking down at my watch, I notice it's half past ten. The whisky has nuzzled itself deep into my veins, and I desperately need to walk it off before heading to bed. That and some aspirin.

"I think I'm going to head out. I'm beat after today."

"Beat? What do ye mean, lassie?" Duncan asks, concern flashing over his features.

An unfamiliar slang to Scotsmen. I laugh. "It means I'm tired."

Ailith nods while turning off the water and drying her hands on a towel. She walks over to me, placing her hand gently on my back.

"I'll walk ye out, love."

CHAPTER TWENTY-SIX
lachlan

I never thought I'd say this, but I think I overdid it on the whisky at supper.

The alcohol buzzes around in my head as I stand outside the kitchen, listening to Avery talk to my family. They're all conversing with such ease, as if she's been here for years. It's effortless, and it has been that way for them since the first day she arrived. Ailith welcomed her with open arms, and Elle fell in love with her instantly.

Tonight, seeing her here, in the house I grew up in...it did something to me.

It would be so much easier to resist this if I actually hated her.

As if I could hate her.

Every fiber in my being is screaming at me to fight this attraction. But I'm not sure I want to. There is a magnetic force pulling me closer to her, and the more I ignore it, the stronger it gets. The harder it becomes to endure.

Stepping into the kitchen, I see Ailith and Avery disappear through the opposite door, leading towards the front foyer. I should stay here, lend a hand, talk to Elle, have a dram with my uncle. Should let Avery get back to the inn on her own.

I should stay away from her.

But I don't do any of that.

I smack Duncan on the back and thank him for dinner as I ruffle Elle's hair and say goodbye. She sneers at me, trying to push me away.

Silently, I make my way down the hallway, my hand grazing the wall for support. Avery stands by the door, zipping up her coat and smiles at Ailith. Her hand hooks underneath her hair, as soft brown curls cascade around her face and back, framing her features like a halo. I want to run my fingers through her tresses, feel their silky texture against my skin. My hand curls into a fist at the thought, my knuckles turning white with the intensity of my unwanted desire.

Avery's eyes meet mine for a moment, but her expression shifts and she averts her gaze. I take a step closer, drawn in by the sudden tension in her body. Her lips part as she inhales a deep breath, and I can see the battle unfold inside her. I want to reach out and touch her, to offer her comfort, to finally give in, but I hold back. Focusing on the way her chest rises and falls with each breath.

I love knowing that I have the same effect on her.

I place my hands on my aunt's slender shoulders and bend down to kiss her cheek.

"Thanks for dinner."

"Are ye heading out, too, Lachy?" Ailith twists her head, looking up at me.

I reach over and grab my jacket hanging from the wall hook.

"Aye, I'm knackered. Mind if I walk with you back to the inn, Avery?"

"I'm not going back to the inn." She clears her throat.

"Where are ye going? It's late, lassie," Ailith says.

"I know, I'm just going to take a quick stroll over to the lighthouse."

"I don't think that's..." Ailith begins to say.

"I'll walk with her." I blurt out without thinking.

So much for staying away from her.

Avery looks from Ailith to me, hesitancy swirling in those amber eyes.

"That's really not necessary..." Avery starts.

"It wasn't a suggestion." I arch my brow at her, a commanding cadence in my words.

Her forehead wrinkles as she tires to get a read on me. She's been doing it all night and I honestly can't blame her. It's the first time I've allowed myself to just be and not push her away. To enjoy the night with Avery and my family, to simply float in the water and stop swimming against the current.

And it felt so fucking good to just be for one night.

Relief fills Ailith's eyes, and I know what she's thinking because I was thinking the same thing. Mike could still be lingering around here, and it's not safe for Avery to be walking alone this late at night. This is a small village and the streets fall dead after sundown. Besides, with the whisky still thick in my system, the reasons to keep my distance from Avery seem less paramount. I want to get to know her, even if it's just for tonight. Push her a little, watch her squirm under my gaze until her lips turn a beautiful shade of red from the abuse by her own teeth.

The truth is, when I'm around her I feel normal. Like I can be myself for once.

The door swings open and Avery disappears out into the night. I bend down to give my aunt a quick peck on the cheek but she pulls me in for a hug.

"Be nice to her. She's hurtin' ye know," she says quietly in my ear but I can hear the warning in her voice.

Ailith stands tall at five-foot-five on a good day, but being short has never deterred her. Her head is always held high, and she is never afraid to give me her wrath, especially when she knows I deserve it.

"I know. I'll make sure she's safe."

Ailith jerks me in for one more hug before pushing me out the door.

Avery is already striding down the street, trying to get away from me. I take off in a run, catching up to her in no time as a gust of wind runs through her hair, permeating the air with sweet notes of coconut and vanilla. Reminding me of the night she tended to my wounds; I was so captivated by her, I couldn't feel the pain.

The wind is harsh tonight, dancing off the loch and singing up the mountains. The city wind is never this sharp or loud. Too many buildings silencing out sounds of nature. I forgot how much I missed the countryside until I got here. When everything started to crumble around me, I knew exactly where I needed to go.

I fill my lungs with the chill air, pulling my cap out and fixing it over my head. Avery turns her face upward, a tiny smile cracks on the corner of her lips.

"What?" I say.

"Nothing." She shakes her head.

"Out with it."

"What are you doing?" Avery asks.

"Right now? Going on a walk." I utter just as a group of young lads stumble out of the pub. A few people linger outside, smoking as they look our way.

"Why?"

"Walking has many health benefits. I can name a few if you like?" I feign ignorance, smiling down at her.

She sighs in exasperation. "You don't like me. Why are you coming on a walk with me?"

"I'll make you a deal. You tell me why you were shaking your head at me just now, and I'll tell you why I'm going on a walk with you."

Avery hesitates. "I don't get why you hide your hair under that hat all the time. A lot of people would kill for hair like that."

She's very perceptive, I'll give her that. But the comment about my hat isn't what spreads the shite-eating grin on my face.

"Second compliment of the night, lass. Careful or I might think you're starting to like me." I lean in, gleaming proudly.

Her eyes pop out, cheeks turning bright crimson as she chews on her bottom lip.

There it is.

"You're an asshole," she whispers, and the sound of my laugh echoes down the street, skating on the loch.

"We need to do something about that crude tongue of yours."

I can think of a few things I'd like to do with that mouth.

No. You can't go there.

She glances up at me. "We?"

My arm brushes her shoulder as I stop in front of her, lowering my mouth to her ear, "Aye, we."

I feel her body shudder as I wrap my hand around hers and run across the street.

The act is completely self serving. There isn't a single car on the road at this time of night. I just wanted an excuse to hold her hand, just so I could feel that rush of ecstasy whenever we touch.

As soon as we're on the sidewalk, Avery pulls her hand away.

I listen to the sound of our footsteps on the pavement as I glance across the water, like small crystals glistening under the moonlight. I breathe it in deeply, feeling invigorated and alive for the first time in ages.

"It's not too late to turn around and go back," she whispers.

"Do you want me to go back?"

"No. I meant for you. You can go back if you want. I'll be fine." Amber eyes under the moonlight might be my new favourite view. She's like a fucking anchor, pulling me under.

"I don't want to go back." I smirk, inching closer to her again; but she takes a step back, correcting my movement.

"I don't need a bodyguard. If that's why you're coming along, you can just go. I'm sure you have better things to do."

"I was planning on taking a wee stroll. Clear my head and my stomach, especially after all that food and whisky." I tuck my hands in my jacket.

Thankfully, Avery stops protesting.

We walk in peaceful silence, our feet moving in sync. The world around us is still, save for the gentle rustle of leaves and the soft murmuring of lapping water. I feel a sense of contentment settle over me. There is no need to fill the void with words, not with Avery. The quietness between us is comfortable and the night is calm but feels far from empty, at least for me. I'm grateful for the simple pleasure of walking alongside her to the lighthouse.

"Tell me what's in your head." Avery's soft voice shatters the silence. Her bold words take me by surprise.

"Only if I get to ask you the same thing."

She blinks up at me. "Okay, but no bullshit. Only the truth."

"Dìreach fìrinn." I say, nodding.

Shadows fall on her face, her big brown eyes stare up at me in confusion.

"It means only truth in Gaelic." My heart aches with longing as I gaze at her, imagining all the ways I could make her happy, if only I were worthy. I picture myself by her side, watching her face light up with colour when she laughs, her soft touch, the feeling of her warm embrace.

Oh, the things I would do for her.

It hurts to know that no matter how much I want to be with her, to experience everything with her, it can never happen. Not in this lifetime. Not with my past and present standing in the way.

Avery heaves a deep breath into her lungs, mustering the courage to ask me what's on her mind. "Why do you hate me?"

"I don't hate you. Sometimes I wish I did," I say truthfully.

"Why?"

"Because it would be easier," I face the moon. "I don't hate you, Avery. I don't think I ever did."

"Oh, then why did you pretend—"

"My turn." I say, not giving her the chance to ask me a follow-up question.

Her shoulders fall but she nods, waiting for my question.

"Why did you run that day?"

"I was scared."

"You were scared of me?" I stop walking.

She pauses a few feet ahead, turning around as the edges of her mouth tug up.

"That's another question. It's my turn again."

Goddammit.

The wind sweeps across the pathway, a strand of curly hair dances in front of Avery's face. Twirling delicately against the ridge of her nose, framing her features in a way that makes my heart skip a beat. She brushes the hair away with a gentle hand, revealing the soft curves of her face. I can't help but stare, mesmerized by the sight of her under the moonlight.

The way she draws me in is completely foreign. Uncharted territory in waters I haven't navigated before.

Despite the heat stirring through my body, I know that I need to stay away from her. I can't let myself get too close, can't risk losing my head and falling for her. But as I watch her, my resolve begins to weaken. A constant fight between what I should do and what I want.

She is like a lit candle in my life, a burst of sudden colour in a world turned black. Every time I see her, my heart twists harder, reminding me that I am still capable of feeling something other than anger and numbness.

But I know I can't have her, not in the way I want to.

"Why were you so angry to see me at the pub?"

I close the distance between us.

"I thought you were someone from work, and everything with my job is complicated right now. I let my anger control my emotions that day and I'm sorry for that." I answer her as truthfully as I can.

"Okay," she utters, turning and resuming her walk towards the lighthouse.

"How old are you?" I ask, needing a light question to fill the heaviness for this round.

"Twenty-six. And you?"

"Older than you." I smirk.

"That's not an answer."

She starts abusing her lip again and I just want to push her up against the wall and take that darn lip in between my teeth. Tugging and exploring that sweet mouth of hers.

Enough.

"I'm waiting," she says.

I almost don't want to tell her. "Thirty-five."

The sweet sound of her laugh fills the air, tightening the rope around my chest. Fuck, what is happening to me? I've turned into a bloody teenager.

"You're old," she coos with a cunning smile on her face.

"Since when is thirty-five old?" I deadpan.

"It's okay, grandpa. You look good for your age." She laughs again and I bask in her glow and the sound of her happiness. I want to fill every room with the sweet melody of her laugh.

Her hair cascades in waves around her face as she walks backwards, facing me. The strands catch in the cold breeze, dancing wildly. I reach out to grab her, intending to show her that I'm not just any ordinary grandpa, but before I can, she spins around and bolts towards the beach.

The lighthouse stands tall in the distance, its bright beam casting out over the dark water like a protective shield. The air is filled with the scent of salt and sea, and I can feel the sand squishing beneath my boots as I chase after her.

Avery stops at the edge of the beach, entranced as she watches the push and pull of light against the dark night. The white beam cuts across darkness, erasing the shadows as it glides on the water. The lighthouse is stunning at all hours of the day, but there is something mystical about it at night.

I've stood in this exact same spot, watching the loch... wishing I would find my own beacon. I used to come here every night in the months before and after Mom died. Sneaking out when everyone was asleep just so I could get away from it all.

"It's beautiful," Avery whispers to the loch.

She gazes out, following the light, but I'm only looking at her. Watching the wonderment in her eyes, and the contours of her face as she takes it all in for the first time.

Aye, she is beautiful.

"Say what's in your head," I plead.

Avery doesn't say a single word for a long time and when she speaks, her voice is haunting.

"There is something about water that has always fascinated me." She looks straight ahead, following the bright light as if she's talking to it. "When everything fell apart, being near water was the only thing that brought me peace. There is something about it. The unknown is mesmerizing and terrifying all at the same time. But I think that's what makes it so beautiful."

There are secrets hidden in her words, but somehow I understand them perfectly. This exact place used to be my only solace once upon a time.

"I know what you mean. I used to come here every night after my mother passed. No one knew and it was so quiet, I would sit for hours, watching the light dance with the water. Sometimes it was the only thing that brought me comfort. It made me feel closer to her."

I've never shared that with anyone until now.

I glance over to see Avery watching me, with only understanding in her glossy eyes.

"I'm sorry," she whispers.

A single tear skates down her cheek. Without thinking I reach out, wiping it away with my thumb. My skin buzzes with a thousand pins of lightning as I trace my thumb over to her lips, waiting for her to step away, or to turn and run again. But she remains perfectly still, locked into my eyes.

My body comes to life, with a single look. A single touch. The feel of her lip against my thumb. Her pupils dilate, the darkness pushing away the amber.

"Lachlan," she trembles.

I want to find whatever it is that haunts her and rip it out of her soul. I want to show her everything she thinks she doesn't need or deserve. Everything she's convinced herself she doesn't want. I want to take over every dark corner of her mind and set it on fire, until there is only light.

I don't want to lose this moment. "Can we just sit for a bit?"

She nods, dropping to the ground, hugging her knees tightly. I sit beside her, shoulder to shoulder on the cold sand. Neither one of us talks, both listening to the soft waves ruffling in the loch. The wind grows colder as it cuts against my skin and I pull my hood up, wrapping my arms around my knees. But from the corner of my eye, I see Avery's body shivering.

"You're freezing. Let's head back."

"No. I don't want to go yet."

I stand up, unzipping my jacket. The flimsy coat she has on doesn't appear to be doing much.

"What are you doing? I don't want your coat, I'm fine," she protests.

"Can I keep you warm then?" I step behind her, towering over her small body, waiting for permission before I get close to her.

She nods quickly. I sit down behind her, carefully placing my hands on her waist and bringing her back to my chest.

"Is this okay?" I ask.

Her body tenses up. "Yes," she whispers.

"I'll keep my hands to myself but if you get uncomfortable let me know and I'll move." She nods, taking in a deep breath and relaxing against me. I wrap each side of my jacket around her, feeling her trembles begin to slow down. With guarded movements, she leans her head against my shoulder.

"You're so warm." She sighs.

I tilt my face down, taking note of the slow rise and fall of her chest and the way her body fits against mine, as if she were made for me.

Avery closes her eyes, her breaths tapering down as she begins to fall asleep. I hold her close, feeling the weight of the world lift off my shoulders. I feel more alive right now than I've ever felt before. There is nowhere else I'd rather be.

Being with her silences my shadows, those dark thoughts and doubts that have haunted me for so long just fade away.

My phone buzzes in my pocket, pulling me out of my peaceful thoughts.

I ignore it until the fourth buzz comes through.

The words on the screen yank me back to reality. Reminding me of who I am, and the life I can't have. I can't be the guy who sits carelessly on a sandy shore at night with a beautiful woman.

I can't be the man she needs, no matter how much I want to be.

CHAPTER TWENTY-SEVEN

avery

I lie in bed, staring up at the ceiling and willing my body to go to sleep.

But I can't stop thinking about everything that happened tonight. The dinner, the walk, the conversations, how safe Lachlan made me feel without even trying, safe enough that I fell asleep in his arms on the beach. The quiet walk back to the inn with his jacket draped around me. He wouldn't let me take it off, wouldn't hear of it. I can still smell him, still feel his arms around my body, the warmth radiating off his skin.

As I stood outside my room, still dazed from the night, I could sense a shift in the air between us. Something had changed, but I didn't know what to do with it. So I shrugged off his jacket, handed it back to him with a small smile, and thanked him for his friendship.

He nodded and my heart felt heavy with a mix of emotions as I turned and walked inside my room.

It's better this way. For us to be friends and keep things professional as I spend my remaining days in Corran. I'm going to be gone soon, and I can't deny the fact that I'm attracted to him. But I have enough self-control to ensure nothing more happens between us.

Or so I thought.

It's currently two in the morning and I can't fall asleep. I can't stop thinking about what it would be like to be close to him, but without all the layers of clothes in between us. What his hands would feel like roaming my body, his fingers pressing tightly into me. My insides coil as heat floods between my legs.

I've never craved anyone like this.

John and I were intimate, of course, but it always felt like a chore. Something I felt I was obligated to do in order to be closer to him, to form a connection with him. It was never forced, but it wasn't something I enjoyed either. It was like any other task. Penciled in below cleaning out the fridge before grocery day.

A part of me believed it was just something else that was stolen from me. Another thing that made me broken and incapable of deep emotions. I didn't think I would ever desire someone this way, because of the overpowering shame and guilt. But right now, as I lie here, all I want to do is charge across the hall and let him have his way with me.

I groan, tossing for the thousandth time and burying my face in the cold pillow.

If I close my eyes and count sheep, I'll fall asleep. Maybe I can map out where I want to go next...plan out my week...say the things I'm grateful for...lick in between every crevice of Lachlan's body.

Are you kidding me right now?

Okay, let's think of not-so-sexy things. Like bugs, spiders, dirty toilets, cute animals, the calming ocean...finally, we're getting somewhere.

I close my eyes, trying to think of more things but I see his piercing ocean eyes, and his lips trailing down my neck as I run my fingers through his hair, pulling on the longer strands as he explores every inch of my body. My nipples harden painfully against my cotton shirt, pressing into the mattress. Every part of my body is sensitive, craving to be touched.

Fuck this.

I throw the comforter away and charge for the bathroom to take a very cold shower.

THREE DAYS HAVE GONE by and no sign of Lachlan.

I'm having a serious case of deja-vu. Does time loop back in this place?

Besides hanging out with Elle, working, and getting in hikes around Corran, I haven't done much else. Although, Elle and I did venture out to Aberdeenshire yesterday to do some castle hopping. It was her day off and she finally agreed to leave Corran with me, if I promised there would be no hiking involved.

The Aberdeenshire region boasts around three-hundred castles, ruins, and impressive homes. I felt like I was dropped inside a fantasy novel.

It was an exhausting day trip, given most of it was spent driving. But the views and the conversation were worth the early morning start. For me, anyway...I think Elle was blown away by the fact that I was willing to drive three-and-a-half hours to look at castles. But I explained to her that one time I spent over four hours in the car driving from downtown

Toronto to Niagara Falls for a job interview. And I didn't even get the job.

When you're stuck in a car with someone for an extended amount of time, especially someone as chatty as Elle, you're forced to open up and expose yourself.

"Did you come here to get away from your ex?" Elle says, her feet resting on the dashboard.

"Not to get away from him, no. He had already basically kicked me out. Not that I would have stayed after he told me about his affair. I had no where to go and I didn't want to go back to Vancouver."

She turns to me, a frown etched between her eyebrows. "Why?"

Shit, I didn't mean to let that last part slip. I didn't want to go back to Vancouver, because being there reminds me of a time when I was damaged beyond repair.

It reminds me of the aftermath from that night. My mind did a stellar job at shielding me from most of the 'after'. But there are images that remain scattered around my head, popping up out of no where from time to time. I remember the nurse's cold hands as she helped me into my hospital gown. I remember looking at the bright orbs of light on the ceiling; they were floating around my head because I couldn't stop the tears. I remember the way my leg twitched when it fell over during the examination. How intensely my body was shaking the entire time. The way my hospital gown kept falling off my shoulder, the cold draft nipping at my bare skin. The way my silent tears pooled on top of my hospital gown until I had no more tears left. But more than anything else, I remember the emptiness and how it drowned me. It was the night everything went dark, shadows spread inside me, touching every corner until there was nothing left.

I shrug. "Wasn't ready to face it. And I still need to go back for the rest of my stuff."

Elle considers this, staring past the words I'm not saying.

"And being here, is it what you expected?"

"What do you mean?"

She shifts in her seat, taking her feet off the dashboard and turning to face me. I keep my eyes glued on the road.

"I mean, being here in the highlands...is it not boring you?"

"Not at all," I say quickly. "It's actually very therapeutic for me."

I don't tell her why immersing myself in nature is slowly healing my soul. She doesn't need to know how broken I am...I **was***. She doesn't need to know how much her kindness has helped me find a certain longing I've silently been needing all this time. I thought I had to do it alone, that I deserved to suffer. But I was so terribly wrong.*

We talked about everything, except for the one thing I desperately wanted to talk about. I waited for Elle to bring him up, ask about our walk after dinner, tell me where he is...give me a single opening but she never did. And I didn't want to be the one to bring him up.

I don't want to think about him.

Waking up this morning in my bed, the first thought that popped in my head was Morvich. I'm not going to wait around for anyone, I'm only here for a short period of time and I need to go back to Morvich.

I doubt Lachlan even remembers offering to take me, maybe he said it in front of Ailith to make her happy.

My phone vibrates in my back pocket.

UNKNOWN NUMBER

Nessi...miss me?

ME

Wrong number.

I don't think so, lass. It's Lachlan.

When did he get my number? The better question to ask is why would Elle give him my number?

ME

What's up?

LACHLAN

What's up? Is that how friends talk?

ME

Sure. What do you want?

LACHLAN

Awfully rude friend you are. Where are you?

The nerve.

ME

Why do you care? So you can keep avoiding me?

Bubbles appear and disappear for a few seconds before a text finally comes through.

LACHLAN

I got called into work. I'm sorry I didn't message sooner, but I figured since we're friends now…It would be nice for me to check in, see how you're doing…and when you wanted to go on that overnight trip.

Because I'm such a good friend. ;)

He's trying to get under my skin about the other night, and it's working. I panicked, okay?

ME

Well, thanks for checking in…friend. But I'm leaving today, so you're off the hook.

LACHLAN

To Morvich?

ME

Yes

LACHLAN

On your own?

ME

Yes…

LACHLAN

You don't know where the cabins are.

ME

I've got Google, I'll figure something out.

LACHLAN

You're not going to wait for me, Nessi?

Why does he keep calling me that? I let out a sigh of irritation as I send one final text.

ME

Focus on your work, I'll see you when I see you…friend

I turn my phone off, tucking it in my back pocket as I scan my room one last time, making sure I have everything I need before heading out.

CHAPTER TWENTY-EIGHT

I park at the Killian Estate, near the Falls of Glomach, making my way towards the start of the long trail. I have a compass in my backpack and a map of the area I had Ailith print out for me. Knowing I'll be spending most of the day here, she packed me two sandwiches and snacks. She wouldn't let me leave without them.

The wind feels colder out here, but the sun is peeking through the clouds and I'm in the best headspace for an all-day hike. Rain, sun, snow, it doesn't matter. I'm climbing up this hill today.

As I make my way down the trail, the crunch of gravel under my boots is the only sound in the stillness of the country-side. I noticed a few parked cars at Killian Estate, but I haven't run into any other hikers yet. The narrow footpath winds through verdant rolling hills that seem to go on forever, each one melting into the next in a collection of greens and golds. The cold breeze rustles the damp grass, sending ripples across the landscape like waves on a sea of emerald.

I walk for hours, the climb becoming more strenuous.

Passing foot bridges, small rivers, and a forest track with billowy valleys, I don't stop. Sweat trickles down my back, my foot slips a few times but I push through it all, feeling more energized with each step. Focusing on my steady heartbeat as my lungs, like the mountains surrounding me, expand with each breath. Reaching higher and wider with every inhale.

As I clear the forest, I begin ascending towards the falls, admiring the river flowing below. The path opens up to Ghlas-bheinn, which holds the most picturesque views. The place is a natural fortress, with sharp cliffs and toothed rock formations that have stood here for centuries. But it's the remote feeling of the place, the silent humming of its power that forces me to pause. I can practically feel its magic as the untamed beauty of the land sings to me. For a moment, I forget who I am, while staring into the endless views of sage, luscious mountains and flowing rivers nestled in between.

I feel so insignificant and the cracks in my heart slowly begin to fuse together.

Inching closer to the falls, I look down as the water roars, dropping with such force that it drowns out every thought in my mind. Glomach is unlike anything else—a full-blooded drop of 370 feet with the river crashing deep into a chasm. I am like a speck of dust standing above, as I look down and drink it in, needing to feel it up close, to reach out and almost touch it.

Glancing at the warning signs, I decide to scramble down for a better view. There is a very short, narrow descent meant for experienced hikers. The steps down to the falls are steep, slippery, and unprotected. But I don't think twice about it as I climb down. I can handle this, having hiked more dangerous terrain in the past.

My skin buzzing with the sheer thrill of it, I carefully tiptoe down, watching my every step. I get to the landing, pushing my back against a rock wall and finally understanding why this place is rated as the best waterfall in all of the United Kingdom. It's heavenly. The sheer power of it from standing this close makes my body vibrate, as deafening water cascades down a steep cliff and collects in a midnight pool of turquoise water far below. The mist from the falls drifts above, floating around like confetti as I inch closer to the edge.

I really did it, I'm here.

I never gave up, I wanted to so many times but something held me back. Something whispered for me to keep going, keep fighting. Maybe I was always meant to find my way here. To go through everything in between so I could finally exist here. I keep having these moments of clarity when I'm immersed in nature, as if its calling out to me.

I peer down and my left boot catches the edge of the wet rock. My body trembles as the wrecking force of wind crushes the breath out of my lungs. Adrenaline pumps through my veins, making me feel high. It's exhilarating standing this close to nature's unforgiving beauty.

Suddenly, my body is forced back as a strong hand wraps around my waist. My back hits a hard body, and I frantically look behind me, not believing my eyes. Lachlan is standing here, pressed against the jagged wall as he holds me tightly. There is nothing but fury in his eyes as he glares down at me, his breaths sharp and fast.

I turn, pushing against his firm grip but he doesn't let go. His chest is heaving, wet from the light dusting of the falls behind us. Not trusting myself that this is actually real, I reach out and touch his cheek. Watching his eyes turn soft, as he gazes at me with concern. He doesn't attempt to speak, there would be no point since it's so loud we wouldn't be able to hear one another. The sound of crashing water is so ear-splitting; I can barely hear my own thoughts. I don't know how long we remain like that but he eventually takes my hand and begins guiding us back up the path. Pausing only to move me in front of him, Lachlan stays right behind me the entire time, keeping a steady hand on me.

Does he not realize I climbed down here without him?

When we get to the top, I attempt to pull my hand away but it's no use, his grip is firm as he pulls me along like he's carrying a toddler in the middle of Walmart. We walk until the sound of water grows a touch quieter. He finally releases my hand and whips around, glaring down at me. His eyelashes are wet, and his eyes are bluer than ever.

"Are you out of your bloody mind?" he roars.

"What are you doing here? And who the fuck do you think you are dragging me around like that?" I storm back, unfazed by his anger.

"You insufferable woman, you were two seconds away from falling to your death!" He gets right in my face, his heady scent distracting me for a millisecond.

"I was fine until you came along!" The sound of the falls still thunders quietly in the background. "How did you even find me?"

I was having a perfectly good time until he showed up. Deciding to be all protective, like he gives a shit. He disappears for days and then just randomly shows up here, of all places!

He stares at me with great ire. His brows drawn together, unmoving.

I decide to storm off, determined to put some distance between us as I make my way back down the narrow path. I don't bother to check if he's following me; I just listen for the sound of his footfalls in the rustling grass. And sure enough, his steps crunch in sync with mine, like an echo of my own gait. I'm torn between wanting to tell him to piss off and secretly feeling grateful that he's here. The sun beats down on my skin, and the breeze carries the scent of wildflowers on the wind.

Eventually my body calms down as nature cools my temper. We walk in silence for hours, and I wait for him to say something but he never does. The sun begins to set, and dark shadows slowly seep into the sky. I glance down at my watch and realize I stayed at the falls for over two hours.

Finally reaching the straight forest path, I pick up my speed, not wanting to be caught in the dark with Lachlan. We're covered by a thick canopy of trees and the wind slows down to a whisper in this part of the forest. The silence is chilling, broken only by the sound of our footsteps crunching on twigs and fallen leaves. I reach out my hand, feeling the rough bark of the trees brush against my fingertips as I continue to walk towards the clearing.

"Avery." Lachlan's dark honey voice casts a shadow above me. I love the way my name sounds coming out of his mouth. I hate how much it affects me.

"Lass, slow down."

I don't, choosing to walk faster.

His hand wraps around my arm and turns me to face him.

"What do you want, Lachlan?" I yank my arm away.

"I just want to talk to you. We were supposed to do this hike together, remember?" There is no more anger in his eyes, replaced by a shade of sadness.

"Yeah, well...I didn't want to wait around. I'm not here forever," I say, crossing my arms over my chest.

"I know," he looks down. I feel a twinge of guilt for my harshness, but I can't take the hot and cold from him anymore. We're acquaintances, at best, so why did he feel the need to come after me today? I thought he was working. I told him I was coming here, alone.

He takes a deep breath, running his hand over the back of his neck. When he finally glances up at me, his shoulders sag like he's waving a white flag. "I got back minutes after you left. I followed you here, decided I'd try to catch up to you."

"How did you know I'd be attempting the falls?"

"Lucky guess. This trek is shorter, and you left after sunrise." He shrugs, offering me a sheepish smile, and my weak side is just about ready to hug it out with him.

Am I supposed to be happy he followed me, or mad that he is handling me like I'm his property? I turn around, hoping we can hike silently back to our cars and go our separate ways. But his hand is on my wrist, forcing me back again. I collide into his chest. My breath hitches in my throat as his arm wraps around my waist.

He presses in on me, hurrying us forward until my back collides with a tree trunk, its rough bark scrapes against my back. A few drops of rain patter on my face. This is the closest we've ever been, and I'm acutely aware of the way his body fits against mine, each plane and contour in perfect alignment. Our eyes lock, and a buzzing desire spreads across my skin, igniting every nerve ending. His warm, solid frame leans into me, creating an ache in places I never knew existed.

I can't breathe. I can't think.

"What are you doing?" I croak.

"Avery...were you going to jump?" His voice is soft, laced with quiet torment.

His words startle me, and suddenly everything clicks into place. His distressed gaze on me now, the fear that flickered in his eyes back at the falls, the way he clung to me as if I might disappear like a wisp of smoke. I lean into him as his quick breaths fan across my cheek. It's like he's trying to hold himself back, but there is a need simmering in his eyes.

I reach up, my fingers brushing against his skin as a jolt of electricity shatters through me. Lachlan's eyes flutter closed and he inhales sharply, as if my touch hurts him. I know he feels the shocks too. I know they haunt him like they haunt me. Soft stubble grazes my fingertips as I trace his cheek bones, up to his nose, and down to his jaw. My finger lingers for a moment on his lips.

"I wasn't going to jump. I just wanted to stand close to the water, feel its power against my skin."

Leaves rustle and trees sway in the darkening sky. My hand falls limply to my side as I drink in the sight of his eyes opening. The cerulean depths of his irises reflect the vast expanse of the ocean, as his eyes find mine, engulfing me in its intensity like the waves crashing against the edge of a cliff.

"When I saw you standing there, I didn't know what to think. It looked like you were about to jump. You had this look of aching sadness on your face, like you were submerged in it. I felt it, Avery. I fucking felt it and it scared me to death." He brushes a damp tendril away from my face, searching my eyes as I drown in the sea of his gaze.

My eyes burn, but I blink it away. "Lachlan, I don't...I'm sorry."

He shakes his head, a look of defeat in his eyes that I somehow comprehend. Sometimes, no matter how much we want to say something...the words just aren't there.

He steps back, casting one final glance in my direction before walking away. I remain glued to the tree for a few seconds, my body mewling at the loss while I try to feel my legs again.

I finally peel myself off and follow him into the darkness.

CHAPTER TWENTY-NINE

"There has to be something else. I'll sleep in front of that fireplace, I really don't care," I beg the clerk, pointing behind me at the grand log fireplace, but she shakes her head as she explains how that's not possible.

Lachlan hands her some cash and grabs the room key. I drag my cold, soaked feet in a daze as I follow him to the one room left in this entire forsaken place. The room we'll have to share for the night.

One room. With hopefully two beds. Two single beds, on either side of the room in this log cabin.

It was late when we got to our cars, and there were only four options available in the area. Three of them were fully booked. This little cabin lodge was our last option, and I was very hopeful they would have two rooms. It is such a small cabin, tucked away in the middle of nowhere, I was certain no one would know about its existence. Especially not this time of year. I don't even know if there is cell service here.

The strong smell of cedar permeates the lodge, seeping from every corner, crevice, and crease. Everywhere we turn there are wooden logs, enclosing us in a cocoon of timber. The door to our room is a horizontal row of small, tightly packed yellow logs, which Lachlan holds open for me. I nervously pass by him, wondering if I should just turn around and sleep in the car for the night.

I stare in horror as soon as I'm inside the tiny room.

On second thought, I will sleep in the car.

"No way. Absolutely not." I turn to leave, but Lachlan steps inside the cabin and closes the door behind him.

Don't panic, it's fine. We just need to find another option. Maybe I can convince him to go to the next town. There must be something else.

"Why don't we try to find another town nearby?" I say, watching Lachlan peel off his wet boots, throwing his hat and jacket on the ground. He runs a hand through his hair, tousling the wet strands.

I groan, turning around and hoping another bed has magically appeared in the last two seconds. It's a small room, way too small to share with someone else. Smack in the middle of the room is a double bed. It's way too tiny for a man his size. There are no bedside tables because there is absolutely no space for them. But there is a plush, round rug tucked underneath the wooden bed frame. Immediately to my right, is another wooden door, which I assume leads to the bathroom. That's it. That is the entirety of the cabin.

"It's late, there is nothing else. And this spot is close to the Five Sisters. I'll sleep on the floor."

Unlike me, he's completely calm. Minus the permanent scowl on his face.

"You know what? That's okay. I'm totally fine sleeping in the car. I used to do it all the time when I went camping with my dad," I lie. We went camping once and it was a disaster.

I turn, reaching for the door as my fingers graze the cold

metal handle. But before I can turn the knob, Lachlan's arm shoots out, his hand presses flat against the door to stop me in my tracks.

"I'm not letting you sleep in the car, lass," he says, taking a step back as he leans his back against the door. "You'll freeze to death."

"I'll be fine," I mutter, already shivering from my damp clothes.

His gaze roves down my body.

"We're friends now, are we not? We can survive one night in this room." His eyes spark with mischief. "Unless you can't control yourself."

Pfft, I'll show him control.

"You're right. Friends can absolutely share a room in desperate times."

His jaw tightens as he looks past me.

I drop my bag on the floor and decide to go check out the bathroom. Behind the narrow doorway is the tiniest stand-in shower, a toilet, and a mini sink with no mirror. I'm not even sure if Lachlan's tall frame will fit in here. But it's one night and we can work around one another.

I walk back into the room to find Lachlan searching around for something.

"I'm not sure you'll fit in that bathroom, but there is one, which is nice. Do you want to shower first?"

He doesn't look up or address me, too busy trying not to rip the place apart.

"What are you looking for?"

"It's freezing in here. We'll need a space heater." He turns, noting my soaked clothes. He's no better off—we got caught in a downpour before reaching the car.

"Go ahead and wash up. I'm going to head down to see if I can find a heater and some food."

"Okay. Thank you."

He walks towards the door and leaves without another word. I'm drained from the day. From the hike itself, then running into Lachlan at the waterfall, the weird encounter we had in the small forest, and trying to find a lodge for the night. Lachlan somehow convinced me to leave my car at the Killian Estate and drive with him. Now I'm stuck here all night.

In one room.

With a guy I was fantasizing about the other day.

This is a total disaster.

I pull out my phone, and there is only one bar of service. I doubt that's enough to call or text anyone, but I'm going to try.

ME

> Becca…I don't know if you're asleep still or just waking up, I can't do time difference math right now. But you remember me telling you about the ridiculously hot guy from across the hall at the inn who fought a douchebag because of me? Well, I'm stuck sharing a tiny cabin with him for the night.

It takes two minutes for the text to show delivered.

Not even a second later, text bubbles pop up.

BECCA

> OMG! My prayers have been answered.
> Please, please for the love of God, tell me there is only one bed.

I close my eyes, sighing in disbelief. Texting her was a mistake.

ME

> There is, unfortunately.

BECCA

Tell me you're planning on banging him…
please bang him.

ME

Becca! We just became friends, like a second
ago, I have no plans on sleeping with
this man.

BECCA

You need this, badly…you're practically a
virgin again. You only live once and this
situation you're in NEVER happens. BANG.
HIM. Do it for me if you won't do it for
yourself.

ME

This conversation is over. Check to make sure
I'm alive tomorrow.

I chuck my phone on the bed a little too aggressively before bending down to pick up my bag. Grabbing a long PJ shirt, my toiletries bag, and a rolled up towel off the bed, I make my way towards the bathroom. Wrestling to strip out of my wet clothes, I pile them on top of the toilet lid and step inside the shower, under the piping hot water.

A wave of relief washes over me as my tired muscles begin to relax. The warmth of the water penetrates into every inch of my skin, melting away the cold that has settled deep in my bones. The tension in my shoulders finally begins to ease, as I close my eyes and allow myself to bask in the comfort of it all. I try not to think about tonight, but my mind keeps wandering to Lachlan.

This would be a lot easier if I wasn't attracted to him. Attraction is putting it lightly. My body reacts to him in a way I can't even begin to describe. I've never wanted someone to touch me more, thinking about the way his body was pressed up against mine as he held me up against that tree...

But this can't happen, right?

He is from here and I'm not. I'm leaving very soon.

But that might be exactly what I need.

There isn't enough time for emotional attachments, but there could be time for some fun. Would it be so terrible to have a physical relationship? Something to help me get out of my head a little bit. I want to hate the idea, but I can't deny the way I want him. The way my skin tingles just now, thinking about him.

I lay my head on the shower wall and close my eyes, turning the dial over to COLD.

WHERE IS MY UNDERWEAR? I'm sure I grabbed it before walking in here to take a shower.

You idiot.

My hair is towel dried and brushed, I'm ready to step out but I forgot to bring in underwear, which means I'm naked under this big ass shirt.

Slowly cracking the bathroom door open, I poke my head out. The bed is exactly as I left it, except there is a wooden tray sitting on the comforter with two glasses of whisky. And a dinky space heater in the corner, emitting a deafening screech that makes it seem like it's on the verge of exploding.

"Lachlan?"

No answer.

I don't waste another second, bolting towards my bag, which is propped open in the middle of the room. I shoot my arm to the bottom, searching aimlessly until my fingers wrap around a string. Pulling up to find a lacy thong.

I always pack extra underwear.

Dumping the contents of my bag on the floor, and frantically searching my things, I quickly realize I only packed one underwear. I do have a clean pair of leggings and socks. Facing the closed door with a racing heart, I swiftly put everything on.

I'm sitting on the floor, placing everything back in my bag when there is a soft knock on the door before it sways open.

Lachlan steps in, holding two Styrofoam containers. I let my eyes trail over him. He still looks good, even after a full day of hiking and getting caught in the rain. Not like the dishevelled mess I was when we first walked in here. I bet he smells good too. He'd probably smell good after spending three days in the desert, with sweat trickling in between his muscles.

Great, now I have that image in my head.

"Hi," he says, knocking me out of my very inappropriate thoughts.

"Hi," I stammer.

"How was your shower?"

"Good."

"Good," he repeats awkwardly.

"I see you found a heater," I say, scrambling to come up with words.

"Aye, piece of garbage, though. Not sure it'll help but it's better than nothing." He frowns, sitting on the end of the mattress. He opens the containers, placing them on the bed.

"Are you hungry, lass?"

I nod, moving towards the bed, and sitting in a kneeling position facing him. A shiver runs through me.

"Are you cold?" He hands me a metal fork.

"A little," I whisper, but I'm not sure if it's from the cold.

He holds out a glass of whisky. "This should help."

"Sláinte," he says quietly, holding up his own glass. "To new friendships."

"To friendship." I smile, taking a long sip of the whisky. This one is a lot dryer and not as smooth as Anam Cara. Shuddering, I force it down my throat.

Lachlan's light laughter fills the air. "They didn't have your favourite."

I take another sip of my bitter drink, hoping to mask my smile.

"Thank you, Lachlan. This is thoughtful."

"It's nothing. I'm sorry if you're uncomfortable with all of this."

I'm not uncomfortable for the reasons he thinks.

"It's fine."

His curious eyes never leave mine as he brings his glass to his lips, sipping slowly. I wish I could sketch him, right here... right now. His towering presence, the way he is looking at me like I'm the only thing he can see. He's breathtaking. It's my thoughts about him that make me uncomfortable, because the truth is, I like being close to him.

He reaches behind him, pulling his sweater off in one swift motion. His black T-shirt rides up his stomach and I allow my eyes to wander.

His eyes fall to my lips, lingering as I gnaw on my bottom lip.

"Stop that," he groans, handing me a container of food with what appears to be brown oatmeal.

Stop what? Biting my lip?

"Have you had haggis yet?" Lachlan says quickly.

"No. I've been meaning to try it."

"It's your lucky night. That's all they had left in the kitchen."

I pick up my fork and dig in. The haggis is warm and

crunchy. With flavourful notes of sausage and oats, seasoned to perfection. There is a dollop of fluffy mashed potatoes beside the crumbly haggis, and I dip my fork in both.

"It's delicious."

Lachlan smiles as if he was expecting to hear something else. "You'd make a good Scot."

"Wow, my first compliment," I retort proudly.

He laughs and the sound is more delicious than the food I'm eating. "First time for everything."

He stares at me, all blue eyes and wet, lawless hair. But he looks relaxed, unguarded even.

I focus on chewing and swallowing, making a to-do list in my head. We'll eat and then go to bed. He'll sleep on the floor like he offered and in the morning, we'll wake up, I'll hike through the Five Sisters, and everything will be great.

Lachlan finishes his food quickly, washing it all down with the rest of his whisky. He stands up, and I stare at his perfectly round ass, while he fishes out some clothes from his bag.

"I'm going to shower," he says.

I nod, trying to swallow down the food lodged in my throat.

He disappears into the bathroom, clicking the door shut. I scarf down the rest of my food and whisky, planning to be in bed and asleep by the time he gets out.

There is only one extra fuzzy blanket on the bed, aside from the faded flower comforter. And two pillows. Bare necessities. I decide to give Lachlan the comforter since he's offered to sleep on the floor. Lifting it off the bed and setting it aside, I wrap the thin fuzzy blanket around myself and lay down on the cold bed sheet. The blanket comes up to my ankle. Tucking in my legs, I try to trap whatever body heat I have.

The temperature in the room seems to be dropping, despite the overworked heater in the corner. The blanket scratches at my neck, forcing me to toss uncomfortably. I don't think I'll be sleeping tonight.

I hear the water turn off and the door open. Sitting up on my elbows, I watch a shirtless Lachlan approach, wearing only a pair of black sweatpants. He's rubbing a towel over his head, oblivious to my ogling. I trace the water droplets crawling down his crafted chest, licking my lips. On full display is a large tattoo of two snakes, one black and the other white, tangled around one another, starting from his lower chest and disappearing to his back.

Jesus Christ, I think I'm melting.

I glance back up at him and he's caught me staring. He smirks to himself as the towel drops on the floor beside his bag.

I wish the bed would open up and swallow me whole.

"Need something?" His voice drips with honey.

I muster the courage to sit up, staring at my hands. "Um... I...uh...left you the comforter. You can have it. It's over there," I point towards the comforter, not daring to look up. "It's yours. Unless you want the bed. I'm happy to sleep on the floor, or the car or whatever."

Shut. Up.

My body is on fire, burning from the projectile word vomit that just came out of me.

Screw the heater, who needs it? Not me.

"I'm fine on the floor," he chuckles.

"Great, grand. Thank you. I owe you, big time."

"Goodnight, Avery."

"Night!" I exclaim like an idiot, flopping down to my side and closing my eyes shut, as I start shouting at myself in my head.

The light flickers off, casting the room in darkness, and the initial excitement fades into silence. However, the biting room temperature lingers, making the air feel thin and icy. I fold in on myself and pray sleep takes me.

CHAPTER THIRTY

avery

I curl up tighter, hugging me knees close to my chest in a futile attempt to keep warm. My teeth chatter uncontrollably, and I'm pretty certain my toes have frost bite. Every breath I take sends a new wave of shivers through my body, and the rough texture of the goddamn blanket is only adding to my increasing discomfort. The cold has seeped so deep into my bones that it feels like a layer of ice has formed inside of me.

"Avery," Lachlan grumbles from the floor. "Are you awake?"

"Ye...ss."

"Bloody hell, you're freezing. Take my blanket." He's shifting around somewhere but I can't hear much over the sound of my chattering teeth.

"No."

"Avery."

"Lach...lan," I bite out.

I feel the weight of Lachlan's comforter on me as a cold draft brushes against my face, causing a stronger wave of trembles. I open my eyes to see Lachlan standing beside the bed, still shirtless, as he tucks the blanket around me.

"No," I protest, shaking my head like crazy.

"I can't sleep with you shivering like that."

"I'm...sorry."

"Fuck, lass. Tell me what you need." He kneels down, brushing a damp curl away from my face. His fingers are so warm. I don't understand how he hasn't turned into an ice cube already.

"Warmth. I need...warmth." I'm not sure what I'm asking for right now. Fire? We have enough wood. Light the place up.

"How can I make you warm?" He sucks in a breath.

Body heat. No...I can't.

Just say it. The worst that can happen is he says no and I can go back to shivering until sunrise.

I close my eyes, taking in an icy breath. "Can you...hold me? Just until I...stop...shaking."

A long beat of silence.

He blows out a deep breath, and I pry my eyes open to see him walking away. My heart starts pounding in my chest, knowing I might have crossed a line I can't trace back. But then, the comforter lifts from behind me, and I sense Lachlan's presence lingering. I turn my head and find him standing there, his gaze fixed on my back.

"Are you sure?" He murmurs, his voice low and gravelly.

"Yes. Get in before I turn into a block of ice."

Lachlan gives me a curt nod, as he moves under the cover and scoots close to me. I turn away, already feeling the warmth of his body everywhere.

"Drop your knees."

I let go, my teeth shuddering faster. My jaw hurts from the intensity of it but I try to breathe through it. Lachlan's arm wraps around my waist and he pulls my back to his chest.

"What the fuck is this shite?" He tugs on the scratchy blanket cocooning me.

"I know, it's awful."

"Can we get rid of it?"

I nod, gratefully shifting as he helps remove the sandpaper blanket, throwing it aside with a frustrated groan. He then enfolds his body around mine, and I melt into his embrace instantly. He radiates heat like a furnace, dissolving the ice from inside my body. Gently, he slides his arm under my pillow, adjusting it to support my head, and places his hand on my forehead. The warmth of his palm seeps into my skin, easing the ache in my bones. It feels like heaven.

"You're so warm." I breathe out.

"Aye, compared to you. You're colder than ice. Why didn't you say something sooner?"

"Why did you bring me to an ice hotel?"

"It's never been this cold."

"Sure...or you're trying to give me pneumonia."

He laughs, his soft breath tickles the top of my head, sending shivers down my spine. "Even frozen half to death, you still have something to say. I wonder what it'll take to shut you up."

"I guess you'll never know."

A pause, as if he stopped breathing all together. "I wouldn't be so sure about that."

My heart drops to my stomach at the subtle promise.

His other hand coasts up and down my frigid arm, creating sweet friction that slowly spreads through my body, easing the cold out of my muscles. Despite the physical comfort, the air between us is tense, heavy with unspoken words. I want to break the silence, to say something, anything to fill the void.

"Do you have any siblings?" I blurt out.

"Only child."

"Same."

"Parents?" His voice is gentle against my head.

"Divorced. I talk to my dad every week and I don't know where my mom is." I don't know why I just shared all of that.

"What happened?" He whispers.

"Oh you know, the usual. She wanted a different life, one without me or my father."

"I'm sorry."

I shrug. "That's life. You can't make someone love you, no matter who it is."

His hand slowly trails over my stomach, his palm flattening as the heat diffuses through my shirt. My heart races impatiently, and the clothes in between us suddenly feel heavy, too much.

"Tell me what you're thinking." Lachlan's voice is low.

I can't say the things teetering on the edge of my tongue because if I do, I'll never be able to take them back.

"It's nice to be warm again." Pathetic, but it's the truth. "You?"

"Your feet feel like icicles even with the bloody socks on."

I laugh, reaching under the cover and yanking off my socks. I press my feet against his shins and he groans, locking his legs around mine. I squirm, trying to get away, only to end up facing him, my palms pressing into his firm naked chest. Realizing the compromising position, I drop my hands quickly, and lie flat on my back, staring up at the ceiling.

"Why did you come after me today?" I rasp, unable to hold it in any longer.

"That's a question, not a thought."

I sigh, not in the mood to play this game with him. "It's what I'm thinking about."

"No, it's not. What is it you really want to say?"

Oh, he's good. Too bad for him, I'm a closed vault.

"I guess you'll never know."

His warm fingers skate down my stomach, trailing slowly along my thigh. My breath hitches, I try to swallow but my mouth is suddenly bone dry. His hand draws close to my core as streaks of pleasure burst through me.

"I didn't want you to be alone out here. And you owed me a hike." His fingers play with the bottom hem of my shirt.

"Is that all of it?" I breathe out.

"I guess you'll never know." He repeats my words back to me, his warm breath brushing the back of my neck.

My heart hammers in my chest, frantic to get out.

"I'm not sure if I trust myself around you." I close my eyes as the truth finally spills out of me.

"Why?" His hand curls under my shirt, as his fingertips graze my bare skin.

I suck in a sharp breath, my body buzzing with anticipation.

"Why don't you trust yourself, lass?" He repeats his question when I don't answer.

"Because my thoughts aren't so friendly anymore," my voice comes out low and breathy as his fingers stretch across my bare stomach, sending small ripples of electricity down my body. His touch is painfully careful. Never approaching my chest or my pant line, even though I want him to touch me where it hurts.

"Look at me."

I open my eyes and it feels like someone took a match and dropped the flame on my kerosene-doused body. I burn under his gaze. His pupils are dilated, eyes the colour of the ocean at midnight. The pads of his fingers skate across my stomach, torturing me from inside out. My treacherous body betrays me as wetness pools in between my legs.

"I came after you today because I needed to see you. I needed to make sure you were safe."

"Why?" I hold my breath.

Lachlan's eyes are intense, burning into me as if he's searching for something impossible. I swallow hard, feeling the lump in my throat grow larger the longer the seconds tick by.

"We should get some sleep." He lowers his head to the pillow. Removing his hand from under my shirt as he turns me around, my back against his chest once more.

I mull over his words, turning them inside out, dissecting the entire conversation into tiny pieces. Until finally I realize that was his way of gently letting me down.

CHAPTER THIRTY-ONE

lachlan

I'm in royal fucking shite.

You bloody stupid fud. What did you think was going to happen when you chased after her?

I'm so fucked.

On top of that, I feel like the biggest arsehole in the world this morning. I've been lying awake for over an hour, trying not to think about the devastated look on Avery's face when I shot her down last night. I wanted to tell her I needed to see her because I couldn't bear the thought of being apart from her. That my fucking heart yearns for her with every beat.

God, she looked utterly deflated when I didn't say the words. I almost took her lips in between mine just to erase that look from her face. Promised I would only say the truth, but I backed out like the coward that I am.

It's for the best.

Is it? Because I'm running out of reasons why.

I'm dying to know what her lips feel like against mine, what they taste like. And I almost went for it. I want to do unspeakable things to her. When she shivered under my touch, squirming and pressing her thighs tightly together, I almost lost it. I bet if I had slid my fingers inside her panties, I would have found them fucking soaked.

Bloody hell.

I groan, shifting as my morning wood grows harder, right below her thigh.

Her naked thigh. I don't know where her leggings went but I'm certain she had the damned things on when I crawled in bed next to her last night.

I've never spent the night next to a woman before. I don't cuddle or share a bed with anyone. This should frustrate me, maybe even repulse me, but the only thing it's doing is making my heart ache in my chest. I've tried to push away, to bury my feelings for her deep inside me, but it's not fucking working anymore.

I can't help but drink her in. Avery's face is pressed against my chest, her palm resting on my shoulder. Her long brown hair is flowing in every direction, curls wild and untamed. The rays of the morning sun peek through the small window above the bed, illuminating her locks with a gentle glow entangled around each individual strand. As if she's a goddess of light and her hair is her crown. She's breathtaking. Avery's dark lashes flutter as she exhales deeply. I want to stay in this moment forever, with her peacefully asleep on my chest.

I want her more than I want my next breath, more than I've wanted anything else in my life. Being next to her is like oxygen to my soul, and without it, I am lost in a sea of darkness. She is the light that guides me.

You can't drag her into your mess. You can't do this to her.

I lift the bedspread, trying to cover her cold arm when I notice her bare arse sticking out. Her black lacy thong is on full display and her shirt has ridden up to her midsection, making me itch to feel her plump cheeks in the palm of my hands.

I grunt, pressing my eyes shut. This is absolute torture.

I should have slept on the cold floor all night. It would have been less painful than this.

Realizing I need to get the hell out of here before I do something stupid, I peel myself away from her. Careful not to rouse her from sleep, I leave a quick note on the bed. I grab my boots and jacket, then slip out the door.

CHAPTER THIRTY-TWO

I woke up to an empty bed, with my leggings laying on the floor and not on my body where I left them before I fell asleep. There is a fuzzy memory of me getting out of bed to take them off because I was boiling in the middle of the night. Quite the contrast to freezing my ass off before Lachlan came in to cuddle with me.

I still can't believe that actually happened.

And even worse, I slept like a baby drunk on milk. And I know that has everything to do with the man currently huffing for air next to me. I didn't think I would be comfortable enough to actually drift off next to him, so imagine my surprise when I woke up this morning from a restful slumber.

We're about three hours into our eight-hour hike at the Five Sisters of Kintail, which is supposed to cover the entire mountain. I was surprised when Lachlan said he was coming with me. I figured after last night he would want some space, but he was eager to start the hike early this morning.

Today has been an uphill climb from the very start, our journey winding through verdant mountains as we ascend towards each summit. We have been at the highest peaks, amidst two points, and on the sides of these sublime hills. Each footstep seems to propel me further into nature, away from the worries that gnaw at my mind. The mossy earth underneath my boots muffles the noises and drowns out the anxiety that lives in my head rent free. Out here, in the tranquil highlands, none of that matters. The myriad of voices in my head fade into the background until they are undetectable.

"This is much harder than I thought it was going to be," Lachlan pants, bent over with his hands propped on his knees as he gasps for air.

"You should amp up your cardio at the gym." I tease.

He quirks a brow, giving me a knowing smile. "If you're doing cardio at the gym, you're not doing it right."

I blink. "What do you mean? Where else would you do cardio? I mean, I know where...what..." I shake the thought away, blushing. "No. Forget about it."

The sweet sound of his laugh echos off the hills.

"This is cardio, going for a run outside is cardio, repetitive motions like chopping wood is cardio. What did you think I meant?"

"Nothing."

He gives me a cocky grin, walking closer. "I want to know."

I cross my arms over my chest, shaking my head.

"Hmmm...where is that sharp tongue of yours, Nessi? Do tell." His deep, honey voice brushes up my thighs.

"No."

He stares down at me gleefully, with victory in his eyes. I push past him and continue climbing towards the third peak. Needing to stop imagining all the different positions Lachlan prefers to do cardio.

Get a hold of yourself.

I clear my throat. "So, you haven't done this hike before?"

"Not this sister. I've climbed the first one," he calls back, the wind loud and heavy in my ear as we walk by rocky steps lining the steep hill.

It's a difficult trek up, I will admit, and I focus on one foot after the other as we make our way up the summit. The rocks are slippery, the grass wet from hours of rain. But I march on. My throat burns as the air pierces my lungs, every inhale harder than the next. At some point, Lachlan passes me and I follow closely behind, using him as a focal point to stay focused. My lower back spasms and I want to stop. I want to give up so badly, but I keep going. Keep moving forward.

We're nearing the top of the mountain when the air suddenly changes and the wind grows louder. A sea of clouds pass us by, licking the top of the mountain peaks. Lachlan disappears for a second as I heave myself up.

The summit finally comes into view.

I forget about all the pain and difficulty as soon as the clearing appears. It's like we're amongst the gods, walking through the clouds sitting atop the mountain. The wind roars like giants, whipping pieces of my hair out of my ponytail. The top of the mountain juts ten feet out, bending into a narrow curve of mossy ground strewn with saw-edged rocks. I walk towards the small pathway and look out beyond the vast land-scape. The view is restricted by low-lying fluffy clouds. I stand still and close my eyes, picturing the heavens as my face kisses the sky.

As I crouch down to perch on the edge of the cliff, my foot slips on a loose rock, causing my heart to lurch in my chest. I quickly plant myself, steadying my nerves before gazing down at the incredible drop. The world around me falls away as the vast expanse of the valley stretches out before my eyes. It's almost too much to take in.

Lachlan approaches, his leg brushing against my back as he

takes a seat beside me, offering his hand to steady me. Our fingers intertwine, a feeling of warmth spreads through me at his touch. I lean into him, drawing comfort from his solid presence. And in this moment, all that exists is us, perched on the edge of the world, together.

The wind quiets and the clouds grow still, surrounding us like thick fog.

These moments in nature remind me to live in the now. There is so much of the world I haven't seen, touched...felt. There is so much I haven't lived. Instead, I have spent all my time resenting, running, pushing everything away because of my fear. Because of my past. What a waste of time. It makes me realize how inconsequential we truly are, and how our life is a blip compared to everything else out there.

Lachlan and I sit in silence for a long time. Listening to the howling of the wind and staring out over the misty clouds.

"You're shivering. Let's go," Lachlan yells, putting his hand under my arm and lifting me up. We walk carefully back down the path, and I turn to look at the evergreen vastness one last time before we begin our descent.

He walks close behind me, reaching out to grab me whenever my foot slips on the wet slop. The descent is much more difficult. But thankfully we are both wearing proper footgear and waterproof clothes. I slip a few times, and Lachlan is there to catch me every single time.

"That was something else," he says once we finally catch our breaths, our feet back on flat ground. We walk side by side down the narrow pathway, heading for the next hill.

"Reaching the summit is always my favourite part. Not because I'm standing at the top, but because along the way there is a stretch of time where I'm not sure I'm going to make it. Where I want to give up so badly. But when I finally get to the top, all the pain from the climb just fades away."

Lachlan's hand gently brushes against my cold fingers. "I felt it just now. Why you stood so close to the falls. I felt the rush, the clarity as I stood on the edge of the cliff and looked down. It was frightening and yet, it made me feel alive," he says quietly. "I have a fear of heights. I wasn't sure I'd be able to get that close to the edge."

He's staring out at the landscape when I ask, "How did you do it? How did you push past the fear?"

A half-smile blooms on his lips. "I just push through and face it head-on. I knew the view would be worth it and I didn't want to miss that. And I wanted the strength more than the fear. The fear is never going to go away. It'll always be there, but I choose to face it instead of running from it. Because every time you face it, you strip its power away. And It can't chase you."

He's right...*If you face the fear, it can't chase you.*

I stare at him in awe, letting his words really sink in. He pauses, looking away quickly, and I swear he's blushing, but it could just be the cold wind leaving a mark on his skin.

"What?" I swallow.

His eyes find mine, ocean blues amongst a forest green background.

"Being here, with you...makes me feel like I could do that over and over again. Like I could face all my fears."

His words envelop my heart, squeezing tightly as another piece of me fuses together. I would be lying if I said I didn't feel it too. Being close to him is like getting lost in nature. He makes the rest of the world fade away. And whenever we're together, I'm tethered to that moment with Lachlan.

But I can't say that, and when words fail me, he intertwines our fingers together. It should feel strange, out of place, but it feels like a lost memory finding its way back to me.

We walked and talked for hours. He told me about the

history of Scotland and the highlands. How they inspired him to pursue his dream of starting his own whisky company, Anam Cara. Lachlan is so passionate about Scotland, and that comes through easily for him. His eyes are usually filled with uncertainty, but when he talks about his homeland, they light up with a newfound spark.

He is good at talking about everything but himself, though. I tried digging more into his personal life, his job, his hobbies, but he gave me vague answers every time. I got the sense he wasn't comfortable so I didn't push. People open up when they're ready.

I think I judged him too harshly. He's clearly battling a silent demon and seemingly doing it alone. Everyone is fighting battles we can't see, and I'm not sure what his story is but it's obvious he's working through it. He dozes off at times, gaze heavy with contemplation and I wish there was something I could do to ease his mind or let him know he's not alone. Sometimes you just need someone to hold your hand.

We're heading towards the final sister and Lachlan starts grilling me with questions again.

"I want to know more." He says.

"I think you already know everything there is to know about me."

"That's not true."

I give him a narrow look. "What more do you want to know?"

"What's your favourite TV show or movie?"

I cringe, biting my lip. "I'm not a TV person—at all."

"What do you mean? How can you not be a TV person? Isn't everyone your age into the Kardashians?" He nudges my shoulder playfully.

I press my hand on my chest, my mouth gaping open in disbelief. "Excuse me! That's presumptuous of you, Grandpa.

But I'll have you know, I'm a book nerd. And when I'm not reading, I'm drawing. Sorry to be a bore."

"What about dates with your ex? Dinner and a movie? Netflix and chill?"

I shake my head, my cheeks heating at the last three words he said. "Never did any of that, not really. I think we went to a movie once with his friends. We did get Netflix and cable when we first moved in together but John cancelled them after a few months since he was too busy with work."

This is the one topic that hasn't come up yet, and I'm not sure I want to know about his dating history. With Lachlan's looks, I bet he gets more opportunities than there are minutes in the day. Now who's being the presumptuous asshole?

A look of disbelief washes over his face. "No dates?"

I shake my head.

"What a wanker."

No matter how hard I try, I can never escape my past. But talking about this doesn't hurt like I thought it would.

"Social media? Celebrity crushes?" He asks.

I shake my head again, staring up at him. "Wasn't allowed social media either."

"What do you mean?"

I release a tired breath. "John is a politician and his image is very important to him. His online presence is clean, and that's always been a top priority. He loves the spotlight, no matter the cost. When I decided to move to Toronto and live with him, in his elected community, I had to get rid of all my socials. I stood in his shadow." I look down, realizing how many red flags I ignored throughout our relationship and how I always put myself last because I never felt worthy of more.

I glance around at the hills, how small we must look from above, squeezed in between jade mountains and tall wispy grass.

I jump when Lachlan suddenly pulls me against his chest. The way he's looking at me feels intimate; emotions flood me as he tucks a loose strand of hair behind my ear. I force my battering heart to settle.

"I want to say what's in my head," he murmurs.

"Okay."

"You deserved better than to be tucked away, left alone in a city you didn't know. I'm so sorry, for everything that you have had to endure," he whispers, leaving a gentle kiss on my forehead.

My heart rattles in my chest, urging me to offer it on a silver platter to this man. This rare man who speaks so freely, and who seems to notice every part of me. Who makes me feel less alone than I ever have before.

His fiery gaze shifts, the light dimming as he battles with his thoughts.

"Avery..." He opens and closes his mouth several times but no words come out.

All at once, the sky opens up, and fat droplets of water smack me in the face as I stare up at the darkening sky.

"Come on. There is a small forest up ahead." Lachlan tugs on my hand and we break into a run. I'm breathless by the time we reach the forest, which forced us to veer off course, but it was the only option as we wait out the rain.

Raindrops trickle down loudly through the small grove. I take cover under a big evergreen, with long branches that extend out. Lachlan stands across from me under a smaller tree, rain pouring down on him relentlessly. I could offer him some space under my tree but I don't trust myself to be near him right now, not after what just happened.

I reach for my ponytail and pull the elastic out, running my hands through my wet hair. The smell of wet bark sways in the wind and I smile, catching droplets of rain in the palm of my hands. My breaths billow out in front of me and I close my eyes, pointing my face up towards the sky. I feel weightless, as if I'm floating on air.

When I open my eyes, Lachlan is still leaned against his tree, covered in a shower of rain as he watches me intently, like he's trying to capture this moment. There is a look of contentment and wonder in his face.

My heart beats violently against my ribs, demanding to be set free. I'm breathless, unable to peel my eyes from his. He pushes off the tree and stalks towards me.

"Where did you go just now?" His eyes glow bright blue, almost teal in colour.

"Just here. This is amazing, the rain, the forest...it's like a small moment trapped in time. I swear, there is something magical in these lands. You have to bottle it up and give it away." I smile.

The air around us shifts, charging with heavy tension. Lachlan's eyes darken, flickering with an emotion that I can't quite read, and his hands clench into tight fists at his sides. It's as if he's struggling against an impossible force inside his own mind, battling some inner demons that threaten to consume him. But he remains rooted to the spot, his body tense and still.

"What's wrong?" I reach out for him but he takes a step back.

"Nothing. We should go. It's probably not safe to climb the final mountain today, with all the rain."

He starts to turn away, but my hand instinctively reaches out to grab his, catching the subtle twitch in his grip.

"Lachlan, what just happened?"

He doesn't turn to face me.

Just let it go.

But I can't let it go. If I try I may detonate all over this fucking forest.

"What happened between now and five minutes ago when you said my name like you were about to tell me something? When you said I deserved better and kissed my forehead? Why are you pulling away? What have I done?" I yell to his back.

The muscles in his back stretch and ripple beneath his drenched jacket, his chest heaving for air.

"You haven't done anything. It's better this way," he says, his voice loud enough to carry in the rain.

"Fine. Let's go then." I release his hand.

And at that moment, he finally turns around, swiftly closing the space between us. Water cascades down the top of his hat, landing on my hairline and stinging my eyes. Frustration boils in my blood, and before I realize what I'm doing, I reach up and knock his hat off his head. He towers above me, his face a mask of tumultuous emotions as he gazes down at me, breathless.

"Tell me this is real. Because God, I feel it all, Avery. And I don't want to. I can't..."

An onslaught of pain and confusion hits me at once. My own emotions turning into a storm, thundering and clashing deep within me. My heart is a drumbeat, pounding so loud I'm sure he can hear it despite the downpour. I try to steady my breathing, but it's impossible when all I want to do is scream at him.

"Fine." I snap, taking a step to the side but he blocks me.

His eyes flash with something akin to pain, but his voice is low and scratchy when he speaks. "Tell me I'm not imagining this."

"Why? So you can push me away again? No, Lachlan... you're not imagining this. That electric pull whenever we touch, I feel it in every part of my body, in my fucking veins. Is that what you want to hear? That I—"

Without warning, he steps forward, his hand cupping the back of my neck as his lips crash into mine.

My body feels like it's been thrown into the sun. A strong magnetic shockwave courses through me, trapping the air in my lungs. He kisses me deeply, starting off soft and inviting before turning ravenous as his tongue glides into my mouth. I grip the back of his neck, arching into him. Lachlan pushes me against the tree, a soft moan escaping my lips. He eats up the sound, groaning as he bites my bottom lip, pulling on the flesh before diving back into my mouth. We're hungry, desperate for one another, like we've been starved for years.

This kiss is all-consuming.

His lips, his tongue against mine, the way he smells, everything about him drowns me in a type of ecstasy I have only read about.

His hands trail down my body. Even with layers in between us, my flesh comes to life under his touch. We remain entangled against one another, as the rain continues to fall, melding us into one. His fingers embrace my face and he rests his forehead against mine. Our faces so close—breaths mingling in shared gasps.

"Lachlan." I pull back to look at him, placing my hand over his heart, and feeling the rapid beat in his chest.

"I don't know what came over me. I shouldn't have done that." He says, shattering our perfect moment.

"Right."

"I'm sorry." His thumb gently caresses my cheek, before he wraps his hand in mine, intertwining our fingers.

The butterflies I had locked up in my stomach for so long finally break free, and I knew in that moment that I will never be able to cage them up again. No matter how much it stung to hear his apology.

CHAPTER THIRTY-THREE

avery

It's late when I pull into the parking lot at the inn back in Corran.

Lachlan's car pulls up right beside mine a minute later.

I can't even look over at him. Not wanting to admit how many times I traced my lips on the drive back, re-living the way we were intertwined under the tree. How could I ever forget a kiss like that?

But then his voice whispers in my ear, the words he uttered after our lips parted by the tree.

I'm sorry.

It hurt to hear it, especially after a kiss like that but if anyone understands needing space and time, it's me. No matter how much I want this, it's not going to happen. And I have to respect that. I have to respect his wishes.

I shouldn't even entertain the thought of a romantic relationship with Lachlan. I'm a tourist, with way too much extra baggage, and it would be so much less complicated if we kept things platonic for the remainder of my time here.

But God do I want him.

I crave all the physical with none of the emotions attached. This would be the perfect opportunity to have that. I'm leaving in the next few weeks, which means there is no time for emotions. He's staying in Scotland and I'm going back home to Canada. There is no future here.

Three weeks ago, I didn't even think I was capable of wanting someone the way I want him. That's profound all on its own, even if nothing comes from this.

I kill the engine, taking in the near-empty parking lot before I catch my reflection in the rearview mirror. I look as scraggly as I feel, but I'm about to go inside and take a hot shower. Scrub the last two days off me. Start clean.

Lachlan and I step out of our cars at the same time.

He doesn't look at me.

We grab our things and walk towards the inn without uttering a word. I focus on the sound of our footsteps hitting the concrete, and the hum of bar music in the background, instead of the weighted silence growing heavier between us. My nerves fire on all cylinders. This is already so awkward and painful, I might have to leave Corran soon.

The foyer is deserted, as it always is at this time of night. The only movement is a delicate wisp of smoke floating up to the fireplace chimney. The remains of a dying fire give off a faint scent of charred wood in the room. The door to the pub is closed, muffling the lively chatter and music emanating from within.

I make my way down the stone hallway, with Lachlan following closely behind me. The low lighting casts long, flickering shadows that seem to dance in the corners of my vision. Eventually, we reach my room, and I fumble for the key in my pocket.

I press my key into the slot, twisting around to catch Lachlan's back as he props open the door. He turns around, and in the dim light, his eyes lock onto mine without hesitation. I can feel my heart race as I take in his appearance—his damp shirt clings to his chest, the fabric accentuating every contour and muscle. Triggering an onslaught of vivid memories from the last night, when our bodies were entwined, and his warm chest pressed against me.

I look away, feeling my cheeks flush with embarrassment at the intensity of my thoughts.

"Thanks for the great adventure." I say.

A painful smile ghosts across his lips before it disappears. He approaches me, standing so close, I can feel the heat shedding off his body. His eyes fall to my lips, as he inhales sharply and taking deliberate steps back in the direction of his room.

"It was unforgettable, Nessi...all of it. Goodnight." He says, disappearing inside his room and closing the door.

All of it.

With a heavy heart, I retreat to my room, drop everything by the door, and head straight for the shower. Stepping under the hot stream, I promise to let my desires go. His actions seemed final tonight. If he wanted to, he would have made a move or said something more.

It doesn't matter that his kiss haunted me the minute we pulled apart, or that I want him to infiltrate my very existence because apparently, I have learned nothing. Apparently, I am willing to get lost in him even if it's just for a very short time.

But he doesn't want to.

He doesn't want me.

I'VE BEEN TOSSING and turning in my bed for hours. Why is tonight the night I have to be impossibly uncomfortable? I've tried tucking pillows in between my legs, behind my back, over my head, on my face. Nothing is working and I can't fall asleep. My body is sore and exhausted after two days of hiking; I should be able to sleep until next year.

Maybe some whisky will help.

I roll over and glance at my phone. Three-thirty in the morning.

My stomach gurgles.

"Ugh, not you too."

I whip off the comforter, rubbing the exhaustion from my eyes. I guess I'll eat a protein bar and try to sleep again. Although, I do recall Ailith mentioning that if I ever get back late and want a snack, I can help myself to the kitchen.

I'll keep track of what I eat and pay her back in the morning.

I head to the bathroom and take in my reflection in the mirror. My curls are damp and wild, since I went to bed with wet hair. Black lace bralette and matching sleep shorts—more like underwear since half my ass is sticking out. I have to do some laundry tomorrow.

I remember seeing a robe behind the bathroom door. Letting out a sigh of relief, I grab the soft navy flannel robe from the hook and drape it across my shoulders. I feel around for the strap to secure it in place, but it's missing. Nothing behind the door either.

Screw it. Trapping the fuzzy material under my arm, I head for the door.

As I take a step outside my room, the old wooden door creaks loudly behind me, the sound reverberating down the dark hallway. I freeze and glance around warily. The hallway is cloaked in complete darkness. The only light comes from the far end of the corridor, casting a faint, eerie glow that barely illuminates the path ahead.

I peer down the hall, searching for any signs of movement or life. The outline of Lachlan's door is shrouded in darkness.

At least one of us is getting some sleep.

A chill runs down my spine as I hurry towards the foyer, tiptoeing carefully to avoid making any noise. As I enter the space, my eyes are drawn to a standing lamp in the corner of the room. It's utterly quiet. And I just remember Ailith telling me the doors lock overnight for the safety of the guests. The inn is small and doesn't have overnight staff, so it's crucial that the doors are secured once the bar closes down for the night. I make my way past the front desk, the click of my footsteps echo in the stillness.

I move through the small, arched hallway that leads to the kitchen. The light from the lamp barely penetrates the darkness here, and I feel my way along the wall until I reach the kitchen. The familiar smells of baking bread and simmering soup wash over me, leaving me with a sense of comfort.

I feel for the light switch, my fingers grazing the uneven texture of the kitchen wall. A weak glow flickers on in the corner. An ornate lamp sits on a small wooden table with papers strewn across it. It barely lights up the large kitchen, but I don't plan on spending too long in here.

My eyes quickly scan the countertop, searching for any signs of food. I spot a bag of bread, lying forgotten beside the fridge. My hand brushes against the cool metal of the fridge handle, and with a small tug, the door creaks open.

The cool air presses against my skin, sending goosebumps along my arms and legs. I release my robe, letting it hang loosely on either side of me. I locate some cheese and reach for it, but my eyes catch on a small glass container filled to the top with whipped cream. There is a note on it that reads, "Elle's - don't touch!"

Too bad she's not here to stop me.

I reach for the bowl and pull open the lid, tossing it on the counter. Dipping my finger into the sweet cream, I bring it up to my mouth and lick the foam off. It tastes amazing. So fresh. Much better than the store-bought stuff Dad buys to put in his coffee. I used to make fun of him for that until I tried it.

I could honestly eat this entire bowl.

"What are you doing?"

I yelp and the bowl nearly slips from my grasp. My back hits the fridge door as I turn; my heart is beating so fast it feels like it's going to launch out of my chest. I clutch the cold bowl tightly, focusing on the cold glass pressing into my skin as I try to calm my breathing.

"Fuck, Lachlan. You need to stop sneaking up on people like that."

He leans against the kitchen doorway in nothing but flannel sweatpants, his bare chest is on full display. His broad, muscular shoulders taper down to a chiseled torso that is taut with strength. The flannel sweatpants hanging low on his hips reveal the defined lines of his abs and the hard planes of his pelvis. He crosses his arms across his chest, his biceps bulge and ripple under the smooth skin. I clench my thighs, looking away from him.

"Couldn't sleep?"

I shake my head, my eyes on the bowl of cream in my hand as I dip my finger inside. "Why are you here?"

Bringing my finger to my lips, I savour the rich cream that clings to my skin. Slowly, I drag it from bottom to top, enjoying the sweet taste on my tongue. Lachlan's gaze turns ravenous, tracing every inch of my body from head to toe, before landing on my mouth. His tongue runs along his lip, his eyes hooded with desire. I hold his gaze, feeling a thrill run through me. With a deliberate pop, I release my finger from my mouth, watching as Lachlan's gaze darkens.

Dangerous territory, Avery.

"Do you want me to leave?" His voice is rough and thick.

I shrug. "You can leave if you want to."

My eyes catch on my open robe, remembering it's missing a belt and my half-naked body is on full display. My cheeks burn as I balance the bowl in my other hand, pinching my robe closed.

"I was hoping some food and whisky might help me fall asleep. Ailith said I could come here if I ever got hungry at night." I murmur.

Lachlan takes a step inside the kitchen, stopping at the far edge of the island.

"Are you hungry?" I continue.

"Not for food." He takes a step closer to me.

Oh Jesus.

More slow steps, and his heady scent surrounds me. My eyes roam down his stomach, taking the opportunity to really enjoy him up close, without wanting to hide or run from my emotions. Lachlan takes one final step, closing the distance between us, as he dips a finger into the bowl. I hold my breath as he lifts a blob of cream and sucks it off his finger. He takes a laboured breath, his eyes on mine as he dips the same finger back into the bowl. I watch as he withdraws it, the tip coated in creamy goodness. This time, he doesn't put it in his mouth.

He leans forward and smears the cream onto the hollow of my neck.

I'm not sure I'm breathing.

"What are you doing?" I croak.

"Tell me to leave," he urges, going in for more cream.

His cream soaked finger traces up my neck, all the way up

to my chin. He curls his finger under, nudging my face up as he stares down at me with the same desperate eyes in the forest at Kintail. Right before he kissed me.

I shake my head slowly.

He reaches down torturously slow, dipping his finger back into the bowl. Raising it up, he traces a path of cream from my chin to my lips. My mouth parts and I drag my tongue across the rough pad of his index finger, savouring the sweet flavour off his skin.

He hisses, closing his eyes.

"Avery," he whispers my name.

I quiver under his touch, my knuckles white from holding onto the glass bowl so tightly. Lachlan grabs the bowl from my clenched hands and places it on the counter behind me.

CHAPTER THIRTY-FOUR

"Tell me to leave, Avery." Lachlan stands frozen, breathing slow through his nose.

"I don't want you to leave."

He glances down, gently tugging at the edge of my robe and releasing it from my hold. The material falls free, exposing my body. The back of his hand brushes along my chest before he removes it, taking in a sharp breath.

"No?" he asks, his fierce eyes on mine as he gives me another chance to turn him away. To reject him.

"Do you want me to ask you to leave? It shouldn't be this hard to want this." Cream drips down my collarbone and his eyes trace the movement.

I remain frozen, holding my breath in anticipation for the incoming chill. He could walk away. Leave me here like this; vulnerable and insecure with cream dripping down my neck.

Lachlan grips the back of my hair, tilting my face up. He bends down, his warm tongue makes contact with my skin as Lachlan slowly licks the cream from my chest up to my collarbone to my neck. Sharp tingles erupt from my spine, shooting down my legs, caressing my knees before settling in between my toes. He tastes my chin, hovering above as he stares down at me through heavy eyelids.

"I've wanted you for so fucking long," his breath falls against my lips. "I tried to stay away from you, but I don't think I can do it any longer."

"Then don't," I murmur.

My words break the tether holding him back as his lips crush into mine. His grip tightens in my hair and I dive into him. With each breathless gasp, I dig my nails deeper into his corded shoulders, feeling the strength of his muscles beneath my fingertips.

I'm on fucking fire.

His rapid heart races against my own. Lachlan grabs my ass, pulling me up onto the counter as he steps in between my legs. The robe slides off my shoulders, pooling around me. And we become all mouth and tongue and hands, as if we're racing towards an imaginary finish line after a triathlon. Pleasure rolls through me as my core throbs with fresh desire.

This feels so good. His touch is comforting and thrilling all at once, and I can't get enough. I'm trapped in a lustful trance and I don't ever want to wake up.

Lachlan trails kisses down my neck, his hand cups my breast overtop of the lacy material of my bra. His thumb grazes my hard nipple, as the rush of pleasure steals the air from my lungs. He pulls my bra strap down, licking and biting my shoulder before he kisses overtop of the bruised flesh. The wide outline of his erection rubs against my inner thigh, and I moan, suddenly needing to feel him all over me. Inside me.

"God, you're the bonniest woman I've ever seen. So fucking beautiful," he whispers against my skin. The tip of his tongue traces my shoulder down to my chest, before he pulls my taut nipple into his mouth. The sensation radiates through my stomach, settling heavy in my clit.

I close my eyes. Needing more of him, so much more.

"Avery, look at me," he commands through clenched teeth. Desire is laced in his beautiful accent, as he says my name like it's the last word he'll ever utter.

I open my eyes, watching as he grates my nipple in between his teeth, lapping it with his tongue while his knuckles trace down my stomach, grazing over my wet underwear. My hips jolt, as he draws lazing circles on my inner thighs with the back of his hand.

I'm going to combust right in this kitchen if he doesn't touch me soon.

I pull on his hair and he laughs softly against my breast, the vibration from his throat sends me into a frenzy.

"Are you teasing me, Lachlan?"

My question is silenced by his lips, hot and demanding as they meet mine. I feel myself drowning in his embrace, losing myself in the rapture of the moment. The question I asked fades into nothingness, replaced only by this all-consuming desire.

"What if I am?" he whispers. "Will you beg me, Nessi? I'd love to hear that mouth of yours beg." His voice ragged and desperate against my lips as he pulls the bottom of my underwear to the side. I gasp as his thumb brushes across my tender skin.

Holy shit, is this really happening?

I run my nails down his chest, hooking my fingers into his waistband and pressing the heel of my palm into his hard length.

Boundaries.

We need to set them before this goes any further.

I lean back, staring at his swollen lips. "Lachlan...if we do this, it means nothing. Just sex," I swallow hard, getting lost in his ocean eyes. "That's all I can give."

"Just sex," he utters against my lips before fusing us back together. I tighten my legs around his waist, surrendering myself, as if a dam has broken inside my mind. I finally let go, as we kiss, suck, and explore one another ravenously. I'm intoxicated by him, by his touch, his lips, his tongue, his hands. I explore his body while every one of my senses kicks into high gear.

Reaching behind me, Lachlan unclasps my bra and flings the material to the side. He cups one breast while his mouth closes around the other, his tongue circling and pulling on my nipple. I whimper, running my nails through his hair and scratching down his back. His fingers brush along the band of my shorts, drawing lazy circles on my skin, as he plays with my sanity. His touch tempers and the closeness of his fingers moves through my body like wild rapids.

I groan and pull on his hair hard. He snickers, pressing a kiss to my lips. "Tell me what you want."

"I want you to stop being a fucking tease," I murmur.

A deep laugh rumbles from within Lachlan as he leans forward, his lips hovering close to my ear. I can feel his hot breath brush against my skin, scattering all my thoughts. "I can't wait to fuck this attitude out of you. See what else this dirty mouth of yours can do."

"I'd like to see you try."

His slow, tender touches are so close to my core that it feels painfully punishing. And right as I'm about to lose my mind; he presses his thumb to my clit, drawing torturously slow circles. I swallow down a moan, arching my back and moving into his touch.

Lachlan's breaths are as ragged as mine. The pressure of his thumb is constant as my need grows stronger, deeper with every stroke. He pushes a finger inside me, igniting my body and we both curse at the same time.

"Fuck, Avery, you're so wet." His voice drips with lust as he works my clit, teasing and playing me like a well crafted instrument. He adds a second finger inside me and I moan into his mouth, as he swallows my whimpers like a starved animal. Our tongues lap desperately against one another, pushing, tugging, biting. I can't get enough, no matter how hard I try.

He nips at my lip, dragging the soft flesh through his teeth as he glances down at my body. Watching me come to life with his touch. Soft moans and short breaths are all I can offer. Everything falls away, and it's just us, only us, in this moment.

His fingers plunge in and out of me, slow and deep. Suddenly the pressure from everything doubles, as an unimaginable pleasure writhes within me. Lachlan kisses my neck, as he makes his way up and down my body, like he can't possibly get enough. The room fills with the sounds of our breathless moans and soft grunts.

I reach for his pants just as a loud cough comes from outside the kitchen.

We both freeze.

But he doesn't stop.

Lachlan's eyes grow darker, wilder as he presses his palm to my mouth while his other hand continues to push in and out of me slowly. My eyes roll to the back of my head, as a life ruining orgasm begins to chase after me.

"Lachlan, is that ye in there?" That voice belongs to Duncan.

Oh my God—Duncan is about to walk in here and see his nephew's fingers plunged inside me with my breasts on full display.

"Aye, it's me. Just grabbing a bite. Go back to bed, Duncan."

"Erm...I...I'll be back in ten to start preppin' the kitchen. Place better be empty when I get back." Duncan's voice drifts farther away with his hurried footsteps.

I try to push against Lachlan to get down, but he stands firm, unmovable like a giant boulder.

"No way I'm letting you leave without finishing. I need to feel you come all over my fingers." He curls his fingers inside me as his thumb expertly works my clit. Lachlan bites down on my neck softly. And the pleasure and pain combination is enough to shove me over the edge.

"Oh fuck...Lachlan." I lose my measly fight. My eyes fluttering shut as ecstasy rushes through me.

He works quickly, his fingers slick with my wetness as he pumps in and out of me. I wrap my hands around his neck, clinging to him as my body shakes with savage pleasure. My mind goes hazy and my thoughts drop like pins all around me.

Lachlan groans, and my nails dig into the back of his neck as I cry out against his lips. My body coils as the orgasm detonates inside me, my legs shudder and my breaths jagged and uneven. His fingers guide me through the swells of rapture and he kisses me as I come down from the high.

He withdraws his soaked fingers and brings them to his mouth. I lean my head back, panting as I watch him lick one finger, then the other, lapping up the evidence of my pleasure.

I stare at him in utter shock, the sight of it only turning me on more.

"I've been dying to know what you taste like." He mewls, licking both fingers clean. "So fucking delicious."

Holy shit. That might be the hottest thing I've ever seen.

He cups my neck, pushing his tongue back into my mouth. His erection pressing hard against my drenched core.

"We have to leave. Duncan is going to be back any minute," I breathe out.

"You go. I've got this." He turns and reaches for the bowl of whipped cream.

"Are you sure? What about you?" I glance down at the hard bulge in his pants.

"I'm fine. Go, before we both get caught." He kisses me for a long second, planting a peck on my nose before releasing me.

I hop off the counter, pulling my robe over my shoulders and grabbing my bra off the floor. Pausing before stepping out of the kitchen, I turn to see Lachlan leaning against the sink, staring after me with an ear-splitting grin on his face.

I rush back to my room. Closing the door shut, and leaning my head against the cold wood, I stare up at the ceiling, smiling. In complete disbelief about everything that just happened.

My body buzzes from the afterglow long after I climb into bed.

But for reasons I can't explain, a sudden wave of shame floods me, right before my eyes close shut and sleep takes me.

I see her face as soon as I open my eyes, and for a moment, I forget she's not beside me. A glorious moment, filled with only memories of last night. The feel of her soft skin against mine, the sound of her breathless whimpers, the sweet taste of her arousal on my tongue.

I think it was the best fucking night of my life. I'm no longer swimming against the current, I'm drowning in it. And I never want to come back up for air.

A light layer of sweat coats my skin as I whip off the blanket, groaning in frustration at my hard dick. I haven't been this consistently hard since I was a young lad with raging hormones.

The problem is I can't stop thinking about her.

I cursed Duncan over and over again for interrupting us as I tidied up the kitchen before heading for my room. I stood outside her door for a long time, considered knocking but talked myself out of it every time I raised my hand. Wanting to finish what we started but I also wanted to make sure she was all right. I'm fully aware of the line she set, about this meaning nothing, but I'm not certain it's that easy for me.

256

My craving for her has only intensified.

Spending the last few days together, exploring the highlands with Avery, my chest burned with an intense passion I could no longer suppress. With each fleeting moment, I found myself drawn even closer to her. Her raw beauty was undeniable, and I could see every emotion that she tried to hide reflected in her stunning brown eyes. I was captivated by her every move, and I couldn't resist the pull. It's difficult to put into words just how I felt, but after we kissed, I knew with every fiber of my being that I couldn't turn away from her anymore.

I'm willing to accept whatever time we have together, cherishing every moment with her. Whatever she desires, she can take from me. I am hers to give. She wants my fucking soul? She can have it.

I came back to Corran in search of answers, and with each passing day, it's becoming clearer what I want.

What I need to do.

Bloody hell, I'm so fucked.

I WALK through the pub doors, spotting Elle behind the bar. She's busy taking a breakfast order, as my eyes sweep the place, looking for Avery. She wasn't in her room this morning, which means if she's not here, she's gone.

Waiting at the bar for Elle to finish, I keep glancing over my shoulder at the door. It's only 7:48 a.m., where the hell could she have gone this early?

"Hiya... you're never here this early. Coffee?" Elle's voice draws my attention back. I offer her a lazy smile and nod.

Grabbing a fresh mug, she fills it with black coffee and hands it to me.

Raising the mug to my lips, I look behind my shoulder again.

"She's not here."

"Where is she?"

"Why the sudden interest, Lachy?"

I sigh, running my hand down my face as frustration hums under my skin. "I'm not in the bloody mood, Elle. It's a little too early for Avery to be out and about, don't you think?"

"No. She's usually up early, finding a new trail or loch to admire," shrugging, Elle grabs clean mugs out of a washing tray and starts putting them away.

"Did you see her?"

"Maybe. Did something happen?" She pauses, her brows furrow as she leans towards me.

"Nothing happened. I just need to speak to her."

A dreadful feeling settles in my stomach as Elle sighs exasperatedly. Did Avery leave and she doesn't want to be the one to deliver the news? What if I crossed a line last night?

"I just barely caught her as I was walking in for my early shift this mornin'. It was dark still, maybe around half-past four. She seemed to be in a rush, mentioned going to Fort William. She was a bit flustered, actually. Are ye certain ye had nothing to do with that?"

"Shit...I don't know. Thanks, Elle." I lift my mug, draining the rest of the hot bitter liquid.

"Woah! Where are you going?"

"Fort William," I say, striding out of the pub before she has a chance to stop me.

Deep down, I know I shouldn't follow Avery, especially if she wants to be alone. It's not fair to go after her when she clearly wants to sort through her thoughts. But she's been doing things alone for far too long. And I'm not going to sit around here, while she navigates through emotions I may have caused, all on her own. There are many things I should do when it comes to her, but I know that waiting around here all day is not one of them. I need to make sure she's okay.

I could text her.

The thought doesn't even register as I run into the carpark, glaring up at the sunny sky as I head for my bike.

Cutting an hour of time on the road by taking my motorbike, I finally reach centre of town in Fort William. I turn the engine off, planting my feet on the dusty cobblestone before lifting the helmet off my head. I run a hand quickly through my hair before grabbing my ball cap and sunglasses. The sky is cloudy but Fort William is always bustling, it being a major tourist attraction, and I can't take my chances here, nor do I want the additional stress.

Pulling up the hood of my jumper and zipping up my leather coat, I get off my bike and make my way over to the small coffee shop across the street.

Fort William is known as Scotland's outdoor playhouse. It is the largest town in the highlands and lies in the shadow of Ben Nevis, one of my favourite places to explore.

Even though it's slow season right now, the streets are still bursting with tourists and early morning shoppers. Avery could be anywhere. She could be at Ben Nevis or Neptune's Staircase, a beautiful walkway on the Caledonian Canal. She could simply be wandering the streets. I have no idea where she is, but I'm not leaving until I find her.

I feel like a stranger to myself. This attraction is new to me; I've never felt such a strong pull towards anyone before. It's overwhelming to the point where I would normally isolate myself and seek professional help, but I can't seem to get enough of her. Like a drug addict chasing that first high, unrelenting and dangerous as fuck.

I tried to fight it, to stay away. Convince myself that I don't want her, that she's someone I shouldn't get close to. That she is better off without me, but I've never been good at lying to myself. I'll keep her safe while she's here and make sure my world doesn't taint hers.

Glancing into the coffee shop and realizing Avery's not here, I begin to make my way up the narrow stony sidewalk. A couple of older women pause and glare at me, but I bend my head down and continue my pursuit. Suddenly filled with fear and excitement at the idea of this mini-chase.

Do I have the same effect on her as she has on me? God, I bloody hope so.

Colourful buildings and stores line the streets, all glued together, in different shapes and sizes, but perfectly mapped out in the historical city. Coffee shops, bookstores, quaint antique stores—it's all here. There is something here for everyone.

My head whips side to side, hoping to catch sight of curly brown hair, but she's nowhere to be found. She could be on a hike. I should just call her.

Maybe you're an idiot and should not have come here in the first place.

Probably...but it's too late for that now.

Breathless from running up and down these streets, I round

the corner, my eyes land on a vibrant green door belonging to a bookstore. The small brown building is situated in the corner, with a faded green stone roof and four tall window displays. Something tells me she could be in there, getting lost between pages of books.

Cupping my hands around my eyes, I peer inside the window, a sea of books and tall brown aisles cram inside the tight space. No sign of Avery. The clerk looks up at me and grimaces. I flash her a smile, stepping up to the green door and pulling on the copper handle.

The door chime sounds loudly above my head, as the smell of old and new pages fill the room with a comforting aroma. It reminds me of the school library when I was a young lad, from a time when life was simple. A time when I was just a person and not an exhibit to be used.

The place looks deserted, except for the bored clerk standing behind the register.

There are four aisles that run down the entire length of the store all the way to the back. I peek down the first two but don't see anyone. Walking over to the third aisle, my body lights up the instant I spot her, my heart pounding furiously in my chest.

Avery is standing farther down the aisle, staring at a couple of books in her hands, likely contemplating which one to buy.

I'll buy her the entire bookstore if it'll make her happy. If I can see her smile, spread out in my bed with a book in her hand...while I bury my face between her legs.

I walk to the next shelf and quietly pad down the cushioned floor. Pausing when I see the outline of her body on the other side, she shuffles and I peer through the small slit above the cascading books lining the shelves. Her olive skin is flushed, likely from the bite of the cold October air. Her chocolate hair is down and in waves, spilling effortlessly around her. She's in black leggings, wearing hiking boots, and drowning in an oversized black jumper. And her perfectly full lips are bare and red, as if she's been chewing on them.

I pull out a thick hardcover, giving myself the perfect window to watch Avery.

She doesn't glance up.

Now that I've had a taste of her, I can't stop myself from wanting more. She's bewitching. Bold eyebrows, full lips, and those big whisky eyes that can see right through my fucking soul.

Look up, Nessi.

A faint smile brushes her lips, her attention gripped by the book in her hand. Her eyes grow wide, and she pinches her bottom lip between her teeth. That sends a shot of desire straight to my dick. She does this a lot, and I don't even think she realizes she's doing it, but it drives me fucking insane. Letting out an exasperated sigh, Avery giggles quietly. I reckon she's reading something dirty. Her cheeks are flushed the same as that night at Ailith and Duncan's, when I caught her reading erotica.

This feels intimate. Like I'm part of a hidden moment that's meant only for her. Watching her in secret, I want to reenact whatever she's reading, just so I can feel her body writhing under me. As she shudders, letting out those breathy moans I love.

I place the book back and the hardcover falls against the wooden shelf, making a loud thud. Avery's eyes snap up but I step out of of her line of sight. Running my fingers along the spines of the books, I walk further down the aisle. Stopping to pull out a bigger hardcover, all about the history of World War I.

A few seconds tick by and a book from the other side is pulled out. Avery gasps just as I glance up to see her whisky-brown eyes glaring at me with shock.

She's utterly flabbergasted and I drink it up, attempting to wipe the coy smile off my face.

Everything inside me feels whole in the span of a second, just from one look from her.

"Lachlan? What the fuck?!" she hisses.

I don't answer her as I gently place the book back on the shelf, blocking her view. She grumbles, and I have to stop myself from bursting into laughter. Practically running down the aisle, I hear her shuffling as she matches my pace from the other side. A giant wall of books stands in between us, but not for long. I'm going to make sure of that.

I pick up the pace and reach the back wall, which is also covered in books from floor to ceiling.

Avery steps in front of me, her cheeks are a deep red, her lips already calling my name.

"What are you doing here?" she whisper-yells.

I shrug. "You seem delighted to see me."

"Did you follow me? Who's the stalker now?" She's got such a prickly attitude, and I want nothing more than to fuck it out of her, right here...up against this shelf. My hard cock presses against the seam of my pants.

Settle down.

"Do you want me to leave?" I reach for her hand, stepping closer to her.

She bites her abused lip, looking down as her fingers play with the edge of a hardcover.

Avery can pretend to be annoyed, but I can see right through her. I close the small distance between us, the tip of my boots brushing hers, but she doesn't step away. Her eyes crawl up my chest as she takes a shallow breath.

I lean forward, brushing her hair with my nose as my lips graze the top of her ear. "Were you running again, lass?"

She shudders, exhaling. "No."

I arch my eyebrow, calling her out.

"Maybe," she sighs.

"To get away from me?" My heart aches in my chest.

"No," she says, placing her hand softly on my thundering heart.

I cover her hand with my palm. "You don't have to run anymore. Not from me. Not ever."

I catch her staring at my lips, and she leans in as if unable to resist the magnetic pull between us.

I fist my fingers in her hair, pulling her into my chest. She smells like the forest after a rainfall. I trace my thumb over her tortured lip, feeling her body shiver.

Every inch of my body yearns for hers in an endless, insatiable hunger.

Avery's eyes grow heavy with lust, and I walk her back against the bookshelves, kissing her with dire urgency.

We collide like angry waves crashing in the untold ocean. Electricity coils down my body, and every single moment, every glance, every touch, every breath, all crashes into me at once.

Her hands are frenzied as they lace through my hair, pulling on my jacket like she is trying to fuse us together permanently. I cup her ass and pull her up, pushing her further into the brown wood. She wraps her legs around my waist and I thrust my hard dick against her entrance.

Planting a hand on the bookshelf above her head, I start thrusting into her slowly. Too many clothes separate us, but it feels so fucking good. She feels right.

"Oh, God....Lachlan...I..." she whimpers against my lips.

I run my other hand up underneath her jumper. My fingers relishing against the warmth of her skin. She's wearing a tight sports bra underneath, and I feel her hard nipples poking through the material.

She pulls away, panting through swollen lips. Not sure why

she stopped, but I move back in for her lips just as she tugs on my neck hair. All the while grinding her hips against me, her back arching off the wooden bookshelf as I hold her there.

"Lachlan...we're in public," she whispers.

I lean in and run my nose along hers. "I don't care. And neither should you. Get out of your head."

"What if we get caught?" she asks.

Those words snap me back into reality, and suddenly I remember who I am. There could be onlookers, or the clerk could recognize me. It could ruin everything. It could put Avery in danger.

Placing her on the ground, I plant a kiss on the tip of her nose and release her, as I reach inside my jeans to adjust myself.

I look up to find Avery staring at my crotch, lips parted as she slowly swallows. Her eyes snap up to mine and she turns beet red, stepping behind me to pick up my hat.

"Are you okay?"

She nods but doesn't look up at me. I grab her chin, tilting her face up.

"Are you telling me the truth?"

She bites her lip for the millionth time, drawing a groan from me. This fucking hard-on is never going to go away.

"Avery, if you don't stop doing that, I'm going to rip off your trousers right here and get on my fucking knees. Is that what you want? You want my tongue inside you in the back of this bookstore?"

Her eyes widen in disbelief.

"Oh, Jesus...you can't say shit like that." Her cheeks turn crimson, and she shuts her eyes.

Maybe she's embarrassed to be turned on, or lacks the confidence to let her body feel whatever it is she is feeling. I'm not sure what type of damage her arsehole ex-boyfriend inflicted for her to lose her confidence. She's the most beautiful woman I've ever seen, and I intend to prove that to her.

I don't ask for permission before capturing her mouth. This kiss is deep, passionate, and meaningful. Because I want her to open up, to show all of herself to me. I want to worship her day and night. I tuck a strand of hair behind her ear and caress her cheek with my thumb. She takes a deep breath, smiling up at me.

"You ready?"

"For what?" She pauses.

"I want to take you somewhere."

She dips her head and I kiss her cheek before wrapping my hand in hers. I bend down, picking up all the books she had in her hands, as we make our way to the front of the store.

"What are you doing with those?"

"Buying them."

"What? Why?"

"Because I want to watch you reading dirty books strewn naked in my bed." I give her a lopsided grin. And the smile on her face is everything I need.

I'll happily drown in her until our time runs out.

CHAPTER THIRTY-SEVEN

avery

"Put it on." Lachlan holds out a helmet as he leans against an all-black, edgy motorbike.

"Absolutely not." I take a step back and my foot catches the edged curb.

Lachlan reaches out, grabbing my arm and pulling me close to him.

"Great reflexes. Now, let's take my car."

"Do you not trust me?" He gives me a sly grin, his eyes a different shade of blue today.

"No." The lie tastes bitter coming out of my mouth.

Lachlan looks at me with understanding as he unclasps the buckle on the helmet, placing it gently over top of my head. I don't stop him. I just stare at him and remember the way his tongue explored mine in the bookstore, last night in the kitchen. And how much I want to feel it against other parts of my body.

"Avery, I would never let anything happen to you."

You're so screwed.

He takes my silence as permission to continue, carefully

tucking my long hair behind my shoulders and around the strap of the helmet. His eyes lock on my lips for a lingering second, before he walks to his bike, lifting one leg over, straddling the seat. His muscles groan and stretch underneath his black leather jacket. The man is a work of art, truly.

Can I take him home when I leave?

No, which is exactly why this situation is perfect. There is no future here, it's just me and him existing in the now. Sharing stolen glances and urgent kisses. And I'm okay with that. More than okay. I want this and I never thought I would. After what happened, I never thought I would feel this kind of desire for anyone. That alone is cause for a celebratory dance.

Chestnut strands glisten in the rain, right before Lachlan's head disappears under a black helmet. He flips up the visor, eyes only on me as he extends his arm. Taking a deep breath, I push away my growing desires and walk to him. He helps me get on the back of the bike, and I nuzzle close, wrapping my arms tightly around his waist.

"You ready?"

I nod and he flips his visor down. The bike roars to life, and we pull out before I can change my mind.

Buildings and narrow streets begin to blur as the cold, sharp wind steals my breath. The thrill takes me by surprise, and I don't try to hide my grin. Adrenaline courses through my body as the bike speeds down winding roads. The wind whips my hair, smacking it around my face. But somehow against all this noise, my heart is quiet. Another stolen moment carved out just for us.

Fort William fades into the background, along with castles and shops. Lochs and hiking trails whiz by my eyes, gone in a flash. The bike slows as Lachlan pulls onto a stretch of road, lined with tall trees and brown stone fences. We pass by random cottages, but for the most part it's just green landscape and water surrounding us, as mountains sit tall in the background.

I squeeze my arms tighter to make sure I'm actually here. That this is really happening.

After I got raped, I couldn't picture myself with a man. Sometimes in therapy, Dr. Samson would get me to exercise imagining the future. A future that was realistic but one where I was happy. Never once did I insert a man into that exercise. It never appealed to me. I didn't have those desires anymore and felt disgusted and ashamed for so long, I could barely stand my own reflection. There was no world where I thought this type of longing would be possible for someone like me.

Eventually I moved on with John, knowing a relationship out of years of friendship would feel safe. That maybe I could finally heal, be happy with someone. But when we were together, I was trapped in my head, unable to let go of that tainted image of myself. The broken woman who didn't deserve to be touched.

But last night, with Lachlan, I didn't even have to think about it. I simply slipped away and free fell with my arms wide open over the cliff. It was everything and nothing.

I'm so lost in my own thoughts that when I finally see it, my body vibrates with pure joy. I heave at the magnificent sight of the hauntingly vast viaduct known as Glenfinnan Railway. A towering structure of rust-coloured brick, stretches out before me, its arches framing the sweeping valley below, dotted with fields of wildflowers.

Being a book nerd, I was obsessed with Harry Potter growing up, so of course, I recognize this place. I've been dreaming of seeing this railway for a long time, and the fact that Lachlan brought me here, without knowing, makes my heart swell.

The bike slows down and Lachlan pulls into an empty, flattened patch of grass. It doesn't look like a typical parking spot, and there is no one else here, but there are definite tire tracks on the ground. I stare up at the arches above, unable to keep my eyes away. The whole thing feels surreal, like stepping into a giant painting. I'm awestruck as I take it all in, my movements mechanical as Lachlan helps me off the bike.

"I knew you'd love it," he says, grabbing my helmet and storing it away.

"It's...amazing. No, it's more than amazing. I have no words."

He laughs, grabbing my hand as we walk up a hill. The place is empty aside from the soft sounds of the wind, the humming of tall grass brushing against our ankles, and the whir of rushing water in the distance.

I needed this today.

My fingers itch to sketch, too bad I left my bag in the car, which is currently parked at Fort William. We walk for longer than I expect, ending at a small forest with the perfect clearing showcasing the railway and the mountains perched behind the arches.

A backpack drops to the ground, as Lachlan lays a blanket down on the damp grass. He sits, patting the spot next to him.

"I didn't even see you carrying that." I laugh nervously, nudging towards the bag.

"Just a few supplies I carry in the bike. I hike a lot, so I like to be prepared," he explains, handing me a bottle of water.

"You just go riding for hours?"

"Aye, getting lost in nature."

I sigh. "I wish I could do that."

"You are." A deep furrow forms between his brows, his gaze intense.

"I mean all the time."

"Ah." He looks out at the landscape. "This is temporary for me. I don't have this type of freedom usually."

"Work?"

He dips his chin, expression suddenly weighted. "Yeah, work takes a lot out of me."

"The liquor business?"

"No." He whispers.

My heart drops at that small confession. It's the first time he's admitted to something else burdening him. But before I have a chance to say something else, he pulls his bag towards him.

"I got you something."

He pulls out a beautifully leather-bound sketchbook and a delicate glass container filled with all sizes of charcoal pencils. My mouth falls open.

"I figured you might want to sketch." He shrugs, trying to pass this off as something small. Even though that's far from the truth.

"It's beautiful, Lachlan," I breathe out, running my hand across the smooth cover. "I can't accept...wait...when did you get this?"

I glance up at him but he's not looking at me, fiddling with his sunglasses in his hands.

"It doesn't matter."

"It matters to me." I whisper.

His jaw tightens as he releases a breath. "Awhile ago. I've been holding on to it, waiting for the perfect time to give it to you."

I throw my arms around him, hugging him tightly. His chest gently shakes against mine, and I can feel his laughter brush my neck as he buries his face against me, tightening our embrace.

"Thank you. That's the most thoughtful thing anyone has ever done for me."

I'm not sure how to process this, or what to do with it even if he had told me exactly when he got the sketchbook. Part of me doesn't want to know. Why would he buy this for me and carry it around in his bike for days, weeks...when it was perfectly clear he wanted me to leave? Maybe he never did. Or maybe, he had grabbed this stuff in the morning. What difference does it make? This is just a very kind gesture and nothing else.

It has to be nothing more.

I waste no time opening my new sketchbook. A comfortable silence settles between us as I start to draw the landscape before me. We remain quiet for a while, with me sketching and Lachlan watching, both of us at ease with the peaceful atmosphere.

"Why did you disappear this morning?" His voice lulls me in.

I was hoping this wouldn't come up, that we could just move past it, but I know Lachlan won't drop it.

"I didn't want to see Duncan."

Which was true, but not the entire reason. I looked up to find his eyes on me, watching curiously as he waits for me to say more. My eyes fall to my lap and I resume drawing.

"Did I make you uncomfortable last night? Went too far? Because if I did —" His voice is quiet, etched in pain.

My brows leap. "No, Lachlan. Not at all."

I take a deep breath, feeling my face grow warm. "I wanted that to happen, I just..."

My words drop dead. I feel Lachlan's molten gaze on me before his fingers wrap around mine. A silent show of support, as he waits patiently for me to work this out.

You just what?

Felt shameful for wanting him or exposing myself in that way, when I've been uncomfortable in my skin for so long. Maybe I felt shame because I didn't feel guilty for enjoying the way my body lit up when he touched me, kissed me, when he licked his fingers clean after they were inside me. I felt guilty for loving every second of it.

"I don't do this, and it all happened so fast...I just needed to sit with it for a bit, I guess. Clear my head—whatever you want to call it. And I couldn't do that in Corran, knowing Duncan probably put the pieces together last night. And you never came to my room." My face is painfully hot as I glance up at him. "I didn't know where your head was at...after."

Lachlan leans in, his lips inches from mine. A bolt of electricity hums under my skin, licking at my flesh like lightening.

"You want to know where my head was at?" he says. "I stood outside your door for a long time, wanting to walk in there and spend the rest of the week in bed with you, exploring every inch of your body. But I also know that you need me to take this slow, and I will because, God, Avery...I want to take my time with you."

He didn't even have to touch me for my body to burn. I could imagine it, his hands, his lips, his tongue...exploring every inch of me, deliciously torturing me until I couldn't take no more. My new favourite phrase in a Scottish accent has to be *I want to take my time with you.*

I need a distraction before I jump his bones right here, right now.

"What's your last name?" I blurt out.

His expression changes and he waits a little too long to answer.

"Umm...Carnell," he says, quickly.

"Lachlan Carnell. Very Scottish." I smile to myself.

"Yours?"

"Harris."

He nods, glancing back at me as the corner of his mouth lifts up. But something about the smile doesn't quite reach his eyes.

"Avery..." His voice is dark again as he inches closer, his breath tickling my ear. "What were you reading at the book-store earlier that made you blush?"

And that distraction lasted a millisecond. I made a mental note to stop reading smut in front of him, because now my face is going from warm to burning hot.

"A book."

"What kind of book?" He smirks.

"I think you know."

"Aye, but I want to hear you say it."

"Romance." I cough, scratching so hard against the paper that my charcoal breaks in half.

"Describe it to me." He whispers, his deep voice sends a needful shudder down my spine.

Nope. I can't. It's too much. It's one thing to read the stuff but saying it out loud to someone is an entirely different thing.

"You practically bought the entire bookstore, including the book I was reading...You can read it back at the inn."

My fingers scratch the paper hurriedly, black coal denting the soft paper.

"By the way, that was stupid...I mean, I can't take all of those books with me. Also, I've read some of those books but I'm sure you can enjoy them when I'm gone or lend them to Elle, we know Ailith—"

"Avery, stop rambling." He growls, cutting me off. "Tell me."

Lachlan cocks his head, his smile broadening.

Are you actually considering this, Avery?

I can do this, but I don't have to stare into his bottomless ocean eyes as I say it. I focus on the dark lines on the paper in front of me, as I continue to trace the outline of the railway.

"It was a random chapter. I like to do that sometimes, open a book midway and read a passage to see if the words intrigue me enough to continue." Lachlan's fingers brush through my hair, causing small shivers to erupt at the base of my neck.

"He had her pinned to the bed, blindfolded, hands tied with a rope above her head. He was edging her, drawing out her pleasure until she was shaking with need. Then he buried his face in between her legs, fucking her with his tongue. And when she was done, he took his fingers and pressed them into her mouth so she could taste her own pleasure."

I can't believe I just said that.

My fingers are white, shaking slightly as I hold onto the soft leather of my sketchbook. Lachlan presses his hooked finger under my chin, turning my face towards him.

"You're going to fucking ruin me, aren't you?" he breathes.

Lachlan's large hand splays across my neck, warm and perfectly rough. His calloused palm rubs lightly against my skin as he closes his fingers. He doesn't squeeze, just rests his hand there, feeling my erratic pulse. It's enough to light something carnal inside me. I shudder a moan, closing my eyes.

Reaching behind him, I pull off his cap.

"I want you, so fucking badly it hurts," I whisper against his lips, throwing the hat somewhere in the grass as I straddle him.

His lips collide with mine. We kiss and suck and clash hungrily. It's primal and desperate and so rough. It's everything desires are made of. Every emotion from the last two days explodes around us, more intense than ever before. He pulls away and I groan at the loss of his mouth on mine. He quickly glances behind him, and then past my shoulder. I follow his gaze but there is no one there. Turning back to face him, I'm suddenly forced down to the ground. The air gets knocked out of my lungs as Lachlan cradles the back of my head, hovering over top of me.

He plants his knees on either side of me, sitting on them as he stares down at me like I'm his next meal. His eyes track down my body, and I feel so utterly self conscious. So out of his league. He pulls off his leather jacket and throws it on the ground. He rolls up his sleeves, showcasing the veins running down his arms and my insides tighten at the sight of him.

This feels like a dream.

I reach up, running my hands under his shirt.

"Fuck...Avery," he groans before he comes down on top of me. We're all hands, lips, and teeth again, and I drift away.

He pulls up my sweater, cupping my breasts before tugging hard on my sports bra, yanking the material over my chest. I hiss as the cold air bites my bare skin. Taking one breast into his mouth, his warm tongue sucks hard, while his fingers tug playfully on my other nipple. Pleasure fills my lungs, equal sensations of cold and warmth pinching my bare skin.

Pulling my nipple through his teeth, he drags it out slowly, eyes never leaving mine. He takes pleasure in watching me combust like this. I watch as his tongue crawls up to my lips, before he kisses me deeply, with complete passion. Running his hand through my hair, tugging at the scalp, he angles my face to explore my mouth deeper. When we're both breathless, he pulls away, leaving kisses on my cheek, nose, eyes. Looking down at me as if he's seeing me for the first time.

"You're so fucking beautiful. Bare to me in the open field, like a true goddess in nature."

His words make me shudder as I pant desperately for air. For him.

"Tell me what you want." He licks my bottom lip before pulling it between his teeth.

"You...I want you."

He leans back, searching my eyes, looking for God knows what. "Are you sure? Because I want you to enjoy every bit of this, and I need you to tell me if it's ever too much."

How does he do this? Make me feel so completely safe and wanted.

"Don't hold back," I say.

CHAPTER THIRTY-EIGHT

avery

I lace my hand through his hair and urge his mouth back down to mine, drowning in the feeling of him. We become a frantic force of pulling and pushing. His heat rushes over me like a tidal wave. I palm his hard cock and run my hand up and down his length. I can tell he's big and wide. Maybe too big. I've never been with someone his size. I know that's supposed to deter me but it only makes me want him more. To feel him inside me. I try to open his belt, but he stops me, tightening his hold around my wrist and pinning it above my head.

"No touching." He growls as he tugs on my nipple. A moan escapes my lips, and Lachlan tugs harder, causing pain and pleasure to skate across my sensitive skin.

Kisses pepper down my stomach, mixed with teeth and tongue, as Lachlan makes his way down my body. Sitting on his heels, he hooks his fingers on either side of my pants before yanking them down, along with my underwear. I try moving my legs, but quickly realize I can't. The tight material of my pants is bunched up close to my feet. My chunky hiking boots block the clothing, acting like a rope around my ankles.

I'm butt naked lying on a blanket, in front of the famous Glenfinnan, in the middle of the day.

Completely bare and exposed to this man, who is going to have his way with me, because I told him to not hold back. This all should scare me, making me want to run away screaming, but it only excites me. More than I care to admit. His eyes drink me in slowly, and I blush, suddenly feeling the need to cover myself up. I reach my arm across my chest, trying to hide.

"Don't you dare," he demands. Lachlan pulls my arm away and holds it above my head again. I whimper, having just been freed.

He pinches my nipple in between his fingers, causing a moan out of me. Wetness drips down in between my legs and I'm worried he's going to see it.

"I need you to get out of your head, Avery. You're safe, I'll take care of you. You are breathtaking, and I'm going to prove it to you if it's the last thing I do." His fingers trail past my naval, softly grazing my clit and pausing at my opening. I gasp at his touch, writhing with anticipation. He watches me carefully, sliding one finger inside me.

"So fucking wet," he groans, lacing his fingers in my hand that's pressed into the cold grass. His eyes pierce me, tracing the contours of my body as he pushes a second finger inside me.

"Oh, my God." I gasp as he leans down, biting my neck and kissing the marks on my sensitive flesh.

I close my eyes, letting the pleasure take hold of me. My fingers dig into his hand, pressing me into the earth while I pull and tug on his hair with my other hand. He moans into my breast, the sound of his pleasure nearly enough to shove me over the edge.

One minute I'm chasing my climax, the next I'm being

dragged into the middle of the blanket by my ankles. I try to sit up on my elbows, protest but his fingers push back inside me. I moan loudly at the unexpected contact. He bends down, capturing my gasps with his mouth.

"Do you still want me to not hold back?" he asks.

"Yes," I plead.

"Then stop fighting it," he orders.

Pulling his fingers out, and running my arousal along my slit, he starts drawing circles on my clit. I groan, my hips rolling forward on their own accord. Suddenly, my legs are in the air, knees pressed to my chest and Lachlan's face is in between my thighs. He just fucking handled me like a rag doll, throwing my legs on his shoulders, as my tied ankles lay against his back. Like a chain, draped around his neck.

What a sight this is, to see him in between my legs like this.

I want to scream, to run, to crawl out of my own skin from the exposure and the sudden closeness of his face to my core. But I can't deny what the sight of him alone is doing to me. It will be seared into my memory until the day I perish.

"You don't have to do that," I say quickly.

"I've been dreaming of doing this for bloody weeks. Do you not want me to, lass?"

I blink down at him, at his lips so close to the apex of my thighs. "It's not that I don't want you to...it's just, I know...it's not...you just don't have to."

He begins trailing kisses along my inner thighs, watching me intently through hooded eyes and not giving a flying fuck about the words coming out of my mouth.

"Avery, I'll happily die right here, in front of your sweet, wet pussy with my tongue on your clit."

Did he just say that?

Lachlan presses his palms into my ass, groaning as he works his way up my thigh. I'm going crazy with need as the shame slowly seeps away, his words erasing all traces of guilt or embarrassment. I'm quivering, dizzy from the contact. He starts circling my clit with his thumb as his tongue dances all the way up to my opening.

My head falls back as pleasure shoots through me.

My mind goes blank, all thoughts and fears rush out the minute his mouth starts exploring me. He leaves no space untouched, lapping and devouring me as his tongue plunges inside my tight opening. He moans, the stubble on his jaw makes my hips buck as my legs try to close around his face. But he forces them open with his shoulder, resting his arm on my stomach as he lashes out on my clit, his tongue like a relentless fighter.

"Oh, Lachlan." My eyes roll to the back of my head, as his fingers find my clit again, working in unison while he fucks me with his tongue. He feasts on me like he hasn't tasted anything in years. I can't think, can't breathe. I'm falling into the abyss.

"Keep calling my name. You taste so good, fuck...I could never get enough." His dark voice cuts through me, my mind stuttering as his breath falls on my clit, before he dives right back in.

I moan, shutting my eyes as I fight to fill my lungs with oxygen. His tongue explores every inch of me, starved, desperate to get deeper. My legs begin to shake as he loops his hands around my thighs, forcing my legs to open wider. His mouth closes around my clit, sucking and licking with such fervour, that I lose my surroundings. Just when I think I can't take anymore, Lachlan shoves two fingers deep in me.

Unable to hold back, intense pleasure coils inside me and I feel my body letting go, as the sounds of my pleasure fill the open air around us. His fingers curl and pump, while his tongue laps my swollen clit. My hands grip his hair tightly, as I hold on for dear life.

I cry out his name, not caring if the whole world can hear me.

He lifts my hips slightly, hitting a spot I didn't know existed as a sudden burst of ecstasy swallows me. Everything fades to black and I succumb to a deep, carnal pleasure as it continues to pull me under. It fills my lungs, my organs, my mind, suffocating me in bliss as it ravages my body and soul.

Lachlan works me through my orgasm as I slowly came back up for air. Feeling like a brand-new person.

Holy fuck, that was earth-shatteringly good.

When my vision returns, Lachlan pushes himself up my body. My legs lay limply around his hips. He brings his fingers up to my lips, nudging me to open up. I can't even catch my breath, let alone protest, as I open up and suck my arousal off his fingers. He groans, licking what's remaining off his fingers, before his lips crush mine.

"Was that how you pictured it in your book?" he whispers against my mouth.

"So much better." I pant.

I'm lightheaded post-orgasm, but I want more. So much more. He holds my hips in place as I began rubbing myself against him, leaving a wet mark on his jeans.

He looks down at us, watching intently as his breathing speeds up. I press farther into him, increasing my rhythm. His forehead falls to mine, as a groan leaves his lips. His chin still glistening, and I can't help but revel at it. We are covered in one another, swollen, red, messy, and quite beautiful.

He shifts without warning, pushing me back down and moving away. I protest at the loss, but he grins, pulling my pants up my legs. I lift my ass, helping him dress me.

"I'm going to make a mess in my trousers if I let you keep going."

"What if I want that?" I say, sitting up and pulling my bra

back down over my breasts. He sits up on the grass, still catching his breath as he watches me eagerly. He looks happy, satiated, even though I was the one who got off. I crawl over and straddle him, running my fingers through the back of his hair.

"My turn," I tell him.

"I'm not having sex with you here for the first time." He wraps his calloused hand over mine. I push away his hand and start to unbutton his pants.

"Who said anything about sex?" I pull on his zipper, his bulge presses impatiently against the opening. "I want to taste you," I whisper against his lips and he closes his eyes, letting out a deep groan.

God, I love the way he reacts to me. The way that type of passion makes me feel, it's addicting.

Sliding my hand inside his pants, I cup his concrete erection. He feels bigger than before, harder if that is even possible. He lifts his hips, helping me work his pants down.

His dick springs free and my mouth goes dry at the sight of it. Hard, thick, and long. A blue vein runs all the way up his glorious dick, and for a second I'm not sure if he'll even fit in my mouth. I spread the pre-cum over his tip with my thumb.

His hand fists my hair, as he pulls my mouth to his.

AHHHHHHH.

We both stop, looking around as muted laughter fills the air. Lachlan gently lifts me, laying me on the blanket as he stands, fastening up his pants. He starts looking around frantically, trying to locate the source of the noise.

He turns swiftly, reaching down to grab his hat and jacket.

"We have to go." He sounds alarmed, like he is itching to get as far away as possible.

"Oyeee, is that..." A female voice screeches.

"Now. Avery," Lachlan whispers, reaching his hand down

towards me. I grab on as he pulls me up. He looks at me for a quick second, planting a rushed kiss on my lips. Even at a time like this, he still paused to kiss me. We waste no time, speedily packing everything up.

When we're done, Lachlan tugs down his hat firmly and reaches for my hand as we start walking down the hill, closer to the arches of Glenfinnan.

Wait...I thought we were leaving, but he's leading us the opposite direction, to where his bike is parked.

"Where are we going?"

"Don't you want to see more of Glenfinnan? A different angle to sketch," he says over his shoulder, not bothering to stop.

"I thought you said we have to leave."

"We will...soon." He doesn't look back.

Something about this entire thing seems odd. The panicked expression on his face as he packed everything up in two minutes. He seemed nervous, as if he couldn't fathom being caught with me, which made sense when we were naked but... now? I can't shake the feeling that I'm missing something, but then again, maybe I'm reading too much into it. Who am I to question him? Everyone has secrets they don't want to speak, things we want to pretend don't exist.

And our time together is short; I don't want to waste it asking questions that have nothing to do with us.

CHAPTER THIRTY-NINE

avery

I'm a ball of nervous energy as I stare at myself in the bathroom mirror.

Sliding my damp palms up and down my dress, I try to practice mindful breathing but it's not helping. I'm not even sure why I'm so nervous. It's not a date, it's just dinner, with a guy I'm probably going to sleep with tonight.

That is all.

All? Who am I kidding? I don't have casual sex.

Are you ready for this?

I want to be, my body is definitely ready for this. But my mind cannot be trusted and there is the fact that I haven't had sex in over a year.

What if I'm terrible at it? What if I've always been terrible at it?

I've never been a fan—it would make sense.

Maybe I should bail.

Lachlan and I got back from Fort William over an hour ago. As we were walking up to the inn, he asked what my plans were for the rest of the night and if I wanted to have dinner with him. His tone was casual, friendly even...but his hands and lips said differently.

Now I'm standing here, overthinking the skintight black dress I'm wearing. I don't want to seem too eager, but I also want to feel his eyes stripping me naked in the middle of the pub. Want that rush of need crawling up my skin.

Becca's familiar ringtone jolts me out of my thoughts.

I get a shot right up her nose as soon as I accept the FaceTime call.

"That is not a good look," I chuckle.

"Oh my God! Hi! I miss you! Woah, you're right. Let me just put you here—" I recognize Becca's blue kitchen cabinets in the background, as she finds a spot to lean the camera on.

"You're home early."

"Ugh, yeah. We got out of work early to get ready for a group pilates class. I don't know what I was thinking when I signed up for it a month ago, but here we are. I'm considering calling in sick."

"No, go, it'll be good for you Becs. Is everything okay?"

Becca looks as if she got about two hours of sleep last night. Her hair is in a messy bun on top her head and she has dark circles around her eyes. She rests her chin in her palm, leaning close to the camera.

"Yes, just haven't been sleeping well. Wait...forget pilates, why do you look so hot? Where are you going?"

I feel my face turning red. "Just to the pub."

"No, that dress isn't for the pub. Oh shit! Is it the mystery man from across the hall?"

"Yeah, about that..." I chew on the corner of my finger.

"O.M.G!" Becca screams as I snatch my phone, lowering the volume.

"Would you stop? Also, it's oh my God, when you're actually talking to someone on the phone."

"No, it's not. Did you bone him yet? Please, tell me you fucked! Also, I need a picture. Like, yesterday. What's his name? It's my duty to internet stalk him to make sure he checks out. And to ensure he's appropriate rebound material."

I chew my lip. "Oh, Becs, it's been the hottest 24 hours of my life," I whisper, but Becca screeches, jumping up and down as her phone falls flat on a surface. The screen goes black.

"Are you done?" I ask, once she leans the phone back in place.

"Never. Tell me, was it good? I'm so glad you're not celibate anymore. Name?"

"We haven't had sex yet and his name is Lachlan Carnell."

Becca disappears, and comes back with a pen. "Why? Don't tell me you're holding back. Do you not want to have sex with him?"

"I do, believe me, I do. But...what if I'm bad at it, Becs? He's so skilled, and well, sex has never really been my thing. And we agreed that's all this would be so, what if I'm terrible? I'm supposed to have dinner with him tonight, and I'm pretty sure it's going to happen after or before. What if—"

"Stop that shit right now, Avery Harris. You're amazing and wonderful and fucking hot. He would be lucky to spend any amount of time with you. Stop overthinking this and go get yourself some much-deserved dick."

"Becca!"

"What? It's true. Okay, now, what happened that was so hot? I need all the disgusting details."

"No, too much. I don't kiss and tell." I shake my head.

"Come on! I tell you everything. Just a little nugget."

I sigh, glancing up at the ceiling. "There might have been some tongue action outdoors," I bite my nail, watching Becca's unimpressed expression.

"And? Everyone makes out outside."

"And, I was naked. Outside. In broad daylight. In public. With his face in between my legs."

She yelps, her jaw dropping.

"Who are you and what have you done with my best friend? FINALLY. Ahhh, I'm so happy for you. Go live it up, and send me a picture of lover boy. Preferably before you gorge yourself on his dick."

I laugh, shaking my head. "You are so vulgar. Have fun at pilates."

"I won't. I love you!"

"I love you too."

"GET THAT DIIIII—" Becca yells just as I end our call.

She may be a bit much sometimes, but I love her. Talking to her always puts a smile on my face. I have a stupid grin as I re-apply lip gloss, giving myself one final look-over. The tight tension is somewhat gone from my chest. Talking to Becca was exactly what I needed before walking out the door, ready for anything the night throws my way.

I STOP at the pub door. My hand grasping the handle tightly, as I take in a deep breath.

Here goes nothing.

As soon as I step into the pub, I'm hit with a wave of sound and energy. The air is thick with the scent of alcohol and French fries. The clamour of voices is drowned out by lively Scottish music. My eyes draw to the back of the room, where a band is set up against the wall, their speakers looming tall and proud. Four older men sway together, their bodies moving in time with the cadence of the music.

The band is in perfect harmony, each member playing their part to create a symphony of sound that fills every inch of the room. Tables and chairs have been pushed to the sides, making way for a dance floor that is now filled with people swaying and spinning to the music. Countless faces light up with joy, their bodies moving in time with the beat.

It is amazing.

I edge my way closer, spotting Duncan, Ailith, and Elle behind the bar, as they happily fill out drink orders. All the bar stools are occupied. My eyes do a quick sweep of the place; he isn't here.

But I can't shake the feeling that he is here somewhere, watching me.

A few heads turn in my direction, as I make my way towards the crowded bar. Ailith's eyes catch mine, her face lights up as she shoves a hand in between two guys standing at the bar. They glance over their shoulders at me, before creating a small space. Heat floods my face, and I apologize as I step up to the sticky table.

"Wow, lass...that's a bonnie wee dress ye've got on."

"Thank you," I yell, leaning closer to her.

Ailith turns, picking a bottle of Anam Cara off the shelf and pouring some into a glass.

She places the whisky in front of me. "What's the occasion?"

I smile into my glass.

"The live band." I nudge my head to the band, just as Elle walks over.

"Woah, Avery! Look at ye. I wish I wasn't working tonight so we could dance the night away, as that American expression goes. But my boss is a bit of a tight arse." Elle reaches over the bar, pulling my shoulders in for a quick hug. Ailith smacks the back of her head and we both burst out laughing.

"Me too." I glance over my shoulder, scanning the crowd again without meaning to. A pang of disappointment hits me square in the chest.

Maybe he changed his mind.

Maybe he had to leave.

Shaking the anxious thoughts away, I take a swig of whisky, catching the eyes of a guy leaning on the bar staring at me. But I quickly look away. If Lachlan doesn't show, I'm heading back to my room. I'm not interested in talking to anyone else.

So much for 'this means nothing'.

"Oh shite, I'll be right back," Elle shouts before disappearing into the kitchen.

I grab my drink, stepping away from the bar to free up space. Suddenly, I feel intolerable standing here alone, in a crowded room full of people.

But what if he did change his mind?

Would he have the decency to text me and let me down easy?

My thoughts begin to run at full speed, filling me with self-doubt. I continue to step back, drawing closer to the door leading towards the inn. The song ends and people fall away from the dance floor, creating a gap for my eyes to roam freely around the room, to the back of the pub. Searching the occupied tables and the band set up in the back corner. The speakers...

My breath freezes in my lungs.

Time seems to stand still as the deep ocean blue of his gaze slams into me with a force that leaves me reeling. The sound of my pounding heart drowns out everything else around me. I struggle to breathe, gasping for air as if I'd been submerged underwater.

The entire world falls away to leave just the two of us. His eyes hold mine, unrelenting in their intensity, and I find myself sinking into their depths. The weight of his gaze is all-consuming, and in this moment, I know without a doubt that I am in so much trouble. Because those eyes have the power to ruin me completely. But I can't bring myself to look away.

I am caught in place, completely and irrevocably captivated by Lachlan Carnell.

CHAPTER FORTY

avery

Lachlan is leaning casually against the back wall, hidden from view by the giant speakers close to the band. He looks different somehow, completely at ease in a way I haven't seen before. He's not wearing a hat tonight, his hair carefully styled, as if he spent a little extra time getting ready.

Not that he needed to; he is always handsome. But tonight, he looks devastating.

He's wearing jeans and a snug-fitting black T-shirt that hugs his chest in all the right places. His perfectly crafted arms are on display, showcasing their impressive definition. It's as if every inch of his body has been sculpted with precision by Michelangelo himself. One foot is propped up against the stone wall behind him, his knee bent as his heavy-lidded eyes trace every inch of my body, causing my heart to sputter.

Pushing off the wall with a single smooth movement, he begins to make his way through the crowd towards me. I count every step, unable to do anything else until he is standing in front of me. The heat from his gaze burns as it sears right through me. God, when was this going to get old? Because my lungs are suffering from the constant lack of oxygen.

Lachlan reaches out, grabbing my waist as he brings our bodies together.

His cheek brushes mine as he leans in close to my ear. "I was worried you weren't going to show."

I slide my hand around his neck. "I was right on time."

"It felt torturously long."

I don't know what it is about the way he speaks, or the gravity of his words, or perhaps it's the way the words sound in his Scottish accent, but they have the power to lull me into a state of delirium.

The music slows down in tempo. Lachlan starts walking backwards, guiding us to the dance floor. I can't remember the last time I slow danced with a guy. Blinking away thoughts from the past, I focus on Lachlan, as he begins swaying us to the music. His hand combs through my hair, resting on my lower back, and I lean into him, closing my eyes, soaking in the smell of pinewood and the heavy weight of his hand against my skin.

"You look absolutely breathtaking, mo gradh." Lachlan's eyes find mine, as his hand draws delicate circles up my back, before resting behind my neck.

Mo gradh. That's new. It could mean asshole for all I know.

The guy has a thing with nicknames. I still haven't asked him what Nessi means.

"And those eyes, they remind me of the forest at dusk and the perfect glass of whisky on a cold winter night." His fingers dance around my face, his thumb lovingly caressing my cheek.

My breath catches as I feel a rope wrapping gently around my heart. This is dangerous territory; somehow it's becoming romantic and that was not part of the plan.

"Didn't take you for a poet." I smile awkwardly, trying not

to think about how that was the nicest compliment anyone has ever said to me. My eyes are brown and dull. I try to look away, but Lachlan holds my face in his palm, forcing my gaze to remain locked on his.

"I'm not, but with you..." he starts, but I place my finger on his lips.

"Don't. You can't do that, remember? Words are powerful and this"—I point my finger between us—"it's short-term. It's fun, right? It's not supposed to mean anything."

His brows knit together for a moment, as if he is hearing all this for the first time. But then, something akin to sadness fleets across his features. He lets out a deep breath, nodding slowly as he leans in to press a kiss to my cheek.

"Whatever you desire, Avery. I'm just happy to be here."

I smile at him. "I'm just happy to be here too. What does 'mo gradh' mean?"

He smirks. "I'm not allowed to use words like that, and I guarantee you won't want to know the meaning of those two words."

Jesus fucking Christ.

"Drink?" I exclaim, a little too excitedly since I'm desperately trying to ruin this moment. I grab his hand, rushing us to the bar. He stumbles behind me without protest. I lean on the table, turning to look at him, and catch his eyes raking over my back, zeroed in on my ass.

I want to just say screw it to dinner and take him back to my room.

The bar is overcrowded with thirsty patrons. Duncan, Elle, and Ailith are frantically filling orders as Lachlan leans against the table, looking side to side. Seeing exactly what I'm seeing, he wraps his arm around me, lifting me at the waist as he pulls me back to him. Lacing our fingers together, he walks to the end of the bar, lifting the partition as we make our way to the kitchen.

There are two older men in the kitchen. One is putting food orders together while the other is standing by a metal dishwasher, filling the tray with dirty dishes. They both look up as we step inside. I wait for Lachlan to let go of my hand, but he tucks me closer to his side.

"Lachy, mate, your food is in the corner. Do you want anything else?" One of them asks.

"Cheers, Lewis. You all right?" Lachlan walks to the table, picking up two large to-go containers.

"Aye, nothing we can't handle. Enjoy your night," Lewis says.

Lachlan nods to the guy he was speaking to, Lewis, before he addresses me. "I ordered for us, I hope that's okay. I figured it would be busy with the live band and I know you love the burgers here."

The notion warms my heart. "That's very kind, thank you. I do love the burgers here."

He winks, turning me into a puddle, as he heads towards a small door in the back of the kitchen. The door is tiny, barely comes half-way up the wall and not nearly big enough for Lachlan to squeeze through. Turning the knob, he presses his back into the wood, holding it open for me.

The other side is illuminated by a dying glow, and all I see is stone, giving me underground dungeon vibes.

I blink at him. "Where does that go?"

"Why don't we find out?"

"You know? I'm not that curious."

Lachlan's laugh echoes as he holds out the food containers to me. I grab them out of his hand, taking a small step closer to peek around the doorway. I find a short landing and a narrow stone spiral staircase that appears to be leading down to Hades.

"Is there a torture chamber down there? Should I be concerned you're not going to make it back?" I clutch the containers and take a step back.

He quirks a brow, giving me a slow smile. "Didn't think you were scared of a little darkness. The drink cellar is down there. I just want to grab us a bottle of whisky since they're busy out front. Unless you'd rather go back in there...completely up to you."

To-go containers of food. A new bottle of whisky. And time alone with Lachlan? My stomach stirs nervously.

"Don't forget to say hi to the ghosts," I say, giving him a bright smile.

Lachlan cranes his neck, laughing as he steps into the dark. "I'll be right back, don't go anywhere." And the heavy door shuts loudly, shaking the walls.

I turn around, pretending to take in the kitchen I've already seen. My eyes land on an empty container similar to the one from the other night, filled with whipped cream. My core aches at the memories of Lachlan's fingers all over my body, his tongue, his bare chest pressed up against mine.

I feel a blush creeping up on my face as Lewis turns, glancing my way as he walks by, holding a stack of clean plates.

"Didn't care to venture down the creepy cellar with Lachlan? The ghosts here are friendly, ye know."

"I'll take your word for it," I laugh.

Lewis turns to face me, his expression suddenly shifting. "I dinnah know if I should be saying this, but I have never seen Lachlan like this. I've been friends with Duncan my whole life, and I've known Lachy since he was a wee bairn. It's nice to see him smiling. Finally happy, after everything he's been through."

Wee bairn, I know that one. Small child.

"What do you mean?" I ask quietly.

Lewis scratches the back of his neck, dropping his head as his eyes fall to the floor. I don't want to push but he started this conversation. Surely I can grab a tiny sliver of something.

He glances at the closed cellar door before he speaks. "Oh, I can't...just, the lad seems happy. Really happy for the first time in a long time."

"Oh...well, that's great. I'm sure it has everything to do with being back in Corran." I smile shyly, not making any assumptions or wanting to insert myself into the situation. Lachlan could be happy for plenty of reasons. And none of them probably involve me.

"Aye, Corran...that's it," Lewis laughs, turning to the dishes on the counter.

He looks back at me, his lips twisting, like he's unsure about his next words. "It's because of you, lassie. I hope you choose to remember that later. He's a good lad, pure heart, the kindest soul. He...he, deserves this." Lewis frowns before turning and walking away.

What the fuck does that mean? Is later supposed to be about when I leave? Is he trying to tell me to stay for Lachlan's sake? No, that's dumb. Who says shit like this to a total stranger? Lachlan and I are just getting to know one another. And even if we had more time, this is strictly a friends-with-benefits-while-I-travel-around-Scotland situation.

Nothing more, nothing less.

"Hey, Lewis!" I call out, keeping my voice low but he doesn't turn or throw me a pity glance.

I consider going after him. But then the door behind me groans loudly, and Lachlan steps into the kitchen holding a tall bottle of Anam Cara. I swear there is a cobweb dangling from his shoulder.

"Got the goods." He holds up the bottle.

I flash him my teeth, offering what I'm certain is the fakest smile. "Fantastic!" I exclaim.

"Everything all right?"

I dip my chin repeatedly.

He narrows his eyes at me, glancing at the guys working in the kitchen but he doesn't say anything else. Deciding to drop the subject and blow past my incredibly awkward expression.

"There is a small office down the hall. More like a storage closet, but we can eat in there, if you like."

Lachlan is still very careful with me, treading gently, offering me choices at every opportunity. It feels like a part of him knows, without ever needing the words to pass between us. He's so in tune with my body, my emotions, my needs in an effortless way. It's refreshing.

"If you want, or maybe one of our rooms would be more comfortable?" I shrug, watching the relief in his eyes as his hand skates behind me, guiding us through the back of the kitchen and towards the inn.

CHAPTER FORTY-ONE

avery

I'm sitting on the edge of Lachlan's bed. The fire is crackling gently in the corner, as flickering shadows dance across the walls; casting a warm, amber glow over the room as I take slow drags of whisky. Lachlan skims his fingertips along the palm of my hand, staring at me like I'm a figment of his imagination.

"You're staring." I say into my glass.

He exhales loudly. "I'm sorry. I can't help it."

"What's on your mind?"

His gaze lingers on my lips before finding my eyes. "You, always you...I can't quite believe this is real." His fingers drift up my arm and across my collarbone, goosebumps shadowing his touch. "And how much I want to rip this dress off you and kiss every inch of your body, until I memorize every part of you with my lips."

I swallow hard. *Good God.*

"What about you?" His voice is deep with desire, but he smiles, leaning back on his hand. He downs his whisky and places the empty glass on the floor.

I tuck my hair behind my ear, hesitating. "I can't believe this is real either."

I don't mention the other thoughts fogging up my mind. The ones where I want to take him deep in my mouth, taste him and feel his body tremble beneath mine. Torture him until he can't take it anymore. Until he takes control, shoving me up against the wall and having his way with me. Intense need coils tightly in between my legs.

I shift, repositioning myself on the edge of the bed.

Lachlan doesn't miss the movement. "What else?"

I bite the inside of my cheek, repressing a smile. "I guess you'll never know."

"I have ways of making you talk, Nessi."

"Prove it." My chest tightens, a hidden pleading tone in my voice.

I need him to make the first move because I don't think I can.

My body is hyper-aware of how close he is to me. Of the way his knee is touching my thigh, causing shivers to prickle down my back as his fingers continue their slow drift across my skin. I chug the rest of my whisky, enjoying the burn and the momentary distraction it provides.

He gazes deep into my eyes, as if he's staring out at the world. And then he kisses me. My empty glass falls to the floor, rolling as we desperately pull at each other. He tastes like whisky and cinnamon, and I want to ravel myself in him forever. His warm hands caress my body, and I do the same, wanting to touch him everywhere, all at once. Taking time to commit him to memory, his every muscle, every curve, every inch of skin. I can't get closer, can't get enough of this feeling, of this need to fuse us together.

I want him so badly it hurts.

You're so screwed, Avery.

Breaking away to steer my dangerous thoughts, I crawl backwards until my back hits the wooden headboard. Lachlan stands, reaching behind his back, and pulls his shirt off. Shadows and light dance beautifully across his naked chest.

"Get over here," I say, curling my index finger at him.

Lachlan smiles and lunges forward. He grabs my ankles and slides me down the bed before I have a chance to react. I yelp, my dress riding up to the bottom of my ribcage. He unzips my boots, pulling them off my legs and dropping them to the floor one after another.

His eyes roam over me eagerly, like he hasn't already seen every curve and contour of my body. His rough calloused palms feel so good as he runs his hands up my legs. Past my knees, to my thighs, stopping at my black lace thong while his fingers twist around the band. His other hand continues to trace up my shivering body, knuckles brushing against my hard nipple beneath the material of my dress. His touch shouldn't feel this blazing, as if a thousand suns are exploding inside me.

Lachlan takes his time, his movements slow and excruciating. His hands find their way underneath my bunched-up dress.

"Do you like this dress?" His eyes lift slowly to mine.

"Yes."

"Then you better take it off before I rip it." His voice is low and rough, brushing against my throbbing core.

I sit up and peel off my dress slowly; ignoring the rapid beats of my heart. Fully exposed to Lachlan again, under the light hue of the fire, I should feel vulnerable and scared. I should want to run the opposite direction, to hide, to cast our bodies in darkness. But as his eyes meet mine, I feel nothing but a sense of comfort and safety. He makes me feel cherished and protected. I trust him with my body, and feel a type of warmth in his embrace I've never felt before.

Every place he touches feels like light; colour replacing the dull, dark shadows on my body.

"Lachlan," I whisper, gripping his arms.

He cages me in, our lips devouring as I wrap my arms around his neck, my breasts pressing into his warm chest. I reach down, working quickly to unbutton his belt, dragging down his zipper and sliding my hand around his thick, hard cock. Lachlan draws in a sharp hiss, biting my lip. His mouth moves to my neck, as he tugs on my nipple with his fingers. He bends down, licking and sucking on my other nipple with enough pressure to drive me wild. The man knows how to use his mouth like it's his full-time job.

I think I may come from nipple foreplay alone. Is that even possible?

His fingers wrap tightly around my lace underwear and he yanks hard, ripping the thin material instantly. I gasp.

Lachlan smirks, grazing my nipple in between his teeth. "You didn't say anything about wanting to keep those."

His knuckles ghost over my sensitive clit, before his hand moves to my thighs, his nails drawing slow circles up and down my flesh. I'm trying my best to remain calm, to not combust right here. I'm trying really hard, but this is pure agony.

"Are you trying to kill me?" I groan.

He bites my neck, sucking and kissing the spot before capturing my lips with his. I rub my palm hard against his dick, grinding my body against his, desperate for any extra friction. Just then, he pushes his fingertips inside me, gathering my arousal before circling my clit.

"Fuck, Avery. I think you're the one trying to kill me." He says against my lips, kissing me deeply. If he keeps doing that, I'm going to shatter soon.

His fingers trace back down, one pressing deep inside me. My hips buck and I moan into his mouth. I claw my nails through his hair, urging Lachlan to slow down but he doesn't ease up. His thumb circles my clit as he slides a second finger inside me. His lips hover over mine, eating up the sounds spilling out of my mouth. My mind begins falling peacefully into the abyss.

"Come for me, lass."

His words pull me apart, and I come hard. My body explodes like a million pins of electricity. But this orgasm only fuels my desires. Only making me more insatiable, more greedy for him.

I push up against his chest, sitting on my knees as my fingers trace down his muscles, pulling on his nipple, gliding over every ridge of his abdomen, and the defined cut leading in between his legs.

"What are you..." he starts, but I'm already pulling on his pants.

"Off," I demand and to my surprise, he doesn't fight.

"Those too." I nod at his boxers, and he drags them down, causing his incredible dick to spring free. A drop of pre-cum glistens on the tip and suddenly, I just want to bend down and taste him. Before he can take control, I push him down on the bed and straddle him.

I kiss his jaw, running my tongue along his chest. Moving slowly, as I lick every line and plane of his body. He shudders under me, chest heaving as I drag out his hunger like he did to me. My tongue slides down his stomach, biting the hard muscle and feeling his cock jump. He lets out a delicious sound as I suck on the sensitive skin in his lower abdomen, leaving him with a small hickey. I wrap my hand around his dick, rubbing the pre-cum with my thumb, as my lips continue travelling down.

"Jesus Christ," he groans, fisting the bedsheet.

This man wants me, I'm doing this to him.

Me.

I lower my mouth, licking the tip of his cock, tasting his salty pleasure. I don't think twice, don't second guess anything as I take all of him deep inside my mouth.

"Oh, fuck. Avery."

Lachlan's eyes are a deep blue, ravenous as he watches me move up, sucking the tip before his cock disappears back inside my mouth. His head falls back, as a deep grunt vibrates through him. He is too big, too much for me to please like this without gagging. But I want to keep going. I want him to fall apart. I want to be the one to please him.

It's intoxicating, having this kind of effect on someone as beautiful as Lachlan.

His choppy breaths fill the room, making me work faster, taking him deeper. His fingers wrap around my scalp as he fists my hair. Pulling out, I lightly blow on his dick before taking him all the way to the back of my throat, while cradling his balls in my hand.

"Fuck." He groans.

His body is mine and I own every single sound coming out of him. I've never experienced this type of desire from pleasing someone else, and I was getting off on it. The way he calls out my name, desperate with lust. I move fast and deep, giving him exactly what he wants for a bit longer, before slowing down, circling his tip with my tongue.

He's too strong, his movements too quick, as he pulls me up, rolling me over onto my back. He presses his body into mine and cradles my head, kissing me deeply, tasting traces of himself on my lips.

"Such a fucking tease," he says against my lips.

I laugh as he grabs my legs and yanks my thighs over his

shoulders, just as his mouth finds my pussy. My head falls back as he feasts on me, groaning in approval and the vibration in his throat hits my clit perfectly, blackening my vision momentarily. He licks down to my opening, fucking me with his tongue. My back arches and I can't hold back my whimpering moans any longer.

I have never felt pleasure like this, God, I am ruined. Every wave feels so much stronger than the next, knocking me off my feet. His movements are hard and unrelenting, moving from my clit to my entrance. Aching to push me closer to the edge.

Not able to wait a second longer, I claw at his shoulders, desperate to pull him up to me. I want him. I want all of him. Right fucking now.

"No," he says. "Not until you come on my tongue."

He sucks on my clit and a low moan erupts from me, as I bury my eyes with my arm. Every moment, every glance, every graze draws me into this moment. My legs begin to tremble as breathing becomes near impossible, skin buzzing with buds of electricity shooting through me. Blinding me from the stark light as I crumble into a million pieces around him.

"So beautiful, I can't fucking take it." He plants a kiss on my inner thigh.

"Lachlan, please," I finally beg. He sits on his knees, looking down at my body as he tears a condom open with his teeth. He quickly sheaths himself and pulls my legs open, lining himself up at my entrance.

He pauses, staring into my eyes. "Are you sure?"

I nod, yanking him down to my lips. Our mouths crash together aggressively, searching for more. He pushes the tip of his cock inside me. I moan, urging my hips forward, forcing him farther in.

"So impatient," he grabs my hips. "And I thought you'd be wrecked by now." He eases inside me slowly. I close my eyes, trying to adjust to his size. He's so in tune with my body, not giving me more than I can take. He breathes deeply against my neck, saying my name like a prayer, until he's fully seated inside me.

He waits for me to adjust before he starts slowly moving inside me. Deep and slow, while his ocean eyes anchor me, a tidal wave of ecstasy pulling me under. Taking note of every reaction, every breath, every shudder. He's setting me free. I run my hands over his strong body, through his hair as he slides in and out, picking up speed, filling me deeper and harder every time.

I wrap my legs around him, and Lachlan lowers his head, planting kisses on my lips. His eyes remain on mine the entire time. Our bodies move back and forth together. It's so sensual, so incredibly intimate. A type of connection I never dreamed I would have.

This can't be real.

But it is, and you're in it.

"Where have you been all my life?" His voice so low, eyes round as if the words just slipped out of him. He doesn't wait for a response, as if he's scared I'll say something he can't bear to hear. His mouth possesses mine, forcing me under water like the magnitude of his words. I feel it too. All of it. I feel way more than I should, more than I will ever admit. Because we're running against time and this, too, will come to an end.

Where have you been all my life?

Dreaming of you.

His movements become faster and harder as our mouths rage, kissing and biting. I drag my fingernails down his back, leaving red marks along his skin. My third orgasm sneaks up and I explode all around him. He thrusts a few more times before he groans, chasing his own release alongside mine. Eyes alight against the glow of the fireplace, he falls on top of me, half his body resting on the bed. Lachlan's heart beats rapidly against my chest as he nestles his face into my neck.

We stay locked together like that for a long time. Catching our breaths, tangled in one another as I think about the collection of unbelievable moments we just shared.

I want to stay in this moment forever, drowning in him.

CHAPTER FORTY-TWO

lachlan

It feels like coming home.

Like I've finally come home after years lost at sea.

I stare at her closed eyes. Her body is quiet and calm. At peace, in my arms. I don't want to leave but I eventually manage to peel myself off and walk to the bathroom.

She feels like home.

How am I supposed to come back from something like this?

When I walk back inside the room, Avery is bent over, grabbing her torn underwear, her dress in her other hand.

"What are you doing?"

She gives me an awkward smile. "I'm going back to my room. That's what happens after this, right? Don't you want me to leave?"

"No. Get your sweet ass back in bed. You're staying here tonight. I'm no where near done with you."

I walk over to the bed, lifting the covers and waiting for her to crawl in.

"Naked?" she whispers, like she's telling me a dirty secret.

"Aye, naked," I laugh but she just stands there, blinking at me.

I consider picking her up and throwing her on the bed but she sighs and drops her clothes. My dick twitches at the sight of her on all fours, crawling to the other side of the bed. This woman has turned me upside down.

I follow behind her, sinking into the pillow beneath my head, and laying on my side. Avery does the same, we lay face to face, her body so close I can feel the heat radiating off her skin. Her whisky eyes, with strands of gold, green, and brown, sparkle in the dim light of the bedroom. I feel myself drawn in, mesmerized by the kaleidoscope of colours.

When Avery looks at me this way, I feel as if she can see through every wall I've put up. I try to commit the moment to memory, every detail etched in my mind like a photograph. I imagine placing each look into a box, but I know deep down that no matter how many boxes I fill, it'll never be enough. I'll never get enough of her.

My head is dizzy, trying to piece together everything from the last few days. It all feels surreal, like I'm trapped in a dream. I want to tell her how she makes me feel alive, how being with her is like finally coming home. But she doesn't want to hear any of that. She doesn't want to know how she's etched herself into my heart in such a short amount of time. So I'll keep my thoughts to myself, content to bask in her presence and hold on to whatever moments we have left.

This means nothing.

Her words from that night in the kitchen keep replaying in my head, like a broken record I can't turn off. What if this means everything to me?

"What?" Avery asks, tucking her hands under her cheek.

"You told me no words." I lean in and kiss her forehead.

She makes a face, scrunching her nose, like she smelled something rancid.

"Why did you just make that face?"

Her eyes shoot to mine, alarmed as she puffs out a breath.

"I was just thinking about how many women you've had one-night stands with." She worries her lip in between her teeth, driving me bloody bonkers.

"Not as many as you're thinking. And nothing like this."

Understanding crosses her features, her golden eyes growing softer at my reassuring words.

"There's been nothing quite like this for me too," she whispers, so low I'm not sure it was meant for me.

The knot in my chest twists painfully at that admission.

Then let me in. Let me worship you. Let me...

"Can I ask you something?" She says.

"Anything."

"Why do you keep calling me Nessi?"

"It's your nickname."

"What does it mean?"

I cringe, not sure how to deliver this one. I gave her that nickname early on, when she was a runaway mystery. But no matter how much physical distance she put in between us, I couldn't get her out of my fucking head.

Her eyebrows shoot up. "Oh, crap. Okay, let's hear it."

"I don't know, lass..."

"It can't be that bad. Just tell me."

"Promise you'll let me explain after I tell you?"

Avery nods and I consider my other options for a few seconds before deciding to just go for it.

"It's a nickname I gave you, inspired by the Loch Ness Monster."

Avery's nostrils flare, as she shoots up to a sitting position, her jaw clenched.

"I remind you of a mythical monster?!"

I lean against the headboard, facing Avery's growing rage with a smile. "You promised you'd let me explain."

She crosses her arms. A taut line of tension runs through her body as she waits for me to speak. I admire her restraint, the way she typically tries to hide her emotions. But when it comes to anger, she doesn't hide. She lets it loose, unafraid of who her wrath might hit.

"Ness is not a monster, not to me. She is a creature of myth and legend, a being coveted by many but seen by none. Those who journey to the shores of Loch Ness hope to catch a glimpse of her, but she remains elusive, a creature of fantasy and imagination. She's rare, impossible even, a cherished dream for those who desire to see her. And for the lucky few who claim to have seen her, she was a sight to behold, a creature of such otherworldly beauty and elegance that their lives were forever changed."

Avery blinks at me several times, but doesn't say a word. Her anger shifts to an emotion I can't quite read. Her brows are drawn, as if she can't quite comprehend what I'm saying, or maybe she doesn't want to.

Come on lass, read between the lines. Maybe she's choosing to ignore it, continuously pushing away our connection and pretending like it doesn't exist. Like it will vanish the minute she leaves Scotland.

"Thoughts?" I lean in, kissing the corner of her mouth.

"Not really," she breathes. "Not sure what that has to do with me."

I grab hold of her hips, lifting her on top of me. She straddles me, holding on to my shoulders. I brush my fingers through her scalp, fisting her hair gently and forcing her to look me in the eyes. Because what I'm about to say is going to make her want to run. I feel a tremble move through her body.

"Maybe you just need me to say it, Avery. Maybe you need the words even if you don't want to hear them." I kiss her lips once, pulling back to look at her.

Her nails dig into my shoulders.

"I never thought I would find you." Another kiss.

"And I'll take every moment of time you'll give me." Another kiss.

"But no amount of time can erase how much you've changed me." I lean in for one final kiss, but she surprises me, pressing her body into mine and intensifying our embrace. I kiss her with a hunger that borders on desperation, driven to frenzy by the force of my feelings for this woman who has completely turned my world upside down, from the moment we met. It was as if she had always owned every part of me, and I had been holding onto it all along just to present it to her. Just to watch her throw it away if she pleased. I am powerless to resist her, and I don't want to anymore. I would give her every-thing, anything, because she is worth it all.

Avery pulls back, breaking our kiss as she gasps for air.

"Lachlan...I..."

"I know, lass. You don't have to say it." I whisper, pulling her back in because if she kept staring me in the eyes, she would see how much of a fucking liar I am.

<h1 style="text-align:center">CHAPTER FORTY-THREE</h1>

<h1 style="text-align:center">lachlan</h1>

An incessant buzzing wakes me from sleep.

Avery is nestled against my chest, her eyelids closed and her luscious lips are slightly parted as her chest rises and falls softly. I memorize every new angle, every new moment with her.

Buzz. From my bedside table.

Another buzz from somewhere on the ground.

What the fuck? Are both our phones going off? What time is it?

My phone vibrates again. Only one person would be hounding me like this. I try to ignore it but the fucking wanker doesn't let up. Reaching out my arm slowly, I grab my phone. I have fifty-plus notifications from Henry. Frustration clouds my vision as I sit up slowly, making sure to not disturb Avery.

HENRY

This is getting bloody old, mate.

Tick tock, Moore. You're running out of time and Edgar is getting very impatient. You know what happens when someone makes him wait too long.

If you don't fucking answer, he's going to send a car to Corran and your precious cover will be blown.

I'm sorry mate, I'm under a lot of pressure. Please call me.

It's important.

ME

What part of 'out of reach' do you not understand?

I place my phone face down on the table, leaning my head against the bed and staring up at the empty ceiling.

I wish I could disappear. Go back to Canada for a little while with Avery, until things quiet down here. Maybe they'll forget about me, move on to bigger things. But they never will. I owe them, and Edgar always collects what he's owed. Especially with such a high price tag on my head.

I finally made the decision to get out but I don't know how Edgar will react to the news. Will he take me for everything I'm worth? Will he tarnish everything I've worked hard to achieve? The whisky business, my real estate portfolio? What if he decides to hit me where it hurts? Send the vultures after Ailith and Duncan? I'd never forgive myself. I can't do that to them. Not to the people who have always been there for me.

Before I say anything to Edgar or Henry or anyone at the agency, I have to find a good lawyer who will do whatever it takes to get me out of this mess for good.

Buzz. Buzz. Buzz.

That's a call, and it's not coming from my phone.

Leaning over the bed, I notice Avery's phone laying on the floor beside her dress. It could be important. I slip out of bed, picking up her phone and noticing an incoming FaceTime call from Becca.

Her best friend. Avery has told me all about Becca, and I'm sure Becca knows about me too.

I contemplate grabbing my hat and answering the call but the FaceTime request ends. Not even a second later, a text comes through.

BECCA

If you don't text me within the next five minutes, I'm calling the Scottish police or whatever they're called. You better be in a ditch somewhere or choking on Lachlan's dick. I'm worried! Pick up the phone.

I can't help but snicker as I click on her name, expecting to be blocked by a passcode entry, only to find Avery's phone is unlocked.

ME

Hi…it's Lachlan. Avery is asleep and I really don't want to wake her. You all right?

BECCA

This better not be a stupid joke, Avery. It's not funny. Send a pic, or I'm calling the entire country.

I love that there is someone out there who is fiercely protective of Avery. I sigh, wanting to get this over with so I can go back to bed. I grab my ball cap off the table, angle my face down and snap a photo. I check the photo before sending it to Becca.

BECCA

Hubba babba…wow, you're…okay…Avery wasn't exaggerating.

Hi…I'm Becca but you probably already know that. Is Avery okay?

ME

Aye, she's grand. Asleep in my bed.

BECCA

Oh wonderful, thank you for looking after her. Can you get her to call me when she wakes up?

ME

Of course.

BECCA

And thank you for responding, I appreciate it.

ME

No problem.

My phone buzzes on the bedside table again and an idea pops in my head. I click on Becca's information, repeat her phone number five times before placing Avery's phone down.

I throw my hat on the ground, turn my phone off and climb back in bed.

"NO…PLEASE…STOP…NO!"

I startle, foggy from sleep to find Avery in a state of panic. Her eyes are closed but she's covered in sweat, fists clenched tightly while she tosses in bed, as if she's being chased by something.

"Avery, lass. Wake up." I grab hold of her shoulders, trying to gently rouse her from sleep.

"No! No, don't touch me. No! Get away!" I let go of her, watching as she continues to scream. Tears begin streaming down her cheeks. My heart aches, watching her struggle like this while I sit here completely helpless.

I can't just do nothing. She has to wake up.

I scoop her into my arms. Sobs wrack her body and she starts to shake, lost in another world fighting demons I can't see. She's having a panic attack in her sleep and I have no fucking idea how to help her. How to stop the pain.

"Lass, wake up. Please, wake up." I run my hand through her hair, shaking her gently and hoping to snap her out of whatever nightmare has taken hold of her.

"No, no, no. Stop...please. Not again, I can't do it again!" She screams so loud, pain etched into every letter. It tears my heart into pieces.

"Avery, wake up, lass. You're safe. It's me, Lachlan. It's just a bad dream. I'm here. You're safe." I keep whispering the words, shaking her a bit harder as I rock her body.

She snaps awake. And dark, panic-ridden eyes pooled with tears stare back at me. Avery looks around, taking in her surroundings as her body continues to tremble. Tears roll down her face in a steady stream.

"What happened?"

She pushes her body off mine, scooting to the corner of the bed as she hugs her knees to her chest, resting her head in between them, taking loud, choppy breaths.

"Nessi, tell me what to do. Please, let me help." I crouch in front of her, trying to get a glimpse at her face but she doesn't look up. I want to touch her, hold her but I don't want to hurt her even more. She's hiding from me, pretending I don't exist, while working through whatever this is alone.

But she's not alone. And the least I can do is let her know I'm here.

This is agony. I can't stand to see her like this. If I can't touch her and she won't look at me, how the hell am I supposed to fix this?

Suddenly I remember a trick I had learned in the depths of my own grief long ago. It had helped calm my breathing and tame the the anger. It always worked when I couldn't breathe, feeling like the pain would never subside.

It's worth a try, I'll do anything to take her pain away.

"I know something that might help. I'm going to pick you up, all right?" My voice comes out rushed, desolate.

She doesn't protest, and I carefully wrap her up in my arms. Avery leans against me, tucking her face into my neck. Her cheeks are drenched with tears, coating my skin. The anger fumes and curls inside me.

Rushing to the bathroom, I turn the shower on, heating up the water as steam begins to fill the small space.

"Just breathe, lass. Slow, deep breaths. Listen to my voice."

She continues to sob as I step inside the shower. Ailith insisted on installing these claw-foot tubs in every room when we decided to renovate the inn. Duncan wouldn't pay for it, so it was my gift to her. If I had known it was going to suck up the majority of the space in the bathrooms, though, I wouldn't have agreed to it. But now I'm thankful it's here.

I stand under the hot water as the tub slowly fills up. Avery doesn't let go, she's pressed into my chest as I hold her trembling body under the warm stream. When there is half a foot of water pooling around my legs, I sit against the tub and press her back to my chest. For a moment, I'm afraid she's going to reject this whole thing and storm out of here. Her body is stiff as a rock, but then she leans back, relaxing into me. Small progress, I'll take it.

Avery tilts her head back, resting it on my shoulder as the shower-head streams water over her body. Her eyes are squeezed shut, and her wet hair clings to my chest. The sound of her ragged breaths fills the steamy air, and I can feel her body shuddering against mine as she fights for control.

"Focus on the water. The sound of each drop as it hits your skin, the tub, the rest of the water pooling around us. Focus on the tingling sensation, breathe through it. Just the water, nothing but the water."

Tears prick at the corner of her eyes, as she releases quiet sobs in between jagged breaths.

"It's over now. Breathe around the pain and let it wash away," I whisper, pulling her hair away from her face. It physically hurts to see her like this. God, I would give anything to erase her pain away.

Steadily, her breathing slows down. Her inhales become longer, more controlled. The shuddering in her body stops. I reach out, holding her fists and prying her tight fingers open. She's so stiff, her body not receiving enough oxygen during the attack. Red crescent moons mark the inside of her palms from where her nails dug into her delicate skin. I struggle to choke down the tight knot in my throat.

"How...how did you know this would...help?" Avery pushes the words out in between gasps of breath.

I've never told anyone about this part of my life. Never let anyone see me at my lowest, because I used to think it made me weak.

I run my hand through her hair, brushing through the knots gently with my fingers. "After my mother died, the grief was constant. I was young, didn't understand why she left me. It tore my world apart. But time dulled the pain, like it always does. It got easier, but it never went away. Grief was like a wave and when it hit me, it fucking pulled me under until I couldn't breathe. The panic attacks would come out of nowhere. It hit me once while I was in the shower, but being in the water, surrounded by the constant stream seemed to help. After that, every time I got hit by another wave, I would hide in the shower, sometimes sitting in the tub for hours. Water helped me breathe through the pain."

She laces our fingers together, grasping my hand tightly in hers.

I don't know how long we sit there, but eventually I close my eyes, getting lost in the sounds of water. Avery brings the back of my hand up to her lips, brushing a kiss before pressing my hand into her cheek. It's such a simple gesture, but it ripples through my chest, stealing my breath.

"Thank you," she whispers, her voice low and choppy. "I'm sorry."

"You have nothing to apologize for. I hope this isn't because of last night." I say, pressing my lips to her head.

She shifts, whisky eyes stare up at me. I twist her body away from the direct stream, watching the remnants slide down her chin, neck, as they skate down her body.

"Of course not. Last night was amazing, Lachlan. This is all me, and I'm sorry you had to see this awful part of me." Avery places her hand on my chest, looking down at her fingers. The strange electricity hums under my skin, ignited by her touch. "I understand if you never want to see me again."

I lift her chin, pulling her eyes back to mine, as they suck the air from my lungs. "There is no part of you that has or could ever be awful. To me, you are the most beautiful person, in all the ways you fail to see. You are a survivor, Avery, and even in your darkest days, you could only ever be beautiful. I see you. All of you."

Her chin wobbles, chest heaving as she grabs the back of my neck, sealing her lips over mine in a passionate kiss. A kiss filled with understanding and true embrace. The magnetic pull between us crackles, intensifying everything I've been trying to hold back.

When we finally pull apart, she lays her head back on my chest.

"Please don't tell anyone about this. I've been dealing with it for a long time, it's nothing new."

I nod, unable to speak. A part of me has an idea about what might have happened to her; the words she was screaming were laced with terrible fear. And I want to ask but not if she's not ready to tell me. She might never be ready, but I'll continue to hold her in my arms, try to erase her pain away. Erase every bad, painful memory and replace it with good ones. Happy dreams.

We lay like that for a long time, and the water starts to get cold.

"Are you hungry?"

She nods against my chest.

"I'm going to go find some food and coffee. Are you going to be all right by yourself, lass?"

"Yes. I'm okay. Thank you, Lachlan. Truly."

Avery stands with me and pulls me into a hug. I wrap my arms around her, remaining in her warm embrace. Wanting to hold on to her for as long as possible. But she takes a step back, and I plant a kiss on her nose before stepping out of the tub.

I get dressed in two minutes, covering myself up as best as I can. I scan the room, my eyes catching on the crumbled sheets. Walking over to the dresser, I grab a clean shirt and sweatpants, leaving them on the bed in case Avery is done by the time I get back.

Securing on my hat and sunglasses, I finally make my way out the door.

Since getting into my line of work, I've been obsessed with

hiding in the shadows, covering my face, my body, anything to conceal myself. To disappear into the dark and cease to exist to the world. Trying so fucking hard to be forgettable. Which is ironic because the more I hide, the more they try to find me.

But I don't want to hide anymore. I want to live freely, love openly. I want a new beginning.

With her.

"Okay...so far, this is all I know. Your name is Lachlan Carnell. You were born in Corran, only child. You are a businessman, dabble in whisky." Lachlan narrows his eyes at me, trying to suppress a smile.

I continue. "You have a house in Glasgow. You ride a motorbike, and you're old." Lachlan throws a grape, attempting to aim it at my head but I catch it with my mouth. Which only makes both of us laugh.

We've been in his room for two days. Talking, sleeping, eating, having sex, puttering around Corran, coming back... having more sex. It's been an Avery and Lachlan marathon and it's been wonderful.

"You're close with your aunt, like to hike and enjoy a bit too much whisky," I conclude.

"No such thing," Lachlan says, while stuffing his face with cheese and bread.

I swallow and brace myself.

"That's boring. I want the good stuff...as much as you can

give me. You know everything about me. Hell, you even spoke to my best friend."

"Aye, she's a strange one, but I like her."

I smile, missing Becca a little more today. "She's the best."

"She was worried about you, wouldn't let up. It's nice."

I nod. "You changed the subject."

He chews, watching me as he thinks about his next words carefully. You'd think I'd be used to his piercing glare by now, but nope.

"Wouldn't it be better if we kept things simple? Since it's 'just sex'," Lachlan air quotes the last bit. "Your words, not mine."

"You agreed."

He sighs. "No. I repeated them."

I blink at him. But I'm not going there, not when he's clearly trying to change the subject again. If I'm going to continue sleeping with this guy while I'm in Scotland, I'd like to know a bit more about him. For safety reasons, of course.

"I just want to make sure you're not a serial killer or something. You don't need to give me anything important or deep. You can keep your secrets to yourself."

Lachlan's head falls back as he lets out a glorious laugh. It's so genuine and contagious, that it brings a smile to my face.

"Wild imagination you have, Nessi. Any more guesses?"

"A male prostitute? There is nothing wrong with that! You are great with your tongue." I blurt out, and Lachlan chokes on a piece of grape. Reaching out for his bottle of water.

"This is going downhill quickly. You're terrible at this game."

My cheeks burn but it's true. It would explain why he's so good in bed.

"Answer the question."

"No."

"A criminal?"

His mouth tilts up, giving me a half-smile. "I'm sensing a theme here."

I throw a cube of cheddar cheese at him. "Stop messing around."

"No."

I nod. "Okay, then why is there no trace of you online?"

"What?" He tips his water back in his mouth, his eyes falling to the floor.

We're getting somewhere. "Becca said there is no trace of you online. You don't exist. Anywhere."

"Neither do you."

"That's different."

He leans forward, challenging me. "How? I'm a private person. I like to keep to myself. I don't like social media."

That is a valid point. There are plenty of people that like to keep a low profile for various reasons. He's an outdoorsy man; it matches his character.

"Is that because you're a billionaire?"

Another beautiful laugh spills from his lips. "No."

I chew on a piece of cheese, staring off and trying to come up with more questions.

"May I have a turn?" Lachlan asks.

"No, we're not done with you yet."

"Have you ever been in love?"

My heart falls to my stomach.

Not this again.

"No."

"Not even with John?"

I take a deep breath, not knowing how to answer that question. So I settle for honesty. "What John and I had wasn't love. It was always just simple, comfortable companionship. He was my safe choice."

Lachlan mulls over that for some time before he speaks.

"What if you meet your perfect person? What then? You won't allow yourself to experience love?"

I was really hoping he was going to drop this. Lachlan sits up, crossing his legs, facing me. Our knees are touching. Apparently, he's interested in my disgust for love.

How do I answer this without sounding heartless?

"No." I drop my eyes and pick at my cuticles. "I've told you before I don't believe in it. To me, love has always been war. Only filled with pain and heartbreak. Why would I put myself through that? Why experience something amazing, knowing the ending will be terrible?"

"How do you know the ending will be terrible?"

"Because it always is."

Love was pain. It broke perfectly whole people in half. It wasn't meant to, but it always did. Love wasn't supposed to tear your heart out and stomp on it. It wasn't supposed to feel like war, like you were slowly watching yourself bleed out on the dry pavement. But that's all I'd ever known. All I'd ever seen. Love was meant to heal, raise you up, not bring you down and pull you apart, thread by thread. Love wasn't supposed to feel like a prison. In a perfect world, love was meant to slow down time, make you feel alive. But then again, how would I know?

We didn't live in a perfect world and if it hurt as much as it did, then it wasn't love. If it made you feel so lonely that you wished you would drift away, then it wasn't love. If it made you wish you were out of time, then it was relentless agony and I wanted nothing to do with it. I'd seen and felt the damage of love firsthand.

It was not worth it.

My parents are the perfect example of this. My mother is on husband number...I don't even know. And my father is still living in my childhood home, hoping she's going to walk through the door one day and profess her love for him. Even though she's broken him a million times, he would take her back in a heartbeat. That's not love, that's devastation. That's called being a fool.

I wait for a reaction. Shock, judgement, withdrawal, but Lachlan just listens and absorbs the information. There is no pity or sadness in his eyes, just reserved understanding. He may not agree with it, but he doesn't argue or make me feel bad about it.

"Have you lived outside of Scotland?" I ask, reaching for some grapes, desperate to get as far away from the topic of love as possible.

"Aye," he says, as he rests his hands on my knee. The warmth from his skin tingles down my legs.

"England, Spain, Italy, France, Turkey, Hungary, and Australia."

"Wow, that's adventurous. Was it for work?"

He nods, his fingers brushing over my kneecaps as he focuses his eyes on them. A clear hesitation. Work seems to be a sore subject for him.

I watch a single brown curl drape across his forehead. Reaching out, I run my fingers through it. Lachlan stills; whatever thoughts were clouding his mind vanish as he takes a deep breath, enjoying the feeling of my fingers in his hair.

I shift, sitting on top of him and his hands immediately grip my waist. I continue running my fingers through his hair, gently massaging his scalp with my nails. He closes his eyes, groaning as his hardening erection presses into my core. And I'm suddenly writhing with desire again, needing to feel him all over me.

"I don't think I can concentrate on your questions if you keep doing that." His eyes remain closed, but he flashes me a brilliant smile.

"I can tell." His palm lands on my ass, making me jump with laughter. He takes the opportunity to roll me on my back as he nestles himself in between my legs, pinning me down. Lachlan's eyes fall to my lips and he leans in, kissing me softly. It's delicate and careful, like he's trying to slow down time. My fingers trail down his chest and dip past the waistband of his boxers, and I pause for a millisecond to see if he's going to stop me, to take control. But he doesn't.

He lets me take the lead this time as he makes love to me. The gentleness of it should send me running because it feels more intimate somehow. But I don't focus on those muddy feelings. I remain in the now with him, leaning into him more—getting lost in him. He turns off every thought in my head and replaces it with silence, peace. Unimaginable pleasure.

This is how it should have been.

This is what I deserve.

And before I know it, I'm falling over the edge. The wild rapids take hold of me, pulling me under the current. And I never want to come back up; I surrender myself to this wild feeling and allow it to carry me into the unknown.

CHAPTER FORTY-FIVE

avery

I open my eyes to complete darkness, to an empty pillowcase beside me, and I remember I'm in Lachlan's room. I've been sleeping in his room for almost a week now, only going back to my room when I need to change or grab more things. A week of bliss wrapped around us like an impenetrable bubble, as we got to know one another and got lost in the electric energy circling us.

What time is it?

Where is he?

I sit up, rubbing the foggy sleep from my eyes. Reaching over to the side table, I tap on my phone screen. Six in the morning. And no texts from Lachlan.

It's frigid in here.

It gets cold overnight and without the fireplace turned on, the rooms become an ice cube. Swaddling myself in a blanket, I beeline to the fireplace, flip the switch on, run back to bed, and decide to hide under the covers until the room heats up. Hoping Lachlan will walk through the door, join me in bed and warm me up with his body. It's still early, perhaps he went to get some coffee or for a jog.

Reaching for the other blanket, I spot a small, curved piece of paper folded at the edge of the mattress.

> *Avery,*
> *I had to leave. I'll be back soon. I'm sorry.*
> *- Lachlan*

My heart drops at those three small, uninformative sentences. I don't have a reason to be disappointed. This is a good reminder that what we have is temporary, just a vacation fling. Flings are supposed to be physical and not emotional. He doesn't owe me any explanations, and I don't need to ask questions. This was supposed to be just sex. I asked for that, I want that.

I still do.

Which means I should probably get out of this bed and get back to my own room, back to my own life and all the plans I had when I first got to Scotland.

I'LL BE BACK SOON, my ass.

It's been twenty-four hours, not that I'm counting. And not even a text message. I could be the bigger person, send a good morning text, feel things out. But I can't bring myself to do it. Not when he's been so damn quiet.

You told him this meant nothing. Just sex, remember?

Yes, I remember but I'm allowed to be angry too. I'm fuming

this morning. Not because this means something more, but because ghosting someone is childish and unnecessary. Silently fighting with myself while getting dressed, I pull up my hair and fasten my hiking boots. I need to get out of here for the day, preferably someplace with no cell service. Someplace that won't remind me of him.

Everything reminds you of him. You're in Scotland, dummy.

There are a few people grabbing coffee at the pub when I walk in. Ailith is standing behind the bar with a clipboard in her hands. Her head lifts up just as I walk in. I smile and give her a half-wave.

"Avery! Top of the morning to ye, lassie."

I decide to steal some of Ailith's positive attitude. I'm determined to have a good day. Shoving my pent-up frustrations to the side, I approach Alith and grab a seat across from her.

"Good morning."

"Coffee?"

"Yes, please. Thank you."

Ailith heads for the kitchen and reappears a minute later with a steaming mug in her hand.

"I was starting to think ye were trying to avoid us, or that ye fell ill. I came to yer room the other night, but Lachlan caught me outside yer door and told me he'd been keeping ye busy...in his room," her cheeks turn rosy. A big, radiant smile spreads across her face, as if there's something else beyond those words that's making her light up.

And then, she winks at me.

Oh God. He told her about us. *Hey, auntie...your favourite guest and I have been shagging like bunnies.*

Can one melt of sheer embarrassment? Because it sure as shit feels like it right now, with the sweat collecting in my armpits.

I cover my face with my hands, groaning into my palms.

"What's wrong?" Ailith grabs my hands and pulls them away from my face.

"Oh, Ailith. You must think...oh, my gosh, I don't know what you must think of me."

Her laugh replaces the morning hush in the pub. "Oh, love, it was only a matter of time. We all had bets. With all that tension, it was bound to happen. It seems only the two of ye were trying to fight it." Ailith lays her hand on mine. "I'm thrilled, Avery. He...Lachlan needed this. He needed ye."

We're going to pass right over that comment.

"Do you know where he is?" The words leave my mouth before I have a chance to stop them.

Real smooth.

Ailith's eyes fall to my shoulder, her smile slowly disappearing. She begins fiddling with the papers on her clipboard. Pulling them out, shuffling them, anything to avoid me and my imposing question.

The acid in my empty stomach burns as worry sets in. "Is he okay?"

"Oh, aye. He had to go deal with a wee situation at work," she finally says.

"Well, I'm glad he's doing well."

Even though he's choosing to ignore me.

"He'll be back soon, lass."

"It's fine. He doesn't owe me anything. We're just friends," I lie. To myself, to Ailith, to anyone with ears that could be overhearing this conversation. But no one believes the words coming out of my mouth, especially me. I should just stop talking before I embarrass myself more than I have.

Ailith happily drops the subject, offering me breakfast, and I absentmindedly place an order of food. I don't remember what, but she disappears into the kitchen, leaving me alone with my irritating and unhelpful thoughts.

My phone vibrates in my pocket. I reach for it quickly, like a pathetic lovesick puppy.

My heart skips a beat seeing his name pop up.

LACHLAN

> I miss you. Wish I was still wrapped up in the sheets with you. I'm sorry I couldn't text sooner.

My traitorous heart thunders in my chest.

I stare at my phone for a long time, not sure what to say.

LACHLAN

> I'm trying hard to get back to Corran. But in the meantime, I got you something.

I glance around the pub, not noticing anything out of the ordinary.

ME

> What?

Bubbles pop up immediately as he types a response. I want to ask him so many questions, tell him I'd prefer answers than some lame-ass distraction. Why is his job so secretive? And it seems like everyone else knows but me. Is he royalty and isn't meant to be involved with a nobody like me?

What does it matter? You're leaving.

LACHLAN

> Any minute now, Nessi.

I begin sifting through the last week and half, trying to figure out if I missed any hints he might have dropped when the street-facing doors to the pub whip open, the loud bang from the door hitting the wall draws my attention.

I blink in disbelief. Tempted to wipe my eyes with my knuckles like they do in cartoons.

I can't believe what I'm seeing.

"Avery!!!! Ahhhhhh!" Becca drops her bags and starts running towards me at full speed.

Becca, my best friend, Becca is here. In Scotland. In Corran, how did she know where exactly to find me...wait... how? What is she—

Before I can finish my scattered thoughts, her body smacks into me, as she throws her arms tightly around my neck.

"Becca? Am I hallucinating? What was in that coffee Ailith gave me?" I pull back, staring at her face. It's Becca. She's here. I pat her cheek, her auburn hair, squeeze her shoulders. She's really here.

"Are you really here? How?" I pull her in for another hug. She smells like peanuts and airports.

"Yes, Aves! I'm here. In mother-effing Scotland."

"How? What?" My brain is jumbled.

Becca steps away, staring at me with tears in her eyes. "Lachlan arranged the entire thing, Aves. Days ago. He said he had to go in for work and he didn't want you to be alone. Can you believe that man? He flew me out here so we could spend time together. It's been too long, Aves. You look so good!"

He didn't want you to be alone.

She pulls me in for another hug, gripping me so tightly the air escapes from my lungs. She's really here, with me. And Lachlan sent her, hoping it will make me happy, but I don't think he realizes what this actually means to me.

Lachlan, the same guy I was just telling myself is only with me for sex. People that are only sleeping together, don't fly best friends to a whole ass country to make them happy.

This is all too much. Becca here, his kindness—I am at a

loss. To see Becca in person, after all this time. My heart feels whole as I grab on to my best friend, not bothering to hold back my tears any longer.

avery

"Where are we going again?" Becca asks, sitting in the passenger seat of my rental car.

We spent the entire day yesterday catching up. She was tired after a full day of travel, so we stayed inside, mostly laying in bed as we talked about everything. Things we normally don't get a chance to say over text or phone. It was perfect.

But today, we're getting out of Corran and I'm showing her around this beautiful country.

"Ben Nevis."

"Have you spoken to Lachlan?"

I arch my brow at her. "Yes, he was texting me this morning."

"Andddd?" Becca drags out the word, as if she's talking to a small child.

"And what? He's doing good. Well, I'm not actually sure. He is very secretive about work but he's seems fine. I've already thanked him a million times if that's what you're worried about."

Becca shakes her head at me. "That's it? That's all you're going to say? He did all of this," she draws a wide circle with her arms. "Thought of it. Planned it. Coordinated it. Executed it. Don't you think that's beyond romantic?"

I pause, glancing back at the road. "It's not like that."

Becca scoffs. "Tell yourself whatever you want, sweetheart. The man is fucking smitten."

"It's not as deep as you think. He's a very nice person."

"Avery! No man is ever that nice. Wake up! We need to discuss the elephant in the room."

"No." My fingers twist tightly around the steering wheel.

"It's going to push us out of this moving vehicle if we don't."

"I don't want to talk about it, Becca. It's not up for discussion. This is a vacation fling, that is all. He's just nice. The unicorn of men."

"Who will be receiving a much-deserved blow job upon his return."

"Becca!! Do you have to be so blunt?"

"With you? Yes. Speaking of, how's the sex? We somehow did not talk about that last night."

"For good reason."

"Come on, Aves. I'm living vicariously through you right now. Unless I can find my own Scotsman to take home, but I'm only here for four days, so I'm not holding my breath."

I chew the inside of my cheek, thinking about all the orgasms I've had in the last week.

"Oh, that's a new look!"

I glance over at Becca. Her body is turned towards me, her hazel eyes bright with interest and she's got a stupidly large grin on her face.

I sigh, feeling the smile break out over my face.

"It's freaking amazing. Like, earth-shattering, body-quivering, I-forget-my-name amazing."

"Oh my God, yes! I love that for you. Only like, five percent jealous."

"It's not good. How am I supposed to have sex again? Not that I was before, but something has been unleashed in me. I feel like a hormonal animal. I'm ruined."

Becca raises both palms in the air. "You don't want to hear it from me. But at some point, I'm just going to come out and say what we both already know."

"You're wrong."

"Am I? Or are you still running, like you always do?" She utters quietly.

Her words inflate like a balloon, pressing uncomfortably between us. I'm not having this conversation. I may be able to hide from everyone, including myself but I can't hide from Becca. She sees right through me and isn't afraid to call me out for it.

"So, Ben Nevis. Highest peak in the United Kingdom. We'll climb, catch the sunset and end the day at a pub with a pint or two. It's going to take us all day but it'll be worth it. Trust me, when you get up there...you're going to have an out-of-body experience. This place is magical. There is a reason J.K. Rowling was inspired by Scotland when she wrote Harry Potter."

"You want me to climb a mountain all day? You're shitting me, right?"

I glare at her. "Listen, we used to hike all the time in Vancouver. Don't even pretend like you hate it. You packed your hiking gear without Lachlan needing to tell you."

"Yes! Because I know what you're like, and I knew you were going to make me work on holiday."

"Okay, so why are you complaining if you already knew? You're here to keep me occupied."

"Pfffft..." I spot Becca's smile from the corner of my eye, and I reach over, grasping her hand.

"Thanks for being here."

"Don't thank me, thank Lachlan."

I change the subject and Becca brings it right back to Lachlan. My best friend is relentless and infuriating, but I love her. And she's here. I couldn't be any happier right now.

"I'M GOING to murder you and leave your body on this mountain as a gift to all the animals." Becca is wheezing, slouched over on a giant rock. I pass her a bottle of water and she snatches it out of my hand without looking up.

"Come on. It's not that bad."

"Says the one who's been doing this kind of shit for weeks AND runs daily."

I cringe, feeling bad for pushing her. "That's fair. I'm sorry. Let's head back."

Becca's head whips up, her eyes shooting daggers at me. "I'm not leaving when we're this close. My mother raised no quitter. There was a family with small children that passed us twenty minutes ago. If those little shits can do it, so can I."

"You need to listen to your body. No one is going to judge you."

"I am! I will judge me. We're finishing this bitch."

Ben Nevis is more crowded than the other spots I've visited in Scotland. It's a popular tourist attraction, even late into the season. The climb has been constant and strenuous, but manageable with enough breaks. And there are plenty of scenic resting spots along the way.

"This place is really beautiful, though," Becca says, glancing around at the sheer size and majesty of this place.

Ben Nevis looms over the surrounding valleys and mountains like a giant. A towering mass of rock and earth, that seems to reach up to outer space. The surrounding landscape pales in comparison, dwarfed by the mountain's immense presence. It feels like we're standing in Olympus, amongst the gods.

"Avery, I need to tell you something but you need to pretend you didn't hear it from me."

Becca's voice distracts me from the view I was admiring. "What is it?"

I approach her, taking a seat on the rock beside her.

"I saw your dad at the grocery store the other day. He was with a woman. It looked like they were buying things for dinner together. He looked happy, Aves. So happy."

I stand up, because this is too big of a news to take sitting down. I stare down at Becca, pressing my hand to my chest.

"Are you serious?"

She nods, her eyes glistening with tears as I reach out, pulling her in for a hug.

It feels like a monstrously heavy weight has been lifted off my chest. I wish I had heard it from my dad but I didn't care, not right now. Not hearing the words "happy" attached to my dad. My dad, who has been nursing a broken heart for as long as I can remember, is in a relationship with a new woman. And he's so happy that it's obvious from someone on the outside, looking in.

"I know. I almost burst into tears in the bread aisle."

I laugh, standing back to look at Becca's face. "What did she look like?"

"Short brown hair. Beautiful brown skin. She is tall, only a few inches shorter than your dad. She seems kind and gentle. I caught her staring at your dad while he was reading the ingredients on some sauce bottle. She was admiring him, with the cutest smile on her face."

Oh my heart.

"I can't wait to meet her."

The woman who had been special enough to enter my dad's life, put him back together in a way no one else could in the past. I just hope my dad is healed enough to allow himself to finally be happy. He's so brave for jumping in, and putting himself out there. Something blooms in my chest, knowing he isn't lonely anymore. That he has healed.

Maybe healing isn't about trying to erase the past or abandon the pain. Life doesn't work like that; broken hearts don't magically put themselves back together. Grief never lets you forget the loss you went through, the emotions you felt sitting in a cold hospital room, all alone. That type of pain will always be with you, no matter who you are. Maybe it's not about forgetting, but learning how to breathe around the broken pieces of yourself, until inhaling doesn't burn. It's about learning how to love yourself after you fall apart.

Finding happiness and light in the aftermath.

"Me too." Becca whispers, wrapping her hand in mine as we head towards the trail.

EVERY STEP IS BECOMING MORE difficult than the last, as the wind howls and the rain lashes against us. We are soaked, our clothes heavy with moisture. I glance at Becca, only finding determination and focus on her face as we continue to climb higher. My lungs burn with effort but we are so close—a few more minutes and we will be at the top, standing above the clouds.

The wind picks up, threatening to knock me to my feet. The weather has changed drastically as we near the top. The air has grown thin and harsh. I know I won't be lingering at the top for long. Just enough to claim the personal victory and climb back down. A pint of beer sounds real good right about now.

Seconds turn into minutes and we finally reach the summit, both of us holding on to our knees, gasping for air. I finally force my body to stand tall as I look out at the breathtaking view. I feel Becca's fingers lace mine, she squeezes my hand tightly.

"We fucking did it," she breathes.

I nod. We have conquered more than the mountain, as we stood, looking at the awe-inspiring view from the top of Ben Nevis. We are on top of the world. I feel unstoppable. Like I could overcome anything I set my mind to.

The vista before us is nothing short of stunning, with uneven peaks stretching out into the far distance, valleys dropped away into the mist. It feels like the heavens. Something almost spiritual grazes me, and I could swear Becca feels it too. I see it in the way she is silently quivering, taking it all in. We stand there, holding onto one another for as long as possible, until the cold begins to seep into my bones, and with one final glance over my shoulder, we begin our descent.

I feel lighter than I have in years climbing back down Ben Nevis.

CHAPTER FORTY-SEVEN

avery

"I wish you could stay longer. Four days is nowhere near enough."

Becca and I are standing outside the inn, her driver is about five minutes away and I'm tempted to throw her in the back of my car and just take us somewhere far away.

"I know, but I have to get back to work or they're going to fire my ass."

"We both know your boss isn't going to fire you. He's been in love with you for years."

Her eyes get thin. "You're insane, Avery."

I sigh, deciding to leave this conversation for another day. "Thank you for coming. It was exactly what my soul needed."

"Me too. I'm so glad your fuck buddy is rich."

I laugh, nudging her and trying to forget about how much I miss a certain someone. When he's all I've been thinking about, day and night.

"I'll be sure to thank him when…if, he gets back."

A black Audi turns, pulling into the carpark.

"Oh, that must be my driver. The app said he's driving an Audi."

"I thought he was supposed to meet us here, by the front door?"

Becca shrugs, picking up her suitcase. "Beats me. Let's go."

As we round the corner, I see Lachlan stepping out of the black Audi that pulled in a minute ago. My stomach lurches to my throat, forcing my legs to stop dead in their tracks. My heart smashes wildly against my rib cage.

He looks up, ocean eyes locking on mine.

I don't think twice about it as I break into a run.

Lachlan sweeps me up in an effortless, warm embrace, as I twist my legs around him, forcing us closer together. His arm sits upright against my back, hand behind my neck as he presses his body into mine. The world disintegrates around us.

"I fucking missed you, mo gradh."

"I missed you too." Tired eyes stare back at me, exhausted and restless, like he hasn't slept in the last few days.

"You did?" he says, sounding surprised.

I lean down and kiss him. He groans, lips melding into mine as his tongue traces my lip, asking for entry. I open up, and he deepens our kiss, not a care in the world about where we are or who's watching. His fingers inch up my scalp, holding me in place as we melt into one another. Our kiss is hard and boundless, desperate with longing.

"I don't mean to break up this steamy reunion but I'm getting very uncomfortable standing here, and my ride just pulled in."

Shit, Becca.

I drop to the ground, breathless as I smooth down my clothes.

Becca is staring at Lachlan as he runs his hand through his hair, wiping the sex look off his face. She sticks her hand out awkwardly, blushing. I smile to myself, watching her try to hold it together. I don't blame her, I had the same reaction when I first met Lachlan. Worse, I was a blubbering mess.

"Nice to finally meet you in person. And thank you, for all of this. For bringing us together." Becca shoots me a look as Lachlan shakes her hand.

"It was my pleasure, Becca. I'm so glad you were able to come on such short notice. Sorry you can't stay longer."

"Next time," Becca promises, both their eyes catch mine. I avert my gaze, my pulse fluttering.

"I'll give you two a minute."

Lachlan steps away, grabbing Becca's bags as he approaches the car that's going to take my best friend to the airport soon. I know I'll be seeing her in Vancouver in a few weeks, but I'm riddled with emotions right now, not wanting to let her go.

"Holy shit, Avery. He's gorgeous," Becca whispers, her eyes on Lachlan's back.

I huff out, "I know, it's really annoying. And he's nice. Which only makes him hotter."

"He looks familiar, I can't put my finger on it. Probably from all my dreams combined." Becca laughs.

I glance back, watching Lachlan place Becca's bags in the trunk while the driver leans against the car, lighting a cigarette.

"Look at me," Becca says urgently, pressing both her cold hands on my cheeks. She's shorter than me, so I lurch over awkwardly, staring at her with a smushed face.

"Jes—"

"Shut up, I need you to listen." Her eyes dart behind me for a second, making sure Lachlan isn't near us. "He's good, Avery. Really good. And he cares about you, deeply. Anyone could see that. I don't care if you both want to pretend this means nothing, but fuck...Avery, let him in."

I step back, grabbing her wrists and pulling them away from my face.

"Becca, stop."

"No, you stop. Stop fighting this. Why can't you just be happy? You out of everyone I know deserves this, Avery. You deserve to be happy."

"I'm not fighting anything. I don't live here, he does. My life is in Canada, with you and Dad. This isn't my home," I say, keeping my voice low.

"That's not a fucking reason and you know it."

"Come on, lassie! I don't got all day!" the driver yells.

Becca puts her arms around me, planting a kiss on my cheek.

"I love you and I just want you to be happy. Promise you'll think about what I said."

I nod and she holds my hand firmly as we walk towards the car.

"SO..." I say, glancing out my window.

After Becca left, Lachlan asked if I would take a drive with him. He has a motorbike and a top-of-the-line Audi. The liquor industry must be lucrative. Likely does other things that make him good money—secretive work no one is willing to share with me. Because if he was gone for whisky business, he would have just told me that.

Maybe it's best I don't know. I need to keep my heart protected and my feelings in check.

"Where are we going?"

"You'll see." He reaches for my hand and guides it towards

the stick shift. I close my fingers around the cool metal, feeling Lachlan's fingers overlap with mine, forming a snug grip.

"I don't really like surprises." I stare down at our joined hands.

I can hear the smirk in his voice. "You liked the last one."

"That wasn't a surprise, Lachlan. That, I don't even know what that was. But it meant the world to me."

His thumb circles the back of my hand, as he shifts gears. The familiar bolt of electricity spreads from my hand, shooting out as it lights up my body.

"I hated leaving but I'm glad it meant you got to see your friend. If I hadn't been forced to, I wouldn't have gone. And you wouldn't have seen Becca, which would have been a shame considering how happy you are around her."

"You didn't have to do that. You could have just left and texted me. You don't owe me anything."

His face falls, hurt flashes in his eyes and I feel instant shame. Regretful for taking a stab like that. But that wasn't my intention. It's just the truth, we don't know one another enough for that kind of grand gesture. We know our bodies intimately, we have great chemistry, but on a personal level, we're both so guarded. Especially Lachlan, he's a closed vault. And that's okay because our story is bound to end soon. It doesn't mean we can't enjoy whatever time we have remaining.

Everything comes to an end—a five-star book, the guitar solo in an amazing song, the credits at the end of a movie, a terrifying nightmare, or a dream you want to remain in forever. A hug, kiss, a touching conversation with an old friend. Sunny days on the beach, rainy ones where you have nothing else to do but lay in bed, reading. They all end.

But it doesn't mean you stop enjoying things that make you happy. It doesn't mean you stop the song midway or turn off the TV before the movie ends. It doesn't mean you stop reading the book. We ride it out, experience it all...good or bad, knowing it will eventually pass.

"That's where you're wrong." He shakes his head, letting out an exasperated grunt. "There are things I'm not able to say, not because I don't want to but because...I just can't. I don't want to drag you in my mess. I want to protect you. And no, I didn't have to do it. But I wanted to, because knowing you're happy makes me happy."

His eyes flick to mine. "I couldn't stand the thought of you alone in that room, thinking I just left. It wasn't fair to you. Our time is short, and I don't want you to spend a second of it thinking I don't..." His jaw clenches, as the rest of the words die on his lips. He glances away, staring at the long stretch of empty road in front of him.

I'm a little taken aback by the gravity of his words, and everything he didn't dare say. I don't want to think about all the ways that sentence could have ended. Not wanting to fight with him or continue this conversation, I decide we need some good music to change the somber mood.

Twisting in my seat, the leather groans underneath me as I grab my phone. My other hand is still trapped under Lachlan's.

The crushed glass screen scratches my thumb, reminding me that I broke my phone after Ben Nevis. I have a text from Elle and Becca, and I respond to both before opening up my Spotify app and search for a good song.

"What happened to your phone?"

Lachlan frowns, his lips twisting into knot.

"Oh...long story. It's not a big deal."

"We've got nothing but time right now."

"It's my fault. After Ben Nevis, Becca and I went to a nearby pub to celebrate and we got a little drunk. I left my phone at the bar and didn't notice it was gone until after we walked out. We ran back in, looking like two idiots rummaging around in the dark. The bartender noticed us, asked what I was looking for, and then handed me my cracked phone. He told me someone had given it to him."

Lachlan's eyes dart to mine, his forehead creased. "Someone found your phone and returned it? Broken?"

My shoulders lift up. "Yeah, it probably fell on the floor, someone likely stepped on it. Who knows? I'm just happy the person was nice enough to leave it with the bartender."

Lachlan's attention is on me, a disoriented look on his face when he should be watching the road.

"The road," I remind him.

"Did you talk to anyone at the pub?"

"Probably, I don't know. It was a long day and we'd had a few drinks. Why?"

"I need you to remember, Avery. If you can."

I shake my head, closing my eyes and exhaling loudly. I don't have the energy for this.

"What is this about?"

Lachlan doesn't answer me. His mouth tightens as he removes the hand resting on top of mine on the stick shift. Reaching inside his jacket to retrieve his phone, Lachlan types quickly, eyes darting up and down from the road to the phone. When he's done, he tucks his phone back in his pocket and reaches over, laying his warm hand on my thigh.

"You're not going to tell me about this one either?" I sag into my seat, feeling defeated with the layers of secrets in between us.

"Do you want a new phone?" He says.

"No. I have insurance. I'll get it fixed when I get back home."

He nods once, his eyes glued to the road, brows still pulled in. He's got a very attractive pissed-off face, and I imagine make-up sex with him would be catastrophically good. But the man is not in the mood today and since I just got him back, I don't want to waste time fighting with him. He should have just stayed in Corran, maybe spent the day in bed sleeping it off.

I tap the large touch screen on the car dash. The thing lights up instantly, showcasing a smartphone interface. Wow, fancy technology.

"You know, you can tell a lot about a person by the type of music they listen to," I say, glancing at him from the corner of my eye.

"Is that so?"

I nod, smiling. "Anything you don't want me to see?"

Lips pursed, he shakes his head.

I swipe the screen, clicking on Lachlan's Spotify app. Playlists populate instantly as his most played songs line up in front of me.

Immediately, I'm drawn to the classical music section. Bach, Vivaldi, Mozart. I click on Bach's "Cello Suite No. 1 in G Major" and the cabin fills with sweet notes of piano and cello. But there is also Ed Sheeran, Linkin Park, Blink 182 and ...excuse me?

"You like Rüfüs Du Sol?!"

He glances at me before checking the screen.

"I love them." He smiles, and it's the best damn thing I've seen all day.

Maybe we can turn this day around, after all.

"I would have never. Aren't you too old for progressive music?" I joke, his hand tightens around my thigh and I laugh softly, pressing play as "No Place" by Rüfüs Du Sol begins blaring through the speakers.

Closing my eyes, I lean back, letting the hypnotic melody of the song pulse along my skin.

The electronic instruments and subtle guitar riffs weave together, lifting me up, as the emotive vocals pierce through my heart. The lyrics speak of meeting a stranger and discovering an inexplicable connection so profound, it feels like true belonging. As if you've always known them. The desire to be with this person is all-consuming, drawing you in deeper and deeper, until you're unable to resist.

I'm left breathless, singing the words to the song. Tingles race down my spine, settling at the base, as if the music has unearthed a buried emotion I've refused to feel. My chest heaves, flooded with something I can't begin to explain.

When I open my eyes, the car is stopped on the side of the road, and Lachlan's watching me. His chest is rising and falling, mirroring mine after listening to the song. His knuckles are white, hands fisted, like he's forcing himself back.

"Lachlan...," I whisper, breaking the silence.

I can't tell who makes the first move. The kiss is a storm, fierce and chaotic, like the ocean during an angry tempest. It shatters through me, leaving me breathless and dizzy, as the waves rage around us, mirroring the wild beating of our hearts. The force of the water drags me deeper and deeper until he is suddenly everywhere—in my thoughts, my senses, my soul...my heart.

CHAPTER FORTY-EIGHT

lachlan

No matter where I go, how far I get, Edgar still has a hold on me. Pushing legal documents in front of my face, giving me threats, trying to control me so that I abide by his commands. And I go, because I'm weak. When he threatens to ruin me or give me away, I run like a wounded dog with my tail tucked in between my legs. And it only gives him more power over me. Every threat becomes worse than the last.

The guy gets off on power and control.

I worked non-stop trying to get back to Avery, to this exact moment, and I wish I could tell her that. She's using my silence as fuel to keep herself guarded, protecting her heart and pretending like this isn't real. We both know that's far from the truth. You can't kiss someone like that and say it means nothing.

You can't kiss like that and have it not change you. A terrifying kind of kiss that buries itself deep in your heart. I didn't even know it was possible until I touched her lips.

I found a lawyer in Inverness and made an appointment to see him later this week, get the legal process started against Edgar. I'll pay extra if it means getting out of my contracts quickly. The sooner I do this, the sooner I can climb my way out of hell.

And tell Avery everything.

The thing is, I remember what it felt like to be free. It was an honest life, but at least it meant something. At least it didn't feel like breathing underwater, suffocating a slow painful death while people stood around, watching. I want to go back to the way things were. Figure out my focus, my future...start new. I want to walk out of my house without needing to look over my shoulder every single time. Without the constant need to fucking hide.

I also need more time with Avery. More time to fuck her, cherish her, protect her, care for her, and love her.

But more than anything, more time to make her fall in love with me. Because I have no idea how the bloody hell I'm supposed to ever let her go.

How do you let go of someone that feels like home?

I PULL into the carpark at Fairy Glen Falls and kill the engine. Avery's busy looking around, taking in her new surroundings, but I don't give a shit about any of that. I just stare at her. She's so goddamn beautiful.

"Fairy Glen Falls? I've heard of this place!"

Avery excitedly unbuckles her seat belt and nearly jumps out of the car with delight. You can't see the falls from here, but the surrounding forest is lush, waiting to suck us into its beauty. She turns impatiently, facing me. Avery tucks her hair behind her ear, soft brown tendrils kissing her middle back. I grab a fistful of it and pull her lips to mine. I hate myself for wasting days away from her. Days I won't get back.

"I'm sorry," I whisper against her lips.

Her hand rests on my cheek as she pulls away, running her nose against mine with her eyes closed. Her thick, brown lashes fan across the top of her cheeks. She's got faded freckles along her face, and I've counted every single one. She usually covers them with product, but today she's not wearing any makeup.

"I forgive you."

I plant kisses all over her face, causing her to laugh. She opens her eyes, running her fingers through my hair. I want to capture every touch. Every freckle. Every crooked smile.

It'll be all I'll have left after...

Her whisky eyes collide with mine, stealing my breath.

No, I can't let her leave. I'm certain this is a once-in-a-lifetime kind of thing.

The words are at the edge of my tongue, but she doesn't want to hear that, she doesn't want to know how she's taken my world and flipped it upside down in the most prodigious way.

"Stay with me," I murmur.

Another kiss.

"I'm right here."

That's not what I meant. I meant, forever.

I have to get out of this car before I say more words and fuck this all up. We've already had a shit start, my mind running over the details she glossed over about losing her phone.

Could it be?

No. That problem was dealt with. I take out my phone anxiously, pulling up my conversation with Henry. I messaged him on the drive over, needing to know that Stephanie was still locked away.

ME

I thought you were always on your phone?

HENRY

Some of us work all day. I just got off the
phone with the institute, actually. They
wouldn't tell me much other than the fact that
she's still there, and will be for a long time.

Relief floods my vision after reading Henry's response. I exhale the breath I was clutching onto tightly.

ME

Cheers mate, I really appreciate it.

HENRY

Remember that the next time I try to get a
hold of you.

I tuck my phone away, grabbing my hat. I lean close to Avery, loving the way her body responds to me as I open the glove box, taking out my sunglasses.

She blinks at me, unimpressed. "It's cloudy, you don't need those."

"You never know with Scotland. One minute it's cloudy, the next sunny, the next it's pissing rain." I flash her a smile, stepping out of the car.

Avery gets out at the same time. Walking around the front of the car, I reach for her hand, lacing our fingers together.

"Are you ready, lass?"

She nods, smiling up at me like the sun. We head for the stony trail surrounded by thick greens. There is no one ahead of us and I look around, checking our surroundings again.

I need to blend in today. No distractions.

Just time with my bonnie lass.

My grip tightens in her hand as I pull her body next to

mine. She squeezes my hand twice, letting me know that she's with me.

"How long is the walk?" Her soft voice blends in with the picturesque forest.

"It's not long. About an hour, and it's all a clear path like this. Switches between stone and wooden trails." Our boots click on the stones that have lined the ground here for decades, each shape different from the next.

"It's so green. I thought with the colder seasons, the trees would have started to change colour by now."

"Some parts stay green but most of the landscape changes in the winter. We even get snow."

"Wish I could see it all." She sighs.

"Why don't you? Stay longer."

"I can't. I have to get back to reality at some point. I can't run from my problems forever."

I glance down at her. "Is the breakup what brought you to Scotland?"

I don't deserve to know more about her, not when I'm keeping important things hidden. Not when I avoid hard questions, only offering her silence instead of words because I don't want to lie to her face.

She hesitates, taking in a steady breath.

"Sort of. I mean, it definitely pushed me to make the decision and head to the airport. But I've been needing to do this for a long time."

"Will you tell me the rest of it someday?" Because I recognize the familiar feeling of pain, the need to run away as far as possible, to pretend to be someone else. Start anew and leave behind everything you hate.

She blinks up at me. "What makes you think there is more to it?"

I lean down, brushing my lips against her cheek. "Because I know you."

Avery forces a smile, averting her gaze from mine.

"How about you? Have you found what you're looking for in the highlands?" She does this whenever she's uncomfortable, turning the spotlight away from herself quickly.

Aye, I'm looking right at her.

"What makes you think I'm looking for anything?"

She's been censoring her questions lately. Not wanting to know things about me, because she believes the more she learns, the harder it will be to pull away when the time comes. But, none of that matters. It's already too late. Her curiosity is a welcome change, reminds me of the night we walked to the lighthouse, discovering things about each other.

"That's why you came to Corran, to get some space, find some clarity. Isn't it?"

I guess I did. My house felt foreign, unpleasant. I left Glasgow, needing to figure out my next move, what I planned to do with the life I had chased for so long, the same life that was eating me alive.

But being here, out in the highlands, I found something even better.

"Something like that."

I glance down at our joined hands, as we walk in silence. The sound of distant birds, rustling leaves, and soft streams growing louder the closer we get to the falls. Raising the back of her hand up to my lips, I kiss her soft skin. Holding it close to my heart.

"Tell me something." Avery breaks the silence.

"What do you want to know?"

"Anything."

I have a million things to say but I push the urge down.

"Did you know your name is Scottish?"

"Hmmm, I'm not so sure about that." Avery's lips quirk, looking at me like I've just said the most ridiculous thing.

A delicate ray of sunlight descends through the branches, casting a soft glow on her bronzed skin. It's the perfect moment to capture on camera. Her beauty never ceases to amaze me, her allure is more than just skin deep; the richness of her soul and spirit. Her gentle heart, woven together with threads of courage, vulnerability, and strength. My own heart swells with an admiration that knows no bounds.

"I'm serious, it means ruler of the elves."

She nudges her shoulder into me and laughs.

"Does it look like I have Scottish in me?" She points down to herself.

Arching my eyebrow, I lean close to her ear. "I'd say you do.

Do you need another reminder, lass? Maybe up against that tree over there? I could fill you with so much Scottish, you won't be able to walk straight."

I drink up her heated cheeks and the small gasp that falls out of her lips. She looks up at me with pure lust and I wonder which memory she's thinking about while she stares at me with those whisky orbs. Which position she is replaying, as her eyes dilate, before falling to the ground. Was it the other morning when I woke her with my head in between her legs, as she screamed out my name, pulling on my hair? Or when I pressed her down in a field, sliding inside her because we just couldn't wait to get back to the inn.

Fuck, I want her so bad I think I let out an audible groan.

Avery coughs, pulling my thoughts away. "You seem to know a lot about Scotland and whisky. Is it a Scottish thing or being in your mid-thirties thing?"

My laugh pierces the air, echoing through the forest.

"You seriously need to do that more," she gushes.

"What?"

"Laugh like that. It's infectious, to see you that free."

Free. What a concept. But I suppose I was, in this moment, free. And it has everything to do with the woman walking beside me, holding my hand.

Avery might be the first woman to compliment my laugh. Not my smile or the orchestrated poses I've been taught over the years, but the reason for that type of happiness. I've heard every variation of compliments and praises in the past, all surface level.

At the beginning, it flattered me, I'm not going to lie, the attention was nice. But over time, the compliments became chaotic and meaningless. Numbers on coffee cups, sticky notes thrown in the cab, pub napkins with hotel room numbers. Quick interactions only. No one was interested in actually talking to me, going to get tea to just chat with me. Get to know the real me. They just wanted to sleep with me to fulfill a fantasy. One time, a woman actually asked if she could call me by a different name.

I went back to my room that night, feeling utterly worthless and alone.

But then Avery came along and treated me like a normal person, didn't even give me the time of day. She fucking ran away from me.

"Are you happy, Lachlan?" she whispers, her amber eyes focused on me.

Her question catches me off guard. I stop walking, grabbing the back of her head and bringing her close.

"Right now? Yes."

And then I kiss her, chasing this moment, and not wasting a single second of it. Avery's body molds into mine. Her tongue dives into my mouth, charging the electricity burning between us, like a thousand fucking suns inside my chest. I won't survive this fall.

We remain like that for minutes, hours, days. I don't bloody know, time doesn't exist when I'm losing myself in her. But Avery eventually pulls away, breathless and staring at me with fuck-me eyes.

"We're never going to make it to the falls if you kiss me like that again."

"Maybe that's my plan," I lean in, whispering against her lips.

"You're just trying to distract me. Changing the subject so you can avoid talking about yourself."

"No, lass. I just can't get enough of you," I rasp.

I am desperate to steer the conversation away from myself but I'm also desperate for her. When I'm with her I'm overcome with euphoria, no control, no thoughts, just the need to be with her. To feel her close to me. I forget who I am and all the things I hate about myself. Seeing myself through her eyes, it's like falling off an endless cliff. All the other bullshit doesn't exist when we're together.

"Besides, we were talking about the origins of your name. Where are your parents from?"

She pinches the bridge of her nose, casting her eyes skyward before she begins walking away from me.

Bloody brat.

"Fine. I'll go first. Born in Scotland, raised in Scotland. Mom was from Corran and I don't know my dad. He took off before I was born."

"I'm sorry."

"I'm not. I had everything I needed."

Her brows draw together. "It's nice that you didn't feel the loss."

"What do you mean?" I ask.

She shakes her head quickly. "Nothing. My parents are Canadian. Dad was born and raised in Vancouver. My mom is Turkish but moved to Canada when she was young. I remember Dad saying I'm part Bolivian, as well, on my mom's side."

Avery speaks fast, as if she's eager to just get this piece of information out and never talk about it again.

"You look like your mom, then."

"Yeah." A flicker of sadness flashes in her eyes, but disappears just as quickly. "I got my dark features from my mom. Copy, paste my dad always said."

"Why do you seem sad about that?"

She stares off into the distance, mulling over her thoughts. "I don't know. I've just never liked my brown eyes. Hair you can change, but my eyes are dull, lifeless. My dad has the most beautiful green eyes. I wish I had a piece of him with me."

Dull? Is she fucking serious?

I stop, grabbing her wrist and pulling her back to me. "Don't talk like that about yourself. You have beautiful eyes. I love your eyes."

She tries to look away, move out of my grasp. "Says the man with ocean-coloured eyes and an alluring Scottish accent. It doesn't count coming from you."

I can't help but chuckle. "What?"

She wrinkles her nose, irritated with me. "It doesn't count coming from you. Your eyes are the colour of the ocean. Not the middle of the ocean where it's dark and deep. But the crystal blue hue close to shore, with white sands. Sometimes they're so blue it looks like they're glowing, especially when you stand in the rain. And other times, they turn dark and stormy...when you're upset or turned on..."

Bloody hell, I love this woman.

Avery's eyes grow into saucers as realization dawns on her. Her face flushes red and my lips curl into a giant smile. She covers her mouth with her hand, groaning.

"I DID not just say all of that out loud. I'm such an idiot...I totally didn't mean it like that, I mean...of course, I meant it. But not in the creepy way it came out. I just—" Her voice is muffled beneath her hand as she keeps talking, trying to take it all back. Tuck the words back into the confines of her mind.

I reach up, flipping my cap around. My heart soars in my chest, taking flight. I take back what I said about falling. This is soaring, high in the sky, so high that I'm grazing the stars in the night sky.

"Avery?"

Her eyes drop to the ground. "Yeah..."

"Stop talking and get over here so I can fucking kiss you."

There are so many things we hide. Secrets, dark pasts, emotions we tell ourselves we don't feel. Pieces that shape us, change us forever. I want all pieces of her. Even the ones she hates, the dark pieces that dimmed her light. I want to fuse myself with all her broken parts and put her back together. I want to hold her hand, prove to her how beautiful and strong she is.

THE DENSE FOREST begins to thin out as we approach the first waterfall. A massive rock formation towers above us, commanding attention. The sound of rushing water grows louder, as two prominent streams trickle down on either side. But that is only the beginning. As we draw closer, one of the falls splits into two separate streams at the top before converging again at the bottom, creating a breathtaking display of nature's power and beauty. The water is so clear that in some parts, it creates a glowing blue hue. Shimmering perfectly, like small diamonds floating in the water.

Avery approaches the falls silently. Her face is utterly awestruck, as she takes in every detail.

I love watching her when she's lost in another world. As if I'm discovering something extraordinary for the first time.

"Legend has it that fairies come out at night, dance and play around in these waters. And if you visit during a full moon and leave an offering of food or drink, they will grant you a single wish," I say.

Avery's eyes dance with wonder, as she extends her arm out to me. I don't hesitate as I reach for her, leading us to a large log laying at the edge of the water.

There is a haunted look in her eyes that reminds me of the night I came here.

The night I almost broke.

I left Glasgow in the dead of night. Drove straight here, sat in this exact spot as I watched the blue waters sparkle, waiting for a sign. Seeking change, redemption, a way out, anything. I would have offered my soul if it meant I could re-do it all, turn back time. I was consumed by pain, anger, and fear, constantly feeling like an outsider. Living a life that was not truly mine. I was a fucking coward. And I hated myself for all of it, especially that night.

Maybe if I had taken the time to deal with my demons, instead of pushing them aside, pretending like they didn't exist, I would not have ended up here that night. Maybe things would have gone differently for me.

"It's beautiful, Lachlan. Thank you." Avery's glossy eyes lift to mine.

She thanks me with tears in her eyes, like she understands. Our pain bonding us together in this moment.

If anyone could understand, it would be her.

"I used to come here a lot. The sound of rushing water always helped quiet my mind. I've never had a wish come true, but I always leave a gift, full moon or not," I say roughly, staring out at the water.

Avery presses her other hand overtop of our entwined fingers. "What did you wish for?"

"To go back in time."

She nods. "Yeah, I think we all wish for that at some point in our lives."

I pause, my gut twisting. "This is the first place I came to after I left Glasgow. I was desperate to get away from the city, and I drove until I ended up here. I sat in front of the falls for hours, hoping to find anything, something in the moving waters."

Avery's grasp tightens in my hand. I keep my eyes on the

continuous stream of water, the sound of my beating heart is suddenly louder than the rushing water. But I want to open up my chest and bare every piece of myself to her.

"There was an incident with a woman I was seeing. I had met her at work, it was casual and never anything serious. I broke it off after a few months, because she was showing up at my house, at events, at my neighbourhood pub, she even tracked down Elle when she was visiting me in Glasgow. Trying to befriend her." I hesitate, taking in a sharp breath and not knowing if I can keep going.

"It's okay. You don't have to." Avery's eyes find mine and she nods, giving me the comfort I need to continue.

"I want to...we had a big fight after that. I told her I didn't want to see her again. A few weeks later, she was fired from work. Not because of our relationship, but lack of performance or some shite. Months passed, and I started to forget about the whole thing. Until one night, when she sent me a frightening text. I was worried she was going to harm herself, so I drove to her house. At some point..." I take a deep breath, glancing down at our hands.

"At some point in the night...she drugged me, I think from a bottle of water...I don't know. I honestly don't remember much. She took compromising photos...of me, with things, using tools meant for...fuck," I lean my elbow on my knee, closing my eyes. "I can never unsee those images. She had a metal cage in her basement." Avery's body goes rigid next to me.

I exhale, trying to pull myself together. "She left me in there for the night. I woke up in the morning naked, on a cold concrete floor, surrounded by a metal rods like a fucking animal. She threatened to expose me. To ruin my career if I didn't choose to be with her."

Avery's breath hitches, her chin trembles in astonishment as she gazes at me.

"I put on my best performance, agreed to it all. She...bloody hell—"

Tears roll down Avery's face, I reach out and grab one with the pad of my finger.

"She even made me prove it to her. And when I finally got out, I ran to the police, I called my manager, confided in my work partner. Things moved quickly after that. The police got in, found the cage—took all the evidence, except for the compromising photos she had of me. We couldn't find that anywhere but there was enough for them to arrest her. My DNA was all over the tools. I put in a non-harassment order. That was over a year ago. But a few months back, I heard she was released and sent to a mental hospital in Glasgow. Edgar, my manager, thought maybe she had improved. That it would be good for me to go visit her. Make the whole thing go away. He said it was bad for business. That's when it all hit me and I realized I needed to leave. And I headed straight to Corran...to here."

A heavy silence falls in between us. I focus on the sound of rushing water, remembering to breathe through the painful memories.

"Lachlan...I don't even know what to say. I'm so sorry."

"You and me both, lass."

"Is this the whisky business? A managing partner you're working with?"

"In part, Anam Cara is mostly mine. Edgar has been managing other contracts and projects over the years. But he treats his clients like absolute garbage—as if we're soulless robots, meant to only fill his pockets. It was okay for the first little while. It helped set me up. But it quickly turned into something ugly and I couldn't do it anymore. I don't want to live that life anymore."

Every time I relive the events in my head, it doesn't feel

real. It feels like I'm on the outside looking in, watching a horror movie.

It will be over soon.

"You're so strong, for leaving. For making such a big change."

"Not strong, just a good actor. I should have done it a long time ago. Before it got bad." I smile awkwardly, glancing into Avery's disturbed eyes.

The irony of it all isn't lost on me.

I breathe in the conifers and bushes circling us. Focusing on the here and now. The way Avery's hand feels in mine. The knowing look in her eyes, when I finally opened a part of myself to her. In the way I don't feel so alone, with her by my side. I bend down, kissing her softly. Feeling weightless for the first time.

<h1 style="text-align:center">CHAPTER FIFTY</h1>

<h1 style="text-align:center">avery</h1>

"Ready to go?"

"Yep, I just need a second," I say.

Reaching into my jacket and pulling out a granola bar, I edge closer to the falls, leaving the bar on a rock overflowing with gifts from other visitors, sitting untouched.

I close my eyes, and make a wish.

When I turn, Lachlan has his eyes fixed on me, smiling with admiration as he takes my hand.

"What did you wish for?"

"That's between me and the fairies."

His laugh echoes, falling gracefully around us like a blanket, as we make our way back to the carpark. I wasn't expecting him to open up to me in that way. Honestly, I never thought he would. I figured we would have our time in the sun and go our separate ways.

Then he shared an impossible part of himself with me. All his rough edges from the first time we met finally made sense. Well, not all. I know there are things he's still keeping close to his chest, but it takes a lot to open up to someone like that. I recognized the familiar look of helplessness in his eyes, the guilt, the fear, the hatred. I knew it too well.

This silent recognition between us has been happening a lot more lately. Sometimes words aren't even necessary. Maybe I don't have to say it, because at times when he looks at me, I know he can feel the things I'm not saying.

Lachlan's strength is inspiring in many ways. His determination, drive, the way he pours all of himself into everything he does.

I'm not sure I trust myself anymore.

The smart thing to do would be to pack up my shit, say my goodbyes and move on. That would be the sensible thing to do. Leave before things get too hard. Emotions were meant to be left out of this agreement. I promised myself that from the very beginning.

I could wrap up our story here. It would be the most perfect ending. Untouched. Preserved in time. No ending means no heartbreak, no war.

But then again, leaving is inevitable. It may hurt a bit more, but nothing can hurt as much as the past. What's a little extra pain in exchange for more time with him? For a once-in-a-lifetime connection I never thought I would get to experience? Shouldn't I enjoy this happiness for a little while longer?

Just a bit more time and then I'll leave.

LACHLAN KILLS THE ENGINE, as we both sit with our thoughts for a few minutes, outside the inn back in Corran. The day at Fairy Glen Falls seems so far away, even though we just got back from there. I left changed somehow, deepened our connection without intending to. And now, I'm sitting here with unwelcome and overwhelming incessant chatter in my mind. I just want to shut my brain off and get lost for a little while.

Stepping out of the car, we make our way towards the inn. The temperatures continue to drop at night, and I wrap my arms around myself, walking a little faster. A jacket falls around my shoulders, and I look up to find Lachlan looming over me.

"Thank you," I say.

He nods, nestling me close to his side. The muffled sound of music carries outside from the pub as we head for the adjacent door to the inn. I pull out my key and speed walk down to my room, hearing Lachlan's boots follow close behind me.

Opening my door, I turn to see him leaning against the wall. He keeps his gaze on me, waiting for an invitation or words I don't have.

He seems nervous, almost shy. Maybe we're both overwhelmed right now but the last thing I need to do is talk about it. I'm done talking or feeling or thinking.

I step inside my room and leave the door ajar. My heart hammers against my chest, as I take my muddy boots off by the door. Heading inside the bathroom, I keep the lights off, twisting the shower on as I strip out of my clothes.

I hear the sound of the door closing and locking behind me. Releasing a sigh of relief, I face the shower, my back to the open bathroom door as I feel his eyes on me, watching my every move. Removing the last piece of clothing clinging to my body, I step inside the hot shower, letting out a quiet whimper as the hot stream sinks into my muscles, warming my bones.

A soft glow shines from outside the bathroom.

I run my hands through my hair, letting the water work its comforting magic like it always does. I hear a belt buckle drop to the floor as Lachlan steps in behind me. I feel him every-where, as he wraps his arms around me, tugging my back against his comforting chest. He envelops me, sliding my hair to the side, and stringing kisses from my shoulder up to my neck.

I want him to reach down, touch my aching breasts or my throbbing core but he doesn't. I'm out of breath by the time he turns me around, still holding me tightly, as if he's worried I'll evaporate right in front of his eyes. I bury my face into the hollow of his neck, sinking into him.

This is too intimate.

Dangerous territory.

Lachlan's hands rove around my ribs, his fingertips pressing into my lower back. He tilts my head up, kissing my jaw, the corner of my mouth, cheeks, eyebrows, eyelids, my forehead, before he finds my lips.

I don't open my eyes. I'm afraid that if I do, he'll see right through me. See the tears I'm hiding under the hot stream. He'll see just how right I feel in his arms. I hate how much I'm feeling right now, how much this close contact means to me. I hate what it's doing to my heart and how I can't seem to stop it.

I clasp my arms around his neck, running my fingernails over his scalp. He hums against my sensitive skin, pushing me up against the wall. His forehead rests against mine as we share desperate breaths, holding onto one another as if it was the last time.

It should be the last time. Before it's too late.

Run.

"Look at me," he pleads.

I can't.

"Avery." His gaze is already on mine when I open my eyes, filled with anguish and deep longing, and a word I cannot bring myself to fucking think.

I glance down at his chest, at my hand resting on his

heart. My eyes travel up, locking on his just as we crash. Becoming an angry storm of desire. I trail my other hand down his back, savouring the feeling of his coiled muscles as they go taut against my touch. Circling my fingers around to his defined V, my hand inches farther down, wrapping around him tightly. Lachlan groans into my mouth, deepening our kiss as I stroke him harder. The kind of kiss that makes the world slip away, and I am chasing that high constantly with him. I can't stop, even if I want to, even when I tell myself I need to.

I hate how addicting it is, wanting him like this. But what I hate more is how much I love it.

He bends down, grasping my thighs as he lifts me up. I tangle my legs around his waist, my slit meeting his hard length as I start grinding on him.

"Mo gradh," he murmurs. And I hate how much I love the sound of those two words. Even though I have no idea what they mean.

"What the fuck does that mean?" I pant angrily.

Confusion sets in between his brows for a millisecond, but then he meets my fire with fire. He tilts my hips, opening my thighs wider, as the tip of his cock sits right at my entrance.

"It means—" his soft breath brushes against my lips. "—my love." And he sinks into me.

I cry out, the thrust hitting so deep, it lights me up from within.

Mo gradh. My love.

I pull hard on his hair, and he just smirks down at me, intensifying his movements. His strokes turn more vicious as he surrenders himself to me. I tighten my legs around him, meeting every thrust with equal fury, turning into a mess of moans and breathless screams. And he eats up every single one, relishing in my pleasure.

God, I hate how much I love hearing those two words come out of his mouth.

And in this moment, I finally allow myself to think it, to feel it...to acknowledge that we were two halves of the same. We always were, from the very beginning. Our two halves were drawing us to one another. A magnetic force I couldn't fight any longer.

And I hate how much I love that too.

"Say it again," I croak.

He leans in, biting my shoulder. "Mo gradh," he whispers, over and over again, all along my skin. And I shudder, screaming out his name, chasing my pleasure into the light as it swallowed me whole.

The last thing I hear before I fall are the words:

Mo gradh.

CHAPTER FIFTY-ONE

avery

Lachlan's fingers lazily draw circles up and down my back, as we remain knotted in front of the fireplace. We made a makeshift bed after the shower, grabbing pillows and blankets from the bed. It's been hours and I have no intention of getting up. My face pressed up against his chest as I listen to the rhythm of his heart, watching the fire dance along the log.

There is no where else I'd rather be right now.

"Tell me what's in your head. One true thing," he murmurs.

My heart pounds in my chest, a wild creature demanding to be liberated. A part of me really wants to let go, confess to everything I've been feeling. Release the shadows that have concealed me for far too long. But the other part of me wants to run far, far away.

"I don't want this to end." I offer.

A thick silence hangs in the air.

"It doesn't have to end. Stay with me, Avery." He says it with such clarity that it frightens me.

Stay with him. As if it's that easy, uproot my entire life once again to be with a guy I barely know. Based on what? Strong feelings of attraction we can't resist? But fires eventually burn out, and our time will come to an end. I can't become someone else's shadow again.

"I can't."

His fingers still on my back, and I feel the crack run down my heart. Saying those words shouldn't hurt this much. Not when he's still here, when we still have time.

He plants a kiss on the top of my head.

"No matter what happens I want to thank you, lass. For bringing me back to life." His voice is soft, etched in pain.

My heart is pounding so fiercely, I'm certain he can feel it.

I lean up on my elbow, facing him. My hair glides down my shoulder, tickling my skin as it drapes across his bare chest. Reaching up, I trace my thumb across his eyebrow and down his cheek, where two tears slide down. My lips tremble at the sight of it.

"Lachlan, you gave me something I couldn't believe in. A feeling of belonging I never thought I would find. And I will forever be grateful for that," I take in a difficult breath. "You helped me heal, erased my ugly marks and replaced them with beautiful touches. Years from now, when I remember our time together, I'll remember everything you gave me. All the pain you erased with just your fingers."

His eyes lift to mine and he kisses me with such rare urgency. Electricity ripples through my entire body, locking me to this kiss, and whatever it is that our souls recognize in one another. A wordless confession we both can't say.

This is as close to love as I'll ever get.

He breaks the kiss, lifting my chin up. "There is no part of you that's ugly. Even the broken pieces you hide so well are beautiful, because they are part of you, Avery. They are the parts of you that turned you into the strong, confident, fierce woman you are today."

Tears pool in my eyes, gliding down my cheeks. If only that was true, if only I could be a slither of those things. But I've always been weak, running and hiding from my problem. I believe him when he says he thinks no part of me is ugly. But he hasn't seen every part of me. He hasn't seen the worst part.

Maybe it's the meaning behind his words, or the intense gaze in those ocean eyes, but I want to tell him, to open up and show him how wrong he is about me. I may not be the same broken girl I used to be, but I was for a very long time. And that will always be a part of my story.

Pressing my back into the ground, my eyes lock on the shadows dancing on the ceiling. "When I was nineteen, I was —" I blink the stinging pain away from my eyes. "—I was raped. By a guy I thought was a classmate. I had seen him a few times and one day he asked me to hang out. We stayed on campus, talked for hours, and watched the sun go down. When it got dark, he offered to walk me to my car. Where he proceeded to steal everything from me in a matter of minutes."

I close my eyes, letting the panic swirl underneath my skin, waiting for it to dissipate before I carry on. "The old me died on that cold concrete floor that night, and I spent years blaming myself. I hated everything about me. And I let the memories of that night continue to haunt me. I was so weak. I allowed it to consume me because I couldn't let go. While everyone simply moved on, living their lives; I stared out at the world behind a glass wall, trapped in a past I couldn't escape."

I expected the panic to keep rising but I felt numb as the words trickled out of me.

"And the worst part? They never found the guy. He didn't even go to my university. The name he gave me was fake. He just vanished, as if he never existed. I was always in a constant state of fear, like he was going to return and hurt me again. You say I'm not ugly but that's not true. I'm covered in marks and whenever I looked at myself, I was reminded of it. And then you came along."

I glance over at Lachlan sitting as still as a statue, silent tears rolling down his cheeks. He doesn't wipe them away. I sit up, resting my hand overtop of his, and he turns his shaky palm up, his fingers closing tightly around mine.

"I never thought I could open up to someone like this. To surrender my body freely and take pleasure in being with someone. To allow you to see the ugliest parts of me. I thought the guilt and shame would always hold me back but when I'm with you, all of that just slips away." I smile through quivering lips. I caress his rough cheek, as a salty tear slips between my lips.

Lachlan holds me against his chest. I hide my face into his neck, feeling safe in his solid embrace. Breathing in his scent, knowing how nice it is to have him here, holding my hand through this. How freeing it is to talk about it without breaking into pieces all over again.

"I'm so sorry. I'm sorry this happened to you. That you had to endure it all alone. I'm sorry the world made you feel ugly. I'm so fucking sorry, Avery." His voice is hoarse as he rests his lips on my forehead. I hold onto him tightly, my chest shaking as I finally let go.

"All parts of you are beautiful, Avery. You are strong, brave, and endless. You are enough. You have always been enough. You're so much more than that night, or any moment that threatens to break you apart. You chose to find happiness, to heal, to be here. You made that decision, and it doesn't matter how long it took you to get here. You did it, Avery. You climbed that fucking mountain on your own. You made it, mo gradh."

We were not brought together by mere chance or coincidence, were we? It is his affection, his heart, his love that make me believe in feelings I thought were impossible. With Lachlan, I learned the beauty of surrendering myself—body and soul —to another person. I've learned to let go, to enjoy the moments, to feel earth shattering pleasure without shame. He has shown me that it's possible for two people to fit their broken pieces together, and make something whole and radiant.

And even knowing all of this, I'm still going to let him slip through my fingers like the clear blue waters of the ocean. But one thing is certain in my clouded heart, Lachlan will always remain a gift, one I'll cherish for the rest of my life.

CHAPTER FIFTY-TWO

avery

"This place is gorgeous." My head is slightly outside the window as I gape at the beauty that is Inverness.

Two weeks has come and gone in the blink of an eye. The internal departure clock grows louder in the back of my head with each passing day. My heart is heavy, as I know my time here is slowly coming to an end. I spoke to my dad yesterday, and he wants me to come home. He had a friend go to John's place, and box up all my stuff, and had it shipped to Vancouver. I couldn't believe it when he told me. The shipping costs alone for all those books must have cost a small fortune, but he said he didn't want me to worry about having to go back to Toronto. To see John again.

I had forgotten all about John.

My dad has always been good about thinking ahead, dealing with problems head-on. Unlike me, who turns around and runs the other way. Go figure.

Lachlan and I have been inseparable. We spent Halloween together last week, and I was blown away by the celebrations here. I should have known that Halloween originated in Scotland. It's rooted to Scotland's pre-Christian culture, where small villages would come together and celebrate Samhain—a night marking the end of summer and the beginning of winter.

The end of light and the beginning of darkness.

The celebration in Fort William was something out of this world. Lachlan was completely in disguise, dressed as Ghostface, which I learned, I apparently have a thing for. Maybe it was the sight of Lachlan's bare chest that turned me on, or the way he took complete control of my body after I asked him to keep the mask on. And the way he lifted it off his face, revealing a mischievous smile, while moving in and out of me torturously slow...

I think it was the hottest sex I've ever had.

We celebrated the beginning of darkness four times that night. I couldn't walk properly for days.

But then, the new month rolled around, bringing anxious energy with it. Lachlan has noticed the change in my mood, too, like he always does, catching every emotion and thought as if there is an actual bond tethering him to me. But even he hasn't said a single word, both of us ignoring the looming goodbye.

I decided to go for a run early this morning to clear my head, and when I got back, Lachlan had packed our bags and was ushering me out the door. I barely managed to squeeze in a quick shower. But now, I understand why he was so excited to bring me to Inverness. Why didn't I come here sooner?

Inverness in movies and travel books does not do this place justice. It's a place of wonder.

"Aye. It's one of my favourite places. Inverness is known as the capital of the Highlands, and you understand why it holds that title when you come here." My perfect tour guide. He should do a couple of commercials for tourism companies and promote travel to Scotland. He's got the quiet, brooding demeanour that's perfect for television.

We drive on the edge of town. A stretch of water on one side, as far as the eye can see, and beautiful historical buildings on the other, with teeming green parks peppered throughout. A perfect balance of quiet nature and bustling city life. A large bridge comes into view as we pass by Inverness Castle, its imposing presence looming over the city. I'm absolutely giddy, pulling out my phone to look up everything there is to see in the short time we're here.

"Lachlan, I want to see it all. How long are we here?" I glance over at his smiling face, eyes facing the road.

"A couple of days."

"Where are we going to first?"

"Wouldn't you like to know."

"I would, that's why I'm asking. Maybe we can do the castle first, and then the cathedral. Or, vice versa. And then a walk through centre town. Oh! Maybe Loch Ness too."

His face lifted. "Can you let a lad just sweep you off your feet a little?"

"A little? I think you've been doing that since the moment you realized you wanted to kiss me."

His eyes flick to mine, holding me hostage. "And when was that?"

"When you came after me in Morvich?" I bite down on my swollen lip.

"No." He says with a straight face.

"No? After? I thought we were friends by then."

"No. I've been wanting to kiss you from the moment I saw you sitting in that field in Glencoe."

My face twists, but my heart quickens with each word.

"That's not true. You didn't like me."

A slow shrug. "Aye, but I was undone from the moment I laid eyes on you."

My cheeks flush, and I look away.

"What's that face for?" he laughs casually, unaware of the way his words have an effect on me.

"You have a way with words. It's impossible not to react when you say those things to me."

He leans in, his hand crawling up my thighs. "That's the idea, Nessi. I want to ruin you for everyone else."

"You're the worst."

"Tell yourself whatever you like but we both know you love every single word."

I roll my eyes, turning to face the window so he doesn't witness me chasing my next breath. Grabbing my hand, he places a kiss on my palm.

He's not wrong. I am fucking ruined for everyone else. How am I supposed to read romance novels now, knowing I got to experience a real-life book boyfriend? It's one thing when they're fictional, but he's right here...and I don't get to keep him.

I know this won't end well and I'll be heading to Vancouver with a very broken heart, but at the same time, I'm thankful to have experienced it in the first place. I still don't believe in love, but I think if I did, this is what it would feel like. The feeling of lightness, as you fly through the cloudless sky. Lachlan gave me wings.

And I know he feels it too. Not because of the thousand kisses and the words he whispers into my ears, that set my soul on fire. But because he seems genuinely happy, light. Walking around like a weight has been lifted off his shoulders since that day at Fairy Glen Falls. But sometimes, late at night, his eyes drift off someplace far away. And he disappears at random times, for a couple of hours in the day and other times, to take a phone call. I know it has to do with his work, but I never dare to ask, worried it's going to burst this perfect bubble we're in. We're on borrowed time and I don't want to risk it at this point. Stupidly, I want to remain in oblivion until the very last second.

Ailith stopped me after one of my runs last week in the inn's foyer. I was drenched in sweat after a two-hour run and desperately needed to shower. But she didn't care as she yanked me down, hugging me tightly. She thanked me four times, as tears ran down her cheeks. She told me she hasn't seen Lachlan this happy in decades. Ailith kissed my cheek, told me the fairies brought us together. And it reminded me of my offering at the water, the wish I made.

But none of that matters; time doesn't care about any of us. And the fact remains that I'm leaving soon. Very soon.

I shake my heavy thoughts away, focusing on what's in front of me. Quaint cobbled streets lined with charming shops and cafes, their colourful facades standing out against the grey stone buildings. The River Ness flows lazily through the heart of the city, its sparkling waters reflecting the bright afternoon sun.

It looks like we've stepped inside a postcard.

Lachlan turns the corner as a large brown cathedral comes into view. Inverness Cathedral's intricate architectural design and rich history immediately draw me in.

"Wow, can we stop and go inside the cathedral?"

Lachlan chuckles. "We're not staying far from it. Let's check in and we can take a walk back."

"Okay." I sigh audibly, craning my neck and watching as the cathedral grows smaller in the distance.

"What do you love about cathedrals?" he asks, flicking his eyes to mine.

"They're so beautiful. I feel like I'm transported back in time when I step through the doors. I've never been religious but something about them moves me. The details, the sacredness of the space...you can feel it."

"I get that, I love the quietness of them."

There is something in his eyes I can't read, and I find my cheeks growing warm under his intense gaze. I look back out the window and notice the car has stopped. I turn to see Lachlan secure his ball cap on his head. He winks at me right before he puts his glasses on.

"Come on, Nessi," he says, and he's out the door, heading for the trunk. I take a second to collect myself before stepping out of the car and standing in front of a grand hotel. There are floor-to-ceiling windows lining the entire first floor. And a doorman dressed in black stands tall by the revolving doors. He starts approaching Lachlan's car.

This place looks way too expensive.

"Lachlan!" I hiss, my eyes following the man as Lachlan hands him our bags.

He walks up to me. Overcrowding me and interlacing both his hands in mine, nestling my body tight against his. I'm forced to stare up at him, watching my reflection in his black-out glasses.

Why does he still wear this stuff if he knows his crazy stalker is locked up in a mental hospital?

"We can't stay here."

His brow quirks up. "And why not?"

I look around again. "It looks expensive."

"Why don't you let me worry about that?"

"But...no." I try to pull away but it's impossible, it's like trying to push a giant rock.

"Avery...do I need to carry you over my shoulder? Take you upstairs and fuck the stubborn out of you again? Maybe occupy that mouth of yours with something else?"

I gasp, opening my mouth to tell him off, secretly wanting

him to do just that when he runs the tip of his thumb up in between my legs. His breath ghosts over my ear, " I know you want it, lass. I can feel your wet pussy underneath these trousers."

I'm speechless.

Lachlan removes his glasses, tucking them into his jacket before he flips his ball cap around. He cups the back of my neck, his tongue tracing my bottom lip before he crushes his lips to mine. I open up for him, kissing him with such conviction, that I forget we're standing on the sidewalk, beside the car. Fuck it, he can have me against the car right now.

I whimper, my knees wobbly as he breaks the kiss, taking a step back to secure his glasses back on his face. He readjusts his hat, grasping my hand in his.

"Grand. That should keep you quiet for a while. Until I get you upstairs." He flashes me a delicious smirk as I follow him into the hotel, my legs moving like jello.

I'm one hundred and fifty percent ruined.

CHAPTER FIFTY-THREE

lachlan

I've stayed at this hotel before. On several occasions for a few exclusive work events. The last event was well over a year ago, and I hope none of the staff recognize me as we step inside the lobby.

The place is best described as historic with a modern twist. Floor-to-ceiling windows with black borders display the streets of Inverness as if you're looking at photographs. Large marble pillars are propped up tastefully, holding the old building in place. Edgar loves using this hotel because he thinks it gives him an edge, but there is nothing unique about being a soulless shark. This hotel wasn't my first choice when I decided to bring Avery here, but I know the backdoors well, in case we need to use them.

I should have taken her somewhere more remote, like Isle of Skye. She's been talking about wanting to go there lately. But every time she mentions Skye, it sounds like the finale. The last stop on her trip. And I can't do it, I can't fucking let her go. So I brought her here, as a distraction, another way to pretend we're not running out of time.

But now that I'm here, I remember how busy Inverness is, how public. Too crowded, with locals and tourists roaming around. I feel uncomfortable just standing here. Reminded of the person I'm working hard to forget. The secret I've been guarding this entire time. I should have just told her at the falls. Avery isn't going to see me in a different light if she knows, so why the hell didn't I just tell her then?

I should have. But it never felt like the right time to finally let it out, to come clean. At this point, Avery is so determined to leave I don't see the point in sharing that piece of me with her. I don't know anymore.

Once the official papers ended up on Edgar's desk, all bloody hell broke loose. Emails, phone calls, texts...I was being bombarded. I eventually got a hold of Henry alone and we talked it through. He was surprised I decided to pull in lawyers and call it quits, but not shocked entirely. He took it a lot better than Edgar did, that's for certain. But even after he spent days with his team, going through each and every word in the documents, he couldn't find anything. Which means, I'm finally done. I can walk away from that life and start again. Break free from my chains.

I just have some paperwork left to sign and a couple of contracts to close out, I even hired a realtor and listed the house in Glasgow. I'm so close, I can taste it.

"Hiya, welcome to the Royal Inverness Hotel. Do ye have a reservation?" the young lass, dressed in a formal pantsuit, addresses us as we approach the lobby desk. Her thin brows pull in as her eyes linger on me curiously.

"Yes, under Carnell." I pull my wallet out, handing her my credit card.

Her long nails clack loudly against the keyboard. "Royal suite, brilliant. I'll also need yer identification card."

I'm acutely aware of Avery's eyes on me as I slide my ID to

the clerk, covering the plastic with my palm. My foot taps nervously on the floor.

"Are you all right?"Avery whispers.

"Just a headache," I say, my thumb circling inside Avery's wrist. It's meant to calm me down more than anything else.

Settle down. Nothing's happened.

I turn just as the clerk, named Millie according to her name badge, glances up at me, smiling awkwardly. I know what she's going to ask before she says it.

"Sir, do ye mind removing yer sunglasses? I'll need to see yer face for just a second."

I don't hesitate. "Of course."

I fold my sunglasses and set them down on the marble desk.

A certain curiosity flashes in her eyes, her cheeks turn red as she glances down at my ID again.

All right, lad. Now is a good time to start panicking.

"Want to get out of here?" I lean in to Avery. She looks at me like I've lost my marbles. And I think I have because I'm two seconds away from going back to the car, and heading straight to Corran.

"Grand. All set, Mr. Moore. You'll be in room 77." I turn at the sound of Millie's voice, and my fucking last name, which she said louder than necessary. This bloody woman is out to ruin my day.

"Wait...Moore? I thought your last name was Carnell." Avery turns, her gaze burning while my heart lodges in my throat, jamming in place.

Frozen in place, I don't turn to look at Avery, while I wait for Millie to hand me the room keys.

"Lachlan," she says with such a bite in her tone, I know she's going to either leave or rip my head off if I don't answer her.

Anger swirling around in those deep whisky eyes. "We'll talk about it in the room. I promise."

She takes a breath and tilts her chin down.

Millie grins, presenting the room keys to me with an outstretched hand. "Yer bags will be up in yer room shortly. If ye need anything, please don't hesitate to dial zero from yer room phone."

"Brilliant, cheers."

When I pull on the cards, she doesn't release them. My eyes dart up to hers, as hot fury bubbles inside my gut.

"I know I'm not meant to say this, but I'm a huge fan. Would it be okay if I got yer—"

"No," I grit out, cutting her off and yanking the cards.

Clutching Avery's hand tightly in mine, I head for the elevators. All I see is red as the storm inside me intensifies, growing taller and louder.

I should have followed my gut, should have chased the bad feeling and left when we got here. I glance behind me quickly, and Millie has her phone out and is pointing it directly at me. The flash goes off.

"Fuck!" I snarl, panic creeping up my neck as I stare at the closed metal doors, pressing the button over and over again.

"It's okay, Lachlan. You're okay."

Avery looks bemused, maybe even hurt but she doesn't say it. She won't, not until it's just us in the room together. She's trying to keep me grounded, her soft reassuring voice calms my ragged breaths as I stay locked on her face.

The elevator doors ding and we rush inside at the same time.

CHAPTER FIFTY-FOUR

lachlan

Avery sits on the edge of the bed, watching me pace the room, as I try to figure out my next words carefully. Because these ones are going to matter the most. I didn't think it would happen this way. I hoped we would be somewhere secluded and not panicked when I finally told her who I am. The reason I've been hiding in Corran and cover my face everywhere I go.

The reason I've been so incredibly alone until she came along.

She's been strangely quiet. It's an unsettling kind of quiet—too dense to ignore—that gnaws at my insides with a growing sense of dread. A sinking feeling that we've reached the end of the line.

"I've known you've been hiding something for a long time, Lachlan. I didn't bother asking because I was afraid it would change things and I guess, I just selfishly wanted a little more time."

I stop pacing, standing five feet away, staring at her mournful face as she mentally prepares herself for the worst.

She's seconds away from demolishing me.

"I need to hear you say it, because I think I already know," she whispers as her eyes find mine. "But not right now. Can we hit pause? I know that's incredibly foolish of me—"

Did she just give me a way out? Saying the exact opposite of what I was expecting to hear? I don't wait for her next words as I rush over to her, dropping to my knees. I cup her face in my hands, staring into her eyes, as she claws at my soul.

"Lass, I promise—" I start but she stops me.

"No, I don't want to know, except..." She pauses, staring at me with jaded eyes. "Was any of it true?"

"Everything I've ever told you has been true. And when I couldn't answer you, I didn't say anything. I never wanted to lie to your face. I know that's not right, but I've always ever been myself with you."

"Except for your last name."

I curse, because she is right. I had lied about that, in a way. "Moore is my last name. But Carnell is my middle name. Lachlan James Carnell Moore."

She nods, closing her eyes to suck in another breath. It's apparent that she's locked in a fierce internal struggle, and it kills me to see her like this. My guilt is inescapable, knowing there is nothing I can say or do to fix this right now. Knowing I caused this.

The finality of this moment feels unbearable.

"I still want to hit pause," she says.

"Are you sure? Because I'll tell you everything right now, if that's what you want."

She shakes her head, her eyes opening up as they slowly find mine. Her hand reaches out, resting overtop of mine, and the small gesture alone nearly obliterates me.

"Not until...I just want one last time." Her eyes drop down to my mouth.

The words gut me from the inside out. I take in her pink cheeks, the shape of her lips, the faded freckles splattered on her nose, the soft rise and fall of her chest. My bed in Corran reeks of vanilla and coconut. How can I go back there without her?

"One last time for what?" I choke out.

"To be with you."

Every word pierces my chest like a sharp blade. I swallow the pain, smothering it beneath a thin composure.

I shut my eyes, trailing my hand up her torso, memorizing the feeling of her body. A shiver runs through Avery as she leans in closer, her lips a breath away from mine. My fingers lace through her hair, savouring the feeling of it in my hands as Avery leans forward, brushing her lips against mine. The softness of her kiss pierces me. It's slow and deep at first, but then she pulls on my bottom lip, sucking it into her mouth. We turn fierce, the energy crackling as it consumes us. We're sucking and licking and biting unlike ever before. Raging against a storm. Desperate for one another, as if it really is the last time.

She whimpers as I stand, wrapping my arms around her and throwing her on the bed. Avery gasps for air as she stares up at me with those fucking eyes.

"Tell me what you want," I say. She called the pause, she can do whatever her heart desires. She's in complete control, of my body and soul.

"Take off your shirt," she demands. I obey, reaching behind my back and pulling the material over my head.

Avery slides off the bed and walks behind me. "Turn around."

I twist around, my calfs meeting the edge of the mattress as I stare down at her. She pushes her index finger into my chest, forcing me to fall on the bed. I follow her every command, happy to just exist in the same space as her. Trying to find a way to turn back time.

Leaning back on the palms of my hands, I watch her eyes as they roam down my chest. She takes in a shuddering breath and steps closer, straddling me. I bite the inside of my cheek as she grinds her pussy against me, holding back the need to flip her over.

Avery's fingers slip under my waistband, hooking the band of my boxers and tugging once.

"Undo your pants," she says, holding onto my legs as she slowly lowers herself to the ground, sitting on her knees. The sight of her like this, in front of me...fucking hell.

She watches as I undo my belt, and then my trousers. My erection painfully pushes against the fabric and open zipper, but I don't pull the material down. I wait for her next order, the anticipation slowly driving me mad.

I know she's dragging this out on purpose, hoping to provide a moment of bliss in the mess I've created. Avery smiles, reaching up and looping her fingers into the hoops on my trousers and pulling on the material. I lift my hips as my dick springs free. Her eyes lock on it, as she inches closer, driving her hands up my thighs. Her face hovers an inch above my hard cock, and it takes everything I have to sit still.

"You don't have to do this," I say.

"I want to." Her breath brushes my cock, and I stifle a groan as she bends down, running her tongue from my base to the tip.

"Do you want me stop?"

"No," I grit out, watching her through hooded eyes, as she tries to take all of me in her mouth. She struggles for a few seconds, adjusting to my size. I stifle a moan, which only makes her go deeper. My hand fists her hair, but I don't push, I just hold her there as I watch her suck me off like she's having her last meal.

"Fuck, that's it."

I close my eyes, letting my head fall back, my legs vibrating with the need to thrust into her mouth, but I hold still. She's in complete control. She cradles my balls in her hand, tugging lightly, as her head continues to bob up and down. Blinding pleasure rushes through my body.

"Avery," I groan.

But she doesn't stop. And I don't think I can take it anymore, the small thread inside me threatens to snap. I need to hold her, touch her, feel her body against mine.

"Let me touch you, please," I plead, and I think she's going to ignore me again but then she pulls back, giving me a single nod.

I pull her up to my chest, wiping away her smudged mascara before fusing my lips to hers. I'm vehement and starved, as I push her down on the bed and begin stripping her. She helps me undress quickly, both impatient as I grip her underwear, feeling the material rip away.

Her bra flies off next, and she squirms on top of the comforter, completely naked and fucking perfect. I groan, taking one of her breasts in my mouth and sucking on her hard nipple greedily.

I hover above her, drinking in her soft pants as I press my hips up, grazing the tip of my dick along her wet core. I circle my hips, teasing her. She presses up against me, trying to get more but I pull away, staring down at her.

I want to give her the world. Anything she asks for, I'll fucking lay it at her feet.

"Avery."

Suspended above her with one hand pressed on the bed beside her head, I guide my cock back to her core. She lifts her hips, rocking herself against me, trembling as she digs her nails into my ass, urging me to to push inside her. I can almost feel her wet cunt squeezing me tightly. But this is so much more than sex, this physical connection between us.

Laying my hand on her stomach, I pull away slightly. Frustration floods her eyes, and she turns away from me. I grab her chin, turning her eyes to my searching gaze.

"Nessi," I murmur.

"No words." She lifts up and kisses me, folding her arms around my neck. Her nipples stroke my chest, as we clash against one another. She reaches down, aligning me with her entrance. I edge the tip inside her, nearly losing all control as she pants in my mouth, grinding up.

I withdraw from her swollen lips, looking down at her. "Say you're mine, no matter what happens. Because I'm yours, Avery. Always yours."

"What?" she breathes, looking dejected and pained. Much like the woman I met sitting amongst the tall grass at Glencoe.

"Do you see me the way I see you? Because I see you. All of you. Forever and always, mo gradh."

I move my hand down to her chest, never taking my eyes off her. My fingertips buzz from the connection and the feel of her beating heart under my palm. Her hand wraps around my wrist tightly. Her eyes plead with mine, but I mean every word.

"Say it," I groan.

No matter what tomorrow brings, I'll hold on to this moment and every second before it. My eyes are always on hers, searching, pulling, reaching out to her. My lungs ache, tightening at the realization that she may not feel the same.

"Yours," she whispers. "Always yours."

The thread around my heart snaps, I hear it at the same time as I feel it.

I drive into her, and our sounds pierce the air. I lean down, kissing her as a single tear of clarity slides down her temple. She folds her legs around me, opening up to me as I move deeper inside her, grinding my hips against her. We are transfixed, our gaze unbroken. Her nails dig into my shoulders as she forces me closer, each thrust deep and patient, because I want this moment to last a lifetime.

She's fucking mine.

I grip her hair and claim her mouth, pushing my tongue inside as our bodies move in perfect unison. I moan into her neck, pulling out slowly before thrusting back in. Her back arches and I lean back, looking down at the way our bodies connect, as we become one over and over again.

My eyes crawl over her, drinking in her golden skin and the way her breasts move up and down with the rhythm of our bodies. Her eyes are closed as she starts chasing her climax. I trail my tongue up to her breast and pull on her nipple, sucking before it pops out of my mouth. She pants and I slow my movements. Her eyes fly open.

"Lachlan," she pleads.

I push into her, relishing in her cries of ecstasy, as she begins to lose herself. She grunts when I slow down again and presses her cheek into the comforter in frustration, my lips quirk at her impatience.

"What are you doing?"

"Savouring you," I say as my tongue skates up her delicate neck.

I pull out again, the tip of my cock nudging inside her. Her eyes fall down to our bodies. The lines on her forehead deepen like something flashes in her mind. She takes a long second before looking back up at me.

"What is it?"

"Can we try something?" She asks nervously.

"Anything you want," I say, slowly pushing back inside her, my eyelids droop as she tightens around me. She groans, her hips twitching as I hold her leg up against my hip.

"Take me to the bathroom. I want to watch us."

"Wrap your legs around me," I said with ragged breaths. I grab her back and lift her off the bed. Avery winds her legs around me, whimpering and biting into my shoulder as I walk over to the bathroom, while still inside of her.

Mirrors line the entire bathroom, providing the perfect playground. I set Avery on the counter, and she recoils slightly as the cold stone touches her skin. I angle her body, and she turns her head to the side, watching as I slowly begin to fuck her. She seems hesitant, a little restless at the sight of us like this, crowding all around her. I pull her earlobe through my teeth, kissing along her jaw, down to her neck. Avery relaxes as she leans back on her hands, admiring us in the mirror.

"Do you like the sight of me worshipping your body, lass? I've lost my fucking mind and you're the reason why."

I move her hips, angling her so the head of my cock rubs into her G-spot. Her mewls echo in the bathroom. Our eyes lock in the mirror as I take her in, watching Avery release everything that was holding her back. I watch her come alive right in front of my eyes.

"Harder..." she demands.

She's so wet I can feel it dripping down my balls. I lift her up slightly, driving into the spot that pulls sharp breaths out of her mouth. Her legs start to shake, and I know she's getting close. And I reach down, my fingers circling her clit.

"Fuck...Lachlan," she cries out. Dragging her nails down my chest, her eyes locked on our reflection. My skin tingles as bright red lines rush to the surface. Her head falls back against the glass, and I continue working her closer and closer to the edge.

She shatters all around me and I chase after her as we fall into the abyss together. My orgasm crashes into me, forcing the edges of my vision to go black. I bend down, kissing her with such fervour that I forget who I am, what I've done, and forget that life exists outside of us. Outside of this perfect moment.

She completely surrendered herself to me. Trusted me to walk her to the edge of the unknown before we even had a chance to talk about everything. She trusted me enough to allow me to do this for her. Avery has been facing her demons from the moment she got here. Finding ways to discover herself and what brings her joy, making new memories and erasing the pain in her heart. Giving me the chance to love her.

I can't pinpoint the exact moment I fell for her, but I know I never landed. With each passing moment, my desire for her only grows stronger, for she is the embodiment of everything I've ever wanted, dreamed of. I only wish we lived in a reality where I could love her fiercely and treasure her for the rest of my life.

CHAPTER FIFTY-FIVE

avery

I'm not sure how much time has passed, with neither one of us saying a word. My naked body is pressed against Lachlan's as I lay in the crook of his arm, listening to his soft breaths. Surrounded by his scent as I soak in these last few minutes of silence.

His eyes are closed, but I know he's not asleep. He's waiting for me to give him permission to speak. To tell me everything I don't want to hear. What does it matter now? The secrets he holds. I had opened up to this man, shown him every corner of my dark mind, been completely vulnerable with him and he still cherishes me. He still treats me with respect and expresses himself without fear of judgement.

Who the hell cares about the rest of it?

But no matter what I tell myself, or how much time passes, I know we can't just brush past this. Not anymore.

We're out of time.

"So...how famous are you?" I ask, ignoring the booming sound of my pulse.

Lachlan goes rigid, my voice breaking our blissful silence as he blinks open his eyes, staring up at the white ceiling.

"Enough to want to hide."

That sounds familiar. The constant stream of hats and sunglasses and hoodies. Lachlan sought out the shadows, hiding from his past, his present, from chains he can't break free from, or doesn't know how. He hides, while I run. Both of us haunted by our fears.

"Start from the beginning," I say.

Lachlan hesitates, his gaze fixes on the ceiling as if searching for the right words.

"I left for London as soon as I finished secondary school. I wanted to get away for a bit, outside of Scotland, find something I wanted to do with my life. I got a job working as a run crew for *Phantom of the Opera*, living with three other flatmates. It was bad pay but I enjoyed it. Reminded me of my mom, when I was little and she used to sing around the house. She had a beautiful voice, one of the things I always loved about her—and how much she loved to sing."

He glances down at me, to see if I am listening before his gaze crawls back up to the ceiling. "After a couple of years, I knew the show real well, had all the lines memorized and one night they asked me to step in. The lead actor had fallen incredibly ill. Henry, my agent, was there that night. He was new to the industry, desperate for a fresh face. He approached me after the show, told me he's in television and thought I would be perfect for a certain role. I went into the London office the next week, read a few lines, and figured I'd never hear from him again.

"Henry called me three hours later and told me I got the job. I didn't really know what that meant at the time. I was bloody broke, had no ambition and no plans for my future, so I went with it. Edgar, the CEO of my talent management company gave me every opportunity those first few years. Sink or swim he would say. All the bells and whistles, and the money started pouring in. They invested thousands of dollars into me, acting lessons, training, photoshoots, everything. And guaranteed me the comfort of being close to home. I would stay in Scotland and only apply for jobs in the UK and Europe. It was good for the first little while.

"But before I knew it, I was drowning in contracts I couldn't leave, obligations I had to meet, even if I was dying from the flu. Parties, interviews, scandals, drinking, drugs...it was a hurricane, and one day, I woke up and realized I had no idea who the fuck I was anymore. Spending my days in a haze, following orders and directions. Showing up where I was supposed to. And my nights were spent getting black-out drunk. Duncan and Ailith helped pull me out, they got me to slow down my drinking, guided me to invest my money and Duncan gave me the idea to start the whisky business, along with real estate investing. It was something I started doing for me, something I was actually passionate about.

"It also helped me see that I didn't want to act anymore. It wasn't something I wanted to continue pursuing. But getting out wasn't an option, not with all the signatures I had signed over the years that kept me shackled. I knew I couldn't survive much longer. Edgar didn't like it when I started venturing outside the management company with my own money. He especially loathed when I started to sober up. I was less amenable. Eventually, I started skipping auditions and inter-views, and he started smacking me with contract breaches, trying to bleed me dry." Lachlan shuts his eyes tightly, his breaths coming in rapid succession.

He is an actor, a movie star. I figured, especially after seeing the way the hotel receptionist was acting towards him. So why are my nerves so shot hearing all of it? Splayed out like that right in front of us?

I rest my hand on top of his. Lachlan interlaces our fingers tightly as if he needs to hold on to something, to remind him that it is going to be okay.

"I hated it so much. The fame, the attention, the loneliness, God...the loneliness enveloped me. I was so fucking empty for so long. And when I stopped abusing alcohol, it all became too loud to ignore." Lachlan shakes his head. "No, not empty...I was rotting from the inside out. Things got really bad with Edgar when I turned down a Netflix series that was going to air in North America. It was going to take me from B-List to A-List, which meant a lot of money and opportunities for the agency. But it's over, none of that matters anymore. I've hired lawyers and I'm getting out, for good."

"You're quitting acting?"

He nods. "That life is a prison. The money, the status, the attention...I don't want it anymore. That life was never meant for me."

Lachlan's gaze meets mine, his eyes filled with a mixture of apprehension and concern, as he patiently awaits my response. Maybe preparing for an outrage, but he's not going to get that, not from me. I just feel an immense amount of sadness hearing his story, knowing how lonely he must have felt all those years.

"Lass, I'm dying over here. Are you going to say something? Scream at me? Because I'll fucking take that over the silence right now."

"Do you want me to be mad?"

"I deserve it." Lachlan's entire body deflates.

"No, you don't. I understand why you didn't want to tell me. I get the need to just escape it all. It makes sense."

He swallows hard. "What?"

"I'm not surprised. I mean, I am a little. You don't seem like the type, not that I would know what celebrities are like first-hand, but I guess, I wasn't expecting you to be so normal... under these circumstances."

"Normal? What's normal?" Tortured eyes bore into me.

"I don't know. You're easy to..." I nearly choke on the word that pops in my head. "Easy to like...and don't seem like the stereotypical money- and power- hungry type. You're also not obsessed with yourself like someone else I know. I'm not trying to be rude. I hope you know that."

He blinks at me several times.

I sigh, and now it's my eyes that find the ceiling as I roll onto my back. "I just wish you didn't feel the need to keep it from me. I would have accepted you either way."

I can feel his heavy gaze on my skin.

"I couldn't risk it, losing you that way. And I know it's selfish of me, and it makes me a fucking coward. But I was so tired. So fucking tired of all of it," Lachlan takes a strained breath, his eyes stuck on my shoulder, zoned out, like he was trying hard to hold back tears.

His voice softens. "I don't know how to put it into words, but when I saw you at Glencoe, I was transfixed. It was like you carried both sadness and serenity simultaneously, and I was captivated by you. As if some kind of invisible force was drawing me to you, like we were meant to cross paths. Some-thing about it was so familiar and intriguing."

I held my breath, feeling the magnitude of his words.

"And then you didn't recognize me and it felt like I was coming up for air. Like I could be anyone, everything, anything. And when I saw you again at the pub, I thought maybe this was a sick joke Edgar was playing on me. Sending a message to remind me that I'll never be free. I thought you worked for him or you were pretending to not know me so you could stalk me, I don't know. Honestly, I wasn't thinking at the time, letting everything from my past cloud my judgement. But as more time went on, I realized I was wrong, and you still liked me without knowing my past, or who I was running from. It was liberating to be myself, and not have the background noise taint what we had. It was perfect with just you and me."

My lips wobble, my throat burning as I hold back tears. I choke on them, push down every emotion because I know what he means. I felt the connection, too, and I had run because I didn't want to feel it. Because I had been scared of it. Hadn't I been doing the same this entire time? Not wanting him to tell me everything because I loved existing in the now with him?

"Avery?"

I turn to see his glistening ocean eyes, beautifully haunted.

"I get it, every decision. I understand why you did it," I mutter.

The relief in Lachlan's face is instant as he pulls me in his arms. "Avery, my darling Avery," he says into my hair, laying his lips against my forehead. The way this makes me feel safe and wanted terrifies me more than his secret. And I can't give life to these emotions because it still won't change the fact that I am leaving.

"Lachlan, our time together has been nothing short of wonderful and this doesn't change any of it. I hope you know that in the end, it was always you and me."

His body goes utterly still, but Lachlan just pulls me closer into his chest and I wrap myself around him, holding tightly. Maybe it's because we both understand how fleeting this moment is; that if we hold on a little longer, a little tighter, it might just slow down time.

WE BOTH PASSED out at some point, holding onto one another. The sound of my phone vibrating rouses me from sleep. I slowly peel myself away from Lachlan, tiptoe to my jeans, and grab my phone.

I have three text messages.

ELLE

You both all right? I miss you, let's have tea soon.

I want to ask her if she knew, but I'm really not in the mood to fight with Elle right now. Of course she knew, they all do. And I understand why they held his secret. It wasn't their story to tell.

I decide to not reply to Elle right now.

BECCA

Are you in a dick coma yet?

I went on a terrible date and I need to tell you about it. Spoiler alert, my fucking boss Greyson showed up midway. I'm in need of a drinking bitch session soon. Tell me when you're free.

I need my best friend so badly right now. I glance over my shoulder at a very peaceful, sleeping Lachlan before picking up my clothes and heading to the bathroom.

ME

I'm coming home soon, so we can do it in person.

BECCA

What?! Why? What happened? Are you okay? When is soon? Does Lachlan know about this? Wait, why would you leave?

ME

Take a breath, everything is fine but it's time. I need to come home. This was never going to be a long-term thing.

BECCA

Can I call you?

ME

No. Lachlan is sleeping.

BECCA

Listen, I love you and I want nothing more than for you to come home but we both know there is nothing here for you. Your dad is settled and happy, although he would love it if you were here. You can work from anywhere, and you have a smoking, caring boyfriend. What reasons do you have for wanting to come back? Remember why you left Vancouver in the first place?

I hate how Becca never says what I want to hear.

ME

He's not my boyfriend. And why do you have to always give me the hard truth? Why can't you just bitch with me once in a while? Or tell me it's going to be okay.

BECCA

What happened, Aves?

My shoulders slouch, weighed down by everything as it suddenly all feels so incredibly heavy.

ME

He's a celebrity. An actor, Becca.

BECCA

Ok, that's hilarious…but seriously, what's going on?

I turn, facing the mirrors as I pull my sweater over my head. My eyes land on Lachlan's handprint, and I reach out, tracing it with the pad of my finger. My skin tingles, like it always does when he touches me. Images of the way we were tangled in one another, right in this spot just hours ago, flash through my mind like a slideshow. I remember being scared, thinking I would hate him after I found out the truth. How desperate I was to have one more time with him because I was convinced I would walk out. And now…I don't know what to think. This might be worse. Because nothing has changed; I still want him just as much.

The water is so muddy, complicated and I don't know what to think anymore.

My phone buzzes in my hand.

BECCA

AVERY!!

ME

Hold on, I'm stepping out.

I grab a keycard and quietly leave the room. Becca's FaceTime request pops up as soon as the door closes.

"Shhhh…I'm in the hallway," I say, walking towards the elevators.

"Go to the lobby, or the stairwell…and start talking, right the fuck now."

Becca is still in bed, since it's early in the morning in Vancouver with the time difference.

"I wasn't joking. He's a TV star. His name is Lachlan Moore, Carnell is his middle name. It's complicated, Becca. So complicated, but if I leave it won't be complicated anymore. It will be over and I won't have to deal with any of it."

"Holy shit! Have you Googled him yet?"

I tilt my head side to side.

"Want to do it together? At the same time?"

I almost burst into tears right then, in the quiet hallway of this hotel room. I nod and we both open up Google. I can't see Becca but we can still hear one another.

"Ready?" she says.

"Yes." I type his name into the search bar. My heart is in overdrive, begging me to stop. To put my phone away, turn my ass around and go back to the room. Pretend like none of this is real.

The page loads.

Lachlan Moore, up-and-coming star from Scotland...Lachlan Moore to star in a Netflix series, production to begin early next Fall...Lachlan Moore takes over charts in Europe, could he do the same in North America?....Lachlan Moore, bringing your Scottish fantasies to life with his charm and good looks... Lachlan voted Scotland's hottest man...Is Lachlan heading towards A-List Celebrity Status? Time will tell...Lachlan drops Netflix...TV star Moore has a crazy stalker...Where is Lachlan Moore? Too spooked to leave his house...

Lachlan Moore spotted in the highlands with mystery brunette...

"Oh my God...you're the mystery brunette."

CHAPTER FIFTY-SIX

avery

"Where are you going?" Becca shouts.

"I just need some air. I'm going to take a walk."

"Take me with you."

"It's fine. I'll call you later."

The elevator doors open to complete chaos in the crowded lobby. There are people everywhere. Staff scurry around as security guards try to usher people out and block others from entering the hotel. In the far corner, the receptionist that checked us in earlier stands with her face to the floor while two people appear to be berating her.

"What's going on? Turn me around?" I forgot Becca is still on the call.

"I don't know. I'll call you later. I love you." I hang up the phone before Becca's protests come through.

An older couple walks by, heading for the elevators. "Hi, do you know what's going on?"

"No idea! Seems rather strange. We just got back from

dinner, it wasn't like this when we left earlier," the older lady says in an American accent.

I give them a wary smile and turn for the doors, needing to get out of here. My chest feels heavy, like the air around me is suddenly too thick. Inverness Cathedral is close to here, maybe I'll walk there.

A guard standing by the door turns to me. "Are you a guest of the hotel?"

"Yes, what's going on? Am I going to be able to get back in?" I say, flashing him my room key.

"Aye. Nothing to worry about. This happens sometimes when word gets out about a special guest staying at the hotel," he explains before stepping out of the way and allowing me to leave.

Lachlan.

Head down, I rush through the doors and step out into the cold November air. Shit, I forgot my jacket, but the adrenaline rushing through me makes it hard to notice the sharp wind. Quickening my steps, I walk down the street towards the water.

Turning the corner, something tugs at my arm, and I hurl back into a narrow alley between two buildings. There stands Lachlan, still holding onto my arm with a stunned expression.

"How did you—?" I look behind him, and there is a door propped open.

"Are you leaving?"

"No, I just needed some air. I Googled you." I confess.

Lachlan's lips tighten into a hard line. He glances behind me, down the street.

"Let's talk about it in the car. We have to get out of here, now, Avery."

"Okay." My teeth chatter. "Did you see everyone in the front lobby? They're here because of you."

"I heard the commotion, that's why I went through the back exit." He stares down at my body.

"Shit, lass, you're shaking. Let's go."

He unzips his jacket, pulling it around me as he starts guiding me by the shoulders to the back door.

A car screeches behind us, and we both turn to see a black SUV with tinted windows stopping at the curb. Lachlan steps in front of me, pushing me back with his arm, instantly on the defense. The side door facing us opens, and a man in a grey suit steps out. He smiles, looking up and down the street before his eyes lock on Lachlan. He takes slow steps closer to us, his eyes as cold as ice.

"Fancy seeing you here, Mr. Moore. I was in town for a business meeting when I heard all the excitement about you staying in Inverness. Had to come observe for myself." He tucks his hands in his pockets and grins, his expression laced with mockery.

"What do you want, Edgar?"

"You're coming with me. I reckon you didn't hire good enough lawyers."

Edgar is tall, maybe a couple of inches shorter than Lachlan. He's fiercely built and reeks of power. His brown eyes are sharp and cunning and he doesn't even throw a pity glance at me. I don't exist to him.

"I don't believe a thing that comes out of your mouth. And I'm not leaving. Whatever you need looked at or discussed, you can contact my lawyers. I believe you have their number."

Edgar looks down at his shiny black shoes, his vicious laugh causing a chill to run down my spine.

"I reckon you'd say that, mate, but it's a jolly good thing I've got this." He retrieves a USB device from his pocket.

Lachlan fists his hands so hard, his fingers turn white.

"Aye, I knew you'd bloody recognize this. Found it while

I was breaking into Stephy's gaff before you and the bobbies rocked up. I ain't lasted this long in the game by pure luck, mate. It's survival of the fittest, and I won't let you tarnish my reputation and my business. Now, get in the motor, or I'll ruin your bleedin' life and everyone else you give a toss about." His cruel eyes cut to mine as he utters those last words.

I turn, facing Lachlan. "Don't listen to him, Lachlan. Let's go."

But he doesn't look at me. He vibrates with fury as he glares at Edgar, who just smiles casually. The type of smile that gets under your skin and festers for days.

"Pleasure meeting you, Avery Harris from Vancouver. Pass on my regards to your folks, Bill and Derya. I hope I got your mother's name right." Edgar winks at me before he turns and heads back to the car.

"That was a bad fucking idea, Edgar," Lachlan snarls.

Edgar's disgusting laugh pierces the air, before he steps inside the SUV and closes the door.

I'm no longer shivering from the cold.

"We're out of time, Lachlan. For good," I murmur, tears rolling down my cheeks.

Lachlan grabs my shoulders, lowering his head so he's eye-level with me.

"I know you're scared, mo gradh, but I need you to listen. Take my keys and head back to Corran." He opens my palm, placing the keys to his Audi inside and closing my fingers around the cold metal.

"Tell Ailith and Duncan what's happened. I'm going to deal with Edgar and come back to you. I just recorded that entire conversation. I'll be all right, and you don't worry about what he said. Edgar is full of threats. He's just doing it to get to me."

I nod vigorously, my vision blurring from the movement and the tears in my eyes.

"Will you wait for me? I refuse to give up on us, Avery." He steps close to me, wiping away stray tears. "I'm so sorry, I didn't mean for any of this to happen."

"Okay," I let out, my breath ghosting the air.

Lachlan exhales, leaning down to press his lips to mine.

"Message me when you get to Corran. I'll see you soon... I..Avery...I..." He pauses, struggling with his words.

But I don't give him the chance to finish. "Go, be safe."

His eyes linger on mine for a long minute, before he turns, walking to the SUV. He glances behind his shoulder to look at me one last time. He lays a hand on his chest, gripping his shirt as if he's clutching his heart. He bends down and disappears inside the car.

His familiar scent of pinewood lingers around me and my eyes prick with fresh tears as I turn, heading back to the hotel.

CHAPTER FIFTY-SEVEN

The limo door swings open as a thousand flashes dance in front of my eyes, causing me to shrink back. A strong hand reaches out, palm open waiting for me. I lean my head down, trying to see who the arm belongs to, but I can't see anything past darkness.

Something inside me stirs as I reach out, grasping his hand. I look down to see I'm wearing a beautiful floor-length red dress. A deep cut runs up the side, revealing my tanned legs. The man hooks my hand into his as we walk together. He is tall. His hair is chestnut brown, on the edge of golden. Or maybe that's because of all the lights and camera flashes. His body is strong, muscular in all the right places, I can tell even through his stunning suit. He is way out of my league. What am I doing here? We're walking down a red carpet, hand in hand. I glance behind me, but the carpet stretches for miles. There are thousands of people standing, shouting on either side of us. Flashes go off every second, and it's almost blinding.

"Just keep holding on to me. I've got you, Nessi." A deep, sultry voice carries down to me, louder than the rest of the chaos around us. He has a soft Scottish accent, and that nickname, it's familiar. I try to look up at him again, urging my eyes to show me a clearer picture. His face remains blurry.

Voices start to become clearer as we walk in front of a green screen. He tries to pull me along, there are hundreds of photographers in front of the screen. Waiting. I'm stuck to the ground. I can't move. I want to but I can't.

"Lachlan Moore...photo with just you. Just you. How are you feeling tonight?"

Lachlan?

"Come on, Avery, we have to go," he says.

But I just stare at his outstretched arm, our fingers inches apart as I reach out to him.

"I can't move. I'm stuck...you go, I'll be right behind you."

He pauses, his blurry face on mine. But then, the image gets clearer. I start to recognize Lachlan's defined jaw and sharp cheekbones. Those intense ocean-blue eyes. Suddenly, I feel completely safe.

"I'll be back," he promises.

I nod, smiling. "Yes, go. This is your moment."

His arm pulls away as he begins to walk towards the middle of the screen. He stops to face all the hungry photographers and interviewers, giving them a stunning smile, one I have never seen before. It looks artificial, as if he plastered it on for this moment. There are so many people, all stepping over one another to get to him. Suddenly, hundreds turn into thousands, like a hoard of zombies.

Suffocating panic creeps up my throat. Lachlan's smile disappears, replaced by sheer terror. He sees it too. This is insane. He's going to get trampled.

A shadow appears on the other side of him, calling his name. He looks over at me before glancing the other way. The shadow *figure extends a hand; his path appears clear, empty on the other side of impending chaos.*

Ice-cold water clashes against my ankles. I look down to see an inch of water flowing past me, as it continues to climb up slowly. I try to move, but my legs are as heavy as stone. I raise my dress, but it's no use. A wave hits me in the knees, knocking me forward. Freezing cold water continues inching up my body.

"Help!"

"We have to go, come!" Lachlan calls out to me, appearing farther away than before. The distance between us stretches somehow.

"Help! I can't move."

I look down again, watching my feet sink into sand. Another wave crashes into my back, shoving me into the freezing water. I'm sinking up to my chest now. I blink and it's up to my neck. My bones begin to freeze as I quickly realize I'm going to drown. I look back and my scream gets trapped in my throat. Only the angry black sea stretches behind me, slowly pulling me in. I glance up at the silent night sky, calm compared to the vicious ocean behind me.

I glance over at Lachlan, watching him approach the shadowy figure.

"No! Lachlan! Come back. I'm drowning."

He stops and slowly turns around, his body facing me as I'm desperately reaching out for him.

"I'm sorry. I have to go. It's my job. It's important. I can't miss this opportunity."

I try to scream but nothing comes out. Hot tears begin to stream down my face.

"I have to do it, for them." He motions his head towards the horde of people about to break through the short barrier.

I watch him walk away.

I watch him follow the shadowy figure into safety a strong wave pulls me under.

I LURCH UP, breathless and covered in sweat as I look around, taking in my familiar room in Corran.

It was just a dream.

Breathe in, breathe out. Just a dream.

When did I pass out? I throw the covers off, reaching for my phone. Eleven at night. And no new messages from Lachlan. The last one was from hours ago when he informed me he was headed into a meeting with his lawyers and Edgar's team.

My breathing is still erratic, and I'm drenched with sweat. It was just a dream. Just a terrible dream.

Great, the sheets are damp too.

I walk over to the bathroom, strip out of my sweaty clothes, and step into the shower. Fragments from the dream flash before my eyes. Red carpet, a horde of photographers, watching Lachlan leave while the deep black sea swallowed me.

I keep my head under the hot spray, tuning out the noises in my head.

CHAPTER FIFTY-EIGHT

avery

It's just after midnight when I get on the road, driving down the dark, narrow streets headed to Neist Point Lighthouse. I couldn't seem to settle down even after taking a shower. Anxious thoughts from that awful dream crowded my mind. I found myself worrying about Lachlan, unable to even get lost in a book. Usually that's my saving grace but even that didn't work tonight.

I started scrolling through travel forums on my phone—a last-ditch effort at distracting myself—when I came across a post from yesterday about the Aurora Borealis sighting at Neist Point Lighthouse. The photos from the previous day blew me away. The author of the post mentioned the light display is the brightest between two and five in the morning.

Neist Point is just over two hours from Corran, so I got dressed and headed out the door. I sent a text to Lachlan, letting him know that's where I was headed. Not that it matters. I'm sure he'll be stuck in a boardroom all night.

I also ran into Ailith on my way out and she gave me a key

to the inn, since the place is locked between certain hours in the middle of the night. Being the sweetheart that she is, she also handed me a thermos the size of my head filled with coffee. I'm sure if I drink all of it, I won't sleep until next year.

THE SKY IS pitch black as I pull up to Neist Point Lighthouse. I followed the glowing stars and the moving columns of light on the drive over, entranced by the view as they guided me. Out of all the nights, this is the night I needed to see this spectacle the most. Just the perfect distraction my soul needs.

At first, the hues are cascades of white light, but the closer I get to Skye, the more the colours began to come to life. Hues of purple and green, sashaying in the night sky. Of course, I read about this, but I never imagined I would be so lucky to witness it up close. The colours are supposed to be spectacular at the tip of Skye, which happens to be Neist Point.

My heart pounds in my chest as I catch a glimpse of the celestial glow in the sky from my car. I don't care that it's dark and I'm alone. I don't even think twice about it. Catching Aurora Borealis is so rare—when am I ever going to get a chance like this again? And standing by a lighthouse, looking out at the deep ocean? It's a once-in-a-lifetime opportunity, and I can't believe I've stumbled upon it by pure luck. There are other cars in the carpark, but the place is so large, everyone must be spread out.

I tighten the straps of my bag as I speed walk towards the trail. The chill ocean air blows over me, igniting me with renewed energy. I pull my hair up into a ponytail as I look out at the dark ocean, the sound of water crashing into nearby cliffs instantly calms my mind.

The landscape is blanketed by shadows, except for the dazzling painting in the night sky that is growing brighter by the minute. The colours glisten in the rippling water, like jewels swimming freely in the vast sea. The tall cliffs over-looking the ocean are blanketed in sage, verdant grass. This spot is a photographer's dream come true. I can't believe a place like this exists, and people are able to fully enjoy the beauty of it. I follow the concrete path leading down to the lighthouse. The sky glows brighter, making me feel like I've entered into a whole other dimension.

I STAND at the edge of the rocky cliff, staring out at the vast expanse of the ocean as I gape upon its mesmerizing beauty. Time stands still as tears skate down my face. Tears of joy and wonderment. I don't even know why I'm crying, the sight is just overpowering, pulling everything out of me. It's hard not to marvel at the forceful display of light.

It's as if I've finally opened my eyes, seeing the world for the first time. The beauty in the quiet night, the calming sounds of the ocean, the buzzing of the sky, the orchestration of light and colour, is a perfect symphony of nature. It all speaks to my soul, taking me apart piece by piece, leaving me completely exposed.

A rebirth.

Everything has led me here.

The highlands healed me, showed me how to accept and love myself for who I am. It was here I finally realized that I'm worthy of affection, love, pleasure...life. How lucky I truly am to be able to walk these lands, to feel the wet grass beneath my feet, the cold wind against my skin. To climb and conquer a mountain.

I finally fought for that broken girl. I climbed the fucking mountain for her, over and over again.

And if she was standing here right now, I would tell her that she deserves everything her heart desires, even the happy endings she doesn't believe in. I would tell her that she is going to be okay, and that she is worthy. She's enough, and she's always been enough, even during her darkest nights. I would tell her that her dark days don't define who she becomes, and they can never diminish her light.

No, it only makes her light shine brighter.

I wouldn't be able to see the Aurora Borealis shine so bright right now without all the darkness surrounding it.

My past will always be a part of me, a never fading scar, but it can't swallow my light anymore. The darkness no longer scares me, it doesn't hold such power over me.

"You have to surrender to the pain, the suffering, the darkness that still haunts you. Learn to love the broken parts of yourself. When you do that, when you let go of the emotional turmoil and the fear...that's when you'll find Wonderlight."

Dr. Samson's words echo in my head, so loud that I barely hear the sob that escapes me. I am the light that shines within. That dances and swirls and lives—despite the darkness lurking behind me. It's now that I see the aptitude in his words as I stand here, on the edge of this cliff, baring my soul to the lights.

I didn't find Wonderlight, Samson.

I *am* Wonderlight.

That epiphany is so thunderous, it shoves me down to my knees.

Gazing up at the sky, I spread my arms out, wondering how it took me this long to see it. To find myself. The love I feel washing through me is overwhelming. And when I think of the word, I think of him.

I found something else in Scotland.

Something I was never meant to find.

Lachlan.

Love.

Can it really be love? I fought it, surrendered to it, allowed it to consume me, and set me free. I always thought love was war, pain, but this feels like clarity. A remedy. Without Lachlan, I would have never experienced something so utterly beautiful. Three months ago I didn't even believe in love.

It has to be love. Because even now, despite everything, the secrets, the pain, the knowledge that I'm leaving soon...I still feel it humming in my chest. Jolting me to life, every time the edge of the live wire touches me. How could I not love the man who pierced through my dark heart and never stopped chasing me, never stopped believing in me? No matter what happens to us, or how this all ends, he brought me back to life too. And I will always cherish him for that. Lachlan was the missing piece I never knew I needed.

He taught me what it means to find love and acceptance in someone else.

I stand there for hours, lost in thought, succumbing to the clarity of it all.

Then the sky begins to change, morphing into scorching shades of orange, red, and yellow as the colours brush the horizon. A brilliant light, the promise of a new day, rises high above as it continues to drown out the darkness. The sun rises just above the sparkling water, a large glowing orb, casting its rays across the sea.

My chest is tight with the sight of it.

A light fog rolls over to the rising cliffs, creating an ethereal scene. I take it all in for one final time, whispering a silent promise to the sea, and turn away with newfound hope for tomorrow.

CHAPTER FIFTY-NINE

lachlan

"That's it, that's all, Mr. Moore. Thank you for trusting me with this," says Mr. Davis, my lawyer, as I hand his pen back to him. "Brilliant strategizing with the audio evidence. Had it not been for that, we would have found ourselves in court. Edgar appears to relish theatrics, and he would have orchestrated an excruciating ordeal."

"I agree. Good riddance to that slimy bawbag. All thanks to you and your team."

Davis laughs, but keeps quiet, staying professional until the very end.

He tucks the stack of paperwork into his briefcase. "Simply fulfilling our obligations, Mr. Moore. I look forward to crossing paths with you in the future, ideally in more prosperous endeavours. And do keep producing Anam Cara—without a doubt, it's my cherished whisky of choice."

I give him a wide grin, slapping him on the back as we make our way out of the boardroom. Thankfully we didn't have to go to Glasgow since Edgar was already in town and Mr. Davis's office is conveniently located in Inverness. Not too convenient, since I selected him based on his close proximity to Corran, knowing I wouldn't want to be away from Avery when I had to come in for meetings. He's also the best, and I needed the fucking best to slip out of Edgar's strangled hold.

Davis was able to make all my existing contracts with Edgar's company null and void, due to harassment laws in place. I am silently going to step away from the entertainment industry. Edgar and his team can manage the messaging around my departure or just let me fade into the background, I don't give a shite. I'm done. And that's all that matters.

I just want to get back to Corran and wrap myself in Avery. We've been apart for less than twenty-four hours and I miss her so goddamn much. It's unreal how much she's a part of me now. Buried so deep within my soul, at times I don't know where she ends and where I begin.

Before we stepped into the never-ending legal meeting, I texted Henry, calling in one final favour. Asking if he could send me a car when I was done, since Avery drove my Audi to Corran. Even though it's nearly two in the morning, Henry pulls through, letting me know a car would be waiting for me once the meeting finishes. I checked in with him an hour ago with an update, right before my phone died, hoping to hell the car is here when I walk out.

With everything that's happened in the last day, I'm not sure where Avery stands right now. I'm terrified she still wants to leave. Her understanding and support when she found out who I was blew me away. A part of me always knew she wouldn't see me differently—we have been through too much, but I figured there would be some resistance. Hesitations that may have pushed her away, make her want to run again. But she listened intently, took it in, looked at me like she understood every thought and decision I've made over the years. It made me fall for her all over again.

But I'm frightened she'll let herself walk away, to run from this, before she admits this is love. The lock guarding her heart is indestructible and I'm not sure if I'm enough for her, if what we have is enough to break it open. I don't know how I'll survive it if she leaves. But I need to try, to fight for us even if she can't, because this type of love travels across the universe. It's a rare, never-ending type of love, and I'm not letting it go that easily. Not without a fight. I'll chase her to the ends of the earth if I have to, to make her see, to believe in us. To give this a chance.

Mr. Davis locks up the back door to his office, turning towards his car as we say our final goodbyes. Nervous tension knots through my neck and shoulders as I walk out of the carpark, heading up the street. There is a white BMW parked outside with its lights on. The driver steps out, a young lad, maybe in his early twenties.

"Are you Lachlan Moore?" he says.

"You must be my ride."

He smiles, nodding. "Name's Malcolm. Ready to go whenever you are, sir."

"Call me Lachlan, since we're going to be stuck together for a couple of hours." I slide into the passenger seat, and the car starts rolling away.

"Do you have an iPhone charger in here, Malcolm?"

He nods, pointing to the glove box. I connect everything, plug my phone in and wait for the apple symbol to light up.

"Straight to Corran then?" Malcolm asks.

"Aye, thanks mate," I say, taking my hat off and resting it on my knee. I run a hand through my hair, catching sight of my faded reflection in the window. I look fucking done for, bags under my eyes, vein in my neck still protruding from the earlier meeting.

My phone starts buzzing, and I look down, as notification

after notification rolls through. Emails, texts, voicemails. I flip to the text icon, opening up an unread message from Avery.

NESSI

> Couldn't sleep, heading up to Neist Point Lighthouse to check out the Aurora Borealis. Let me know when you're heading back to the inn and hopefully I'll beat you there. Hope you're okay, and remember, you're so much stronger than them.

> And no, I'm not running. Just need a break.

ME

> I'm heading back now, and I better find you naked in my bed when I get to the inn.

I release a shaky breath, glancing outside as the quiet streets of Inverness fade into the darkness.

"Everything all right, sir?" Malcolm asks. "I mean, Lachlan. Sorry, never had the chance to chauffeur a movie star like yourself before, ye ken."

I smirk, watching Malcolm anxiously adjust in his seat. "I'm just like everyone else, mate. Plus, I just got a career change, so no need to feel nervous."

Malcom's face twists as he turns to me. "What? Why? You're living the dream."

Oh, to be young again. "How old are you, Malcolm?"

"Twenty-two."

"Just give it ten more years, and you'll realize some dreams can quickly turn into your worst nightmare. But hopefully you won't have to experience that firsthand."

Malcolm nods, mulling over my words silently. He doesn't say anything else. Maybe he's tired or maybe he thinks I'm full of shite. Doesn't make a difference to me either way, I'm going home.

Home. To her.

I have never been so excited and scared in my fucking life.

Just then, my phone buzzes with an incoming text.

UNKNOWN

Miss me? Because I've missed you for 523 days, 12 hours and 36 seconds.

Time stops and my heart falls, landing on the car floor with an audible thud.

UNKNOWN

Why didn't you come visit me? I waited for you.

Didn't think you'd forget about our love so soon, you're my lock n' key and I'll never let you go.

You'll never escape me.

Come find me, I'm going for a drive.

An image of Avery's back pops up, her brown locks blowing in the wind behind her as she reaches for her car door.

Fear wraps around me, consuming me like a blazing fire as the voice inside me screams. I knew it was her this whole time. She's come back for me.

I remain frozen, as ice and fire fight in my veins. I can't live with this. I won't.

I have to get to Avery.

CHAPTER SIXTY

lachlan

I don't remember how we got here, I don't remember the things Malcolm said. I just know he drove like his life depended on it, while I spiraled the entire time. Begging whatever God is out there to keep Avery safe, until I could get to her. Begging the universe that Avery remains untouched, and I don't find her...

No. I can't go there. Not again.

Not as we're about to pull into the carpark at Neist Point. The sun is just breaking through, the sky turning into a melody of orange and red hues, brightening up the vast stretch of land in front of me. I scan the area, not spotting Stephanie or Avery. Agony, hope, despair, rage, guilt...it all blinds me with unmanageable thoughts.

Jumping out of the car before it comes to a stop, I start running towards the lighthouse. Malcolm yells something from behind me but I don't hear him. I just scream out her name, shaking with fear and rage as I run.

Please God, please don't take her away from me. Not when I just got her. I'm begging you. I've waited forever to find her, to love her. Please, I will do whatever it takes. Give up every part of myself to hold her again. Please let Avery be okay.

I breathe through the cavernous hole in my chest, running as fast as my body allows me. This is all my fault. I did this to her, led Stephanie to her, put Avery's life in danger.

I did this.

I don't deserve her. Don't deserve that pure heart of hers, that accepts and sees me for exactly who I am. So perfect, kind, and loving. God, I did this to her. The moment I stepped into her life, I placed her in danger.

She deserves so much better than this.

I RUN TO AVERY, and she smiles, confused and maybe a bit stunned right before I throw my arms around her, embracing her so tightly, it feels like my heart is about to burst from pure joy.

I pull away, holding her cheeks as I scan her body. "You're okay, you're okay."

Her eyes are red, like she's been crying, and she appears tired but she's okay. She's here, standing in one piece. In my fucking arms.

I turn, scanning the area wildly, looking for the psychopath bitch, but I don't see her.

She's not here.

Where the fuck is she? She can't be far.

"Lachlan? Are you okay? What's going on?"

"We have to leave."

"Why? What's happened?"

I pause, so bloody happy to see Avery in one piece, in my arms...I send a prayer up to the heavens.

If I don't say it, I'll regret it like last time. "I have to confess something and I need you to let me say it."

Her eyes widen, but she doesn't stop me.

"Avery..." I lean in, brushing the hair clinging to her damp cheek. "I love you. You are the best thing that's ever happened to me. The very best. I am so fucking in love with you. It was over for me the minute I laid eyes on you. I didn't know it at the time, didn't know how much you would turn my life around. How meeting you would be the end of life as I knew it. I thought I needed a bigger purpose, that chasing stars would make me happy, but it turns out I just need you. Please don't walk away from this, from us."

Tears fill her eyes and my heart feels like it's going to fall out of my chest. But I keep going because she needs to hear this and I've been needing to say these words for far too long.

"I love you, mo gradh. Across all space, throughout every moment in time, and in every corner of the endless universe...I am yours. Forever and always."

"Lachlan," she breathes, her face crumbling at the impact of my words. My confession. At those three words I said over and over again.

I lean down, closing my eyes as I press our foreheads together. I breathe her in, holding her tightly. Avery's palm falls to my chest, right over my beating heart, the one that beats for her. And only her.

Her eyes finally open, filled with water, and so bright they almost look green. She's torn, I can see it. Her mind and heart are at war.

"You don't have to say anything right now. Let's just go home. Will you come home with me?" I say, pressing my lips to hers. She nods against my lips, kissing me back.

"How romantic. You started without me? Boo."

A nauseating feeling trickles down my throat, settling like lead in my stomach as I turn towards that voice. The voice that still haunts my every nightmare. I grab Avery's arm, forcing her close behind my body. With my other hand, I reach into my back pocket and click the side button on my phone five times, alerting the police. I just hope it bloody works this time.

"You crazy bitch—how the fuck did you find me?"

Stephanie laughs, tsking at me. Her red hair is already frizzy, her eyes crazy and hollow underneath from obvious lack of sleep. She's wearing men's baggy clothes, that she likely stole, and her pupils are blown out. I'm certain she's high on something. Avery intertwines her fingers with mine.

"That's no way to speak to your future wife." Stephanie winks at me, taking a step forward.

"I've been following your little pet around for a few weeks. I got bored waiting for you at the institute, so I left. Figured a reunion was in order, since you clearly couldn't find me. Why else wouldn't you have visited me or bailed me out?"

"I want nothing to do with you, Stephanie. You already know that. The arrest, the harassment order. They weren't for nothing." Avery and I both take two steps back.

Stephanie corrects it, walking closer. "Oh, you're just confused, baby. You'll come around. Remember your promise to me in our love cage?"

"Oh my God...You were at Ben Nevis. At that pub," Avery says, stepping around to stand beside me.

I fucking knew it. I felt it that day, when I saw Avery's broken phone screen. But Henry told me at the falls that she was still locked up. He had called the institute—unless he lied. None of this is adding up.

Stephanie's shrill laugh echoes, causing my rage to coil

tighter. "Oh, she's smart. I like this one. Too bad she's not going to be around for much longer. So terribly sad."

Stephanie pouts while I glance behind her, trying to spot Malcolm's car or any movement, sirens, lights, something, but I can't see anything this far out. I need to distract her long enough to give Avery a running start.

I tilt my head down close to Avery's ear. "When I say run, you run."

Avery shakes her head. "No. I'm not leaving you."

"Yes, you will." My gaze locks on hers. But she keeps shaking her head—in denial or shock, I can't tell which one.

Stephanie takes another step closer. "Louder please, I'd like to be part of this conversation. It's too bad I'm so possessive, otherwise we could all share. Might have been fun. Oh well!"

Stephanie reaches behind her back, withdrawing a gun.

Avery gasps, and I step in front of her, blocking her from Stephanie's line of sight.

Sheer, unfiltered panic drowns my vision. My worst fucking nightmare is coming to life. I need to think fast, do something before it's too late.

"Are you out of your mind?"

"Lachlan, baby, if you like brunettes, you just had to ask and I would have gladly dyed my hair for you. But you see, this won't do." She tsks again, flashing the silver gun between the two of us. "If I let her live, you'll never come to your senses. This is the only way, baby. And then we can be together forever."

It's getting harder to think past my growing rage.

"Let's talk about this somewhere else, Stephy. Just you and me."

"I'd love that, baby. But let me deal with this situation first, and then we can run off into the sunset together. Or, rather, sunrise..." She steps closer and I shove Avery back. Steph cranes her neck, trying to lock eyes with her.

"Move away from her, Lachlan."

"Step the fuck back."

I make myself as large as possible, charging towards Stephanie. Her face lights up like a deranged fucking animal. She's sick, completely out of her mind.

I get right up to her face. "This ends, right here...right now. You're going to turn around and get back in your car."

Her eyes cut to mine as a vicious smile curls her lips. "Tempting, but I didn't track her down and drive all the way here just to leave. You can either come with me, or I'm taking your girl."

"Okay, let's go."

"Dead, of course." Stephanie laughs and I'm so close, I could strangle her.

"The only way I'm leaving with you is if you promise to let Avery go. Otherwise, this is going to get fucking ugly," I snarl.

"Ugh, such a party pooper. FINE. She can go." Stephanie rolls her eyes, puffing out a breath.

Dreadful fury snakes its way through me as I realize I'm going to be leaving again. And this time, I'm not sure when I'll be coming back. I turn to Avery, she's sobbing uncontrollably as she moves to close the distance.

"Avery, no." I shake my head, urging her to stop walking.

"Lachlan, you can't go with her. I won't let you. She's going to hurt you again."

An empty blackness licks at the edges of my vision, offering to pull me in. I grit my teeth, giving my back to Stephanie as I face Avery.

"It's going to be all right. I'll find you again."

"No. I'm not leaving you."

"I love you," I whisper, running my nose along Avery's before I step away, leaving my broken heart in her hands.

Stephanie grabs my hand and we start walking away.

It all happens so fast.

Avery's body flashes by, and Stephanie jumps as she takes a step back, pointing her gun. I throw myself to the side, blocking the gun just as a loud bang pierces the air. The booming sound reverberates through me, throwing me to the cold, wet ground. I try to move, stand but pain radiates through my bones. My body is failing me. I keep yelling Avery's name, or I think I am. A screeching sound blares in my head. Have I gone deaf?

Blinking through the cloudy images in front of me, I face the sky. Just a minute of rest, then I'll get up. Water droplets fall on my face, landing all around me as a blinding pain pulses in my chest. I try calling for Avery again, but this time nothing comes out. The blackness seeps deeper, pulling me in as everything begins to fade away.

Another shot pierces the air, penetrating through the deafening pressure in my ears...but this one is so quiet, like a gentle hum, as I finally close my eyes.

Avery.

Drifting into the darkness, Avery's smiling face flashes before my eyes right as sleep takes me.

CHAPTER SIXTY-ONE

avery

I didn't even get to tell him I loved him.

I didn't get to tell him that he had changed my entire world, helped me find my light, healed me. That he had made me believe in love.

It was too late. I was too late.

He stood there, pouring his heart out to me and I just stayed quiet. He was always fighting for us, always finding me when I didn't even know I needed him. He fought for me. Took a fucking bullet for me. He came to warn me, to make sure I was safe.

Across all space, throughout every moment in time, and in every corner of the endless universe...I am yours. Forever and always.

His voice keeps replaying in my mind as new tears roll down my cheeks. I just want to turn back time, take it all back, I want to be anywhere but in my rotting mind. I want to erase the images of myself kneeling in the mud beside his lifeless body, my hands covered in his blood. My screams travelling across the rolling hills, over the ocean.

But it was too late.

He couldn't hear me. I'll never forget the image of his body, cold and still as someone tried to peel me off of him. I still feel the burn in my throat as I kept screaming his name.

It's been two days.

Two days of me sitting in this cold room, on this hard metal chair, staring at a blank grey wall and blaming myself for everything. Maybe if I hadn't gone to Neist Point none of this would have happened. Maybe if I had just waited for him...

A sob wracks through me as I bend over, letting the blinding pain drown me over and over again. The wave of grief eventually pulls back, my breaths slowing down. The door creaks open but I don't look up. I wish I could just fade away, into dust and disappear.

"Lass, ye have to leave this room. Ye need to eat, take a bath." A hand squeezes my shoulder.

I shake my head, sitting up.

Ailith's face appears in front of me. Her tired eyes look at me with such deep sadness. She went home earlier. I don't know how long she was gone, but she's back now. I haven't left once. I'm still covered in mud. I'm still covered in his blood.

"I brought ye clothes. Yer going to wash up. Come on, lassie. It's not up for debate."

"No." I glance over at the bed. Multiple monitors beep in the background. "I don't want to be gone in case he wakes up."

"Ye won't miss it. Besides, ye don't want him to see ye this way, do ye?" Ailith reaches out and wipes the muddy tears away with her thumb.

I don't care what I look like. I just need to be here, when... if...

"He's going to be all right. He's a strong lad, he will pull through." Her blue eyes fill with tears, but she blinks them away quickly. Someone needs to be strong and it sure as shit won't be me.

"He needed heart surgery, Ailith. It's my fault he was there. It's my fault she came after him, that she found him again. It was because of me, she wanted to hurt me. He's here, lying in this bed, because of me. He jumped in front of that bullet to save me. And worst of all..." I blink, choking back the sob crawling back up my throat. "I didn't even get to tell him how I feel."

The sob ripples through me as I glance at Lachlan's still body. He looks so broken with pipes and machines attached to him. I would give anything to look into those ocean eyes again. I don't care what happens, I just need him to wake up. I need him to live.

Ailith's hand lands on my cheek as she turns my face to her. She's a blurry mess, I can't see anything. Can't feel anything but excruciating pain, as if someone is chopping my heart up into tiny pieces. It all hurts too much.

"Lass...listen to me. He knew how ye felt. He knew this was something worth fighting for and he will continue fighting because ye are his world. He will pull through, even if it's just to see yer bonnie face." She pulls me in for a hug, but I push her away.

"No, I'm going to get you dirty," I protest but Ailith pulls harder, a gruff chuckle escaping her mouth.

The door swings open and two nurses step inside.

"Avery, you're still here...and still have not washed." Nurse Jane scrunches her nose, releasing a heavy sigh and moving over to one of the machines. The other nurse, whom I haven't seen before, is already busy checking Lachlan's vitals.

Ailith and I watch them work silently, waiting for them to give us a new update.

"All right...we are ready to pull out his breathing tube." My heart drops to the floor, and I jump to my feet. Ailith looks up, thanking the heavens out loud.

I approach the bed and Jane puts out her hand. "We have to wait for the doctors. And ye, lassie, have to shower. The room reeks and it's completely unsanitary. Since ye refuse to budge, ye can use our facilities. Technically speakin', I shouldn't even permit ye to be in here."

"Is he ready for this?" Ailith's hand wraps around mine.

"He's ready. The doctors should be here by the time you've cleaned up." Jane looks at me, her tone completely serious. The other nurse won't even make eye contact with me. I'm sure it's always awkward when you have to tell a hysterical loved one they stink.

I don't waste another second as I grab the bag of clothes from Ailith's hand.

AN HOUR HAS GONE BY, and still no sign of the medical staff. Elle and Duncan arrived while I was in the shower. We're all waiting for the doctor and nurses to return and begin removing the machines that are currently breathing for Lachlan.

Henry also showed up to check on him, and to tell us that he was going to do his best to keep this out of the news. He told me Lachlan had messaged him when he saw my busted phone, and apparently the person he spoke to at the mental institute had mixed up the patient files. He wouldn't stop apologizing and I had to eventually kick him out.

The police also stopped by for the third and final time, to get another statement from me. I honestly don't remember much after Lachlan was shot. I was too lost to even notice Stephanie had put the gun to her own head until the sound of it going off hit my ears.

She was so devastated over shooting Lachlan that she took her own life.

I'm pacing the hallway, trying not to replay the events in my head while the minutes crawl by. Her gun was aimed at my head, and if Lachlan hadn't stepped in, thrown his body in front of the bullet, it would have gone right through my skull. He saved my life. But the bullet landed in his chest, grazing the bottom of his heart. They placed Lachlan in an induced coma for the surgery, letting us know they would pull him out of it within forty-eight hours if there were no post-op complications or bleeding.

We're at the forty-eight-hour mark, and they're going to be here any minute now, to wean him off sedation.

Please come back to me.

I turn, prepared to walk down the hallway for the eight hundredth time when a small group of doctors and nurses round the corner, heading this way. My breathing hitches, and I lurch for Lachlan's room on shaky legs.

"They're coming," I announce a little too loudly.

Ailith walks over, looping her arm through mine. Elle joins me on my other side as we stand in the middle of the room, waiting with shaky hands.

The doctor walks in, talking to us about Lachlan's stats and detailing the same things he had informed us after surgery. I try to listen, but nothing registers as I hold my breath, trying to keep the impending panic attack at bay. The nurses begin working, switching off the extra machines and putting away the cords. One of them hands the doctor a needle, which he injects into Lachlan's IV.

As more hoses are detached and pulled away, nothing happens.

"Ready?"

None of us say anything, we don't even dare move, all of us holding on to one another tightly. The room is terrifyingly silent as the doctor begins pulling out the large breathing tube running down Lachlan's throat. Anticipation hangs thick in the air as we all hold our breaths, waiting to hear Lachlan's soft first inhale.

Seconds feel like years.

Every memory from the last few months lines up in front of me, like neat tiles. The first day I met him in Glencoe, the way his ocean eyes always called out to me. The electricity pulsating between us, always bringing us together. The sound of his laugh, the way his body pressed against mine as he coaxed me down from a panic attack. The way he told me he loves me.

Lachlan's chest begins to rise and fall. Slowly at first, as the machine beside him beeps, and again, indicating a normal heartbeat. Ailith and Elle jump, as laughter fills the small room, prayers are whispered, and tears are shed.

But I'm frozen, stuck in place as I watch him. Not able to really believe what I'm witnessing. I'm terrified to blink, scared it's all going to fade away and I'll be back in that hell. Everything is in slow motion as I continue to watch Lachlan's body take slow breaths, in and out.

Breathe in, breathe out.

I finally move, creeping slowly to the edge of his bed. Lowering myself on the empty chair as I reach out, gently taking his hand in mine. The familiar magnetic current rushes through me, forcing a relieved breath into my lungs.

He is coming back to me.

A soft squeeze and my heart melds back together. Tears

cloud my vision and my heart is beating so fast I'm worried it's going to climb up my throat and suffocate me. My skin buzzes with anticipation as I wait for Lachlan to open his eyes.

He turns his head and his ocean blues find me once more. The world falls away as we stay locked onto one another, the current fusing us together. His eyes feel like a warm embrace, breathing life back into my bruised lungs.

I can't wait any longer to say it, to tell him what I never got to say. What I refused to acknowledge but have felt for so long.

"You came back to me," I whisper, pulling his hand up to my face and kissing the rough skin.

"I love you, Lachlan Moore. Across all space, throughout every moment in time, and in every corner of the endless universe...I am yours. Forever and always." I say, repeating his words back to him.

Lachlan blinks as if I'm an illusion. But then he smiles, slow and bright just like the sun.

"Have I died and gone to heaven?" he croaks.

I laugh through a sob, kissing his hand again and again.

"I'm going to need you to say that again, Nessi." His voice is coarse as he reaches out, touching my face.

"I love you."

He takes a shuddering breath, tears welling in his eyes—glowing bright blue.

"Again."

"I love you, Lachlan. Forever and always."

And in that moment, the final piece of my heart clicks into place.

I am finally *home*.

epilogue

LACHLAN

One year later

"Where are you going? That's not the way!" Avery yells from behind me.

I bite my lip, trying to suppress my laugh, glancing behind me at her furrowed brows and her tight lips. Her hair billows in the wild wind. The sun peeks through the clouds, rays casting down and highlighting her beautiful face.

Her whisky eyes lift up to mine, and she stops walking, looking two seconds away from kicking my arse. "You're going the wrong way, that's not the way to summit."

"We're taking the long way, you stubborn woman. Just come with me."

"Why? Shouldn't we save our energy and take the shortcut? I don't want to go the long way."

Pain in me arse, Nessi.

Just a little bit more, around that big rock formation and

she'll see why I'm taking her this way, which happens to be nowhere near the summit.

She crosses her arms over her chest, glaring at me. She thinks it makes her look serious, but all it does is turn me on. Makes me want to bend her over my knee, slap her round arse before I have my way with her up against a rock.

We're at the Quiraing, in Isle of Skye, and I've been planning this day for months. It's the perfect day, the sun is shining, there isn't a single cloud in the sky, and my lass is pissed to shite. Didn't plan that part well enough.

"Will you just stop being a pain and come with me?" I extend my hand out, waiting for her to take it.

She sighs, rolling her eyes before she finally walks towards me. I grip her hand in mine, leading us around the large rock formation, where I know all our loved ones are waiting for us.

"Thank you." I lean down, whispering in her ear. I can't help but stare at her.

"I'm still annoyed with you." She tightens her lips together, trying not to smile.

How did I get so fucking lucky?

She has always been beautiful, in every phase of life, but when she smiles, her happiness radiates as bright and warm as the sun. Lighting up my entire world every single day.

It's been the best year of my life, and I can't wait for countless more years with her.

Her eyes find mine. "You're acting weird."

"I don't know what you mean."

I came to the highlands searching for answers to questions I couldn't find. But I found all the answers in her. Avery brought me back to life, and every day since then has been nothing short of inspiring. She is my beginning and end.

Her cheeks are flushed a deep red, but her smile is unwavering as we approach the bend.

I spot Ailith, Duncan, Elle, Bill, and Becca standing at the edge of the clearing, amongst the vibrant lavender and pink colours of the heather and Scottish thistle wildflowers. As they sway in the warm breeze, their sweet fragrance fills the air around us. Duncan is holding two bottles of Anam Cara gin, a new line I introduced recently, named Mo Gradh. Dedicated to my love, Avery.

We're nestled between the jagged peaks of the Trotternish Ridge that rise high above the sprouting valleys below, casting long shadows in the soft light of the afternoon sun. The sight is unlike anything else, but it's the woman holding my hand that takes my breath away.

"Lachlan?" Avery stops, glancing up at me with glossy eyes. "What's going on?"

My heart pounds in my chest as I pull her to me.

"Surprise." I lean down, kissing her.

I feel the wave of happiness wash over me. This is the meaning of forever. This is what I imagine heaven feels like. Maybe I died that day and I got to live my happy ending with her. It feels like that some days, it feels too good to be true. Like this sort of happiness shouldn't exist.

"Why are they all here?" Avery's voice shakes.

My eyes burn and I blink as I reach inside my pocket, closing my fingers around the small velvet box that's been burning a hole in my jacket for weeks.

"You have made me the happiest man alive. I want to be the first thing you see in the morning and the last thing before you close your eyes at night. I want to be the one you run to, and I want to be the one to wipe all your tears away. I want to experience everything life throws my way with you. I want to hear you screaming my name in the middle of the night when I'm buried deep in between your legs. I want to spend forever with you." I pull her lips in between mine, swallowing down the nerves and steading my breath.

"I haven't been the same since you ran away from me in Glencoe. You are the best thing that will ever happen to me." I pull my hand out of my jacket, popping open the velvet box. I drop down on one knee.

Avery gasps.

"Will you give me forever, mo gradh? Make me the happiest man alive? Because you are it for me, Avery Harris. Forever and always." The round diamond catches the light, shining bright as sparkles dance across Avery's face.

Tears well in her eyes as she gapes down at me. She glances between me and the ring several times, flabbergasted at what she's witnessing. I'm not sure any of it has registered for her yet. I wait for her to answer me, but she surprises me by dropping to her knees in front of me. Wrapping her arms around my neck as she crushes her lips to mine. We cling to one another, getting lost in the kiss and this moment.

"Yes," she utters softly against my lips. "Forever won't be enough time with you, Lachlan."

I lift her up, smiling and laughing, as I kiss her over and over again. In the distance, our family screams with glee, the sound of their shouting and laughter fill the air like confetti.

I kiss Avery fiercely, just as starved as the first time our lips touched. Pushing the ring up her shaky finger, Avery stares down at the diamond before burying her face in my neck. I hold her against my beating heart as I look up at the blue sky, thanking the heavens for bringing her into my life.

Knowing that amongst darkness, I found a bright sun that will forever light up my universe.

The End

also by tina spencer

Shattered Obsession (Hudson Yards Book #1)

Shattered Hearts (Hudson Yards Book #2)

Untamed (Hudson Yards Book #3)

Watch Me Burn (Hudson Yards Book #4)

Mine to Hunt (Hudson Yards Book #5)

acknowledgments

Where do I even begin?

If you've made it this far, I want to thank you from the bottom of my heart. Sitting here, writing this part of the book doesn't feel real to me and I'm not sure it ever will. When I sat down to write *Wonderlight* I never thought I would finish it, let alone share it with the world.

I've always known I would write and publish a book, but I was never certain about the timing or how it would happen. I wasn't sure I had what it takes and that scared me more than anything else. Characters have come and gone, but none really made a mark on me until now. My previous manuscripts, gathering virtual dust, serve as evidence to that. Maybe it's because I was trying to suffocate my romantic side for so long, until I finally decided to embrace it. I can only thank other romance authors for that. Your bravery inspired me to start writing my own story.

This book, these characters, came from the heart; not as I had envisioned them, but as I needed them. Through early mornings and late nights at my laptop, writing this story became my salvation. I cried, grieved, laughed, loved, and healed alongside these characters. And I hope this book resonated with you in some way.

Maman and baba: thank you for sacrificing everything and moving to Canada so I could live this beautiful life. I feel so blessed to even have the opportunity to write like this. Books filled with hardship, strength, and endless love. This would never have been possible if you hadn't left your home country and given me a second chance. Thank you for allowing me to pursue literature. This was always it for me.

Thank you to my beta readers. You were the first ones to read my messy draft and I will never forget your role in this journey. Laura Johnson: the northern lights are for you, my dear friend.

To my book friends and the book community: I am so grateful this journey led me to you. Thank you for your friendship and for giving me a chance. You were one of the first to read my book and you have no idea what your words, reviews, and beautiful reels mean to me. You all bring light to my life.

A huge thanks to all my ARC readers for giving my book baby a chance. I have read every single review and am so thankful for the conversations we've had.

Thank you to my editor and proofreader for helping me polish this book.

To my high school teacher, Ms. G: I don't know if you'll ever read this or if you even remember me. But I'll never forget the day you told me I was born to write. Thank you for encouraging me to follow my dream from a young age.

To Scotland, the country that will forever have my heart. Magical lands with endless healing powers. I have had the pleasure of going to Scotland twice and I'm already planning my next trip. Who wants to come with me to go to every place Avery visited? Because that's on my bucket list now. Maybe we'll run into Lachlan.

To my readers: thank you for believing in me. Many of the themes and challenges in this book came from a personal place. If you're facing struggles and found resonance within these pages, I want you to remember that you are your own guiding light. You are worthy and capable. You can do hard things. You will always be enough. And even during your darkest moments, know that you are not alone. You are never alone. Feel free to reach out to me anytime, my DMs are always open. I am forever grateful for your support.

And last but certainly not least, to my beautiful children: you are my whole world. I love you. Across all space, throughout every moment in time, and in every corner of the endless universe...I am yours. Forever and always.

Tina Spencer is an international bestselling Canadian romance author known for her dark, emotional, and addictive stories that blur the line between love and obsession. When she's not writing about dangerous men and fierce heroines, she's spending time with her family, trying to take a nap, or wrestling with her never ending to-do list. You can find her at www. tinaspencerbooks.com.

If you made it this far, we're basically best friends. Come hang out in my newsletter where you'll receive exclusive content including bonus scenes, early access, and fun giveaways.

facebook.com/authortinaspencer

instagram.com/tinaspencerauthor

goodreads.com/authortinaspencer

tiktok.com/@tinaspencerwrites